Scout's

A NOVEL
Honor

DORI ANN DUPRÉ

Copyright© Dori Ann Dupré, 2016

Printed in the United States of America
First Printing, 2016
Publisher's Cataloging-in-Publication data and copyright number is available upon request.

ISBN:
.mobi - 978-1-941541-93-7
.epub - 978-1-941541-94-4
TPB - 978-1-941541-95-1

Cover Design: Dionne Abouelela for French Press Bookworks
Interior Design: Dionne Abouelela for French Press Bookworks
Distribution and Printing by Ingram Distribution Group

Reviews

"Scout's Honor thoroughly engages us from the moment we first meet the engaging Scout Webb, a sort of female Holden Caulfield whose lifelong struggles with love make a compelling read and teach us much. First-time novelist Dori Ann Dupré does a terrific job telling her story through an array of interesting characters while demonstrating a keen eye for detail and a true gift for exploring the joys, heartbreaks, complexities and deep truths of human relationships. Scout's Honor will capture your heart."

-**Mark Ethridge**
author of *Grievances* and *Fallout*, screen writer for *Deadline* (the movie adaptation of Grievances) and two-time Pulitzer Prize for Public Service recipient as managing editor with the Charlotte Observer.

"Open the first chapter of this book and step into the mind of a fourteen-year-old tomboy named Scout. Join her in the outfield as part of her mind is trying to keep up with the baseball game she's actively involved in, while another part is reminiscing about the good times she's had at summer camp. Plus there's her pleasant anticipation of the impending camp as she daydreams about the counselor who captured her heart with his good looks and outgoing personality.

It's almost impossible for readers to hear the voice of a young girl named Scout without thinking wistfully of Harper Lee's plucky heroine from To Kill A Mockingbird. Wisely, author Dupre admits to her protagonist being named after the famously fictional adolescent, and you accept the homage in hopes that this new relationship between you and Scout will be as simpatico as the one you shared with her namesake. Setting is made specific by exact reference to locale, and time is cleverly alluded to through the use of video game names that clearly place it in the somewhat distant past. While you may not know exactly where this story is going, an appealing feeling of nostalgia is present in this first chapter that makes you want to turn a few more pages just to see where it all may lead."

-**US Review of Books**,
First Chapter Reviews

For my three kids:
Apple, Pookie and Mom

This book is dedicated in honor of my husband, Eric DeJong, whose courageous fight is our family's battle cry and who has shown me the true meaning of grace, under fire.

"But man is not made for defeat," he said. "A man can be destroyed but not defeated."

— Ernest Hemingway,
The Old Man and the Sea

Part I

August 1983

"...he was led like a lamb to the slaughter, and as a sheep before its shearers is silent, so he did not open his mouth."

Isaiah 53:7, The Holy Bible, New International Version

SCOUT WEBB, AGE 14

The ball flew toward me in a mad spiral as I stood, stomach churning, wrapped up in anticipation. It was coming to my left so I turned my legs back and ran to position myself to catch it. I don't know exactly how my body knows what to do and when to do it at the right time, but even "for a girl" my body knew just the same. My gloved left hand reached just high enough to snatch the speeding baseball out of flight and I stopped myself from stride so I could get the throw into the cutoff man at shortstop. Also known as Charlie. My best friend.

"Good catch, Scout!" I heard someone yell. I felt a sense of relief come over my whole body. I did my job. I caught the well-hit fly ball that should have been a single. The boy who hit it was pissed off, no doubt, because some stupid wiry girl in the outfield caught it and *how embarrassing is that* and *I hope she falls and breaks her arm.* Heard it all before.

I love summer. Summertime is baseball season. People like to complain about the heat and humidity here in Haddleboro, North Carolina, but it doesn't bother me all that much. It doesn't keep me inside playing Space Invaders or Pong on Atari or watching reruns on TV like my brother Jonny and his friends. It doesn't keep me from sleeping, even if I'm dripping in sweat on my bed all night and have to wrap a cool wet towel over my head. No homework, no worries but for my paper route — and the promise of Camp Judah ahead.

On Sunday, I get to go to camp for three weeks. I've gone every year since I was seven. It will be my last summer there because I'm aging out. The next time I can go back is as a counselor after I'm eighteen. I'm turning fifteen in a couple of months, so that is a long time. Three whole years. Actually more like four because I won't turn eighteen until October when camp is over for the summer. What am I supposed to do for the next four years? Get a job or something? No one will hire me next summer because I'm too young. I've only ever had camp to look forward to.

Charlie turned around and hollered to me, pulling me from my Camp Judah daydreams. He shouted that I needed to be ready because the last time this kid hit, it went in between us for a single.

"Move in! He can't hit it over your head!" I moved in closer to Charlie, who held his spot at short.

Bobby was pitching. He's too slow at everything. He moves slow, preps the ball slow, kicks around dirt on the mound slow. Even chomps on his Big League Chew slow.

I'm getting anxious again, on high alert, scared to let my team down by screwing up. My stomach's in knots, but it's not clear if it's because of how close we are to winning this game or how close I am to going away to camp.

I stand ready, waiting for Bobby to pitch the ball, then watch the batter swing and miss. And again. Foul ball. Then my mind goes back to Camp Judah and to Brother Doug with the ice blue eyes, the gorgeous lifeguard who I've been practically in love with since I was seven years old.

At Camp Judah, we always address the counselors and other people who work there as "Brother" and "Sister."

"Why do we call all the counselors Brother and Sister?" I asked Brother Doug a few years ago, as I helped him carry some life jackets back to his storage shed.

"Because here at Camp Judah, we are all family. We are brothers and sisters in Christ and all of us are God's children," he answered with a wink.

When I saw Brother Doug for the first time, my camp group (the Lions for Jesus!) was coming out of the lake because our allotted time for swimming was up for the afternoon. A tall, fit, tan man stood at the foot of the water wearing swim trunks that matched the color of his eyes. He counted us as we came out and directed us where to stand to meet our counselor.

I was the last one out of the water, of course. I was always the last one out. I never wanted to leave the cool lake water because the sand was always hot on my bare feet. Some of the kids had flip-flops to put on, but I didn't.

As I walked up the wet sand from the water, Brother Doug said to me, "Hey Shorty, I like your chubby cheeks." I looked up at him, the sun blaring down on his almost-white, blond hair. He looked back down at me with squinted eyes, expanded his cheeks with air, and put his fingers on both sides to pop them. Then he smiled. "Those things are so big you should be able to pop them like that."

He became my favorite person right away.

"I'm Brother Doug. What's your name?"

"Scout," I said.

He laughed. "Really? That was my dog's name when I was boy!"

Heard it before. Someone always had or knew a dog named Scout. Never a cat, though, I noticed.

I've learned to become proud of my name over time. I'm named after the main character in one of the most beloved books in American fiction — from my mom's favorite book, *To Kill a Mockingbird*. And since my mom was a reading teacher at Haddleboro Elementary School, she knew something about books.

So Scout, the little girl in the famous novel, is my namesake. Really, her name was Jean Louise and Scout was just her nickname. But my *name*-name is Scout. Scout Elizabeth. Elizabeth for my grandmother.

After reading the book when I was eleven years old, I was at ease with my unconventional name. I liked the name

Scout and, the truth is, there were too many Jennifers and Lisas and Michelles anyway. Scout was a different kind of name and I was a different kind of girl. My friend Jenny (*see?*), who is a year older, told me that in ninth grade English, her class read *To Kill a Mockingbird* and everyone was talking about me and my name.

But since I was only seven when I met Brother Doug, and I didn't fully understand the significance of my name, I felt a little uncomfortable about it being so unique. Because I didn't want to make this Brother Doug person laugh at me, I just asked him if he missed his dog, Scout.

He grinned and said, "Sure I miss him. He was a great dog. The best one I ever had."

I think Brother Doug noticed my uneasiness, so he got down to my level. He peered into my eyes, still grinning, and put his hand on my shoulder. He continued to squint from the bright sunny afternoon. His unusually light blue eyes were no doubt affected by the sunlight more than other peoples' eyes. "Hey, I will give you a special name, just between me and you, okay?"

I nodded, wondering what in the world he was going to call me.

"I will call you Squirrel-Girl because you got the fattest, cutest cheeks I've seen at camp this whole summer — just like a squirrel hiding acorns in them."

He waited for my reaction and I could tell that he was trying to make me feel comfortable with him. It worked.

He had my complete trust at that moment and for the next seven summers.

Smiling back at him, I said, "Okay, Brother Doug."

As I started to walk away toward the other campers, I stopped and turned to him, inflated my cheeks, and popped them like he did earlier. That one gesture became our special greeting every summer.

Now, I couldn't wait to pop my cheeks at him on Sunday. No matter how much time had passed since I met him as a little girl, I was still his Squirrel-Girl and we always popped our cheeks at each other. I hoped he would be back again this summer because I hadn't heard from him in a long time.

While waiting for Bobby to move along with his pitches, I started thinking of how scared I am that Jesus and the Rapture might come tonight as I lay sweating in my bed. I pictured myself hearing those "Trumpets of the Lord" and then getting raptured up with all the other Christians. Then I'd have to miss out on going to camp. I think I would demand that Jesus let me go back so I could go to Camp Judah — but then I realized that all the people at camp would be raptured, too, so it would be a waste of an argument with the Son of God.

I said a quick prayer as we all watched Bobby taking his sweet time on the mound, "Jesus, please please please don't come again until after camp is over." I often said this kind of prayer on Christmas Eve, on the eve of the first day of school, and on the eve of Halloween.

The boy up at bat strikes out and the game is finally over. I'm relieved. My mind is too cluttered today for this game. I'm too excited, too jumpy, and too anxious for everything. Especially Camp Judah and Brother Doug.

Really, for Brother Doug.

I jog in from the outfield and my team's coach, Mr. Faulkner, who's also Bobby's dad, congratulates us on doing a great job.

"We have four more games this summer," he said. "We are undefeated, boys," he stopped and looked at me, "and Scout," he added with a wink. "Not bad for a team full of scrappy kids just out of junior high." He looked around and continued, "We need to practice on Sunday and Monday, so don't miss. We can go far with this group. I just know it!"

Mr. Faulkner sounded pretty excited and he never sounds excited.

When everyone dispersed, he came over to me and said, "I'm sorry you're going away to camp, Scout. We need you."

I was glad he said that, but humbly replied, "There are lots of boys on the bench who can play just as good as me. I hate to miss so much, but if we win the rest of the games, I'll be back in time for regionals."

To be honest though, if Brother Doug wasn't at camp anymore, I would have considered missing my final summer at Camp Judah to play baseball instead. I'm kind of over all the Bible verse competitions, the devotionals every morning, and the constant segregation of boys and girls in the teenager groups.

Last summer, this boy named Carlo from Philadelphia liked me and tried to kiss me. He was a nice boy, but I didn't want him to kiss me because I'd never want Brother Doug to hear about it. It really wasn't a big deal, though.

"Scout, I think you're pretty," Carlo said to me. "Can I kiss you? Just one time so I can remember you?"

I was flattered because Kelly was the prettiest girl at Camp Judah that summer — and probably every summer. All the boys wanted to kiss her. But Carlo liked me instead.

"I don't think so, Carlo. I don't want to get in trouble," I told him.

Well, some girl named Pepper, who nobody liked, went and told a counselor about what Carlo said to me. Poor Carlo got in all kinds of trouble. His parents were called and he missed a whole day of activities. They probably would've sent him home if it wasn't so far away. So some of the camp rules are starting to annoy me.

But Brother Doug *is* there. At least, I hope he is. I think he is. He has to be! And I know he misses me. He has told me so in his letters.

Mr. Faulkner told me before the season started that I'm lucky I can play baseball at all. He had to do some convincing with the people in charge of the county because there were no other girls playing this level of baseball anywhere in the state. Since there wasn't a summer softball league for girls, and I was just as good as the boys, they decided to let me play.

Usually by this age, girls and boys go their separate ways in sports. Girls chase softballs or chase dreams of being on some stage or just chase boys. Once I overhead someone's dad say, "Teenaged girls are chasin' either one set of balls or another." I didn't think it was funny, but the other dads sure did.

I played softball in the spring with the county league last year, but it was boring and everyone stunk except for some girls from another town called Black Hill. I couldn't stand the fact that most of them actually did throw like girls and I hated the bigger-sized ball. So instead of doing that again, I got permission from the principal to play boys' baseball for the school team. Since they didn't have a softball team for the girls, he told me that the baseball coach agreed to let me try out. Well, I made the team and had so much fun playing with the boys and Charlie all the time.

Next year, I could only try out for the girls' high school softball team and not the boys' baseball team. I was warned about that. "The girls in high school will be much better players. Some of those girls from Black Hill go to Haddleboro High," Charlie had promised me.

"I hope you're right," I said, unconvinced. But really, I was sad that I would not be playing with Charlie.

The thought of going into high school both excited

and terrified me. I was excited to be able to experience new things and meet new people. But the thought of not being with Charlie all the time was scary. We were a pair. I didn't want things between us to change too much.

"Listen, you can't worry about stuff like that," Charlie told me last week, while we were walking into town for an ice cream. "Nothin's gonna change. I promise."

"I don't know Charlie. It's so much bigger there and maybe you'll meet people you like better than me," I said, feeling really stupid and insecure, especially because of how much attention he had been paying lately to a girl named Katie Smith.

He stopped me on the side of the road and made me face him. "Scout. Stop it. You're my best friend. It will all be just fine." Then he put his hand on my head like I was a puppy. "I don't know what I'd do without you."

I felt a little better about it all after he said that.

After Mr. Faulkner let us go, Charlie and I hopped on our Schwinn banana-seat bikes and pedaled off to his house, which was just three blocks away from the town baseball field. His uniform was covered in dirt from one messy slide into third base. I only managed a grass stain on my knee this game. I hoped I could get it out in the laundry. I hated a dirty uniform for the start of a game.

****

Dear SG,

September 12, 1982

I was so happy to get your letter. It made my day. I was having a tough day at school because one of the younger kids got hurt in a game we were playing and he may have broken his foot. I felt really bad about it, so your letter cheered me up a lot. It sounds like you are doing good. I know it was hard for summer to end, but you should enjoy your last year in junior high because it will go fast. Before you know it, we will be racing down the water slides again.

You asked me if it was OK if you wrote to me. Of course it is! I love getting letters from my campers.

Well, I am going to close for now. I hope you have a great school year. Keep in touch!

Your friend,

Brother Doug

CHARLIE PORTER, AGE 15

Scout and I got to my house and no one was home. The back door was unlocked, like it always is, and I guess it's a good thing that we live in a safe place where nobody messes with anybody's house. They might steal a bike from out front if it's left outside, but no one breaks in or anything. It doesn't seem to matter, though, because whenever my mom's not around overnight, I still get scared that someone is going to break into the house and kill me in my sleep. It's why I keep a knife under my pillow and a bat next to my bed.

We stand in the kitchen and I grab a batch of cookies from the pantry. Scout takes a few and starts to eat them like she's never eaten in her life. She shoves two in her mouth, chomps like a horse, her already-big cheeks looking like a chipmunk, and has crumbs coming out the sides of her mouth.

"What the heck, Scout! You a horse?" I asked her, about to laugh.

"Sorry," she said through a cookie-filled mouth. "I'm starving to death. Haven't eaten anything all day."

Scout's been my best friend since we were in

Kindergarten. It was hard for me to see her as a girl. Even though she is. But now it's easier. I can see she has boobs through her uniform shirt. Only a little bit, though, because the shirt's baggy.

I remember when Mr. Langley, our fifth grade teacher, had to pull her aside and tell her that she should start wearing a bra. We were standing in line at school, waiting to go to art class, and I was the line leader. Scout was behind me. Mr. Langley walked up to her and quietly said, "Scout, dear, you should talk to your mama today when you get home about getting yourself properly fitted."

I sure didn't know what he was talking about, but I could see Scout's face turn bright red and her eyes well up.

"What's that mean?" I whispered to Scout when Mr. Langley walked away.

Tears started seeping out of her eyes and I felt bad for asking. I didn't mean to make her cry. "It means I need to get a bra," she whispered back to me.

When we walked home that day, she cried the whole way. I felt bad for her. She was wearing a yellow tee shirt with big numbers on it and I could see lumps underneath of the numbers. It was pokey-looking so Mr. Langley was right; she needed to start wearing a bra. That was really the first time I noticed.

I don't know if she was crying so much because she was embarrassed or because it finally occurred to her that she would no longer be the same. Her body was changing.

Ever since then, I've tried to treat her like nothing's changed.

"Look," I told her, "I'm still me and you are still you and we will always be best friends."

But then a couple of years later, we played Spin the Bottle at Lisa Wieland's house at her boys-and-girls birthday party in seventh grade. I noticed that I didn't like it when Jason McLean got to kiss Scout when the bottle landed on him. Actually, it really pissed me off. I was hoping the bottle would land on me and she would have to kiss me instead. I wondered how she would've handled it and what she would've done — if she would've kissed me at all. I know I wanted her to.

Scout was my first kiss, but it's not like it was something special or romantic or anything. When we were eleven, she was over my house. It was cold and raining outside and we were playing Hangman in my room. I told her that Katie Smith wanted to kiss me.

"Katie gave me a note at lunch and it said she wants me to meet her in the woods behind the playground after school and kiss her," I confessed. "Don't you think that's weird?" I did not want to kiss anyone at that time, let alone Katie Smith. "She's been wearing the same green sweater almost every day. It stinks!"

"Charlie, I don't think she has a mother," Scout said.

"Well, nobody's told her that she should wear deodorant and change her clothes."

But it didn't stop her from trying to get me to like her.

And I did feel bad for her having no mom and all. People were always telling me how nice I was: how no one could ever not like me, how I always seem so happy, and how I "don't know a stranger." I guess Katie thought that because I was nice to her, it meant that I liked her and wanted to kiss her. Who knows what girls think?

As she put up a letter on her Hangman board, Scout looked over and said, "Are you gonna do it? Are you gonna kiss her?"

"I don't want to," I said, looking down at the carpet feeling my face turn red.

"Why? Because she stinks?"

"No, I just don't want to."

Scout eyeballed me for a few seconds, her eyebrows raised up like she had a question. "Do you even know how to kiss?"

That was the real problem. I had never kissed anybody before and it was embarrassing, I guess. But I just hadn't ever wanted to. Or, I've never been around a girl I'd like to. I didn't answer Scout, but she knew. She knew me better than anyone on this planet and if I had kissed someone, I would've told her.

Scout pulled herself up off the floor and grabbed a pillow off my bed. "Here," she said holding it out for me.

I took the pillow. "What...am I supposed to kiss the pillow? Practice on it?" I laughed. "No way, that's so stupid."

Scout shrugged. "Well that's what I do. That and the

back of my hand."

I gave her a face. "Do you want to kiss someone? Is that why you've been practicing?"

Scout didn't like any boys that I knew of and I sure didn't like the thought of her wanting to kiss someone.

"I want to be prepared if it ever happens is all," she answered.

She came much closer to me and looked right into my face with her intense, dark brown eyes. She had light freckles across the bridge of her nose and her long brown hair was thin and resting over her shoulders. She had full, round cheeks that always looked like she had some gum in them. If I had been older, I probably would've thought that she was a pretty girl.

"I will kiss you, Charlie."

I wasn't expecting that. I didn't know what to think of it at the time because Scout's not a *girl*-girl. She's my best friend. We've played matchbox cars, built forts, played war, gone bike riding in the woods, gone fishin', shared clothes, played on the same baseball teams, and hollered for the New York Yankees for more than half of our lives. The only time I was reminded that she was a girl was if I had to use the bathroom after her — the seat would be down. But kissing?

"I'll be your first kiss and you can be mine. We can practice on each other so when we like someone enough to want kiss them for real, then we'll both be ready."

I just sat on the floor feeling stunned. Scout stepped

over her Hangman board and sat down next to me. As I watched her, I felt like what I thought a drunk person would feel like. In a haze or something. Scout leaned over, her face close, and said, "Just put your lips against mine."

So I did.

We kissed with our lips pressed together for a quick second. I didn't feel anything special. I thought kissing was supposed to be like some exciting thing.

Scout pulled away and looked at me thoughtfully. "That was a peck. But what we need to practice is the long kissing, where you put your tongue in my mouth, like they do in the movies."

That sounded gross to me, but Scout seemed like she wanted to try it anyway. So she leaned in again, we put our lips together, and she put her tongue in my mouth, which felt really weird. Then she pulled away briefly and said, "Now you have to put yours in mine." So I put my tongue in her mouth and, before I knew it, we were exchanging our tongues in each other's mouths like snakes trying to strike out at someone. It didn't feel good, but it didn't feel bad either.

After a couple of minutes, she just leaned back and said, "Well, that's not what I expected. But we did it. We are each other's first kiss and, if you want, we can practice once in a while so that when it's time to do it with someone we really want to kiss, we'll be ready and we won't be bad at it."

Sounded good to me. But I still didn't want to kiss

Katie, no matter how good I would get at it. And I wanted to know who Scout wanted to kiss. I mean, why was she practicing?

"Charlie, I have to go home. My mom needs to go to the store, and she wants me to be at the house with Jonny because he's sick," Scout said pulling me from my memory, our shared memory, and then left my kitchen. I put the cookies away and watched her ride off on her Schwinn, butt in the air, ponytail bobbing through the back of her ball cap.

My mom's working at the hardware store, I think. Or maybe she's at her latest boyfriend's house. Not sure. I hope she's at work because the thought of her being at that prick's house makes me mad.

I sit down on the couch after I turn on the TV and find a *Brady Bunch* rerun. Alice was running through the kitchen and hollering something, but the volume wasn't loud enough. I'd have to get up again and go turn it up. But instead, my mind drifted back to the kissing.

Scout and I haven't kissed again, not since that one time years ago. We never practiced, like she said we could. As time went by, and opportunities came up, she never said anything about it and I wasn't going to. I did want to practice kissing with her so I could get good at it, but I was too embarrassed to ask. I figured she didn't want to — or liked practicing on her pillow better.

But I do know that a couple of years later, when I did cave in and kiss Katie Smith in the closet at Lisa's party during Seven Minutes of Heaven, Katie didn't stink anymore, so someone had taught her about deodorant. She never wore that green sweater anymore either, so maybe someone taught her how to change her clothes. Maybe she got a new mom because she always brushed her auburn hair real nice and wore pretty blue makeup above her eyes. And when she came in the closet to kiss me for Seven Minutes of Heaven, I let her. For all seven minutes. And I liked it.

And I think she did, too, because ever since that party, I've kissed her a lot more times.

****

Dear Brother Doug,   9-17-82

I got your letter three days ago and wanted to write you back right away. I was so happy you wrote back to me. But then I had to do some chores for my mom and couldn't. I started to write you back when I was in my English class (don't be mad), but then I lost the letter I had started. Then I had to write something about the Falkland Islands in my social studies class. So here I am trying again. I'm in my room and I don't want my daddy to know I'm up this late because he might not let me get my own phone in my room, which is what I want for Christmas.

I've missed you so much since coming home from camp. I was so happy that you worked with my group so much this summer because I got to do more stuff with you.

It was the first time that I even knew you were married and had a baby boy. Your wife must be so pretty!

8th grade is easy. I am in the chorus at my school and, even though I don't think I'm any good at singing, the teacher said that she wants me to sing a solo part in the Christmas show later. My mom was happy about that.

I just got my 8th grade picture, so I am sending it to you so you will remember me. My mom didn't think I smiled enough, but my daddy liked it. I hope you like it, too. Don't forget me!

Please write me back! I am so glad we can write each other letters now. I miss you a whole lot!

Love,

Squirrel

****

DOUG DEHAAN, AGE 32

Taking a sip of my Cheerwine, I looked at the big calendar posted on the wall in the camp office kitchenette.

"The last group of campers comes on Sunday so just three more weeks of this shit!" I said, probably too loudly.

Chris, one of the counselors, sat close by, thumbing through a Bible. "Three more weeks of screaming kids, three more weeks of being on alert for several hours a day, three more weeks of this shitty food for lunch, three more weeks of 'Jesus this' and 'Jesus that!'" he said back to me, clearly ready to go back to college.

I wanted to continue with, "And three more weeks of my wife Cammy nagging me to do <insert whatever household chore she doesn't want to do herself> as soon as I get home after these long hot days out in the sun," but I thought better of it. No one needs to hear about my marital woes. Then I realized that, of course, she'll just be nagging me after long days at my real job instead. "At least it won't be as hot," I said under my breath.

"This summer's heat and humidity seem to be worse than last year," Chris said, standing up to stretch his legs.

"Maybe. Or maybe I'm just getting too old for this crap," I quipped, taking another sip of Cheerwine.

I've been a lifeguard since I was seventeen and working at this camp during the summer — every summer — since I got out of college. Ten years later and here I am. Still.

"I don't know why I don't just let this place go, Chris," I said, looking out one of the windows, observing the haze over a steamy afternoon. "I'm a thirty-two-year-old grown man with a family to support and, for some reason, every summer, I come back here to lifeguard these kids."

I can do it because I'm a teacher and the extra income is good, especially since my son Paul was born two years ago. Plus, we need the money, so who am I kidding? If I was smart — which I'm not — but if I was, I would leave this place and go work at some other kind of summer job that pays more money and has an easy schedule, like teaching driving school.

Chris laughed, "You do it for the great pay and benefits." He closed his Bible and fell to the floor in a pushup position, completing one after the other. "I haven't seen that girl from last summer come through yet. The one with the chubby cheeks that you like so much."

I looked over at him, his head bobbing up and down, his skinny arms set too wide. The coach in me wanted to correct his form, but he caught me off guard with such an odd reference to Scout. He's right. Only one more group of campers left to come through for the summer and Squirrel-

Girl still hadn't been here.

"Yeah, she hasn't come. I thought for sure that she told me last year she had one more summer left before she was too old." The truth was that I hadn't heard from her in a while so I wasn't sure when or if she was coming back at all. "That kid is the measuring stick for the other campers, year after year. She's a great little girl with a dare devil streak in her."

Chris stopped doing pushups and got up, heading toward the kitchen. "Yeah, she was pretty funny and sweet, and I remember that she was always helpful. What do you call her? Don't you have a nickname or something?"

"Squirrel-Girl. I've called her that since she was little. When I first met her, I could tell there was something special about her. She was a great little sport: was one of my best swimmers, listened to instructions, followed directions, and always respected authority. Cute as a button, too. The plumpest set of cheeks I've ever seen on a kid. I thought for sure she'd lose them when she got older, but she didn't."

About to head out the door, I hollered at Chris, "Hey, are there any chips back there?"

"Yeah, I think so."

I went back toward the mini fridge, grabbed some Lay's potato chips sitting on the counter, stuffed them in my mouth and dreaded the pimple that I would no doubt get from it. Then I'd have to listen to Cammy say, "Did you have Lay's chips? When are you going to learn that they give you pimples?" Blah fuckin' blah fuckin' blah. Good Lord. Shut up, woman.

I stuffed a few more handfuls in my mouth for good measure and then ventured back out in the heat for another afternoon of watching kids splash around in a small, man-made lake.

Today is Friday. Later, all the parents will come to pick up this three-week session's little blessings from God. Then, it starts again one last time on Sunday afternoon with a fresh set of little blessings. Yay. Thanks, Jesus! But seriously, thanks Jesus because it will be the last of them. I am all blessinged out.

Walking down the dirt road in my swim trunks and a white tee shirt, which already started to accumulate sweat patches, I could hear all kinds of squeals from the dining hall area. The kids were all at lunch now and my first batch of swimmers will arrive soon after. I was always taught that kids weren't supposed to swim until an hour after eating, but the Camp Director didn't seem to think that was true. I had to wear my tennis shoes because the ground was so hot today, too hot for bare feet.

I started thinking more about Scout — how long I've known her and how she was one of only a handful of kids I watched grow up at this camp. Scout grew into a pretty teenaged girl, and I'm sure she had herself a boyfriend by now. I know I would've liked her if I was her age. Last summer, I found myself feeling a bit out of place around her because it was becoming evident to me that she was not a little kid anymore.

"Squirrel," I said to her sharply as I walked up behind her on the beach. I was trying to make her jump. She stood with her back to me, her body outlined in her camp-approved, one-piece bathing suit, the small of her back inviting me to put my hand on it. Startled, she turned around quickly and I immediately noticed how much fuller her breasts were since the previous summer.

"Hey, Brother Doug," she responded, smirking, and in a different tone — one I had never heard from her before. It sounded older, almost like, if we'd been in a bar, she would've been coming on to me. But she was certainly not coming onto me and I was pissed off at myself for even thinking it. I didn't want to think that way about her.

That split-second interlude at the lake made me realize that she was turning into a young lady. She had a woman's body and I felt like she was developing a bit of a reserved flirtation toward me, probably a crush. I had to keep reminding myself that she's still just my little Squirrel-Girl — and that was mostly true. We had a hell of a lot of fun last summer. I spent a lot more time with the teens. But still, she had grown up a lot in a year and that didn't go unnoticed by me.

I've been around teenaged girls enough to know that they think I'm "cute" and "hunky" and, after three weeks around each other, some will get a crush on me. I get it.

Part of the job, same with being a gym teacher and coach. A lot of young girls look up to me because I'm in authority and I'm nice to them and I like to have fun. Just got to keep myself professional at all times so nobody gets the wrong idea. That's even part of our training.

A few summers ago, before camp started for the season, the camp owner, Mr. Houghton, came over to my house for a cookout. This was back during the time period when Cammy and I invited people over, or as I called it, "BP" — Before Paul. Mr. Houghton sat at my kitchen table and said with a straight face, "Doug, we're adding a new training program for the counselors and staff this summer. It's called 'Understanding Teenaged Girls.'"

I almost spit out my Cheerwine. "What?"

"Well, I feel like we need to have the young men be more educated on the matter."

I laughed and said, "I'll sign up for the 'Understanding Women' class if you have that one."

But what that class didn't address is that we are still guys with guy thoughts. Most of us have no problem managing them and I'd wager that most of us don't even think anything inappropriate about the girls at camp. We are adults with our hearts in the right place. But for some of the younger counselors, the age difference between them and a camper isn't very wide and Mother Nature is Mother Nature.

There have been a couple of counselor-camper scandals over the years. There's only so many Bible verses and

"Come to Jesus" praying sessions that can help a nineteen-year-old young man keep his distance from a seductive, well-endowed, and mature fifteen-year-old girl who is throwing herself at him. It's still wrong, yes, but in a year, they could be boyfriend and girlfriend and no one would care.

I always feel bad for the younger male counselors having to deal with the teenaged girls. There have been a handful of doozies over the years. Mr. Houghton generally puts the young men with the younger age groups, but there are times when one will be assigned to the teens. It's why I sometimes have to work with the teen groups on some of the larger outings and events.

"I want you there, Doug, with the teens, when you can be," Mr. Houghton told me last summer. "It's good to have an older and more experienced man of God around. It helps keep everybody honest."

"Thanks for your confidence in me," I replied to him. I liked how he made me feel important, appreciated, and needed.

As much as I dread going to Camp Judah each day and then dread going home to face whatever stupid shit Cammy wants to piss and moan to me about, I care about Mr. Houghton and his wife. Great people. Done a lot for me over the years, including letting me stay in a closet-sized apartment above the staff housing for free for two years after college. They treated me like family so it's hard for me tell them that my camp lifeguard days are done, although I'm sure they'd understand. After all, I'm a husband and father now and people do move on. But I'd still feel like I would be letting them down. And the thought of that just physically hurts me.

Last summer, after camp was done and the school year was in full swing, I had received a letter from Squirrel with her school picture. She had signed the photo on the back with "Scout Webb." Almost like she wanted me to take her seriously now. Like I could take anyone named "Scout" seriously!

I can't believe her parents would name her something like that. Scout is a cool name and all, but it's a dog's name. There are no lawyers, doctors, or executives named Scout. I understand that she's named after a character in the "Great American Novel", but people who do the hiring do not appreciate nifty, trendy names. Cammy and I were sure to give our son the kind of name that was rooted in tradition and family. Paul is the name of her grandfather, a World War II fighter pilot who doted on her and her sisters. Paul was also one of the greatest apostles of Jesus in the New Testament. No one names their dog Paul.

Scout's school picture had your typical gray background. She was wearing a nice blue shirt and her long brown hair was laying neatly along her shoulders. She smiled slightly, looking a bit mature, no big toothy grin. I guess those kind of school pictures were done with when you hit eighth grade.

I receive letters from campers sometimes because they liked me or they wanted to thank me for a fun summer. It's nice to get fan mail when you're just some nobody Joe like me, even if it's from a bunch of kids or goofy, lovesick, teenaged girls.

Squirrel's letter to me was cute, written with bubbly letters and dotted with little hearts. She had gone and grown up on me and I would only have one more summer to pop my cheeks at her and make her laugh that raspy giggle she had. Only one more summer to toss her off the pier and into the lake or race down the water slide. Only one more summer to sit with her camp group at the bonfire and sing songs about Jesus and "His light" and how He "loves everybody in the world." I would miss seeing her in the summer. And I'd probably never see her again.

So I did what I normally don't do and I wrote her back.

She mailed the letters to me to the Camp Judah address, like she must've thought I lived there all year. I thought that was kind of sweet and tried to imagine what she pictured I lived like. Did she think I lived in one of the cabins? Eating in the dining hall with my wife and son? Cammy pulling Paul's high chair to one of the ten-seater tables?

Her letters were always happy and upbeat, like she was. Even the negative stuff was happy and upbeat. No hint of teenaged angst. She'd tell me about how school was going, what she was up to, that her parents had gone on yet *another* trip without her. She'd talk about baseball games and basketball games and what she saw on MTV at a friend's house and how she wanted her dad to let her put a phone in her room. I gathered that her best friend was named Charlie, but I didn't know if it was a boy or a girl. It could be short for Charlene or Charlotte.

I would write her back eventually after I received her letters from Mr. Houghton, who actually did live in his house at the camp. It was like we became pen pals.

Thankfully, Mr. Houghton never asked me any questions about why this camper would send me letters because, really, I wouldn't know what to say about it. I mean, it was totally innocent. Mr. Houghton knew Scout since she's come to camp the last several summers.

In my letters, I would tell her what was going on in my life, at school, in the PE classes I taught. I would tell her about Paul and how he was growing so fast, how he was starting to talk. I never talked about Cammy — mostly because there was nothing good to say. Not anymore anyway. She was always pissed off about something and inevitably it was about how I wasn't doing something good enough or the way she wanted it. So instead, I would tell Squirrel about the softball league I played in or if I had a family outing or a holiday thing or sports. Light stuff. Good stuff. All normal-life stuff.

Squirrel's letters became something I looked forward

to. Kind of silly for a grown man to get excited about a letter from a kid, but I did nonetheless. I suppose I was desperate for a happy thing in my life, other than my son.

I always addressed her as "Squirrel" or "SG" and she signed her name that way. But she signed the last few letters "Scout Elizabeth." I figured she was trying to act older, let me know in her own way that she wasn't a little girl anymore. A part of me still wanted to see her that way, though. To me, Squirrel was a small, innocent, breath of fresh air, an escape from all the bills and responsibilities, all the nagging and noise from adult life. Squirrel meant happy summertime memories with a good kid who made me feel like what I did with my life mattered. She looked up to me and I liked how that felt. I thought maybe she didn't get a whole lot of attention from her parents or something so it was nice that I could pay her some attention, even from a couple of hours away.

Sometimes, in her letters, she'd tell me that she missed me and couldn't wait for summer so she could see me again. I kept my letters noncommittal and maintained an emotional distance — after all, she was just a child. But the truth is that I missed her, too.

Every year for seven years, Scout Webb was my favorite three weeks of camp.

****

Dear Squirrel,   October 15, 1982

I am sorry that it took me so long to write you back. I've

been real busy and just got some time to sit down and write back. Thanks for your letter. I'm happy that you're singing in a chorus, but I'm not surprised about you singing a solo. You seem to be the kind of girl who is good at everything. I hope school is going good for you so far. Is your dad going to let you have a phone in your room?

My son Paul is finally going to go trick-or-treating for the first time this year. He is going to dress up as a baseball player. He is starting to talk a little bit now and it is neat. I am still teaching gym at my school and right now the classes are focusing on fall sports, like football, volleyball, and running. I hope you are having a fun fall and keep in touch!

Your friend,

Brother Doug

****

SCOUT

"Are you done packing yet?" I yelled up to Jonny, who was still packing his suitcase for camp, as I stood at the bottom of the steps rubbing the belly of my little dog, Stretch. "This is ridiculous. Mom! I've been packed for a week and it's time to go! Get on the stick!" I wanted to leave. Now. "I wanted us to be the first ones checking in so I could go to my group, unpack and say hey to everyone!" I think my impatience was wearing on my mom, who was never in a hurry about anything.

Really, I wanted to head off to the lake to go for free swim because Brother Doug would be there. I hoped, I prayed, I expected. He had better be there!

I've been waiting almost a whole year to see him. He stopped answering my letters a few months ago, so I hoped everything was okay and that he'd be at camp. I had written to him three times with no letter back so I stopped writing him just in case I was being a pest or something. I didn't want to be a pest. I had no idea why he stopped writing me, but maybe he got really busy. I mean, he's a teacher and he coaches sports and he plays on a softball team and he teaches Sunday school at his church and he has a wife and a little boy. So perhaps he got too busy to write little ol' me. But I know there is no way he forgot about me, not after so many letters.

Jonny started dragging his suitcase down the stairs, large thumps accompanying each footstep. "Don't get your panties in a wad," he said. "Jeez, you're so bossy!"

My parents were kissing each other in the living room. *Ew.* My mom was going to take us to camp and my daddy had to go into work at Lee Webb Automotive, the garage he owned, so he could help his friend with something on his truck. He wouldn't see her again until tonight and, well, it was just unbearable for them to be apart for that long.

"Rae, don't be gone too long from me," I heard him say to her. That was what he always said whenever they parted ways. I wanted to throw up, but a part of me wished someone would say something like that to me.

"Never, sugar," was her response, as always.

My parents had that love story type of love, the kind that fairytale or romance authors write about. Once, a woman at church told me that fairytales aren't real and I thought to myself, "Um, you don't know my parents." They've been married for what seems like a hundred years and act like it's their wedding day, every day. They kiss and hold each other in front of us, my daddy buys her flowers and little gifts now and then, and they pat each other's butts and say nice things. I guess the alternative — having divorced parents, like Charlie, where he never sees his daddy and his mom has a new boyfriend every month — is kind of tough. So it's good I don't have to worry about the kinds of things that some of my friends do: things like divorce, separation, fighting, silent treatments, abuse, and alcoholism.

So that church lady, the one who didn't believe in fairytales, I reckoned she was just a "Bitter Betty" who never had the good fortune of knowing true love.

But it can be lonely for the kids, being the offspring of true love. I always felt like I ruined their time together by being born. I intruded on their love story, an uninvited guest. I crashed their lifelong party.

I know that's stupid and not true — they love me and planned to have children — but that's how I felt sometimes. Don't really know about my brother, though, because we never talked about it. We didn't talk much at all. He annoyed me. And I annoyed him.

But I knew what true love is: I saw it in my parents and felt it in my heart about Brother Doug. Silly girl like me in love with an older married man. Sounds like a Shakespearean tragedy in the making. I was sure that he was my true love. Even at fourteen — *almost* fifteen — and even though he was married and so much older than me, it was still fate that we would be together. Maybe not now, but someday, when I'm older, he will see me as a woman and feel about me like I feel about him. Maybe he won't be with his wife anymore because *they* can't possibly have true love. How can he have true love with her if he's supposed to have it with me? At least, that was how I saw it. But these are just thoughts in my head. I'd never have the guts to say these things to Brother Doug!

Daddy gave us a squeeze, I hugged Stretch one last time, and we loaded up in the Skylark.

"Scout, you need to calm down. We'll be there in about ninety minutes," my mom said, clearly in no rush.

"Well, I just can't wait to get there."

"Have a great time, y'all," Daddy said to us as we drove off.

Michelle, who's been my camp friend for five years now, would be waiting for me. I wasn't sure if I'd know any of the counselors this year, but Brother Kevin and Sister Lynn would probably be there leading the camp games like they did every summer. Brother Doug at the lake. Mr. and Mrs. Houghton, Sister Dawn and Sister Angie working in the dining hall. All these kind people who have watched me grow up, grow in Jesus, "grow in grace", as Mr. Houghton said to me every summer.

The only thing that stinks about going away for three weeks, other than missing the rest of my baseball season and letting down my teammates — and missing my dog, of course — is leaving Charlie behind.

"You never get to go anywhere," I said to him last night while we sat on my front porch.

"I got to go to the mountains last year to see my

grandmom," he said, taking the last sip of his sweet tea. He put the glass down on the top step and stood up to go, picking up my paper route's collection book. "I'll just live off of your stories when you write to me and then again when you get home and tell me everything that happens."

"What are you gonna do while I'm gone?" I asked him.

"Play baseball and cover both of our paper routes, just like last summer," Charlie replied, about to pick up his bike off the grass. I could tell that he was keeping the rest of his plans out of this conversation. I knew he was going to be spending his time with Katie Smith. I'm not stupid. And I don't like her.

It's not like I go anywhere, either. I got to go to Disney World once down in Florida. I was nine and my daddy's friend, Mr. Horton, begged him to take off a week of work and take us all with the Horton family so his kids would have friends to enjoy Disney with them. Mr. Horton and his wife were divorced and he didn't want to be alone with his kids because he wasn't sure what to do with them. At least, that was what my daddy told us.

It was a lot of fun for a whole week, even if the three Horton kids were annoying me the whole time, and it's the only vacation my family ever took with all four of us together. That's it for me. Camp and Disney. Then Raleigh once in a while to see my aunt. We'll go to the big mall up there and to the state fair each October. Charlie's mom took us to Durham for a Bulls baseball game when we were ten. I went on a field trip to the USS North Carolina in Wilmington with my sixth grade class. That's the extent of my travels.

There are a couple of kids in my class who have been to England and a boy named Jack went to Hawaii with his grandparents last year. He showed me pictures of himself in Hawaii near a waterfall and I've never seen anything so beautiful. I hope I can go there someday. Maybe I can go with Brother Doug. Maybe we'll be able to go to Jack's waterfall and kiss underneath of it and someone will take our picture. Maybe the picture of us kissing will be used in a magazine or a book.

The rising amount of butterflies in my stomach, flapping like trapped hummingbirds in a dark box, began to overwhelm me with the thought of such a scene in my future life. I looked out the window of the front seat with endless summer green going by fast — but not fast enough — my mom humming quietly to a Patsy Cline song on the radio, Jonny sitting in the back seat with his eyes shut, left hand rested on his suitcase next to him.

"Three weeks of camp, then one week after that before school starts again," my mom said to me, grinning. "Are you excited?"

"Not really," I responded, watching trees go by in the window.

"Nonsense," my mom snapped. "Making new friends,

playing on the sports teams, maybe trying out for the musical in the springtime, goin' to football games on Friday nights." Then she looked over at me, "Homecoming dances…Prom."

"Haven't thought much about it," I said, clearly disappointing her in some way. My mind is so consumed with seeing Brother Doug again that it's hard for me to feel like a normal soon-to-be freshman in high school. I don't feel as young as I am. I feel older.

What's fourteen supposed to feel like anyway? The boys in my class at Haddleboro High School will be the same boys I've known my whole life, except for the ones coming in from Black Hill and the farms nearby — but really, aren't boys all the same no matter where they're from? Except for Charlie.

And while it'll be neat to be in some classes with the older and bigger boys like the juniors and seniors who have cars and jobs, they're all just immature anyway — smoking Camels and trying to look cool, drinking Budweiser at Jasper Lake, and trying get into girls' pants. At least, that's what my daddy told me and I believe him. My daddy doesn't say much, but when he does, it's usually important and worth listening to.

Unlike those boys in my school, Brother Doug is a man. A real man. He is a man who still likes to play like a boy and have fun. But he knows how to treat people, too. He knows how to treat girls — girls like me: girls who aren't the prettiest or the best dressed, girls who don't care about having painted finger nails or coloring their hair or wearing a bunch of makeup on their faces, girls who have scars on their knees from playing too rough outside, girls who like baseball and the Yankees. Brother Doug is what I imagined Charlie would become someday. A really nice, sincere, caring, and fun loving hunk of M-A-N.

Thinking about Charlie as a grown-up makes me realize that I don't know who I'll be without him. But I needed to start dealing with it. Someday, maybe even someday soon, Charlie is going to meet a girl that he really likes, like differently and a lot better than me, a girl he will want to kiss all the time. Maybe a girl he wants to have sex with. And I don't want to think about any of that.

Sometimes, I'd try to think about Charlie as an actual boy, a boy I would want to kiss. After we kissed that one time in his bedroom years ago, it occurred to me that I liked kissing him. I didn't want to stop kissing him and felt like I wanted him to put his hands on me. It scared me how it felt because I had never felt quite like that before.

"Scout, that was really weird, but it felt good at the same time," Charlie said to me after we stopped kissing with our tongues. That was the first inkling I had that maybe we could've been boyfriend and girlfriend. He leaned into me so close that I could feel the heat from his face. "I like doing this with you," he whispered, eyes closed.

I wanted to tell him that I liked it, too. But I didn't. I made it sound like it felt weird and that we weren't any good at it.

Heading home on that day after we kissed, I knew that if he became my boyfriend instead of just being my best friend, and if we broke up like all the boyfriends and girlfriends our age did, then I would lose him as my best friend. And the thought of that terrified me. It wasn't worth it.

So, while I do think Charlie is a cute boy with his salty blond hair, blue eyes, and string bean body, and I admit that I got jealous when he told me he liked Katie Smith and had been making out with her at his house when his mom wasn't home, my heart just wouldn't let me think of him how I think about Brother Doug.

Nope. No love story for me and Charlie Porter. I loved Charlie and always would. But not like how I loved Brother Doug — who was now only fifteen minutes away from this Skylark. I hoped.

****

Dear Brother Doug,   10-22-82

I was so so so happy to get your letter today! J It was the best. It has been a bad week in school but getting your letter made me so happy. I hope you are having a good week.

I love trick-or-treating still even though my mom says I'm too old for it and some of the folks in my church frown upon it. Me and my friend Charlie are just going to put on baseball uniforms and go out and get candy. I don't care what my mom says. But that is so neat that your little boy will be a baseball player, too.

It seems so far away until I can come back to camp for my last summer. I want it to be here so I can see you, but I also don't want it to be here because it means that I don't know when it will be that I will ever see you again. I can come back to be a counselor when I'm eighteen but that will be a really REALLY long time to go without ever seeing you. Maybe we can still write to each other though? Maybe when I'm eighteen, I could come help you lifeguard or something. Or maybe you could become a counselor, too, and we could be in charge of the same group together. I know, I am thinking ahead! But I always do that.

My church is starting the Bible verse competition again soon, so I need to get studying the verses so I can win the money so my parents will be able to afford to send me to camp. This time, I think I will have to memorize the whole first chapter of John! That is a lot of memorizing, but I have a great memory.

Yesterday was my birthday. I'm finally fourteen.

Can you believe that crazy story on the news about people dying from cyanide in their Tylenol? My mom threw ours out and won't buy it anymore!

I am writing a report on a famous person for my reading class. I chose to do it on Richard Petty. My brother thought I should do it on Dale Earnhardt but I like Richard Petty better. Who is your favorite driver?

Well, I will go now. I miss you so much and I hope you are doing good. Please PLEASE write me back soon!

Love,

Squirrel

****

CHARLIE

I came downstairs to the kitchen and saw my mom sitting at the little wooden table drinking some coffee or tea in a white mug that said "MOM" in black print. She had the radio on the oldies station and Frankie Valli was singing about seeing someone in September. The kitchen window was open a smidge and the warm air coming inside wasn't too bad yet.

"It thunderstormed something fierce last night and cooled things for a short while," my mom said looking up at me. It was late in the morning, I guess about 11:00 or so. So that meant Scout would be gone by now. "Did you do Scout's route today?"

"No, that's tomorrow."

"That takes up a lot of time."

"It's okay. I get all her money and tips for three weeks. And she's got better tippers than me. That'll go right into my car savings."

"You still have all your money in that bag under the mattress?" she asked, smiling.

"Yes, ma'am. I have $479.69 saved up so far," I stated

proudly, walking to the fridge.

"Scout save up that much, too?"

I laughed. "Scout told me she has $40.00 in the little piggy bank in her room. She used to have almost as much as me. I don't know what she does with her money because she sure don't spend it on clothes and makeup and other stuff all the girls at school are always buying. She bought a new glove with some of it."

Since Scout is gone for three weeks, that means that I can spend a lot more time with Katie without feeling bad about it. I like Katie and we like to get together and make out. Katie doesn't talk a whole lot, which is strange for a girl, so I do most of the talking. I think it bothers her that I talk so much sometimes, so she just starts kissing me in order to shut me up for a while. That's okay with me. I don't mind making out instead of talking.

"You gonna see that girl with the auburn hair while Scout's away?" my mom asked me.

I nodded.

"You like her, dontcha?"

"She's a nice girl, mom."

Katie is the only girl I've ever seen with auburn hair. She wears her face all done up in pretty makeup and her hair always looks nice. She does it in big curls some days, feathered on the sides other days, and sometimes she wears it back in a big ponytail.

"Well, she seems a little on the dark side to me,

Charlie," my mom said, lighting up a cigarette.

My mom is right about that. Katie isn't the kind of girl who smiles all the time or giggles at dumb jokes and cuts up with everybody. She doesn't have any girl friends that I know of. But I think the two of us bonded because we both know what it feels like to be abandoned and missing a parent.

"Her mom died when she was only five and it was real ugly. Then her dad raised her by himself for a while until he got married to her stepmom," I explained. Katie doesn't talk about a whole lot of things, not like me and Scout do, but she does talk about the sad stuff sometimes.

I've told Katie about how my dad left me and my mom when I was only three, how I don't know him, how my mom has never gotten over it, and how she's dated shitty men ever since. Not that my dad wasn't also a shitty man — I mean, what kind of a person just ups and leaves his wife and young son? With nothing? For good? A shitty man does. Why my mom keeps dating men who would do the exact same thing to her, I don't know, but I'm glad she hasn't married another one, forcing me to deal with it, too. It seems to me like she knows that she dates bad men and feels like she can't do anything about it. So she keeps it away from me. I've met a few of them over the years. Thankfully, none have moved in or tried to become stepfathers to me.

I saw my dad once a couple of years ago, just for a few hours. He showed up during one of my baseball games. After the game was done, he walked over to me and looked me over.

"You want a burger, son?" I knew he was my father as soon as he opened his mouth.

"Okay," I said to him, a little short on words, which is rare for me.

Scout stood over near the dugout, dumbfounded, wondering why I was going off with some strange man.

"I've been living in Tennessee, near Nashville. You hear of it?" he asked me as we drove over to the Soda Shop in town. "I'm pretty sure I got me a gig writing songs and playing guitar for a new fella, a singer from North Carolina. You'd like it out there in Nashville," he said. "They call it 'Music City'. It's where all the good singers go to make it."

"But you're not a singer," I snapped, trying to keep my simmering anger in check, but not doing too good of a job. I used to wonder if I'd be happy or mad if I saw him again. It was both. I was happy to see him at first, but when I saw he had no guilt about anything he's done to us or any plans to be my father again, I got irritated that he bothered to come to Haddleboro at all. And I think he could sense that I wasn't buying his bullshit.

"Look, Charlie, I don't expect you to understand. You're just a dumb kid who don't know anything about real life. I'm a musician. So I got to go write songs for the people who can sing them. And you and your mama need to stay here away from all of that. The music business is no place for a family. And a family is no place for a musician who is gonna go on the road all the time. It's how it is."

"Then why'd you get yourself a family if you didn't want one?" I asked him, holding back.

He shook his head, ate his burger, and didn't say much more to me at all. He never asked how we were getting along without him all these years. He only talked about himself and his big music dreams. Then he dropped me off back at the baseball field and I haven't heard from him since. I never told my mom about his visit.

I didn't know much about country music, so when he told me the singer's name, I had no idea who he was. I'd always liked The Eagles because I thought my dad looked like Glenn Frey when he was younger. Something about the song "Take It Easy" always made me think of my dad and how life could've been if he would've stayed with us.

One day, I heard the country singer's name on TV and remembered that he was the one my dad had told me about. So ever since then, I looked for songs by this Randy Travis singer. If I'm ever in a record store or a place with a juke box, I try to find his music, just in case my dad is mentioned or just in case I can tell the lyrics might be his. I listen for him on country radio, too, even though I don't like country music all that much.

A few years ago, my mom got me a used guitar from a yard sale.

"If you can't have your father, then you should at least be able to share something with him, something he truly loved — and Lord knows, it's music," she said, handing me the guitar. "The Godfather's gonna teach you."

The Godfather was my neighbor, a crusty and funny old black man who used to play in some blues group years ago. Playing the guitar is the one fun thing, other than baseball, that I'm good at. And I guess now I could add "kissing Katie" to this list of things I'm good at.

Katie feels bad for me that my dad would leave us like he did, especially because it was his choice. Her mom died. It's not like dying was her choice. She had some kind of strange virus that Katie never heard of before. Her dad said that she got it from doing drugs before they were married. So Katie's mom didn't abandon her — God did. At least, that was how Katie felt about it.

One time I told Scout about what Katie said about God having abandoned her by taking her mom away. Scout got really upset and I could tell she kept her distance from Katie, more than usual, after that. Scout was a little sensitive about God and people blaming him for the bad stuff that happens in life.

"What does she mean God abandoned her?" she asked me.

"She thinks that because God took her mom away, God Himself abandoned her." I tried to explain how Katie saw it, but since I didn't quite understand it myself, I probably messed it up.

"That's ridiculous." Scout looked offended. "God didn't

take her away. She did drugs and suffered the consequences of what happens to people who do drugs."

I thought that was really harsh, especially coming from Scout, who was usually so nice and understanding toward people who were less fortunate. She knew Katie had no mom. It was odd to hear her be so hardnosed about it.

"Well, Scout, we both have our moms so we don't know what she feels like. People have told Katie that it was God's will that her mom die. Even her dad told her that. Why wouldn't she think that God is responsible for taking her away?"

"God's will is God's will. It doesn't mean God's responsible. It means that her mom had free will and chose poorly, so God let it be. He isn't going to swoop in and clean up the messes we make."

I guess that made sense. Or maybe not. Either way, I wasn't bringing up Katie or her mom anymore. I didn't like upsetting Scout and feeling confused about God and God's will — whatever all that even meant anyway.

But I wanted to know why some people who clean up their lives get rewarded by dying — and others who never clean up their lives get to live and continue to hurt people? Why do some people, who do the best they can and try to raise their families, just suffer through life — and then why do other people, who are blessed with a family, up and leave and go to Tennessee to play guitar and write songs and never know their son?

"Mom, I'm gonna head out to the park," I said, watching my mom as she sat at the table. She looked like she was fifty-five instead of thirty-five. Her blond hair was frizzy, turning gray already, and her face was tired, worn, and yellow from so many years of smoking. Her cigarette burned out slowly in the ashtray next to her coffee mug.

She looked up and smiled. I think I was the only thing, other than a Donna Summer song, that could make her smile anymore. "Okay, sweet boy. Are you meeting Scout there?"

"No, remember, she's gone to her camp today." It was like she completely forgot that we already talked about how Scout was gone and I was going to meet Katie.

Mom sighed, "I sure wish I could've had the money to send you to camp, Charlie. It sounds like she has a great time every summer."

"It's okay. I don't need to go away for so long and leave you all alone."

While I'm sure I would've had a great time at Scout's camp, I didn't belong to her church. And besides, I meant what I said about my leaving my mom alone. I couldn't do it. I was all she had, and three weeks was a long time to be away from home.

But I would miss Scout. A lot. Even though I liked Katie and spending time with her and trying to figure out what goes on in her head and making out with her, she wasn't Scout. I loved Scout. I wish I had the nerve to tell her that.

* * * * * * * * *

Dear Squirrel,   November 10th, 1982

Thanks for still writing me. I am doing good and am starting to get excited about the holidays coming up. We are going away for Thanksgiving to my parents' house in Blowing Rock. It has been a couple of months since they saw Paul, so they will be happy to spend some time with him. Plus, I don't have to help with any turkey — just eat it. I hope you and your family are going to have a great Thanksgiving feast, too.

Basketball season is about to start and, if you're playing, let me know how it goes. I know you got a jump shot on you! I remember from last summer. Miss ya, kiddo! We will have a great time this summer. Just you wait!

Oh, yes, my wife threw out our Tylenol, too! The world is scary place sometimes. But you have Jesus (and me, too!) on your side. My favorite driver is Darrell Waltrip, but I think Richard Petty is a good choice for your report.

Oh and before I forget, Happy Birthday! The Big 1-4. To think I remember way back when you were knee-high to a grasshopper.

Your friend,

Brother Doug

* * * * * * * * *

CAMMY DEHAAN, AGE 30

I am exhausted.

Pulling into my driveway, I see that there are no lights on in the house and Doug will have to leave soon. That means he's not up taking care of Paul before he heads off to work, so I will have to do it instead. I park our car, turn off the ignition, and look down at the stains on my top from when the orderly dropped a patient's vomit pan just as I was about to leave. I did my best to get it out, but the stench has overtaken the car and now I feel nauseated.

I quietly glide into the house and slip into Paul's nursery. Looking down at my baby boy, sleeping soundly in his crib, I can hear Doug rustling around in the bathroom. All I want to do is go to bed and sleep for fifty years. Nobody tells you how much a toddler will take out of you. Nobody tells you how you might look forward to going to work so you can get a break from it all.

I love my son. He is the most perfect, cherub-faced, ball of cute that ever existed and I'd gladly lay down on a set of railroad tracks to be run over by the biggest, fastest, loudest train if it meant Paul's life was spared. But he's going to be the death of me — not the train way, but the slow way, running me down and burning me out.

Sometimes, I wondered if it would be easier on me if I didn't have to work. Like some of the other mothers I know who don't have to work. Their husbands must make more money than my husband — or they just don't care about the money and survive somehow.

Truthfully, I don't know how I would fare as a mother who stayed home all day with her kids, cleaning up and cooking meals. There is nothing wrong with any of that, of course. Hell, my mama did it and her mama before her. I've had a job and made my own money since I was eleven years old and now I'm contributing something meaningful to the world as a Registered Nurse at Carolina Memorial Hospital. It's not like raising my sweet Paulie Boy isn't contributing something meaningful, but I always saw myself as doing more with my life than being somebody's mama or somebody's wife.

My mama was somebody's mama and somebody's wife for her whole adult life. She never had anything else but keeping a home, raising me and my sisters, and doing her wifely duties for my father. Then we all grew up and either went away to college or went out to work and she was left — alone — in an unhappy marriage with a man who had been skirtin' around on her for years. My father owned his own car dealership and so my mama never wanted for anything — except things like love, kindness, fidelity, and attention.

"Why do you live like this? With him? Still?" I asked the last time I saw her, as I made her a cup of coffee in my kitchen. She looked at me like I just broke some unspoken rule of life: you don't ask your mama her reasons for staying with your father.

"What do you mean? Live like what?" she replied, playing dumb.

"Why do you stay with a man who treats you like you're nothin'?"

"Campbell, I don't know what you're talkin' about. Mind your own marriage and I'll mind mine."

And that was the end of that.

I heard Doug close the front door behind him and get into the vomit-smelling car. He didn't bother to say anything to me before he left. Since Paul was still asleep, I went into my bedroom and left the door wide open so I could hear him if he woke up. Then I stripped off my vomit-covered top and bra and then down to my panties, falling into bed. Still smelling Doug's scent on my pillow, I tried desperately to fall asleep.

Thinking about my mother and the life she led, I always wanted more for myself, whether in a marriage or career. Always in the back of my mind was the escape — the possible escape I would need from any marriage, just in case it wasn't what it was supposed to be. And with that, the ability to take care of myself and be independent of any man and his money.

The one thing my father gave me that was worth a damn, other than my natural smarts for math, was a great example on what I did not want to marry. I like to believe that he didn't start out as a self-centered dick who treated my mama like a doormat and charmed an endless parade of women. But who knows? I suppose that if a person is an arrogant asshole for most of his adult life, then maybe that's just who he is and who he's always been and who he'll always be.

So I found myself Doug DeHaan, man-child.

My Doug, so so very cute, so so very sexy, not too ambitious — there would be no owning of car dealerships by Doug DeHaan and certainly no medical school or curing of cancer either! — a hell of a lot of fun, great with kids, and great in bed. One thing I liked about Doug was that he was a safe choice for a girl like me who was a bit cynical on marriage.

He had a natural charm to him and could make me laugh, but really, I knew he had been smitten by me. What is it that other men call it? Pussy-whipped? Whenever I hear that term, I laugh. Men call other men pussy-whipped because they are just jealous. They have never been so enamored by a woman and in love before, so they have to put down the ones who have been smitten with such a derogatory term. The poor, stupid assholes don't know what they're missing in life.

"I'd do anything for you, Cam," Doug told me once, as

we snuggled together on the couch watching TV. We hadn't spoken for at least an hour and, out of the blue, he said that to me.

I turned my face to his, "Would you kill someone for me?"

"I'd kill anyone for you," he said, grinning and then kissing my nose. I knew that he was joking around and would never harm a soul, but the way he said it was still kind of sweet in some twisted and dark way.

As a woman, it's a double-edged sword to have a man feel like that about you. It is great because you *know* he loves you, you *really know*. But it's bad because you have all the power in the relationship. He will always love you a little bit more than you love him. Some women like having all the power. I'm uncomfortable with it.

I'm aware that it's like that between us.

"You could walk out on me if I piss you off and I'll come crawling on my knees through shards of glass to make it right with you," Doug told me. "Even if I don't think I did anything wrong!"

"I know you would."

But if he left me? I didn't have the heart to tell him that I'd let him go. And then wait for him to come back to me after his pity party was over.

Since I'm conscious of this, I do everything I can not to manipulate him too much. I'm not always successful and, yes, sometimes I can be a real bitch because I want what I want, but I don't intend to take advantage of the love he has for me. I know how lucky I am to have a man love me like that and, precisely because of growing up in my house with my parents, I appreciate it.

"I married up when I married you," he said to me on our wedding night, seven years ago. He has said on more than one occasion, when he's vulnerable, as we lay naked and entangled in bed after a great evening of sex, "I have everything because I have you."

"I do, too," I said back to him.

"Cam, my greatest fear in life is if I were to lose you," he added, rubbing my temples. "I don't think I'd be able to go on."

"Me too, hon," I responded, more for his benefit than my own. I knew deep down, as much as I loved him, I could go on without him.

He'd compliment me all the time. "Baby doll, you sure look pretty," he'd say, as I stumbled into the house in my crumpled nursing uniform after a long shift and feeling like shit. He used to tell me how much he loved my long brown hair and then run his fingers through the short parts near my temples. He'd touch me gently in the small of my back whenever we'd walk around, kiss me every time we greeted or said goodbye. He'd give me strong hugs, the kind that let me know he would crush me into his chest if he could.

He appreciated my sarcasm. "You keep me on my toes, Cam!" He took a perverse comfort in the fact that I was feisty and had a sharp mouth.

"I'm sorry, Doug," I told him once after a really bad day at work. "I shouldn't cuss so much and I know it must get old to hear my complaining all the time."

He just smiled, pulled me into him, and then kissed my forehead. "Don't ever apologize for being you. I know that you'll always be able to take care of yourself and no one will ever mess with my girl."

It was so nice to have a man who appreciated me just as I am.

When Paul was born, he doted on us both like we were the most fragile, precious things he ever saw. I knew without a doubt, when I saw him with our baby, I chose well. He loved me and he loved our son.

So where the hell has that guy gone?

For the past year or so, I've felt like a single parent. I work the graveyard shift at Carolina Memorial and raise our little boy. That's it. That is all I do. I don't go out, I don't belong to any groups, and I rarely meet up with my sisters and their families. I eat, sleep, work, and take care of this house and our son.

But Doug? He goes to work, stays late to coach whatever sport is in season, works out at the school gym or on the school track, plays on a church softball team, and goes to church on Sundays to teach some Jesus class to ten-year-olds. Basically, he does whatever the hell he wants.

Since I work most Sundays and I'm just not much of

a church person, I don't go with him.

"Doug, I really don't want to. I am not Presbyterian, the pastor is a big fake and I'm just not really all that interested in God," I tried to explain to him after he pleaded for me to start going with him.

"People think I'm married to a woman who doesn't believe in God," he said, trying to reason with me.

"I do believe in God, but I think those things are private and see no need to go to church and give my hard earned money to a brass plate."

Doug looked dejected.

When school is out for the summer, he spends long days at that Christian camp he's worked at for years. He's gone early in the morning, six days a week, and since he said that the Camp Director has asked him to continue working with the teen groups, he doesn't come home some nights until late. We get Saturdays together, but he spends most of it sleeping or playing with Paul.

"Please, Doug, just let that job go!" I begged him last year.

"Sorry, Cam, we need the money and you know it," he said, defensively.

"Then can't you do something else in the summer? Teach Driver's Ed or something? Then you can come home at a reasonable hour!" I tried to make the point that perhaps he is being overworked and taken advantage of — for not very much money.

"Look. I'm *needed* at Camp Judah. The Houghtons are family to me."

"You have a family right here in this house! And we need you more!" I hollered in frustration.

He walked away. But he has to know I'm right.

The sex is just wham-bam-thank-you-ma'am. No emotion, no tenderness, no intimacy. It's like he isn't my Doug anymore. His mind is always elsewhere. If I thought he had time, I'd think he was having an affair. But he's not. I have a spy at that school and she has told me there is no one else — Doug is as clean as a shiny new penny.

Whenever I ask him to do things around the house, he does them, but I can tell he's annoyed, like instead, I asked him to climb Mount Everest for me or something. In the past, he'd shout, "Of course, my dear!" and then either change the light bulb or sweep the back porch wearing a make-shift cape out of a sheet, only in his boxers, singing "That's Amore" in some fake Italian baritone.

Now when I ask him to do something, he gets quiet, and I can tell he wants to say something nasty to me. But he doesn't. He keeps it inside. I wish he'd just scream obscenities at me sometimes. Something!

Is this my life now? After seven years of marriage, one perfect son, and two amazing years of dating before that, and he is already sick of me?

"Do you still love me?" I asked him two days ago.

He kept doing whatever he was doing and replied, "Of

course!"

That was the first time I didn't *just know* anymore.

* * * * * * * *

Dear Doug,   11-16-82

Thank you for the letter. I was so so so SO excited to get it. Now all I can think about is turkey and mashed potatoes. I hope it's OK if I just call you Doug instead of Brother Doug. Really, you're not my brother and instead you are my friend, so if it's OK with you, I'm just going to call you Doug from now on.

For Thanksgiving, we are having my Mema and Pawpaw over. My mom is going to make the dinner because my Mema doesn't cook. Isn't that weird? A Mema that doesn't cook? But it's going to be great and I'm going to try to bake my first pie. I love Thanksgiving because it makes me feel warm in my heart.

Basketball starts next week. I'm going to play and I'm pretty sure I'll be the point guard again since most of the girls don't know how to dribble. Are you going to coach basketball at your school?

I wish I went to your school. Then you could be my coach and we could be together having fun every day.

I miss you and summer cannot get here fast enough so you can throw me into the lake again. I hope you and your family have a wonderful Thanksgiving.

Love,

Scout Elizabeth

SCOUT

We pulled onto the long, forest-lined gravel road leading us into the field where we could park the car. Jonny was awake now, quietly tapping his fingers on his suitcase, his dark hair falling into his eyes.

"You're gonna need a haircut after three weeks," I said to him. "You should've had one before we left."

"Who cares?" he barked.

My heart was in my throat and the butterflies were flapping in my stomach so hard that I was about to throw up on the floor. My mom turned off the radio and spoke up after a fairly long silence.

"You know, I'm goin' to miss y'all so much," she said, in her rural North Carolina drawl. Her brown hair was short and permed and her lipstick was bright red. She always looked so put-together. Today, she was wearing a blue scarf over her hair along with a pair of big sunglasses. She looked like a countrified Audrey Hepburn. If she pulled out a cigarette (she didn't smoke) and took a long drag, I would've felt like we were in a renegade version of *Breakfast at Tiffany's*.

"I'll miss ya, too, Mommy," Jonny said. Then he kicked

the back of my seat three times.

I turned around and hollered, "STOP!" Annoying little brother. "I'll be so glad to be away from you for three whole weeks!"

"Feeling's mutual!" Jonny snapped back.

"Mom, do you and Daddy have plans?" I asked, pretending to sound interested, knowing that surely they did have plans.

My mom smirked and said, "Well, we do plan to take a trip for a few days over to the Outer Banks. I want to go to Ocracoke." She seemed excited about her time alone with Daddy, hand-in-hand, dreamy eyes and kisses on the ferry. Not that I know what the ferry looks like. I've never been to the Outer Banks or on the ferry.

"Well, that should be fun. You won't miss us too much," I said.

As we pulled into the field, several cars were already parked and kids were unloading their suitcases.

Camp Judah was once a big cotton farm. Mr. Houghton told us that he bought it from a black man who had been a sharecropper and whose parents had been slaves on the farm. My parents attended all-white high schools and my Pawpaw used to say ugly things about black people in town. I also heard that my mom was a bit of a rebel about segregation when she was a girl. She would do things like drink from the black water fountains and sneak her friend Cessy, a black girl in town, into her house to listen to records while my

Pawpaw was at work.

Whatever kind of world she grew up in didn't take a hold on her like it did others. She taught me early on when I was a little girl, "Scout, there's only one kind of folks in this world." I later learned that sentiment was from *To Kill a Mockingbird*.

My mom always knew that she wanted to name me after young Scout Finch. "I could've named you Catherine or Elizabeth or Jane or Anne. But those are everybody else's names, too!" Being the daughter of a reading teacher exposes you to a lot of books, different worlds, and ways of thinking.

Because of the stained history of my parents' upbringing and of my favorite place on earth, Camp Judah, whenever I walk around the camp grounds, I try to remember that once upon a time, where I was walking and where I was eating and sleeping, other people once walked and ate and slept — enslaved.

After finally parking and unloading our suitcases, a young man was directing us, "Put your belongings into the pickup truck near the entrance! The truck will drive everything to the camp residence area!" Jonny's luggage would go to The Holy Ghost Town, which is a bunch of cabins for the younger kids. My luggage would be dropped off at The Lord's Reservation, which was where the teenagers had their residence.

Everything was segregated into boys and girls, meaning there was one side of The Lord's Reservation that was girls-only and one side that was for boys. And since I had no interest whatsoever in any of the boys at The Lord's Reservation, I didn't care if they were shipped to a deserted island on the other side of the world.

I was here to see Brother Doug.

There were already a bunch of campers checking in with their parents. Counselors were taking names and forms from parents, as well as checks or cash for the camp store purchases. We weren't allowed to buy stuff from the camp store, but my mom gave us each some money so we could buy candy or an ice cream once in a while.

I stood with my mom and Jonny, scanning the area for any sign of Brother Doug. Was he here?

"Hey, Scout, good to see you again," a peppy blond in her Camp Judah tee shirt said, as she took the money from my mom. It was my counselor from last year, Sister Debbie.

"Oh, hi, Sister Debbie!" I exclaimed, sounding too excited, even for me. "Are you my counselor again this year?" I asked, my voice raising several octaves.

"No, not this year. You have new counselors for the girls, Sisters Abby and Ally." That sounded like a couple of nuns to me.

"Oh, okay," I said, disappointed.

"No, really — they are actually sisters. Twins! How cool is that?" Sister Debbie shouted.

I liked Sister Debbie. She was a tiny college student from New Jersey who would tell us dirty jokes, even though she wasn't supposed to. I thought she was funny and liked how she wouldn't be so pushy with her Christian beliefs and never made me feel guilty for every unchristian thought that came through my head. I mean, I love Jesus and I fear the Lord, but sometimes the counselors would make you feel like you were going to Hell just because you had some "carnal" thoughts about things once in awhile. From memory: "For to set the mind on the flesh is death, but to set the mind on the Spirit is life and peace." Romans 8:6. *Blah.*

"You will like Sisters Abby and Ally, Scout. I promise. I'll see you during the evening chapel time and, this year, I'm in all of the skits," she beamed. "They are freakin' hilarious because I wrote them."

I loved her New Jersey accent. It sounded so tough.

She handed my mom a receipt and we made our way over to the station where the staff would look over the medical forms to be sure we were properly vaccinated. I looked around to see if I knew anyone — anyone at all. Whenever I'd see kids who looked around my age, I didn't recognize them from years past. Is it possible that a lot of people I grew up with at this camp aren't coming back for their last summer?

No sign of Michelle. No sign of Brother Doug.

Then, out of the blue, I felt two arms grab me from behind and a hard nose stick right into my neck, tickling it.

"Boo!" said the voice loudly. That deep baritone voice, that cracked and parched sounding voice, that voice of an angel, Brother Doug's voice.

I curled up my body in response to the surprising welcome and the tickling sensation on my neck and was so overcome with happiness and excitement all at once. He was here. He saw me. He came to say hello to me. He touched me. His beautiful nose was on my neck! I could just go ahead and die right now on this spot under the awning outside of the main chapel area. My life was full. It was complete.

After regaining my composure, I turned and threw my arms around him. "Brother Doug!" I hollered, hugging him with all of my strength and with my forehead buried in his chest. He was almost a whole foot taller than me.

"Hi, Brother Doug," my mom said grinning at this picture perfect man hugging her daughter. "Good to see you back."

"Yes, Mrs. Webb, I can't seem to outgrow this place," he said, releasing me from his clutches and smiling that beautiful smile I've missed for so many months.

"Well, Scout sure is glad you are back. I think she was worried you wouldn't be."

Brother Doug looked down at me, his eyes squinty, his smile turning into smirk. "You were?"

I was speechless, so rather than attempt to respond, knowing that I would stammer and trip over my words, I just stood there looking like a complete idiot *which was so much better.*

"No way, couldn't miss Scout's last summer here. We

both kinda grew up together exactly on this soil. Right, Squirrel?"

Looking up at him, he popped his cheeks at me. Excitedly, I popped mine back at him. Jonny rolled his eyes.

"Well, listen, y'all, I've got some staff duties I need to take care of before I head out to the lake," he continued. "Mrs. Webb, great to see you again. Jonny, I'm expecting to see you compete in my relays this year. And win." Then he locked his eyes on mine, "Squirrel-Girl, I'll catch ya later."

He headed off over toward the camp staff building and left me standing there, a puddle of mush.

My mom eyeballed me. "I declare, that man gets more handsome every summer," she announced.

"I know," I thought to myself. "As if that were possible for him to be even more handsome." My mom might appear to be a flake sometimes, but she is no dummy. She was well aware of my years-long crush on Brother Doug DeHaan.

Jonny piped in, "Scout loves Brother Doug. Ha ha. You're so dumb. He's old and he could never love a girl like you."

"Shut up," I snapped at my brother. Thank the Lord in Heaven above that I won't see much of him!

"Well, sweet babies, I guess I'd better give my hugs and kisses goodbye now. I'll miss you both so much," she said, hugging both of us and kissing our cheeks. "Me and Daddy will come get you in three weeks' time and I'm sure we will stop at Tara's Ice Cream Palace on our way back home."

Goody goody gum drops.

We said our goodbyes and my mom headed back to the Skylark and back to my daddy for her childless three weeks of no work and all play. But all I could think about was how happy I was that Brother Doug was here, that he hugged me, and that he was happy to see me. He seemed so bouncy and giddy toward me, not polite like his letters, but more like the real him. In his letters, he always sounded like a teacher. But in person, today, we could've been a couple kissing under a waterfall in Hawaii. Or at least that was how I felt about our reunion.

****

Dear SG,   December 1st, 1982

I guess you can call me Doug if you want, but just keep it to your letters, okay? I don't want the other campers to think you're my favorite camper or anything (wink, wink). J I enjoyed my Thanksgiving with my family. We had a nice visit up in Blowing Rock and little Paul got to go on his first Christmas tree farm visit. He had a lot of fun.

I am coaching basketball this year but just the boys' team. So far we only played one game and won by a lot. We have one kid who is really good, should be able to start Varsity next year no problem.

Let me know how your season is going. Miss ya,

kiddo! Have a Merry Christmas!

Your friend,

Brother Doug

* * * * * * * * *

DOUG

Well, I have to admit that it's a little silly for me to be this happy about the last three weeks of camp. While I'm genuinely happy because it's the last weeks of this exhausting job and I can go back to school and coaching and finally get away from this place — maybe even for good this time — I'm extra happy, excited even, that Scout is here. She came back. I honestly didn't know if I'd ever see her again after not having heard from her for so long. Not only is it the last three weeks of Camp Judah — for maybe my entire life! — but I get to spend it with my Squirrel-Girl. One last hurrah for us both.

I had a small box in the camp office where I've kept a few personal things over the years. Earlier today, I took it out of the overstuffed closet, opened it, and saw the small pile of letters Scout had written to me this past year. I kept expecting her to get a little bored with my letters. Really, how exciting is it to hear about some guy's little kid or his job? But she kept writing.

She started to get a bit bold with me though, so I had to be careful. I knew that. To me, she was still the little

Squirrel with the chubby cheeks, but between the lines, I could tell that she was trying to sound older than she was.

Then the letters stopped. It was weird. And when they stopped — and I hadn't heard from her for two weeks, three weeks, a month, three months — I became concerned and thought about looking up her father's name and number in the phone book to be sure she was okay. I found myself missing her letters. It's ridiculous and not something I'd ever admit out loud.

Things at home with Cammy have been shitty for a long time. It's gotten to the point where I avoid being there when she's home and I'm happy when she has to pull a shift that doesn't let us cross paths.

I don't feel like myself anymore. Nothing is fun. Everything is about Paul-Paul-Paulie-Boy. I love my son, but as soon as he was born, he was the only thing she cared about. The only interest my wife seems to have in me is any extra money I'm bringing in from coaching, and then wanting me to fix shit around the house, and then having me take Paul from her so she can take another fucking nap.

"Seriously? You need another nap?" I snapped at her last night when I came in for supper.

"I'm tired, Doug! What am I supposed to say?" Then she went to bed.

She never wants to have sex, never wants to do anything, never wants to get a babysitter so we can just go out to the movies or something.

"You know what Cammy? I'm living my life and doing the things I want to do. Just because we had a child doesn't mean that we have to stop being people who like to have fun. Or at least it doesn't mean I have to stop being a person who likes to have fun," I told her, frustrated and fed up.

My escape from her nagging and whining has been work, working late, working out, and the innocent letters from a teenaged girl who has a crush on me. It makes me feel good, as pathetic as that sounds.

When I got back to the staff office, Chris was licking an ice cream cone. "Dougie, what are you doing here?"

"Turning in all this paperwork: the inspection of my equipment at the lake, the inspection of the lake facility, and the inspection of the boys' camp area at The Reservation," I said checking off boxes and putting my binder on Mr. Houghton's desk.

"You coming on the canoe trip and the Desert Wanderers three-nighter this time?" he asked, in between chomps.

"I haven't been asked to do the Desert Wanderers trip," I replied.

"We need you. We need another male," he said.

The canoe trip with the teens was always a lot of fun. I've done it for the last two summers. Lots of great stories come from those, involving throwing some of the girl counselors in the Catawba River and then watching them try to get back in the canoe without any help. Or flipping their canoes and watching them try to turn it back over. Yes, Cammy is right. I'm so *immature*.

"I'm in for the canoe trip, but I've never done the three-nighter before. Not in all of my years working here."

"It's four days, three nights," he said, throwing his napkin in the trash. I knew that the excursion takes the teens into the wilderness — or more accurately, our "wilderness" of a dead cotton farm. "It's a great opportunity for them to learn how to pitch a tent and cook outdoors and evade capture by a swarm of mosquitoes and gnats," Chris explained.

"And if a camper doesn't want to do it, then they don't have to go, right?" I asked him.

"Yeah. The remaining campers stay in The Reservation with a couple of counselors and do other things. But they sure miss out on a great time."

"Okay, let me talk to my wife. She works shift at Carolina Memorial and it's hard for her with the baby and all."

Inside of my head, I hollered, "Hell yeah, three nights away from home!" Cammy would not be happy, but I was doing it. I would tell her that I had already committed to it and it was too late to back out. She'd just have to cry martyrdom, yet again, and deal with it. She likes playing the victim anyway, so I should let her be martyred so she has another thing to complain to me about.

After dropping off my binder, I stood on the balcony of the staff offices and looked across the welcome area. The chapel sat at the center. All of the buildings were heavily-treated wood with concrete floors and screened-in doors and windows. They've been around for years. The chapel itself had long wooden benches where the campers sat for church services, game time, song time, and show time. There was a stage with a pulpit. Sometimes, the chapel area was used for small groups, devotionals and skits or other performances. In the offseason, the camp was used as a retreat center for local churches, where they'd come and spend the weekend "communing in nature and in the Word of God."

There was a camp store where folks could buy a souvenir, which was really just cheap crap. The kids bought stamps and mailed their post cards or letters. Then across the way, there was a snack bar where they'd buy candy, ice cream, popsicles, that sort of thing. Each evening after chapel time, the snack bar would open up and they'd swarm the candy and ice cream as if they don't get fed at all during the day.

There's a couple of outhouse-type bathrooms and then some ponds full of fish and snakes and frogs and pond scum. The only bad thing about that part was the dead fish smell when you got too close.

About a half mile from the main part of Camp Judah is where The Ghost Town is located, which is made up of several cabins housing about twelve kids each in bunk beds. There are shower facilities and bathrooms for the campers on one side of the cabin area, where they walk down with their shower kits and towels and attempt to clean up. I think the girls' side of the shower facility is much more heavily-used than the boys' side.

The dining hall is right next to The Ghost Town, full of huge, round tables. When the campers come in for breakfast, lunch, and dinner, they do so singing a prayer song called "Bless This Food." They need to use their manners at all times during the meal and there are counselors checking on violations. If a camper puts his elbows on the table or doesn't put his napkin in his lap, then the whole table loses a point. The table with the most points at the end of the day is rewarded in some way, usually just bragging rights and the "Honor Cabin" flag hanging on their cabin door.

About a quarter mile from The Ghost Town is The Reservation. The teens have to walk a bit to get to the dining hall, but they have their meals brought to them and they eat outside sometimes. They do a lot more things on their own and in small groups. The Houghtons believe that the best way to reach teens for Jesus is in a smaller setting, more individualized attention, and more personal interactions with young, Christian adults who can more closely identify with them.

Mr. Houghton was a youth pastor so he is pretty well-versed in dealing with teenagers. In their small group devotionals, they talk openly about how Christianity fits into their lives. They are encouraged to grow spiritually in their relationship with God and to look to the Bible for guidance and direction in the difficult choices they face as they grow older. They address issues like dating, drugs, alcohol, music, pre-marital sex, and all the angst — even simply unspecified angst — that teens internalize.

I know that if I had to do things over again, I would've made a good youth pastor. But I'm not Jesus-y enough for some people, so I'm happy to make a positive difference in some other way with the youth.

The whole place has several small ponds, but another quarter mile from The Reservation is my lake. I say it's *my* lake because I've been the head lifeguard of this lake for a long time. It's manmade, but it has a big pier that stretches out in the middle of it with two huge slides attached. The campers have to pass my swimming test to be able to get out to the deep end and use the slides. There is a lifeguard chair on the sandy beach and another on the pier. Usually, the teenaged girls just want to lay out in the sun and that's okay with me — less kids to have to watch in the water.

Mr. and Mrs. Houghton bought this place about thirty years ago with some kind of inheritance. It was their dream to have a Christian camp that would partner with churches and their organizing authorities in all the Christian denominations to offer scholarships to kids through their local churches. They especially wanted to be able to reach out to the children who lived in the more rural areas of the state, who didn't necessarily have the means or opportunity to go to a camp. So Camp Judah was born.

Eventually, this place got so popular that some campers come from the northeast to attend, as well as Georgia and Florida. It is really a special place and the Houghtons will always be like family to me.

"I need everybody to line up with their group!" I heard Brian, the camp director, yell out. The parents were all leaving the site. I could see some counselors folding up the chairs at the check-in area. Others were moving to stand with their groups to welcome their little blessings from the Lord.

When everyone quieted down, Brian hollered, "Welcome to Camp Judah, y'all!"

Some of the older campers cheered.

"This session, The Ghost Town has six girl groups and seven boy groups. Each group has their own counselor. And the Lord's Reservation has sixteen girls and twenty boys."

Brother Chris hollered out, "The girls like their odds!"

I couldn't believe he just yelled that out loud. Dumb ass. God, I hoped Mr. Houghton didn't hear that.

Brian continued above the giggles, "The Reservation has three sisters and three brothers. All of the counselors are students at God-fearing, Christian colleges."

I could see Scout standing near Abby. Abby was one fine young lady I enjoyed looking at all summer. Lust of the eyes. *Oops.*

Scout had grown a lot since last summer and had filled out some more. I know it's wrong for me to notice, but she does look like a woman now, except for her round-cheeked baby face. Her hair was much longer than I remember, full and wavy, and if I didn't know otherwise, I would've guessed she was a counselor out there. Her legs were thicker and appeared strong. She wore a New York Yankees tee shirt, jean cut off shorts, and tennis shoes that looked like they were bought on clearance from Rose's.

It was great to see her again. And I meant that.

****

Dear Doug,   12-10-82

Guess what? I think my daddy is going to let me get a phone extension in my bedroom! I am so happy! If I give you my phone number, maybe you could call me sometime. But maybe you couldn't because it would be long distance.

My friend Charlie and I are listening to records in my room right now. We like listening to Eye of the Tiger. It makes us want to be boxers like Rocky. We also keep singing Freeze Frame and then stand frozen for a second between each "freeze frame." What kind of music do you like to listen to?

I don't think I've ever told you this, but I have a dog named Stretch. He is part dachshund so he has a long body. We don't know what other breed he is though. Do you have any pets? I love dogs more than anything in the world.

My basketball season is not going so good because we

keep losing. But it isn't because of me! The girls on my team just aren't that good I guess. I still like playing though, even if it is frustrating.

Christmas is coming and my mom put out all of our decorations. My daddy put up some lights on the house and it looks really pretty. We got our tree the other day from the tree lot near the main part of town and this weekend me and my mom (and maybe my brother) are going to put up our ornaments. My mom likes to string popcorn as garland but it takes too long to do it. I don't know if I want to do that again.

This year, all I want is the dumb phone for my room. I will be so happy.

I miss you so much Doug and I hope you have the best Christmas ever. Still a long way to go until we can see each other again, but it will be great!

Love,

Scout Elizabeth (Squirrel Girl)

CHARLIE

I rode my bike down to the park and could see Katie sitting on the swings. The whole place was deserted but for her, and now me, so I pulled up to where she sat, dropped my bike on the grass and sat down next to her on the other swing. She smirked at me.

"Hey," she said.

"Hey."

"So are you now off…Scout-free?" she asked sarcastically, emphasis on the "Scout." It bothered her that I was so bonded to Scout. She once said it was like we were tethered together by a leash, with Scout doing all the leash leading. She was right.

"Yeah, she's gone off to camp."

"Good," Katie said. "Now I get you all to myself."

She got up from the swing, walked over to me, and put her legs on top of mine in the opposite direction so that she was sitting on my lap and facing me. Then she lowered her face toward mine and started kissing me. It was immediately uncomfortable sitting that way because of the boner that popped up underneath my jeans. In less than a second, I had a hard-on. It was like that every time the girl touched me. Because I needed to think of something else in order to keep myself in check, I stopped kissing her and started singing the lyrics to "Swingin'" by John Anderson. Katie laughed because she knew exactly what I was doing.

Katie and I haven't had sex yet, but we wanted to. Every time we were making out in my room and I was sure we were safe from any interruption, we would go a little bit further. Katie was a lot bolder about things than I was, but I let her do whatever she wanted because it felt so good. I didn't know what I was doing anyway and she seemed to.

Once I asked her if she'd done this stuff before.

"I swear, Charlie, I never have," she said with her lips hot on my neck. "It's all coming natural to me."

I don't know if that's true or not, but I didn't care. It was nice that at least one of us knew what the hell to do. The last time we were together, I put my hand up her shirt and felt underneath her bra.

"They feel really nice," I told her. "All soft and billowy like a cloud." It sounded stupid, but that was the best description I thought of in that moment. Katie didn't say anything back. I think she gets annoyed by how much I talk sometimes.

Maybe I just needed to get the courage to take off her bra so I could really touch what's underneath. I was scared to go further with Katie because, while I really liked her a lot, I didn't feel about her like I felt about Scout.

"Charlie, if you ever decide to have sex with a girl, you should be certain that you love her," my mom said to me one day as I stood in the kitchen, in my britches, trying to wash a stain out of my baseball uniform in the sink. "Sex for a girl is different than it is for a boy. Girls think sex is the same as love and boys don't look at it like that."

"Okay, mom," was all I responded with, my voice dripping with embarrassment.

I guess that made sense because I felt myself wanting to have sex with Katie, but I didn't think I loved her. But I sure liked her a lot. And I was scared that if I had sex with her, she would think I loved her. I wasn't sure if I even knew what love is. All of this pressure was starting to get to me.

My mom, while on a roll that particular day and having no problem telling me exactly what she thought about these types of things added, "As a man, you should be very careful of confusing the two things. Don't you ever use a woman and her heart and feelings just so you can get your rocks off."

Still scrubbing at the stain, I replied awkwardly, again, "Okay, Mom."

"If you want to get your rocks off, then that's why the Good Lord invented your right hand."

I dropped my wet uniform on the floor at that. And then she added, for full effect, "Oh, and if you do have sex, you'd better use a rubber, boy." It was pretty uncomfortable to hear her say things like that to me. "I'm sorry, Charlie, but I have to tell ya all the things your daddy was supposed to tell ya. So the best I can do is give you my point of view. You will make a better man and husband someday if you can see things from a girl's perspective about these matters of the heart."

I guess she was right. My mom, despite — or maybe because of — her failures with men, probably knew better than most how to raise a man who would care about women and would want to actually know them, not just screw them.

The whole thing is way too complicated for me. I can understand why parents don't want us to have sex when we're young and why Scout's church is always telling teenagers to wait until they're married. Because they don't want us to have babies!

I stopped kissing Katie briefly and said, "I can't for the life of me understand how anyone waits until they're married to have sex."

Katie, probably foreseeing more talking and less kissing on my part, smiled sweetly, and began to kiss me again, rubbing on me with her hand through my jeans. That shut me up just fine.

I finally understood why some people I know got married as soon as they graduated from high school. So they could have sex! Without any fear or guilt! I didn't have the Jesus-guilt thing like Scout did. The only time I went to church was at Christmastime or to the youth program when there was a lock-in. When I was younger, I went to Vacation

Bible School in the summer. That was fun. My mom only went to church on Easter Sunday. She liked it when the choir sang the Bible story about Jesus and the cross and Him raising from the dead on the third day. We weren't regular churchgoers like most folks around here and I figured it's because of all the shame my mom carried around with her, like her own cross of sorts.

But I believed that if God loved everybody, then He loved *everybody* — no matter if they smoked, got a divorce, had mean boyfriends, and never went to church. I had to imagine that He loved my mom. She had the biggest heart, just like Scout, and she always did her best with almost nothing. If God doesn't love someone like my mom, then I felt like that wasn't much of a God to believe in anyway.

Katie pulled away from me and got off of my lap. She sat back down on her swing and started swinging like she was that eleven-year-old girl again, the one with no mom, who stunk and had a crush on me. She started pumping her long, pale, freckled legs harder and harder, making herself go higher and higher.

"I like watching you swing!" I hollered up to her, her long auburn hair hanging back as she held her face up to the sun. She wore a halter top with strawberries across the front and a pair of jean shorts. "You look so happy!"

"Swing with me, Charlie!" she hollered back as she whizzed by, back and forth, starting to sing the "Swingin'" song like I had earlier.

I started swinging and singing it along with her, my legs stretched out in my soiled blue jeans and dirty white Converse tennis shoes, which have seen better days. In the hot, humid summer afternoon, I could feel the sun beating down on my shoulders, barely covered by a white tee shirt.

I felt good, excited about the rest of my baseball season, excited about spending time with Katie — and for the first time in a long time — I wasn't thinking about Scout Webb at all.

* * * * * * * *

Dear Squirrel,   January 2nd, 1983

Happy New Year, favorite camper! I hope you had a fun Christmas and got your phone. I'm sorry that I probably won't be able to call you on it, but never say never! I have surprised even myself at times.

Paul loved his Christmas. He was spoiled by all his grandparents and aunties and uncles. It has been nice being away from school for two whole weeks, sleeping in late, and making breakfast for my son.

To answer your question, no, I don't have any pets right now but I hope to get Paul a dog someday. I had a dog named Scout (ha ha) when I was a boy and it was the best dog I ever had, so it would be nice for Paul to have one, too. Maybe we will name it Squirrel in honor of you! Ha ha

You take care, SG, and drop me a line sometime when

you have a chance.

Your friend,

Brother Doug

****

SCOUT

The first week of Camp Judah was so much fun. I didn't see a whole lot of Brother Doug, but I did see him every day during teen swim. He'd come and talk to me whenever our group was there. And when I say talk, I mean, like, personal talk.

Each day, we raced down the slides, he'd throw me into the water and he challenged me to race him in a swim once. I'm pretty sure he let me win. He would do that kind of stuff with some of the other kids, too, just so it didn't look like he was showing favoritism to me. At least, that was what I thought.

Then he'd come and talk to me on the beach. He sat down on the sand and started yapping about the little things going on in his life at home.

"Last night, I got back home right after Paul had his supper and so I took him to the park near where we live. There's a couple of baby swings there, but they were being used by some other people. So I sat him on my lap on a regular swing and we went back and forth a little." Then Brother Doug just started to laugh.

I smiled at him, trying not to let my eyes light up too much from all the pounding in my heart. "What happened?" I asked him, wanting him to go on.

He started laughing harder, his light blond hair gleaming along with the sun.

"What? Tell me!" I demanded, sounding like a stupid little girl who was a bit too excited about this story.

He calmed down and continued. "The poor kid got really scared, even though I was holding him as tight as I could. There's no way I'd drop him and we weren't going real high or fast at all."

"And that's funny? Scaring your little boy?" I asked, a little confused, because while I didn't see how it was that funny, he sure thought it was. I loved looking at his face as he told this story.

He peered at me and winked. "No, Squirrel, that's not what's funny. He was so scared that whatever he had for supper seeped out of his diaper and through his shorts and onto my lap."

Then it hit me. Brother Doug was trying to tell me that he'd literally scared the crap out of his son. And, yes, that was pretty funny.

He told me about where he grew up, way up in the Appalachian Mountains in a town called Blowing Rock right near Grandfather Mountain. He told me what his life was like as a boy.

"I told you that I had a dog named Scout when I was

a kid," he said, looking right into my eyes.

"Yeah, you told me that the day we first met," I said, suddenly feeling a little embarrassed, like I had revealed a long-held secret.

He was staring directly into my eyes, not looking away for even a second, starting to make me a little uneasy with the length of the pause, before he responded. Then his smile became soft, his lips came together, and he licked his bottom lip gently.

"You remember the day we first met?" he asked, his voice quiet.

I nodded nervously. Now, I was mortified. I felt like I'd been caught taking a cookie from the plate that was set aside for the church picnic. But I wasn't going to turn away from him. He held my eyes in a trance of sorts and I probably couldn't have turned my head away even if I wanted to.

After a minute or so of just looking at each other, Brother Doug turned away and then gazed out toward the water where the other lifeguard was running a relay race. He said, "Scout was a Jack Russell Terrier. He was a great dog. He got hit by a car when I was fourteen. Broke my heart."

He told me about the sports he played and how he always wanted to be a teacher because he liked working with kids.

"What better way to combine sports and kids than be a gym teacher and a coach?" he said, explaining his thought process for his career choice.

"Well, aren't you really just a grown up kid anyway?" I asked, feeling bolder than ever, but my words still coming out shy.

His eyes again held mine, the gazing grew longer and the smiles on his face seemed to be inviting me into them, rather than simply wanting to play with me. He made me feel more at ease with the way he was looking at me, more like an equal and a friend, not some kid at Camp Judah.

He told me about the Houghtons and how, when he was just out of college, he applied to their camp to be a counselor. They asked him if he was lifeguard certified and, because he was, they requested that he'd consider being the lifeguard instead of a counselor.

"They let me live here for two whole years. Rent free," he said. "I got to save most of the money I earned teaching so I could eventually get myself a better car and an apartment over in town."

"Mr. Houghton sure is a nice man," I agreed. "I always like how he says that I'm 'growin' in grace' every time he sees me. I think that's his camp phrase."

Brother Doug looked between his legs at the sand and started digging a hole with fingers. He got really quiet for a bit and then said, almost in a whisper, "Little girl, you sure have grown up a lot since I last saw you." He wasn't looking at me anymore, just kept digging in the sandy hole. Then he added, "You've grown into a truly beautiful young lady."

My heart about popped out of my chest when he said

that and I did my best to contain my desire to get up and run away. I mean, he has to know I have a huge crush on him. He's no dummy. But he just called me a "beautiful young lady." Out loud.

After a couple of minutes of silence between us, and a lot of calming down on my part, I whispered back to him, "Thank you for saying that, Doug."

He stopped digging in the hole and looked away toward the other campers who were laying on the beach. "They treated me like I was their son."

Confused, due to the fact that I was still swimming in my head on the "beautiful young lady" comment, I asked, "Who did?"

"Mr. and Mrs. Houghton. You know they had a son named Judah who passed away when he was a little boy."

"No, I never knew that." All this time, and I never realized that Camp Judah was named for a dead little boy. I thought it was named for the Israelite tribe.

I learned about his college — a nice, small, private school in Virginia. When he graduated from there, he wanted to make it on his own and without his father's help. His daddy made good money doing some sales thing with computers that didn't make any sense to me, but Brother Doug had no interest in that kind of work or making a lot of money. Instead, he wanted to go out into the world and make a difference in kids' lives.

I let him talk to me the whole time. He rarely asked

anything about me and my life, but that was okay with me. I'm just a girl from Haddleboro who has never been anywhere or done anything interesting. My life revolved around sports, church, stuff with Charlie and other friends in town, and singing "Jessie's Girl" into my hairbrush while standing in front of the mirror in my room. There was nothing much else to tell him.

Brother Doug told me so much about his life and the things he thought about, like his hopes and dreams and some of his fears, how having a son changed him and solidified his faith in God.

"A lot of the Bible stories started making more sense to me after I became a father," he said.

"Like Abraham and Isaac?" I asked him.

"Yeah. Like how much faith a man would have to have in God to be willing to sacrifice his son. I don't think I could ever have that kind of faith. That showed me how strong Abraham's faith was and how far I have to go in my walk with the Lord," he said seriously.

He confided in me, like I was an adult or something.

"I think I should leave the camp after this summer and maybe go do something else," he said at one point.

"Well you'd be missed here, I'm sure."

He turned back to me and gave me a smirk. "Well, there's no reason to be here anymore since you won't be back."

My heart jumped again, the butterflies swelling. I felt

so alive. I could float.

Then he got quiet. "It's hard to do it. I don't want to let down the Houghtons."

He talked like he wanted to tell me everything about himself. And I let him and listened to every single word he said. It was nice to learn so much more about him, about his past, about the life he had before I knew him, about the life he had away from this camp. I loved hearing about the real him, who he was deep down inside — what I couldn't get from his short little teacher-like letters all year.

The whole time he talked to me about himself, it was as if I wasn't a fourteen-year-old girl at all, and he wanted to tell somebody his life's story — just never had — and then met me, just the right person to listen to him. It made me feel good. Other kids, especially Charlie, liked talking to me because I was a good listener. But it was even nicer that Brother Doug, an adult, liked talking to me, too, and trusted me enough to share so much of himself with me. It made me feel important. It made me feel like an adult myself. It made me feel appreciated. It made me feel like I mattered.

The only thing he said about his wife — apparently named Cammy, "short for Campbell" — is that they met while he lived at this camp, dated for two years, and then got married.

"We've been married for seven years now," he said turning toward me.

I cocked my head. "Wow. That's basically the whole

time I've known you! How did you meet?" I asked him. I was especially interested in that part because all girls enjoy a good love story.

"I met her in a hospital," he said abruptly, and then stood up, his bare feet covered in sand. His entire demeanor changed in an instant. "Squirrel, I need to give Joe a break," he said and walked off leaving me there. And that was all I'd get in regards to his love story.

Brother Doug came to the last two evening teen events of the first week. At the end of the first week, the teens had a campfire and Sister Ally was playing a guitar. The boys and girls were all together and singing praise songs.

While singing "In His Hands", Brother Doug walked up out of the tree line and sat down on the log bench right across from me. Through the whipping fire, I looked over at him and saw that he was looking right at me, just like he had at the beach during our talks. There was something special about the way he looked at me. Then he smiled and winked. My heart almost burst from my chest. I think Michelle, sitting next to me, must've heard my heart pumping because it was so loud.

After we were done singing the praise songs, and a couple of girls asked the other kids to please pray for their families during Prayer Request time, the campers started to disburse and head back to our teepee tents for the night. Michelle ran off to the latrine because she had to pee like a racehorse. So I started walking down the path to our teepee alone.

"Squirrel," I heard that cracked, baritone voice quietly behind me.

I turned around and was able to make out Brother Doug's shadow near the trees leading back toward the campfire area. Slowly, he walked toward me, and I could see his swim trunks and tee shirt come into full view in the darkness.

"Aren't you gonna give me a hug goodnight, little girl?" he asked.

Once again, I was about to pass out from sheer happy-panic.

"Oh, I'm sorry," I said shyly. I walked closer to him, wrapped my arms around his torso, and put my head right into his chest, which made me feel so small next to him, but protected and safe. "Goodnight, Brother Doug. Can't wait to see you on Sunday."

He hugged me back, pulling me tightly into him and slowly rubbing my back with one of his hands. If I could've melted into his body right then and there, it would've been the most spectacular ending to my short life. He put his hands on my head and pulled it back from his chest and kissed my forehead. Then he pulled back from me, looked right into my eyes, and stuck his fingers on my cheeks, popping them.

"Good night, Squirrel-Girl," he said, backing further away from me and then walking back toward the path. As

I stood there, completely dumbfounded and weak-kneed, I heard him holler back, "I mean…Scout Elizabeth!"

My heart was racing a million miles a minute and it was all I could do to keep myself remaining standing on my feet. I headed back to my teepee, skipping — no, *sprinting* and skipping — and wanting to scream out something into the nighttime sky. I was in love with a grown man! A married father-gym-teacher-coach-lifeguard who just held me tight and kissed my forehead and looked me in my eyes like he could read all of my thoughts! And I think, because he looked into my eyes like that, he had to be in love with me, too!

After I got back to my teepee, Kelly and Mary Catherine, two of my tent-mates, were putting on their pajamas. Kelly was brushing her hair. She'd brush each side of her hair for one hundred strokes every night. It was kind of annoying, but she swore that it made her hair grow thicker. Her mom was a hairdresser so she knew this to be true.

"Did you see how Brother Doug came up and sat down at the campfire again tonight?" Mary Catherine asked me, as I started to rummage through my suitcase to find my nightgown.

"Yeah," I said, hesitantly, wondering why she would ask me that. Did she see our embrace in the woods?

"Kelly thinks that it's because of her. Can you believe that?" she asked.

Kelly stopped brushing her hair and said out loud,

"Fifty-nine." Then she said, "He has come to our campfires two nights in a row and I always catch him looking at me at the lake."

Kelly was one of those super pretty girls with lush blond hair — maybe there was something to that brushing ritual of hers — who always thought that boys were looking at her. And maybe they were, but Brother Doug wasn't a boy. He was a man.

"Maybe he was there to see me...or Scout even!" Mary Catherine said, as she sat down on her sleeping bag.

Kelly smirked. "Look, he is always staring at me at the lake. I know he's old and all, but he is still gorgeous and I think he keeps coming to our campfires to stare at me some more. I mean, doesn't he have a wife and baby? Why wouldn't he just go home to them? He doesn't have to be at our campfires. He's not even a counselor!"

I stayed silent. I know why Brother Doug came to the campfire — and it wasn't to stare at Kelly from Kannapolis. He wasn't shallow like that.

Michelle walked in. She was a Lumbee Indian from Lumberton and my only long-time camp friend. She had short curly black hair, a stout build, and a beautiful round face.

"What do you think, Michelle?" Mary Catherine asked.

"What do I think about what?"

"Kelly thinks that Brother Doug comes to our

campfires to stare at her."

Kelly started counting brushes again. "Sixty, sixty-one, sixty-two."

"No way," said Michelle. "I think he has been coming because of Sister Ally. She is a good singer and has a huge rack."

I laughed. Michelle knew how to phrase things.

Mary Catherine shrugged. "I guess that would make more sense."

I started to get irritated. They were talking about him like he was a street dog looking for someone to sniff.

"Maybe he's there because he cares about all of us and wants to be a part of things," I started. "He has a wife and baby. Why would he be after a bunch of fourteen-year-old girls or a college student? Brother Doug is a good man with a heart of gold. He loves the Lord. I've known him since I was seven so I know him better than anyone at this camp."

"Well, he does talk to you an awful lot Scout," said Mary Catherine.

"And you two do that silly cheek popping thing all the time," piped in Michelle.

"What do you guys talk about on the beach?" asked Mary Catherine, genuinely curious.

"We just talk about sports," I said. "He's a coach and I play sports. Plus, we both like the Yankees." After a pause, I added, "I've known Brother Doug for half of my life, y'all," just to make my point that I was the authority on all matters concerning Brother Doug.

But I didn't want to talk about him anymore. I can't imagine what they'd say or think if I told them about what happened on the path to our teepee and how jealous they would all be. No, my moments with Brother Doug are between me and him only. No one else ever needs to know the extent of our special bond.

I couldn't wait for Sunday to get here.

****

Dear Doug,   1-9-83

Happy New Year back at you! Summer is just five months away. We haven't gotten our packet yet about camp and the weeks that we can pick from, but, in about a half a year, we will be back together. Partners in crime ha ha!

Yes, my daddy got me a phone for Christmas and it was so awesome. He hooked it up to a thing called a jack in my room and so now I can call my friends and talk as long as I want in there. I don't have my own private number or anything, but at least I can have a conversation without everyone in my house listening.

I also got some new clothes and a few new 45s and a new pair of roller skates. I didn't do a whole lot over break, just hung out with Charlie and then my other good friend Maybelle. My mom did take us to Raleigh one day so we could go to a mall. The only thing I bought with my

Christmas money was some candy in the candy store and a button with a picture of a dog on it. I want to save the money so I will have some to use at camp. Since it's my last summer, I will want to buy a souvenir from the store so I will always remember my time with you. Not that I need reminding or anything!

I just can't bear the thought of not seeing you ever again, so we will have to stay in touch after camp. OK? Maybe someday you will be able to make a trip to come see me play in a softball game when I'm in high school. Or maybe my high school will play a high school near where you live and you could come. There I go again…getting ahead of myself and making plans. Sorry, I guess I just don't want our special friendship to end just because our camp years end. I can't wait to hear from you again. Oh and in case you do want to call me, my phone number is in the phone book under "Lee Webb."

Love,

Scout Elizabeth

✱✱✱✱✱✱✱✱

DOUG

Lying awake in bed, my eyes stared up at the ceiling fan, just turning, turning, turning with a faint squeak to it. It was pretty early in the morning, had to be at least 3:00. Our buzzer alarm clock was broken so I didn't know for sure. Our ceiling fan hadn't given me much relief from this summer heat at all, so I wasn't sure if I couldn't sleep because of the heat or because my mind was racing. I need to get an air conditioner already.

Cammy was working the night shift for one of the other nurses who was sick. It was good when she could pick up an extra shift because it seemed like we always needed the money. No matter how much we both worked, and even the fact that we saved money on babysitting by working opposite schedules a lot of the time, it never seemed to be enough.

The mortgage on this older house, which wasn't completely falling apart, but needed some expensive repairs now and again, was killing me. The car needed to be replaced at this point. I didn't want to get a new transmission and I didn't want to put four new tires on it when it's about to die.

Cammy wants a second car and, no matter how much I've told her we can't afford one, she keeps harping on it.

"My father will sell us one at factory price!" she screamed at me.

"I don't like your father. I want no favors from him! I will take care of my own family."

"Well, if you don't want to ask *my* father, then ask your own for some help!"

If she only knew how insulting it was to a man to suggest that he needed to run to his daddy for money in order to take care of his family.

"I don't know where all of our money went, but, somehow, some way, it's gone somewhere!" I shouted back at her, frustrated. Cammy bought some new furniture last month that we didn't need and now I have to pay for it.

"That couch is gross, Doug!" she yelled at me during a different argument about money. "You've had it since your bachelor days at that damn fucking camp! You want your child playing on it? For God's sake, I found a seven-year-old potato chip in his mouth the other day!"

"There is nothing wrong with the couch! So what? It's old! And there is no way in hell you can possibly know that the potato chip you found was seven years old," I responded back, sarcastically.

Let's just say, that conversation didn't go well for me.

"How can you not even care about your own son's safety?" she started yelling, her voice going up several octaves, almost in a fit. "I bet you don't even care about me! Or our family! Paul could eat that potato chip and die from some bacteria on it from seven years ago and you don't even care!"

I couldn't win. Nothing I did was ever right or enough for her.

So tomorrow morning — hell, in a few hours — Cammy would be home and we'd have our "family day." I had no idea what she wanted to do, but I wasn't making any plans because they would be wrong. Hip hip hurray.

My solace from all of this angst in my home life lately has been at Camp Judah. I was both so sick of the place and then longing to be there at the same time.

This past week has been great, like I've gotten a shot of adrenaline in my ass. I've liked all the kids in this latest crop of campers and, more than anything, surprising even me, all I have wanted to do is be around Scout. I know she is just a kid, but she's so easy to talk to, so sweet and fun, and she hangs on every word I say. She looks at me like I'm the greatest guy who has ever lived and she smiles so shyly at me, it's almost hard for me to remember where I am and who she actually is: Squirrel, a young lady I've known since she was a little girl!

But she's not seven anymore. She's almost fifteen, with a lean and hard body and a full, happy round face and, if she was three years older— *just three years!* — it would be perfectly legal and acceptable for me — if I wasn't married

— to ask her out to the movies.

"What do you want to see?" I asked her, in the fantasy going on in my head.

"How about something action-packed like *Raiders of the Lost Ark* or maybe something sporty like *Rocky III*," Scout suggests, her trusting eyes looking up at me in the dark. "No stupid, sappy love stories about impossible love affairs! We already have that in real life," she says, giggling.

"And no Academy-Award-nominated, artsy-fartsy shit!" I said back to her, eyeing that round face, wanting to put it in the palms of my hands.

No, Scout and I would go see something totally stupid and immature, like *Animal House* or *National Lampoon's Vacation*, and laugh and laugh and laugh.

"How about *E.T.*?" she asks, reaching out for my hands.

"Maybe *Poltergeist*," I smile at her, hoping she'd get scared so I'd have a valid reason to pull her into me and hold her the whole night.

No matter what we'd pick, I knew it would be great because hanging out with Scout was great. She found fun in the simplest of things, no doubt a byproduct of a simple upbringing in a working-class, southern family.

Then maybe afterward, we'd go grab a burger and fries, share a shake, and I'd take her back to her college — because in this fantasy, she's in college and maybe I am, too. And I'd kiss her goodnight in front of her dorm. Just a simple, sweet kiss that told her how much I enjoyed spending the evening with her.

I know these thoughts are wrong. I know that there is no way on God's green earth that I should be laying here in the dark in my bed thinking about Scout like this. But I am. And no matter how hard I try to think about other stuff, no matter how much I am simultaneously asking God for help with controlling these thoughts, I just keep thinking about Scout instead and making up various scenarios about things we could do if she was eighteen and I wasn't married and circumstances were different.

If I was a pervert, I'd be thinking about sex with her. But I'm honestly not thinking about that. *Yet.* It's about just being with her, around her, enjoying her company and being appreciated for the man I am — not the man Cammy wishes I was. It's intoxicating for a man to be accepted for who he is and desired just as he is.

Scout and her raspy voice. We both have matching raspy voices. Scout and her full, adorable cheeks that I want to put into my hands and squeeze. Scout's tight little ass that I want to grab and goose. Scout's untouched rosebud lips that I want to kiss. The small of her back, so strong and petite. The way she puts her head in my chest when I hug her, like Cammy used to do years ago — before time and a baby turned her into a raging bitch. Scout's ability to see the positive in everything, to bring confidence to every doubt I have about myself — doubts she doesn't see in me at all. Her legs with lots of little scars on them, simply because she has no fear and likes to take risks, unlike Cammy who's grown to be chicken shit thanks to the stuff she sees at the hospital. Scout's gentleness when she looks at me, her kindness toward me, her effortless beauty. I know she cares about me. She has written me letters for almost a whole year! I don't think Cammy has ever written me one letter in all the years I've known her.

My mind is down the rabbit trail of Scout and how easy life would be with such a sweet girl like her. *If she wasn't in high school. If she wasn't just a kid. If being with her wouldn't be a scandal and end with me in handcuffs and with divorce papers.*

I wondered aloud to myself, "Is Scout a virgin? Has Scout ever kissed a boy? Does she have a boyfriend? How far has she gone?" And for some reason, I knew the answer to all these questions.

Scout was innocent and that was why I loved her. There was nothing promiscuous about her. She was genuine, authentic, real — and blameless. Her heart was pure. She was unfailingly honest. She didn't play the same games that the other teenaged girls did. She didn't flirt with me, blow kisses at me, act like she had something under her shirt that I wanted — like that blond Kelly girl who thought she was hot shit.

While I knew she had a big crush on me, it was just a crush. A long-time, typical, innocent crush. Scout has never treated me in a way that screamed, "JAIL BAIL ALERT!" I know what that feels like. Several teenaged girls through the years have treated me like that, no matter how much older I get.

I knew that she'd never come onto me, never touch me inappropriately or try to get me to do something to her. She just wasn't like that. I'm not saying that she wouldn't want me to do something to her, but she would never instigate anything or make advances toward me whatsoever. I found that extremely comforting.

I wasn't worried about Scout. But I was starting to get worried about myself.

What I did after the campfire last night was nuts. I don't know what came over me, but all I've wanted to do is be close to her. Someone could've seen us embracing on the path, but while I was in that moment, I didn't care if someone did. All I knew was that I wanted to hold her, to pull her into me, to let her know that I really cared for her, too, and to look at her in her brown eyes. I had felt like that for a solid three days, so much that I couldn't think about much else. So last night, just a few short hours ago, I saw my opportunity to share a mostly innocent, but also quite intimate moment, with a girl who means more to me than she knows. I don't care how young she is. She captured a piece of my heart seven years ago and now she just has more of it.

Yes, I decided I am definitely going on the Desert Wanderers trip with the teens. A lot more time with Scout and probably the last real time I'll have with her.

I got out of bed and walked down the hallway to the kitchen. The clock on the wall said it was almost 6:00. So basically, I've been laying in my bed wide awake for almost three hours thinking about a girl who is almost fifteen years old and entering high school.

What the hell is wrong with me?

****

Dear Squirrel,   February 6th, 1983

Hi kiddo. I am so sorry it has taken me so long to write you back. I promise I will try to do better, OK? Been real busy with work and coaching and haven't had much time to do much of anything. You asked me before what kind of music I liked to listen to and I forgot to answer you. I like Led Zeppelin. They might be a little bit before your time, but that is my favorite band. Hope things are going good for you. Camp will be here before you know it!

Your friend,

Brother Doug

****

CAMMY

After another failed attempt at mending my family life with "family day," I am starting to feel beyond defeated. Saturday, the only day both Doug and I have off from work together — the first day in a few weeks, actually — I decided that, despite my sheer exhaustion from working all fucking night, I was going to somehow stay awake when I got home.

My plan was to slip into the house, slip into the shower, and then slip into bed because maybe Doug would want to make love. I can't remember the last time we had sex when I didn't feel like a piece of meat on a slab as Doug writhed around like an angry dog.

Then, after the great sex, and hopefully some tender snuggling, I'd get up, make a full breakfast for both of my boys, and we'd head off to the zoo in Asheboro, which was about forty-five minutes away. We all love the zoo and, even though it's hot, it would be fun.

After a peaceful and invigorating day at the zoo, we'd drive home and stop at Bubba's Backyard Barbecue on the way back for some of the best Eastern North Carolina barbecue ever made. Then, because the day has been so wonderful, and by now I'm about to die since I've been awake for basically two days, Doug would tell me that he is going to take Paul to the park so I can rest. Then he'd tuck me into bed and kiss me on my forehead like he used to when we first started dating.

In my fantasy, this was exactly the day we had. In reality, it was not even close.

First of all, I couldn't slip into the house. I pulled into the driveway, attempted to slip into the house, and found Doug already up and laying on my new couch watching TV. He was eating potato chips. At 7:30 in the fucking morning. And getting crumbs on my new fucking couch.

I was purposely trying not to let it piss me off so it wouldn't ruin my fantasy, which now needed to be slightly altered. So I let him munch his chips without a word from me, knowing full well that they would only cause him to get a huge pimple. Instead, I walked over to him and kissed his cheek.

"Mornin'," I said as sweetly as I could fake it. Girls raised in the South know how to fake the sweetness when necessary. It's one of the first things my mama taught me.

"Morning," Doug replied, not taking his eyes off the TV.

"Is Paul up?" I asked.

"Don't think so," Doug answered, distanced and removed.

What the hell? He didn't even check on Paul this

morning? I kept my mouth shut.

I walked down the hallway and peeked into Paul's room. His little light yellow head was still lying flat and sleeping next to his Paddington Bear, a gift from his Auntie Trish.

I took a long, hot and steaming shower, getting all the hospital shit off of me, hoping that Doug might come back into the bedroom. After drying off, I laid naked in the bed and waited for him. For about thirty minutes. Eventually, it occurred to me that he was not coming back into bed.

Then, I heard Paul stirring. He was talking to himself in his room. This was how Paul would wake up most days. I laid there and waited to see if Doug would get the hell off the couch to go get his son and change his diaper. Well, I really should go into the predicting-the-future business because, as expected, Doug did not get the hell off the couch and deal with his son's diaper.

He knew I had been up all night at work. He knew that I would want to sleep, and I still have to get up and go take care of my son while he watches mindless TV and eats chips on my couch. I hoped that the fucking pimple he'd get would consume his entire body.

Now I was pissed. So I made a big production of opening the door and going into Paul's room and loudly declaring, "Awww, Paulie boy, nobody came to change your diaper?" as if there is a choice between Doug and the Diaper Fairy who would otherwise do it.

Then I changed his diaper — and still — no movement, no nothing from Doug. The TV continued to blare and I swear to God it was louder than when I first got home, like he must've literally gotten off of his ass and turned the volume up or something! He can get up to adjust the volume, but he can't get up to go get his son?

I took Paul out to his father and said, "Here, could you watch your son while I make breakfast?"

Doug pulled Paul into his side and hugged him. "Hey buddy, you're up now!" Then he kissed his face. I wanted to punch Doug in the head at that moment. He knew Paul was up and needed a diaper change. He just didn't want to move from the couch and knew that I'd do it.

"His diaper was sopping with piss, Doug," I made sure to inform him.

"Sorry," Doug responded, clearly not giving a shit.

So I made some eggs, bacon, and toasted up some English muffins. I was going to have a good fucking family day if it killed me.

After I started setting the table, Doug walked into the kitchen.

"You made breakfast?" he asked surprised.

Yes, I made breakfast, you idiot! What the fuck do you think I've been cooking in the kitchen for the last twenty minutes?

"Uh, yeah, I thought we could start our day out right," I said, containing my frustration.

"Sorry, Cam, but I'm not really hungry," Doug said.

Then he went into the fridge and took a sip of orange juice directly out of the carton.

So I'm thinking, number one: that is disgusting that anyone could stand the taste of orange juice after eating a bunch of greasy salty chips; and number two: how many times have I asked him to please use a glass and not drink directly from the carton?

I'm just fed up at this point. No sex and snuggling, no family breakfast — what's next? No zoo? I don't know why I'm still awake at this point. He clearly doesn't give a shit about a nice day with me and our son.

I grab Paul, who is sitting on the floor looking at the TV, put him in his high chair, and feed him some of the eggs. I give him a cup of milk. Paul makes a bit of a mess, but does okay overall for a two-year-old. After he's done, I wipe him up and take him back to his room to change him into his little sailor outfit so he'll look cute as a button at the zoo today.

As I walk back to Paul's room with him on my hip, I see that our bedroom door is closed. I peek in and see that Doug is in bed, asleep and snoring.

Holding back my tears and the rage boiling inside of me, I just turned around, grabbed Paul's stroller from the front porch, packed a day bag with diapers and crackers, got into the car, and headed out to the zoo.

If Doug did not want to spend any time with us or participate in this family on the one fucking day we get to be together, then screw him. Paul and I will go have a nice day together at the zoo and Doug can sleep all day or go do whatever it is he does.

****

Dear Doug,   2-12-83

I am enclosing a small valentine that I made for you. I make valentines for the special people in my life and you are one of them. I just want you to know that.

Are you and your wife going to do anything special for Valentine's Day? My parents are going away for a couple of days to Charleston, South Carolina. My daddy's friend owns a plantation house there that he made into a hotel and he invited them to come and stay there for free any time they could make the trip. I have never been to Charleston, have you?

Since I don't have a boyfriend, I don't have special plans. But I do like making valentines for special people.

My parents won't get cable so I have to go over to my friend Maybelle's house to be able to watch MTV. Do you ever watch MTV? I think it's so awesome to see songs come to life like that. There is this video called "Come On Eileen" where the singers are walking around singing in their overalls. You told me that you like Led Zeppelin. I haven't seen any of their videos yet. But I will let you know if I do.

Our basketball season ended last week and we only

won two games. That was pretty bad, but basketball isn't my favorite sport anyway. Baseball is. Since our school doesn't have a softball team, they let me play baseball instead, as long as I make the team. I hope that the coach won't not pick me because I'm a girl. I'm pretty nervous about it. Tryouts are in two weeks. If I make the team, though, I might be able to play in the summer league, too. So that will give me something to do this summer other than wait to go to camp to see you! I miss you, Doug, and I hope that you will write me again soon.

Love,

Scout Elizabeth

****

SCOUT

"Dear Charlie,

Camp is flying by. Other than the usual things that we do here, like talking about Jesus and the Bible in small groups, singing songs, swimming and games, I've enjoyed kayaking on this other lake that we aren't allowed to swim in and learning about some of the plants and foliage that are native to this part of North Carolina. A park ranger came in and taught us about survival skills. I got to do some painting in arts and crafts and made my favorite counselors, Sister Abby and Sister Ally, each wooden plaques to take back to their college with them. Another counselor taught me how to use a bow and arrow, something I've never tried before. I wasn't very good at that. See you soon!

Love, Scout."

I folded up the quick, sloppy letter, stuffed it in an envelope, threw Charlie's address on it, and walked off to the camp store to get a stamp to mail it. Passing by the lake, I could see Brother Doug off in the distance organizing a relay race on the beach with the little kids from The Ghost Town.

I'm already sick to my stomach about having to leave. We are more than half of the way through our time here and I cannot believe all that has happened so far. It has been a dream come true.

The teens already had our day-long canoe trip on the Catawba River, which was basically one day of constant laughing. Michelle and I turned our canoe over three times and, one time, it took Michelle fifteen whole minutes to get herself back into the canoe.

"Ugh, this water does not feel good!" Sister Abby yelled, as she got out of her canoe and into the Catawba, scuttling over behind Michelle, who had been trying — and failing — to get back into the canoe. She started pushing Michelle up by her butt.

"Your hands are on my butt!" Michelle hollered at Sister Abby, trying to keep herself from laughing so hard.

"Well, that's the biggest part of you!" Sister Abby hollered back, pushing upward.

Michelle was not a very strong girl in her upper body so we just laughed and I tried to pull her back in once she got a leg over and was balanced with Sister Abby's hands holding her up.

Once Michelle got in, Sister Abby was coughing. "This water is disgusting. I must've swallowed a gallon of it. I had better not get some weird bacterial infection!" Then, when Sister Abby was back in her canoe, she screamed, "Oh my God! Look! My bathing suit!"

We looked over at her sitting in the middle of her canoe. The once-white bathing suit was now a lovely rust color from all the red clay in the water.

"Well, that's why you don't wear a white bathing suit to Camp Judah, genius!" I said to her, trying to keep my laughing fits in check.

Brother Doug helped out that day, but he was assigned to be with a group of boys so I didn't see him very much. But when I did, he'd make sure to check on me.

"Squirrel," he'd whisper. Then he'd pop his cheeks. I'd pop back. He'd wink. I'd blush and feel my heart tizzy.

Otherwise, I've spent so much time with Brother Doug. He has been coming to every teen campfire that he can, unless he has to be home to watch his little boy. Every time we have teen swim at the lake, he spends almost all of his time with me. He has the other lifeguard lead all the relay races and keep watch on the slide side of the lake. After he gets everything organized, he nods for me to come over and sit with him while he is on the beach side of the lake keeping watch. Then we talk.

Brother Doug did most of the talking at first, but now he asks me lots of questions about my life back home, my feelings about God, what I want to do with my life after high school, and what I think about things like current events. He asks me about what scares me in life, what makes me happy, if I like artwork or have an interest in learning an instrument, like the piano.

"My friend Charlie plays the guitar. I think someday I'd like to learn how to play one, too. It looks hard to me, but when he plays, he doesn't need to look at his fingers at all," I told him. It was the first time I had talked much about Charlie to Brother Doug.

"I bet you'd be great at any instrument, little girl. You are one of those people who can probably teach herself or learn to play just from listening to something — play by ear," he replied, his light blue eyes gazing at me softly, daring mine to meet them.

I was getting more comfortable with whatever this had turned into between us. My heart pounded and the butterflies flapped wildly within me as I sat next to him on the beach, but it's felt more serene and normal than panicky. He made me feel wanted and interesting. Our talks became more intimate — not so much because of the subject matter, although it was pretty mature sometimes, but because of how we looked at each other, how our voices seemed to have changed into different pitch levels, how there seemed to be an invisible pull between our bodies as we sat together. I noticed that his forearm or his knee would touch me accidentally, more often than before — and he wouldn't pull away.

He'd talk about song lyrics he likes and poetry. I don't know any boy who talks about poetry.

"Robert Frost ones, mostly," he responded to me, when I asked him about his favorite poems.

I smiled to myself, remembering when I made Charlie go see *The Outsiders* at the movie theater over in Fayetteville earlier in the year. The last thing he wanted to do was go see a movie with a bunch of girls squealing in the audience over all the cute boys on the big screen.

"Nature's first green is gold," I said to Brother Doug, which caused him to face me.

"It is. You're like that. You're young. Everything about you is gold: pure, new, shiny, full of value and promise." Then he paused, looking into my eyes again and said, "You're perfect." He stopped with that, and I became so red-faced from all of this romantic attention from him. I didn't know how to respond to it at all. Nobody ever talked with me like this and certainly not in such an adult way, where all of this unspoken stuff is being said out loud, where I'm feeling like Brother Doug and I have become an actual couple in some way. My conversations with Charlie can get pretty deep sometimes and we talk about everything, but it's just different with Charlie because we know each other so well and we're the same age.

Brother Doug talks to me like he wants to really know me, the me deep down inside, the me only Charlie knows. There was so much more to Brother Doug than meets the eye. I had no idea how much was inside of him and wondered if he had ever talked to anyone like he talked to me. Then, as if he had read my mind, he answered my thoughts.

"Scout," he said at one point, after an extended silence

as he looked over the water, which yielded only two campers swimming at the moment. "I have never talked to anyone like I talk to you. No one, not ever. Not even my wife."

"Well, I'm happy that you feel you can."

"You seem more mature than most of these girls here. You know a lot of things for someone your age and have thoughts way beyond just boys and movies."

I smiled to myself as he said that, thinking about how the poet Robert Frost made me think of all the cute boys in *The Outsiders*. But I was flattered. "That's probably because my mom made me read a lot of books," I said. "It forces you to think about things and to see another world beyond your own."

Most of the time, a lot of the teens are in the water and a few of the girls lay out in the sun, so no one bothers us during our talks. I do catch Kelly staring at us and Michelle has asked me more than once why I sit with Brother Doug all the time instead of going in the water or laying out with them. But I can't tell her the truth. The truth is hard for even me to grasp.

Three nights ago, after the campfire, Brother Doug asked me to go for a walk with him. It was really dark out and I didn't have my flashlight.

"It's okay, I know the paths like the back of my hand," he whispered to me, calming my fears. "Besides, everyone is getting ready for lights out, so you won't miss out on anything."

"Okay, let me run back to my teepee real quick to tell Michelle where I'm going," I said, starting to walk away from him.

"No, no, don't, Scout. It's fine. I already told Sister Abby that I needed to speak with you privately about your brother Jonny," he said, stopping me.

So off we headed down the path away from The Reservation and toward The Ghost Town. After a short while, Brother Doug put his arm around my shoulders.

"You doing okay?" he asked me, sensing my tension. My heart was racing. I was alone with Brother Doug on a path in the dark and this time, different from the other time, no one was close by. A part of me was excited and overwhelmed and the other part of me was scared to death. Where were we going? Was there something wrong with my brother? He was touching me and I was so used to his hands now because he hugged me so nicely every opportunity he had. And I gladly let him.

We veered off down a side trail that I've never noticed before in the daytime and eventually he led me to a small clearing that had a tree stump that looked like the kind of artistic chair you'd find at the flea market in Raleigh. He sat down on the stump and pulled me onto his lap so I was sitting on his right thigh with my legs in between his legs.

"Is this okay?" he asked me.

I was on autopilot, in a Brother Doug-infused daze. *Is it okay?* I didn't know what in the world to do. I've never sat on a man's lap before who wasn't either Santa Clause, my daddy, or my Pawpaw. He had his right hand around my waist, resting on my hip, and his left hand grabbed my left hand, which sat limply on my lap.

"Yeah, it's okay," I said to him, not knowing what else to say.

He looked at me and, through the darkness, I could see the crystal blue of his eyes and the longing within them. He was going to kiss me. Really kiss me. I could feel it. And since the last time I kissed an actual live boy was Jason McLean a year and a half ago at Lisa Wieland's party, I was a little terrified about what was to come. I haven't been practicing on my pillow lately, either.

"Scout, I've wanted to just sit alone with you ever since you got here," he said.

I didn't know what to say to him, so I said nothing.

"Can I give you a kiss?" he asked, like we were both teenagers on a first date. But there was nothing uncomfortable about it.

I was so happy and scared at the same time. My chest was about to cave in from all of the pressure building up. Brother Doug wanted to kiss me and I was paralyzed to do or say anything.

My eyes gazed into his, saying all the words that could not come out of my mouth. My body leaned slightly closer to his chest, which apparently meant yes, he could kiss me, because at that moment, he released my hand and put his hand up to my face, pulling it to him.

He kissed me, fully and without restraint.

I felt like I was a live performer in a dream. Out here and in the dark, alone with this man I've been in love with for so long, this grown man, who wanted me, too, like I was a woman and not a girl. He kissed me so softly and gently and I suppose I was kissing him back okay because he kept going. There was so much pent-up passion releasing itself between us and now it was on full display in the woods, on this strange stump in the dark.

Everything came naturally to me and I didn't understand why I was ever scared. I was meant to kiss this man like this. He held my face and then his hands moved to my back, slowly going underneath my shirt and onto my skin. No one has ever touched me like this — or even tried before. It all felt so good. His hands felt so, so good — strong, rugged, calloused, manly.

Brother Doug ran his fingers along the back of my bra, gently, like he was teasing himself. Then he moved his fingers to the front and ran them along the outline of the cups. I let him.

He said nothing and continued to kiss me, running his hands all along my bare skin. He pulled away for a moment and looked at me like I was a long lost love who had been away on a journey, like in a book. He put his fingers on my cheeks and rubbed them softly and then ran them over the outline of my face. He picked up my hand and kissed it. I let him do whatever he wanted because it felt so nice — I never wanted him to stop.

Then he put his hand on the back of my head and played with my hair, again slowly and gently. I thought to myself: this is real love, this is tenderness.

"Was that okay, Scout?" he asked me, quietly.

I nodded yes and then put my head back down to his face and kissed him like he did to me. I think he was relieved at my initiative and it put him at ease with what was going on.

"I love you," I said to him. "I've always loved you."

He smiled. "I love you, too, Scout," he responded and kissed me again.

When we finally stopped, which I did not want to do at all, I asked him, "What happens now?"

He sighed and said, "You are very, very special to me. You are the best little thing that has happened to me. We'll just have to enjoy whatever moments we can have together."

That was okay with me, since this entire experience was already more than I could've imagined in my head. Kissing Brother Doug DeHaan was now officially the greatest thing I've ever known in my life.

"I don't want camp to end," I said. "I want to kiss you every day."

Brother Doug stood up and pulled me close to him, hugging me tight and running his hands up and down my back. I did the same to him, with my head against his chest.

He pulled me back again and leaned down to kiss me and, if I'm being truthful, if he had simply picked me up and put me on the bed of moss below us and took off my clothes and had sex with me, I would've been okay with that, as well.

"I have to get you back, little girl," he said. *Little girl.* I wasn't sure if he meant that as a term of endearment or if he was trying to remind himself that I was indeed still a little girl. Term of endearment, I decided.

We walked back down the path holding hands and, when we got closer to The Reservation, he told me to go the rest of the way on my own, that he had to get back home. He said that we could meet at that spot every night that he was able to come to the campfire, to just slip away like I was going to go talk to Sister Abby or Ally or like I was going to brush my teeth or something.

I understood. This had to be kept a secret. I couldn't tell anyone, not even Michelle.

Then he cupped my face and said, "Goodnight, Scout." He kissed my forehead and walked away as I watched him disappear quietly into the darkness.

And that was how the first greatest night of my life went.

****

Dear Squirrel-Girl,   February 28th, 1983

Thanks so much for that great valentine you made me.

One of the highlights during the school year when you are a teacher is Valentine's Day. I really like it when my students give me one. Makes me feel special. So thank you again.

I know you are looking forward to baseball season and I am looking forward to the church league softball season. We will have to compare batting averages when we see each other again. Don't you worry, camp will be here before you know it. I miss you, too, kiddo.

Your friend,

Brother Doug

****

DOUG

Rummaging around in the storage shed at Camp Judah, my head is spinning and I'm almost dizzy. All I can think about is the teen campfire tonight. Well, not the campfire — more like after the campfire. Since I was home yesterday, supposedly spending the day with Cammy and Paul, I haven't been able to see Scout since Friday night. All I can think about is Friday night and how I wished I'd kept her with me longer.

It was rushed. We were rushed. I was trying to get her back to The Reservation so no one would notice she wasn't there. Then trying to get home at a reasonable hour so Cammy doesn't get even more pissed off at me than she already is — and has been — since God-knows-when. But I don't care anymore. I feel drunk or high or drunk and high.

Scout's lips are so pure, so full, and she felt so good to kiss and touch. Her body, hard and strong, full breasts. She felt like a woman. She *is* a woman. Hell, in other places, places even in the Great North State, fifteen-year-olds are getting married. Fifteen-year-olds are having sex. Fifteen-year-olds are having babies. Scout is a woman.

My heart is racing and my stomach is churning and I feel like a teenaged boy on his prom night. It's wild and crazy, I know, but I can't think of anything else but Scout on the tree stump in the clearing — our spot — for the last few nights. The smell of summer freedom when I kiss her soft, untouched skin, how it feels when she touches me.

Her kisses were so sweet and nice. She knew exactly what she was doing. Not in an experienced way, but in a natural way, like we're two people whose lips fit just right and were finally able to be joined together.

"You smell so good, like vanilla ice cream," I whispered to her one night with my nose in her hair.

"Breck," she said.

"I want to go buy some Breck so I can sniff it when I can't be with you."

Cammy's mother has stayed with Paul the past several evenings because she's had to work and I've been telling her that I have to work late at camp and there's nothing I can do about it. And it isn't a lie. I actually feel like there is nothing I can do about it. I needed to see Scout. Cammy took off from the hospital for the days covering the Desert Wanderers trip and was not happy about it at all. But I don't give shit. This is all the time I get to have with Scout so I'm going to make the best of it. I might never see her again after camp ends.

Tonight is another teen campfire and Scout will meet me at our spot afterward. Then tomorrow is the start of the

Desert Wanderer's trip, which will force me to find us a new spot so we can be together after lights out. But since we will be out in the so-called wilderness, we might be able to get away with being alone together for a little longer. No one will be doing tent checks.

My hands are furiously moving along all of the junk in the shed, digging in crates of rusted tools and old equipment looking for a goddamn hammer. I probably would've found it by now, but I can't think of anything else but Scout. I know these campgrounds better than anyone and, so far, I can think of a couple of places where we could go that are secluded.

Last night, while she sat on the ground in between my outstretched legs with her back against my chest as I kissed her neck, she said, "Doug, I've never had sex before. I'm a virgin." I'm not stupid — well, yes, I am pretty fucking stupid — but of course I knew that she was untouched. "I love you so much. I want you to be my first time and the only man I'm ever with in my whole life," she continued, innocently.

So sweet, my beautiful, little Scout. She wanted me to take her. And I've thought about that so much the past few days and nights. I want to take her. I want to make love to her and make her feel like she makes me feel: desired, wanted, close, connected. There's nothing like it and she's never known it before with anyone else.

"It would be my honor to be your first and only," I whispered to her, my breath still hot on her neck.

Finally locating a hammer resting on the shed's windowpane — right in plain sight — I walk outside and back toward the lake. I need to hammer down a couple of planks out on the pier. But it's just busy work. My mind is consumed. I need time to just pass by already.

Each night that Scout and I have been together, things between us have been more and more intense. The only thing that has stopped me from picking her up, laying her down on the ground, and making love to her, is the timing. I don't want to rush our first time and make her regret anything with me. It has to be right.

Scout trusts me — completely — and that's such a good feeling to have as a man. She knows that I want her, too, that I don't see her as a little girl anymore, that I will protect her and never hurt her. When I finally do make love to her, it will be gentle and tender, like what we share between us right now. And since she is unblemished, I know that it's a really big deal for her. She is giving me a gift — a gift she can only give once in her entire life — and that means something to me.

Nothing about my intentions with her are selfish. I want her to feel how much I care for her, the love I'm holding in my heart. I don't want to hurt her or scare her or do anything that makes her uncomfortable. I know that I have to be extra careful if it does happen. *God, I want it to happen so fucking bad.*

I spent my day off yesterday packing for the trip.

Cammy took Paul and went to visit her sister, Trish. She didn't ask me if I wanted to go so I stayed home and took care of a few things, enjoying the peace and quiet. Cammy has been strangely quiet lately, no nagging or saying annoying shit. Or maybe she has been, but my mind has been so obsessed with Scout that I've shut it out completely.

I have a backpack with a few changes of clothes, a blanket, and my two-man tent. I'll be alone in there for sleeping purposes. The thought even crossed my mind for Scout to sneak into my tent late at night. But that would be crazy. Someone could easily need me in the night and find us in there together. I don't know why I'd even think of it. Oh yeah, because I'm fucking stupid!

"Doug!" I heard someone yell my way, stopping the flow of thoughts. I turned my head to see Chris walking toward me, barefoot.

"Hey," I replied, sitting up on the sandy beach facing my lake, having been alone with my completely inappropriate thoughts. It's all so surreal. I know I'm doing wrong, but I know I'm doing right at the same time. There's no guilt or shame. What the fucking hell is wrong with me? I must have the proverbial devil and angel on my shoulders. And the devil has sawed off the angel's head and fed it to the wolves at this point.

"Hey," he said walking up to me, a bit out of breath. Then he sat down.

"What's up?" I asked him.

"Nothin' man, just tired. My campers are with the dude with the reptiles. I needed to get away for a bit. Haven't been sleeping good." He laid back on the sand and shut his eyes.

I knew how he felt. I've barely slept either. But it's been the good kind, the kind where instead of sleeping, I'm thinking about a beautiful young woman and all the things I want to do with her.

With his eyes still shut, he asked, "You ready for tomorrow?"

"Yeah, I'm all set."

"We're hiking out after breakfast. So meet us over at the dining hall. I'm putting you with Abby and Ally for the daytime stuff and then you'll be with me and Kevin at night. We got a lot more boys going than girls. Actually, all the boys are going. Ten of the girls are staying back. But I don't know if Abby and Ally can handle this stuff so I want you to be with them."

Cool, I will get to be with Scout most of the time.

"Who's staying back?" I asked him, pretending that I cared about this conversation.

"Grace and Amanda will come over to do it. Should be a boring four days for those princesses," he laughed. "I don't understand girls. They come to camp and don't want to do camp things." He paused. "But your Scout likes to do camp things."

That comment jarred me, caught me off guard. "My

Scout?" I asked, a twinge of defensiveness behind it.

"Yeah. Your Scout," he said laughing a bit. "The other guys know she's your Scout, so don't worry, we keep our distance."

"What the hell do you mean by that?" I asked, surprised and even a bit offended.

"Doug, relax. I've been a counselor long enough to know that we like certain campers better than others sometimes. We get a favorite now and again."

I tried to play off the whole paranoid vibe I was feeling.

"Well, I suppose Scout's been my Scout since she was seven years old. So yeah, I suppose she's my favorite camper. Known her a long time. Hell, I've watched her grow up." Then I added for emphasis, "When Cammy and I have another baby, I hope it's a girl. And I hope she'll grow up to be just like Scout."

That wasn't a total lie.

****

Dear Doug,   3-5-83

Guess what? I made the baseball team! I really wasn't sure if I would, but I did and I am so so happy! But not as happy as I will be when I finally get to see you again!

We started practices, but it's been a little cold. I hope

it warms up soon because I don't like the cold. Do you think the Yankees will be any good this year? Did you start playing in your softball league yet? Please tell me all about it.

I finally completed all of my memorization work for church and all I need to do is attend Sunday school for two more weeks and I will get my last Camp Judah scholarship. The weeks that we are probably signing up for will be the last session. It seems to be when will work best for my parents. I don't care when I go. I just want to see you again!

Brother Doug, I've missed you so much. You have meant so much to me all these years. You have been so nice to me and everyone at camp and you make me feel like you really care about me. Sometimes I think about if I was older and if you would still like me. I know it's silly, but do you know how people say that everything happens for a reason? Well, I think there was a reason I met you. I don't know what it is yet, but I bet it is a good reason.

Write me back soon! Love ya!

Love,

Scout Elizabeth

****

CAMMY

Standing alone in my bedroom, I felt like I've been struck by lightning. I felt as if my heart stopped beating completely and I was going to die on the spot, at the ripe old age of thirty. Instead of dying, which honestly would've been much better, this feeling of horror, of dread, of out-right insanity took over my brain and my feet became cemented on the carpet. I was unable to move, unable to think straight, unable to speak.

The phone ringing in the kitchen is what snapped me out of this state where time had stopped. That is, the phone and then the sound of Paul knocking something over in the living room. As I looked down at the piece of paper in my hands, a bit crumpled, but completely legible and fresh, I read, "Dear Doug, Your love is the greatest thing I've ever known. I will love you forever. When camp is over, I hope you will come me see so we can be together again. Love, Scout."

Who the fucking hell is Scout?

I knew it! I knew something wasn't right with Doug. He has been so different and removed for so long. He's been a jerk, an asshole, an uncaring and apathetic dick. And why? Because of some whore named Scout? And what kind of name is "Scout" anyway? It's a fucking whore's name!

A million questions and obscenities and scenarios started flying though my head as I dropped the note on the floor and ran down the hall into the living room to see what Paul knocked over. It was just a large book of photos and as he looked at me with his hand in his mouth, I hopped into the kitchen to answer the phone. But I was too late.

"MOTHER FUCKER!!!" I screamed into the phone to no one in particular, scaring even myself.

Good. I didn't want to talk to anyone anyway. I wanted to scream a primal, murderous, ferocious shriek. I wanted to kill this slut who has seduced and stolen my husband. I wanted to kill my husband for doing this to me. I wanted to kill myself for not being enough of a woman that he'd seek the love of another woman instead. Then I wanted to kill something, anything, because my life as I knew it was over. I married my father and ended up as my mother, after all.

My mind was racing and I knew I had to calm down. My son needed me. I had to be rational about something completely irrational! Doug, my Doug, the Doug I've known for almost a whole decade, the Doug who has listened to me ramble late at night, the Doug who has told me that he has never even looked twice at another woman, that I was the only girl for him, who said there was nothing I could do to drive him from me — that Doug — is fucking some tramp named Scout. Is it some nickname that he gave her? Doug is all about his little fucking nicknames!

But how is it happening? When is it happening? The note referred to camp.

Then it hit me like a big bag of stinking shit. "Oh my God. It's a fucking counselor at Camp Judah!" I shouted out loud. "It's some little college whore at that so-called Christian camp! It has to be! Some little twenty-one-year-old pixie with a perfect cheerleader body."

He's always coming home late, making excuses to be there longer, to go on the overnight trip — even having me miss work when he damn well knows that we need my income just to pay our bills every week. He is fucking some stupid young little twit and leaving me at home with our son in order to do it!

I'm ill. I want to call Trish and cry. I want to open all of his drawers and go through all of his pockets. I don't know where this note came from because it was barely sticking out from under the bed, but it doesn't look old or like it's been washed with his laundry. For all I can tell, it could've been written yesterday.

I yelled up at the ceiling, "DOUG IS SO FUCKING STUPID!" What kind of a moron who is cheating on his wife brings home a love note from his mistress? My moron does, that's who!

Sitting on the floor in the living room, Paul walked over to me holding his little toy xylophone, all colorful and innocent, just like my little boy, now the son of a cheating bastard. I sat with my back against the couch looking at Paul. My mind was flooded in anger, pain, betrayal and just... sadness. My life was a lie — a big, fat, fucking lie. And I didn't know what to do.

So I put my hands over my face and started to sob. Like a baby. Suddenly, I felt two little hands on my head, rubbing my hair gently on my temples, just like Doug used to do, saying, "Ssss'okay, Mommy."

* * * * * * * *

Dear Squirrel-Girl,   March 15, 1983

I really appreciate all the nice things you said to me in your last letter, kiddo. You are a bright and shining light in a sometimes difficult world. I am lucky to know you. Do I think that things happen for a reason? Well, sure I do. I'm a Christian man and I believe that God has His reasons for everything, good and bad. I might not always understand the reasons, but I trust in Him to know what He is doing.

You are a special young lady "Scout Elizabeth" and I am quite sure that we met for a reason all those years ago. One reason I am sure is that you help me remember why I went into teaching and coaching and working with young people. Sometimes it is hard being a teacher and sometimes I have bad days, just like anyone. But then I get a letter from you, a young lady who I have watched grow up over the years, and your kind words to me are a source of inspiration to keep on going. You might not understand all that yet because you are a bit young, but someday when you choose your path in life, you might have a really bad day and wonder why you bother doing what you're doing. And then someone might say something nice to you and remind you exactly why.

So Squirrel, it goes both ways. I, too, think you are something special. Camp will be here before you know it, and it will be great!

I hope that you are happy and having a great baseball season. You tell those boys not to mess with MY SG! OK?

Your friend always,

Brother Doug

****

SCOUT

"Dear Mom and Daddy," I wrote neatly on my light pink stationery, a Christmas gift from one of my paper route customers. "The Desert Wanderer's trip has been a whole lot of fun so far. It's been so much better than last summer. We've done so many things and I think I'm finally getting the hang of starting a campfire with just a pair of glasses. It was scary to do it at first, but I understood all the science behind it."

I put the pretty paper off to the side in my tent and began to scratch my legs, feasted upon by mosquitoes and other critters. I stared at my hands and could make out all of the red clay lingering on and in my skin. It's been difficult to wash my body out here. As much as I don't mind sweating, the red clay in some parts is hard to avoid and I didn't want to be gross around Brother Doug.

"Little girl, don't you worry about that," he told me when I complained how disgusting I felt at the end of the first day. "The time we have together is the only time we get to have so we'll make the best of it no matter the situation out here."

Rubbing my hands together with a damp washcloth, I sat back down on my sleeping bag and continued with my letter to my parents. "The group has done long hikes, set up camp, and learned all about how to survive with minimal equipment. We've cooked our meals over a fire and used stream water to wash our dishes. I pitched my own tent, helped set up the girls' latrine area, and dug a cat hole. Thankfully, there's a pickup truck that brings us fresh water and the food from the dining hall each day. I sure don't want to have to live off of berries and creek water or something. Even I have my limits! But the staff is trying to make the experience as tough as they can without making us miserable and wanting to leave and go back to The Lord's Reservation. It would've been a lot easier to stay at The Reservation with Kelly, Mary Catherine and Michelle, but I love a challenge. There are only six girls that decided to challenge themselves."

What I didn't tell them about Desert Wanderers is that Brother Doug was on this trip, and I was not going to miss our last few days together for any reason whatsoever. If I was the only girl who volunteered, I was still going on this trip.

I've barely thought about Charlie for the last two weeks. The only time he crosses my mind is when I receive his letters at mail call and then when I think about how he'd enjoy whatever our group was doing at the moment. For example, Charlie would love the game Capture the Flag and he would love cooking his food outdoors.

I've been so lost with Brother Doug and all that's happened between us, I haven't thought about home much at all — about my parents, my other friends, my baseball team and how the season ended up without me. I was going into high school soon after I return home from camp and it's been the furthest thing from my mind, almost like the world outside of this place has stopped in its tracks and nothing else exists or matters anymore.

The first two days that Brother Doug and I have been together have been magical. I feel like a princess, or at least what I think a princess might feel like when she's so consumed with love. I'm a sweaty, itchy, and nasty princess, but a princess nonetheless. No matter what activities we're doing in the daytime, Brother Doug helps out with the girls. He always makes sure to be near me, talk to me, make me laugh with a couple of jokes or some kind of stunt. But he doesn't make anything too obvious, so he tries to do the same kinds of things with the other girls. Then after the daytime activities are done, Brother Doug turns into my prince who rescues me in the late nighttime darkness.

"Now, this is what you need to do during lights out. Wait for Charlotte to fall asleep. Then get out of the tent, real quiet like, and make sure that no one else is outside and could see you," Brother Doug instructed me.

"But what if someone might?" I asked, scared of this very real possibility.

"Just watch and wait. When you see them disappear

from view, just discreetly follow the path of matted grass over to the girl's latrine area. If you have to, just crawl over near the higher brush area. No one will be able to see you near there."

The latrine area is made up of a tarp that provides a cover for us while we clean up and take care of our business.

He continued, "When you get to the latrine, just leave your flashlight next to the tree closest to the path for later. Then walk back toward the third large tree directly in line of the tarp. And I'll be waiting there for you," he said, smiling that dreamy smile.

When I found him at the third tree, he walked me to our new spot somewhere much further away so we could be together, all alone, no getting caught.

Tonight will be our last night together. The last two nights, we have spent kissing each other so long and passionately. I let him touch me everywhere he wanted and kiss me everywhere he wanted. I felt no shame or embarrassment at all about anything he was doing to me so I knew in my heart that it had to be okay. If it wasn't okay, I would have felt bad about it all or uncomfortable with him. I was sure of that. God would've let me know it was wrong in some way.

It all felt so good, so wonderful, like I was in some movie being carried away to a happily-ever-after ending. I couldn't understand at all why my mom and the church people and pretty much all the adults I knew said that we young'uns shouldn't be doing these things. Since it all feels so amazing, why shouldn't people in love with each other be sharing such happiness? What good is keeping yourself from enjoying these things with the one you love? Why is it considered wrong or improper? This wasn't lust of the flesh, it was love. I have never felt so close to anyone as I do to Brother Doug. Not even Charlie. And that couldn't possibly be wrong. That couldn't possibly be a bad thing.

Brother Doug is so patient with me, so kind and gentle.

"Little girl, can I kiss you?" he always whispers to me before he does it. "Can I touch you? Is this alright with you?" he always asks me, before he does anything. "Are you comfortable with this? I don't want to do anything you aren't okay with," he's told me a few times. "If you ever want me to stop, I will. No questions asked." He is such a gentleman.

I figured that was what my daddy meant when he told me about boys only wanting to get into my pants. A boy wouldn't ask permission. A boy would just do it and not care what the girl thought about it. But Brother Doug asks first because he cares about me. He is a man, not some stupid boy. He respects me.

Since he knew that I've never done these types of things before, he shows me the kinds of things that he likes me to do for him. But he only talked me through it because I asked him to. I wanted to please him and make him feel like he makes me feel and I wanted us to feel the same things together. But mostly, I wanted him to feel how much I loved him.

And while I'm glad that I never did these things with a boy before, it would've been nice to know more about it. I didn't know anything about how to use my hands and mouth to make a man happy. The mouth part scared me at first, but then it was fine — it felt fine to me.

When my mom gave me "the talk" a couple of years ago, she never told me about all the other sex stuff. She only told me about sexual intercourse or "making love." Even in school during health class, the teacher never talked about all the other kinds of intimate things people do together. She taught about the mechanics of how a baby is made, not at all about how it made you feel inside, how you could be in a dream that you never wanted to end.

We haven't had intercourse yet, but we came really close to it last night. I think tonight we might go ahead and do it because it's our last chance.

"I have a rubber with me and I'll use it on myself if you really want me to," he said the first night we were out there. I've never seen a rubber before, even though I've heard about them from Maybelle.

"It's okay if you don't wear one," I said. "I don't mind. You're my first and I want you to be the only man that I'm ever with like this," I told him. "I don't want anything coming between us, not even a rubber."

I'd wait forever for him, just in case things don't work

out with his wife. I wanted him to know that I was his girl, his alone, that I'd never give myself to anyone else while I'm waiting for him.

Last week, I slipped a small note in his shorts pocket telling him how I felt about him, just so he'd have something from me that told him, something he could see. I love Brother Doug so much. How could I ever love another man like this again? I couldn't. There's no way that I could ever feel this much inside of me for anyone else again.

I love how he likes to hold me when we're done kissing and touching each other. He whispers to me, tells me how beautiful I am, and how much he loves me and cares for me.

"I hope I'll be able to see you again someday after camp is all over," he said one night with his hands resting along my waistline. "I've never felt like this before. What we have is real and special and if my circumstances were different, we would be together."

I believe him. I believe everything he tells me. I felt the same way about him. "I would have to get my parents to sign the papers that would let me marry you," I said to him, all nestled up into his chest. "Or you could just wait for me to turn sixteen and then we could go off on our own."

When we talked like this, he'd rub my back and the hair on my temples and he'd kiss the nape of my neck so softly. I never wanted our moments together to stop.

But they do have to stop. When we're done, Brother Doug whispers that we need to get back. Then we do the reverse down the pathway, and I make myself look like I just went to the latrine in the dark. My flashlight is always hidden next to the tree at the latrine and, because my eyes are adjusted to the darkness, I'm able to find my way back with no problem. Then I get my flashlight, turn it on like I've been there all along and go back to my tent.

Brother Doug sure came up with the perfect plan, just as he said he would.

CAMMY

I've spent the last two days trying to wrap my head around the following: the possibility — no, the probability — that Doug is in fact cheating on me; and, if correct, how I'm going to confront him. Do I throw the note in his face at Holy Jesus Holier Than Thou Camp Judah and humiliate him in front of the very people who think he walks on water? Or do I wait for him to come home and scream at him? Or do I throw all of his shit out in front of the house and set it on fire? There's also the additional terrifying thoughts about divorce and child support and visitation and moving and finances; and then finally, in between all of my raging tirades, forcing myself to remember the things between us that are worth saving and suggesting that we go to a marriage counselor immediately.

The most important thing was finding out for sure and, in order to do that, I need to go to the camp tomorrow and sniff around. But I knew in my gut that he was cheating on me. My mama told me that gut instincts is all a girl really has in this world. Why she never did anything about hers, I'll never fully understand. But damn it, I'm doing something about mine.

Doug is away for only one more night at that camp. I don't know how he is fucking some dumb bitch there while he is supposed to be working and watching the kids, but that place is huge and I guess there are lots of hidden places that they could find. Lord knows in our younger years, we found plenty of dark corners.

I'm trying to keep all of the rage and pain within me, flailing around like some out-of-control fire, under control because I have a little boy to protect from all of this fucking shit and I need a cool head if I'm going to figure out my next move.

But first, I have to sure! I have to know the truth, what is going on, if he is in fact now a younger version of my asshole father. I can't help but be in some kind of denial about it all. But at the same time my gut is screaming, "HE'S CHEATING ON YOU, CAMPBELL! WAKE UP AND RUN!" I mean, it is *Doug*. My Doug. My sweet, doting Doug who's maybe going through a tough time for some reason, or it's a normal rocky phase in our marriage — marriage is hard and everyone has ups and downs and challenging times — and money is tight, but he wouldn't cheat on me over it. Would he?

Maybe that note I found was from some stupid little teenager who has a crush on him. Maybe he saw it and laughed, brought it home to show me, and forgot it was in his pocket — and because it was from a teenaged girl, he knew it wasn't a big deal if I saw it because…it was from a teenaged girl! He knows I understand that kind of silly bullshit comes with his career and I'd see it and laugh, right along with him — all over a cold beer. It's happened before. Doug has worked with teenaged girls for as long as I've known him, and plenty have had a crush on him. I would've had a crush on him, too.

But I couldn't shake the gut feeling. I couldn't reason away the reality that he's so changed, removed, distant, aloof, detached — just gone, really. A completely different person. Not my Doug at all, in any way: in conversation, intimately, even the way he is with Paul.

I watched this kind of subtle drama my entire childhood so I know what it looks like, what it feels like, what it smells like. What do they say? "If it walks like a duck and quacks like a duck, it's a duck."

"Is Doug a duck? A fucking-a-college-whore duck?" I asked myself, standing in my bathroom while looking in the mirror at my pale, stressed, and tear-stained face.

I wanted so badly to talk to my sister, Trish. She understood me. But if I was being paranoid and if I was overreacting, and if everything I was thinking and feeling wasn't true, then she would have this horrible image of Doug every time she sees him. And that wouldn't be fair to any of us, especially him. Doug has been a great brother-in-law to her for a long time and a fantastic uncle to her kids.

Thank God I'm not working. I wouldn't be able to

concentrate. But my plan is set. Tomorrow, I'm taking Paul with me and we're going over to Camp Judah. But we're going early, much earlier than Doug needs me to pick him up. So early, in fact, that he will be surprised if he sees me. I'll go to the camp office and ask Mr. Houghton to see if he can summon Doug. When Doug arrives, I'll show him the note and ask him who "Scout" is. His reaction will tell me everything I need to know. He's not a good liar.

Even though my gut knew otherwise, I still held on to hope that all of this angst I've been dealing with and the emotional roller coaster I've been on for the past two days is all over nothing.

DOUG

Holding her, partially clothed in my arms, with her perfect body against mine, has been the greatest joy of my entire summer — hell, my year — maybe even my life. Her hair is right under my nose so I can smell the Breck scent and my hands are wrapped around her bare waist, our legs intertwined, two lovers without a care in the world. That's exactly the way this should feel and I can't remember if I ever felt like this before with a girl. My head is so far gone with her in our own universe out here in the trees.

We're lying on the blanket I brought with me, but haven't actually used, because it's been too hot. But I wanted to make love to her and I wanted her to be completely comfortable.

"I'm comfortable, I swear," she promised me when we were done. "I'd be comfortable with you anywhere."

I kiss her hair. "Everything, Scout. Everything that's happened between us these past couple of weeks, days and especially tonight, have been beautiful and right."

"I know. It's been amazing, better than I ever imagined."

"If this was wrong, we would've felt like it was wrong.

I never felt like that. Not once," I confessed, caressing her collarbone with my fingers.

"I feel the same way, like this is meant to be. That we belong together someday."

While I don't know what the future holds for us, I have to make sure she understands that she can never, ever, ever tell anyone about this. She can't tell her best friend, her parents, her pastor, not even her dog. She has to keep it a secret because I could get in a lot of trouble. No matter what we think about the love we share, society will crucify me and I'll lose everything: my family, my career, my good name. I'd probably even go to jail. But more than anything, I can't lose my son.

"Scout?" I whisper in her ear as she ran her fingers up and down my forearm, still wrapped all around her.

"Hmmm…" she whispered back. I could tell she was smiling.

"You understand that everything — the love we have, the love we share, the love we made tonight — it all has to remain a secret. You can't tell anyone about it, ever. You know that right?" I asked.

"Yes, I know," she whispered back. "I'll never tell, I promise."

I felt relieved. I knew that she knew she couldn't tell anyone, but I guess I felt like I had to be sure and make it clear to her. She was quiet, not talking at all, and I wasn't sure what was going through her head. She didn't appear to be troubled or anything, but her silence and the stillness about her had me a little concerned. The last thing I wanted to do was make her feel like what she'd done with me was somehow wrong.

I wanted to ask her, again, if she was okay. At a minimum, she'd put my rising fears to rest if she just spoke. Suddenly, the thought of her letters popped into my head and I became curious about why she stopped writing to me. In an effort to get her talking, I decided to ask her about it.

"Scout?"

"Hmmm…?"

"I was thinking about how you'd write me all the time over the past year."

"I loved writing you," she said. "That gave me something to look forward to."

"Why did you stop?"

"Stop?" her body tensed up for a second. She turned around and we lay together face-to-face, our noses almost touching.

"Yeah, your letters. They just suddenly stopped coming, back in March, I think."

Scout looked perplexed. "No…I wrote you like three times and never got a letter back. So I thought maybe I was bothering you and stopped."

That was weird. I never got those letters. I wondered what happened to them and why they never arrived. Surely Mr. Houghton would've given me my mail.

I kissed her nose. "Well, I guess they got lost in the post office."

This was our last night together and tomorrow afternoon, Scout would go home. I would go home. And I wondered to her, "Will I ever hold you like this again?"

CAMMY

Pulling into Camp Judah, I knew that what I was about to do was going to go one of two ways: either my life as I knew it was over or Doug would be pissed off at me for overreacting and making a scene, embarrassing him. Just another thing for him to be mad at me. But at least I would know. At least the torture of this is-he-or-isn't-he would come to an end and I'd either kick his ass out of my house or apologize to him, hoping that he'd see the need for us to talk to a counselor.

I wanted my man back. I was sick of this shit.

Camp Judah was humming. It was mid-morning and there were all kinds of happy noises surrounding the main area. Campers were singing in their groups inside the screened-in chapel. Walking onto the grounds, with Paul on my hip, I quietly observed the rowdy kids, who looked about third or fourth grade, singing camp songs in competition style.

The sun was bright and strong in a Carolina blue sky and I was already sweating from the heat and humidity. I walked over to the camp office area, where I always met

Doug on nights that I had to pick him up — the silent toils of a one-car family.

Paul and I went up the steps and walked into the office. I was expecting someone to be in there, but no one was. There was a break room with a kitchenette and an indoor bathroom. Mr. Houghton's desk was somewhat cluttered, but today it was much neater than I've seen in the past. There were a few old photos on the wall, photos from camp years' past, and one framed picture of Doug from about ten years ago, his light blond hair looking almost white. He didn't look much different now. The man does have some youthful genes.

I put Paul down on a side chair and started to look at all of the things in the office: other photos, a couple of magazines on a small table, a white mug with old coffee sitting thick and cold, forging a nasty brown ring on the inside. And, as I walked closer to Mr. Houghton's desk, I saw something that caught my eye. The word "Scout."

With my heart in my throat, I looked closely at the envelopes on the desk sitting on top of a Christian devotional booklet. I picked up the first envelope and then realized there were two more just like it underneath. They were long, white envelopes with "Scout Webb" written in girly handwriting with a return address from some town I've never heard of. They were addressed to "Doug DeHaan" at Camp Judah. I turned over the envelope and it was still sealed, with the letters "S.W.A.K." written across the flap.

My heart was racing. It hit me that I stumbled on the very thing that I had hoped to find at this place, something that would lead me anywhere to the truth, or at least an answer about what the flying fuck was going on with my husband. I had already planned to ask Mr. Houghton if he had a counselor named Scout working for him, under the guise that I wanted a babysitter. But here are three letters from a "Scout", all addressed to Doug. This is no coincidence.

Looking over at Paul, sitting quietly on the chair and looking sleepy, I ripped open the first letter. My head and heart started to become completely flooded with emotions again. My eyes flew over the gushy words, all in teenybopper handwriting. I read phrases like, "I miss you so much" and "I can't wait to see you again" and "XO" written after her name. I read comments like "You are the best" and "I can't wait until we're together having fun again" and it's all I can do to hold back the tears.

"Who the fuck is this Scout person and why is she writing love letters to my husband?" I hollered out loud, startling Paul. I want to run outside of the office and scream those very words into the thick summer air.

Just then, Mr. Houghton, the sweet seventyish-year-old man who came to our wedding and our son's christening at Doug's church, walked into the office. He looked surprised to see me and immediately went over to Paul, bent down to his face and said, "Hey little buddy, how are you doing?" Then he stood up, wiped his hands on his old faded jeans, sweat appearing on his tee shirt just under his armpits from the heat. "Hey there, Cammy, how's it goin' sweetie?"

He walked closer and kissed my cheek. I always felt like Mr. Houghton didn't think I was Christian enough for Doug, but he was honestly one of the nicest men I've ever met in my life, genuinely kind, and I doubt he had it in his nature to say a mean word about anyone.

"Hi, Mr. Houghton," I said nervously, my stomach clenched, reminding me of why I was here.

"Are you here to pick up Doug already?" he asked, grinning. "I saw him over at the lake. He just got back with the Desert Wanderers group and it looks like he was getting ready to close down the lake for the summer."

I stared him, his gray hair a bit messy, his glasses sitting lopsided on his nose, probably because his nose was sweating. He walked over to his desk. At that moment, the tears that had been welling up in me, suppressed by sheer will all morning, started escaping my eyes. He looked up, surprised. "Cammy, what's wrong?"

I held out the letter I had opened and the other two I had yet to read. He studied them briefly and pursed his lips, sighing.

"Mr. Houghton, who is Scout?"

Mr. Houghton took a breath and eyed me, realizing what I must've been thinking. He came over to me, hugged me gently, and said, "Cammy, it's not what you think, hon."

My heart was in my throat. The tears were still leaking

from my eyes. Paul looked from the chair at the strange scene that was unfolding in front of him.

"Sweetie, I'm sorry, but you don't need to be thinking anything bad about Doug and that letter. Scout's a little girl who's come to this camp since she was just knee high to a grasshopper and who has a big crush on Doug. She has written him letters here since the end of last summer."

And, as if I was paroled from my rather extended darkness, with those words, a wave of relief swept over my body. His words, "a little girl" and "big crush on Doug" marched in the air like soldiers, my heart accepting them, the very thing I was hoping for all along. My tears immediately turned to tears of relief.

He continued, "Scout's just fourteen. She's a good girl, but she's got some sort of fixation on Doug. She wrote him a bunch of letters and, well, at some point, I started getting worried that it might make Doug look bad. So I stopped giving him the letters with the hopes that they might stop coming." He paused. "And they did! See? These letters are from March and April. Scout didn't send anymore after I stopped giving them to Doug."

Stopped giving them to Doug?

"He knows about the letters then?" I asked. He sure never mentioned them to me. He never mentioned a fourteen-year-old girl with an infatuation writing him letters all the time.

I pulled out the small note I found under the bed and

handed it to Mr. Houghton. He read it and looked up at me.

"Cammy, you know about this stuff. Doug's a good looking young man and he's been a charming fixture around here for a long time. And you know how teenaged girls get crushes on lifeguards. Heck, some of my girl counselors get crushes on him, too, but that's all they are. You know your husband. He's a professional, a teacher, a counselor of young people, and more than anything — he's a man after God's own heart, just like King David in the Bible.

Didn't King David sleep with another man's wife and then have her husband murdered?

Mr. Houghton continued, "Doug knows how to deal with it. My guess is that, to him, it's just another minor nuisance." He paused again. "Scout's just a lot more expressive, I guess. You know how girls that age can be."

Everything he said was sinking in and made complete sense, but the gut feeling was still lingering on throughout my body. Something wasn't right. Something was off. The brief relief I felt was dissipating and the dread was coming over me like a dark blanket.

"Why did you keep the letters?" I asked Mr. Houghton, still searching for answers to quell the rising tide of dread and sadness within me.

"I was gonna give them to him today when he left. Scout's been here all three weeks and everything's been normal, no issues or problems that I've been able to tell. No one's reported anything about Scout misbehaving or

Doug being given a hard time. But I wouldn't expect Scout to misbehave. Like I said, she's a good girl with a big crush is all."

This Scout person has been here these last three weeks?

My brain was on overload and I no longer cared what I looked like or sounded like anymore. I was angry. How could Mr. Houghton let an obsessed crazy girl come to his camp and put my husband in some sort of compromising position like that? How could Doug not tell me about some insane girl who's writing him all the time? What the fuck is going on? Why is no one talking to this girl's parents and demanding she see a psychologist?

The emotions start to get the better of me and I can feel all the highs and lows of all I've been dealing with for the last year in a full-out war within me. There is a fucking psycho nymphomaniac trying to seduce and steal my husband. And no one is doing anything about it.

My mama taught me when I was young, after I had been suspended from school for punching a girl in the face who had pissed me off, that I had to learn how to find a productive way to deal with the pent up rage within me. I figured my rage had something to do with my home life, but was never quite sure. As I grew older, I learned to deal with it. Whenever I felt the rage churning, I cleaned the bathroom, I painted pictures, I ran for miles, I vacuumed the car.

But the rage that had been building in me for a long

time, the rage that had been knocking on the door of my head like an aggressive encyclopedia salesman over the past couple of weeks, the rage that was now exploding in my chest, decided it had other plans. There would be no cleaning or painting or running today.

Startling both Mr. Houghton and Paul, I demanded, "I want to see my husband immediately and I want this Scout to come to the office!"

"Now, there's no reason to bring Scout into this. She's just a child and it ain't appropriate for you to confront her about anything," Mr. Houghton said calmly.

I didn't fucking care. She was old enough to know that she shouldn't be pursuing a married man. I wanted to look at her face and let her know that Doug HAS A WIFE AND A SON and that she has no fucking business writing him love letters and notes.

"Cammy, I will radio Doug and tell him to come to the office, but under no circumstances am I sending for Scout. I know you're upset, hon, but it's just not appropriate." He was so calm, like an earthquake could hit us and he'd have no problem shepherding everyone to safety.

I didn't give a fuck if Scout was just a child. I was dealing with this nightmare head-on and putting that little slut in her place.

Mr. Houghton radioed for Doug into his walkie-talkie and I heard Doug's chopped up voice say, "Okay, give me a minute." My head was spinning.

And as if on cue, a comely girl with long brown hair and round full cheeks walked into the office holding a binder. She looked a bit rough, like she had been in the heat for a few days, but she was young and fit and wearing a tee shirt with the New York Yankees logo on it. I figured she was a counselor. She looked over at me, smiled, and then turning toward Mr. Houghton, she said, "Mr. Houghton, Brother Kevin asked me to bring this to you." She walked closer to him and handed him the binder.

He took the binder from her and said, "Thanks, Scout," and then, realizing what he had just said, looked at me with a fearful glare.

Scout said, "You're welcome..." and seemed to want to say something else and continue into a full-blown conversation, but Mr. Houghton was brushing her off, motioning for her to leave.

All at once, rage won its war within me and blew like fire out of my mouth.

"So you're Scout?" I asked sharply, in a tone that would scare the stink out of a skunk. "You're the little twit who has been writing love letters to my husband?"

Scout stood there looking at me and said nothing. The irony of this little bitch having so much to say to my husband in her letters, but nothing to say to me, was laughable. I eyed her over and was disgusted.

Then the rage continued.

"What kind of a so-called Christian throws herself at

a married man? What's wrong with you? Not enough little boys back where you're from in Haddleboro? Or are you trying to steal other husbands back there, too?"

Mr. Houghton interjected. "Cammy, I told you, this is not appropriate. Please." He looked at Scout. "Scout, honey, you need to leave."

But Scout just kept standing there, frozen in her spot, as if she knew that she indeed deserved the tongue lashing she was receiving from this desperately angry woman I've morphed into. And since this day was going to go the way I wanted it to, that thing called "God's will" must've arranged for Doug DeHaan to walk into the office at this exact moment. Because he did. And when he realized what was going on, he too, stood speechless, paralyzed in his footsteps as he listened to my rage roll out all over Scout.

"Who the hell do you think you are? Just you wait until someday when you're busting your ass trying to raise a family and some little bitch decides to throw herself at your husband! See how you feel!" I took a deep breath, and then kept going. "What's wrong you, little whore? Your daddy not pay enough attention to you? Can't get a boyfriend your own age?"

Then, Scout, who had been shaking, started to cry.

DOUG

The sheer horror of seeing my wife in Mr. Houghton's office had to be evident on my face. There is no way I could've hidden it. Watching Scout as she stood there, being verbally accosted, hit me like a two-by-four and almost knocked me back into the door. In all of the years I've known Cammy, I knew she could be nasty and pretty mean from time to time, but this was a side to her that surprised even me.

I wasn't ready, really, to address anything related to Scout. Certainly not right now. Certainly not in this ugly moment as I watched my wife's face turn into a contorted mass of pain and anger. What did she know? What has she seen? What has she been told?

A million questions went through my mind and, as I watched Cammy's wrath-fueled tirade at the frightened and sobbing little girl in front of me, the words melted into the background — and all I could hear was the sound of a train.

As a boy, I loved trains. My father took me to the train tracks to see them go by every Sunday afternoon. I had a small toy train that we'd put around our Christmas tree. We built a rather elaborate train set when I was ten, which we housed on a large table in our basement. But this train was not like those trains. This train was conjured up in my head, lightening fast, and it headed right at me, at Cammy and Paul, and at Scout.

As I stood there, hearing it coming, and as I watched Cammy's mouth rapidly going on and on, firing obscenities and accusations at Scout — my sweet and innocent Scout, my Squirrel-Girl, a beautiful light in this dark world who's been nothing but kind and loving toward me, a friend to me, someone I believed I loved — my stomach tightened to where I was about to puke, my head became overwhelmed, and I could think of nothing but this impending massacre via the oncoming train.

"And YOU!" Cammy screamed at me, shaking me from my speechless state. "How could you allow some obsessed little slut send you love letters for a year and not do anything about it?"

And then, as if a light bulb went off in my head, I realized that there was my way out. A gift, really. And it came from my pissed off — to the point of being maniacal and miserable — wife. She thought Scout was just some young girl obsessed with me, a fairytale-powered teenager living in some fantasy world about a man carrying her off and being with her forever. Cammy didn't know anything. She didn't know the truth.

I decided then and there that she could never know. And neither could anyone else.

Looking at Mr. Houghton, who stood at his desk, completely dumbfounded and very concerned, not knowing quite what to do, I shifted in my spot. I gazed at Paul, who was starting to cry as he sat in the corner of the office, confused and scared about what was going on in front of him. I studied Cammy, who now stood still and quiet, looking at me with her face so full of hurt, just dripping with the angst of my betrayal, so emotionally drained to exhaustion. Then I looked over at Scout, my little girl-woman, sobbing quietly. She stared at me directly into my eyes, waiting for me to say something, anything, to stand up for her, to stop my wife from screaming at her, to help her in this horrible moment, to protect her, to comfort her, to make her feel like everything I shared with her over the past three weeks was real and had meant as much to me as it did to her. And, as I heard Paul say "Daddy", the proverbial oncoming train arrived, I pulled my wife and son to safety — and pushed Scout right in front of it to meet her demise.

"Okay, everybody needs to calm down," I started. "Scout, you need to go back to your camp and get ready to leave. I'll call your parents and tell them what's happened. You are not to write letters to me anymore. You understand me?" I spouted off with the authority of a calculus teacher.

Scout stopped sobbing as if I pushed a button on her and just stared at me, both horrified and lost.

"WHY ARE YOU LOOKING AT HIM? STOP LOOKING AT HIM!" Cammy screamed at her.

Scout's eyes remained fixed on me. Absolutely terrified about what she was going to say or do, my stomach was in my throat and my heart on pause. She could destroy me right now. She could ruin my life with one word. She could cry "rape" or tell my wife that I said I was in love with her, tell her all the things that I've said to her, all the things that I've done with her, all the things I had her do to me. It was like the air in the room was ripe with a thick gas, about to knock me out in an instant. And at this point, that would be preferable.

As I observed Scout, I saw her face slowly change into something else altogether — sad and resigned — and I knew she was going to let it happen. She took the hit of the train without a word, without even flinching, without one utterance of the truth about us and what we've done. She let everyone in that room believe the story they were told — hook, line and sinker — that she was an obsessed, teenaged nymphomaniac who threw herself at me and tried to "steal" me away from my wife.

Some deep, sick part of me knew all along that she would accept her fate in this situation, all because of the trust and love she had for me. I always had her in my back pocket and knew she'd never betray me, no matter what I did to her.

So I went ahead and betrayed her — I couldn't believe how easy it was for me to do it, too. And then, as if a fan turned on in the office, the thick air disappeared, the wreckage from the train parted, and Scout Elizabeth Webb turned her eyes away from me and simply walked out the door.

I knew that I would never see her again.

"Greater love hath no man than this, than a man who lays down his life for his friends," I thought to myself, instantly reminded of the Bible verse. Scout bought into that stuff — sacrifice and true love and all that. We'd had plenty of conversations about that very thing during our many talks this summer.

But what does that make someone like me? A man who sacrifices the honor of an innocent girl who has been nothing but kind to him? A man who willingly accepts the pure love and trust given to him because he knows it's a precious gift, only to throw it into a fire? And all the while doing it willingly and in the name of protecting his family?

At least, that was the bullshit lie I was telling myself at this point. I did it for my family.

But I knew that my actions had nothing to do with saving my family and all to do with saving myself.

SCOUT

In the early evening of the worst day of my life, I laid in my bed with the covers pulled up over my body. Stretch was under the covers with me, his warm body against my leg. It was so hot outside, but my daddy brought home the air conditioner that used to be at his garage and put it in my window. He did it right after we got home from Camp Judah.

The cold consumed the stale dead air in my bedroom and it flowed over me, making me feel some kind of slight relief from the unimaginable agony I now found myself in.

There was a different level of pain that I never knew existed until today. This kind of pain felt like God's hands went inside of my body and ripped out my soul, thread by tiny thread, the kind of pain that makes you wish you were dead.

For the first time in my life, I understood why some people kill themselves, why they want the pain to stop so badly that they decide to end it all by slitting their wrists in a bathtub or hanging themselves from a tree or shooting themselves in the head. I suppose it's good that we don't have a gun in the house and I'm too grossed out by blood to attempt slashing my own body.

Earlier today, my daddy had come to pick us up from camp. My mom stayed behind in Haddleboro to help out with the church yard sale. My suitcase was taken with the others in the pickup truck to the front of the camp and I sat on a bench with a tear-sodded face and a shattered heart in the chapel area while we waited for our parents. One by one, or two by two, just like Noah's Ark, campers left the site and headed home.

But when my daddy arrived, I saw Mr. Houghton pull him into his office. I caught a glimpse of Brother Doug stealthily ducking inside the office, too. About twenty minutes later, my daddy emerged alone and walked over to the chapel to take us home.

That one glimpse was the last time I saw Brother Doug DeHaan.

I didn't speak the whole car ride home — not to my daddy, who was also not speaking, and not to Jonny, who was rambling about all the fun he had and then fell asleep for the last hour of the drive. Daddy said nothing to me when he first saw me. He said nothing on the car ride home. He said nothing when we finally arrived at our house.

All he did was park the car, carry my suitcase up the stairs, and kiss my cheek when I got to the top. Then he left the house for about an hour. When he came back, he had the air conditioner with him. He knocked on my bedroom door and, when I didn't respond, he just walked into my bedroom, installed it into my window, turned it on, and walked back out. He said nothing.

For three weeks, I hadn't seen or talked to my daddy and, because of one twenty-minute conversation with Mr. Houghton and Brother Doug, I could tell that anything good and wonderful that he must've thought of his daughter was now a thing of the past. Did he even love me anymore?

The last thing I ever wanted to do was disappoint my parents. And it looked like I let my daddy down in ways I never imagined I had the ability to do. If he only knew the truth of how badly I let him down, what I had done, and how horrible of a person I actually was. He could never know the truth because he would never forgive me. At least the lies they told him at Camp Judah weren't as bad as the honest truth was.

Charlie knew I was coming home today. We'd written a couple of letters to each other so I knew he was waiting for me. But I didn't want to see him. I didn't want him to come over and see me like this.

How could I ever look at my best friend again, knowing what I am? A dirty whore who fell in love with, seduced, and then gave her virginity to a married man. Charlie would never understand something like that. He might even not want to be my friend anymore.

I was the worst kind of human being: a liar, a Jezebel, a husband stealer, a slut. Even God himself couldn't love that. There had to be a special place in Hell for girls like me, the worthless, wretched, sinner girls. Cammy DeHaan was right. She was right to hate me. And I was so sorry for what I've done.

After my daddy left my room, I took a long shower and stood there while the hot water attempted to wash off three weeks of Camp Judah and a short lifetime of girlish dreams. Then I cried so much that there were no more tears left in me by the time my mom came upstairs.

It was still early, but I was in bed. I wanted so badly to fall asleep and never wake up again. My stomach was so knotted up in grief that I couldn't eat anything so I stayed put, in a ball under the covers. My mom opened the door, walked in, and came over to me. She looked at my face, having been able to see that I'd been crying. She rubbed my forehead with her fingers going up through my hair.

"Scout, it's gonna be okay," she said. "Give yourself a few days and you'll feel better." I can only imagine what my daddy told her and what she must've thought about me. She kissed my face and told me that she loved me, but I know that I don't deserve her love.

I doubted that I'd ever feel better. How does someone recover from a pain so deep and powerful that even staying alive doesn't appear to be a very good option? How do I go on with my life, off to high school next week, when everything I am is just garbage?

I didn't know what to say to my mom. She'd never understand this. She'd never believe the truth about what really happened between me and Brother Doug and I knew I could never tell her. No one would believe the truth anyway. I had been branded the silly teenaged girl with a fixation on the flawless Doug DeHaan. I was the villain in all of this and I accepted my fate because I loved him. And I knew that I would never again be the same.

CHARLIE

Pulling up to the Webb house, I relaxed my bike against the front of the porch. I walked up the steps, knocked, and Jonny opened the door.

"Hey," I said. "Scout here?"

Jonny let me in. "Yeah, she's upstairs. Something's wrong with her."

That surprised me because nothing was ever wrong with Scout.

"Is she sick?"

He shrugged.

"Did y'all have a good time?" I asked, trying to see if I could get more information.

"Yeah, it was the best. I didn't want to come home," he said.

"Where's your parents?"

"I don't know where my dad is, but my mom's in the back yard hanging up clothes on the clothes line," Jonny answered and then plopped himself down on the green couch in front of the TV.

Not quite sure what to do, I told him that I was going

to go check on Scout. Jonny didn't seem to care much about anything other than finding something to watch on channel four so I carefully went up the stairs to Scout's room.

The door was shut so I knocked quietly, in case she was sleeping. There was no answer. I cracked the door a bit to see if I could catch a glimpse of her. There was a big humming noise coming from her window, an air conditioner. That was new.

I missed Scout so much. I didn't realize how much I missed her until last week when I wanted to come over to her house to tell her about my new job at her dad's garage and that our baseball team lost our last four games because she wasn't there and that I had cooked an entire chicken dinner for my mom with no help from anyone and that Mr. Windham from her paper route died while mowing his lawn.

In all the time that I spent with Katie Smith these past few weeks, I noticed that she didn't care about things like that, which to me were the real things. I'd tell Katie about the stupid boring stories in my stupid boring life and all she wanted to do was make out and put her hands on me. Not that I minded all the making out, but she's just not Scout. Scout likes my stories and my mindless guitar strumming and talking about the Yankees and listening to old rock music with me. Scout's everything. I loved her.

The couple of letters I received from her sounded like she was so happy at camp. I felt a twinge of jealousy that she didn't seem to be missing me like I was missing her. But now she's home for good and something is wrong with her. I expected her to get home and come to my house. That's what she's always done before. But this time, she never came over.

I saw her hair poking out from underneath the covers and her head up on her pillow. She turned toward me and caught me peeking into her room. I felt like I intruded on something, something bad. But I didn't care.

"Scout?" I whispered loudly.

I walked inside, shut the door behind me, and I could see her watching me creep toward her. "Scout, you okay?" I asked. But she was not okay. I felt scared and a bit wigged out. She said nothing.

As I got to her bed, I sat down on the side and she peered up at me and started to cry. I had no idea what in the world she was crying about and she didn't say. Seeing Scout cry physically hurt me. It's like seeing my mom cry. I just can't take it. But this time was worse. She wouldn't say anything to me at all — she just sobbed into her pillow.

Not really knowing what to do, I got underneath her covers, laid down next to her, wrapped my arms around her waist, and held her as tight as I could until it got dark.

Part II

November 1987 – August 1988

"Whoever can be trusted with very little can also be trusted with much, and whoever is dishonest with very little will also be dishonest with much."

Luke 16:10 – The Holy Bible, New International Version

SCOUT WEBB, AGE 19

What I've learned about married men in the last several years is that some of them seem to be big cowards. Not all of them, of course, but what I've gathered as I've grown older and started to observe people is that some men who get married either turn into cowards or marriage itself brings out the inner coward that's already there.

I'd been pretty sheltered when I was little and thought that marriage was how my parents did it: lovey-dovey, kissy-kissy, flowers and bottom gooses and hand holding and sweet little nicknames. Husbands bought their wives flowers or even picked them from the side of the road on early Sunday mornings before church. Wives made the husbands their favorite pies in the winter and massaged their backs at the end of a hard day. And everybody lived happily ever after.

But then I saw how Charlie's parents' divorce affected him so much during his whole childhood and how lonely his mom was all the time. It didn't only affect Charlie. It affected Ms. Porter, too. In high school, I learned that some kids had fathers with drinking problems and their mothers were crying all the time. Sometimes, it was the mothers with the drinking problems because the husbands went off and never came back. I heard rumors about Mr. Herrin, the postmaster, having an affair with a girl who worked in the Piggly Wiggly bakery and then how Mrs. Herrin drove his prized cream-colored Caddie into Jasper Lake when she found out about it. Once, I overheard Pastor Rhodes in his office talking to Mrs. Jennings who was sobbing into her hands, "Remember, darlin', you vowed for better or for worse." Later, I found out from Maybelle that Mr. Jennings was caught with some videotapes of questionable origin showing teenaged girls having sex with each other. I had never even heard of such a thing before! Then there was Brother Doug and his being married with a little boy and all. If marriage was so great, then what was he doing with me? Maybe I've watched too many movies or read too many books, but my overall assessment is that real marriage ain't at all how my parents have it. They're the lucky ones.

Some of these men run away from their responsibilities, like Charlie's dad, leaving the mother to have to deal with everything all alone. Some are confronted with an uncomfortable or inconvenient situation that might involve dealing with emotions — *oh, the horror!* — so they do nothing and say nothing, rather than face it. Some are confronted with a mess of their own making, so they lie to protect themselves, blame someone else, and then let everyone around them — usually the women — clean it up. Then there are the abusive ones: the ones who either physically or emotionally beat up a woman and then tell her they are "sorry" and they "love" her, all while slowly chipping away at her dignity and self-respect. This happened to Maybelle's mom. She had to go to court to get a restraining order against her husband. I suppose women can be like this, too, but I only ever heard about the men.

There's the sad sacks who just do what their wives want them to all the time — always giving in to their demands, hopping around like silly chimpanzees at the zoo, swinging from tree branch to tree branch and constantly trying to make their wives happy without realizing that they can't. But they're too afraid to be alone or to lose all of their hard-earned money to alimony payments and lawyers' fees and child support. So they put up with it for the rest of their lives, dying inside each day a little bit more, maybe even finding a little relief now and again with the company or affections of another woman or a bottle of Jim Beam or poker or golf. I think that might've been what happened to Mr. Herrin and why he was skirtin' around with the girl at the bakery. Everyone in town knew Mrs. Herrin was always ordering everybody around and demanding things all the time. After the whole drama unfolded, my daddy said to my mom, "Well, I suppose he went and finally found a little bit of happiness for the price of his beloved Caddie. He can always go find a new car. Don't think he cares all that much about losing that woman who's been so ugly to him all these years." My daddy usually never commented on the personal lives of others, so the fact that he did so on the Herrin matter made me realize that he didn't care for Mrs. Herrin and how she treated her husband.

And then there is the narcissist. These kinds of people, most often men, are the self-absorbed manipulators with no soul. Opening my blue spiral notebook, I looked down at my increasingly sloppy penmanship and read aloud quietly:

"Narcissists seduce their victims with their God-given charm, especially if the victims are emotionally vulnerable, and then they take advantage of them. They pursue their victims at first by dazzling them with attention, making them feel special by pretending to care about them. Narcissists behave as if they're genuinely interested in what their victims have to say. They get their victims to care about them and trust them by opening up, usually about something perceived as an emotional vulnerability or a tragedy, and allow victims to think that they have a special connection to each other. They tell their victims that they're special.

"Narcissists have grandiose opinions of themselves, an excessive need for admiration, and an arrogant and authoritative manner. They are secretive and project mystery, which is a part of their whole seduction. They get rooted into their victims' heads. After they get what they want, they move on to their next victim.

"They're incapable of having empathy about their actions.

"The narcissist's possible goals include: love, affection,

attention, intimacy, friendship, trust, money, sex.

"Narcissists are habitual liars who disguise themselves as honest people. They never take responsibility for their actions and never apologize to the people they victimize. They rely on the naivety and natural goodness of others to perpetuate their façade.

"All sociopaths are narcissists, but not all narcissists are sociopaths."

Thinking about the narcissist further, I've concluded that they know exactly what they are deep down inside: cowards. They hate themselves for it and fake their entire lives with grandstanding, trying to make themselves look superior in order to glean admiration from other people. This gives them a little relief from how miserable they are inside. The textbook says that narcissism is a disorder, but I think it's just a fancy word for a coward.

I don't think I've known a real live narcissist before. Brother Doug was a coward, but I had a hard time fitting him into the textbook definitions of the different personality disorders. I've been trying to figure out if I have my own personality disorder. But as a first year college student, I've enjoyed learning about what makes human beings become who they are — behavioral patterns, pathologies, personality disorders, and how all this stuff affects society as a whole. I find it all interesting, much more interesting than anything I learned in high school, that's for sure.

Today, I'm trying to get a handle on narcissists, so

I'm running through my notes from class while I'm at work doing food prep in the kitchen. I have a test tomorrow in my psychology class, which includes an essay question on their many characteristics. I need to be thorough so I can get an A in this class. I'm doing great so far in my first semester at North Carolina State University.

Back in August, I started waiting tables at Marty's Place, a working man's restaurant in Raleigh. An older waitress named Judy warned me about some of the men who come in here. "Scout, a lot of these men come here to escape the doldrums of their lives. Some are just plain lonely, so they come here to eat some good down home cookin' and talk to me or the other ladies working here. I'm warning you because you're young and pretty and a lot of them will want to talk to you. Are you okay with that kind of attention?"

I wasn't really, but I just nodded. It was easier that way.

When I wait on the lonely ones, I try not to get too bothered if they say something that makes me feel uncomfortable. Not all of them do that, of course. Most of them are perfect gentlemen, but a few have made me feel strange. They're usually overly nice to me and I'm now aware enough to know why. They like me because I represent a bit of a fantasy away from their boring or, in some cases, miserable lives.

"Well, aren't you cute?" this one grimy man said to me during my first week. He was old and fat and covered in dust from whatever job he did out there in the real world. "Haven't seen you before."

Embarrassed, I thanked him and went about my business. But when I walked away, I heard him talking to his friends, also covered in dust. "She's got nice tits. The life hasn't been sucked out of them yet."

Whenever that particular group of men came in, I'd let Felicia or Judy deal with them.

Another man named Swepty, who told me he's fifty-three years old, comes in almost every day. He works down at a warehouse near the State campus, is married, and has two sons. One is at Wake Tech and the other is in the Navy. Last week, he told me that he liked talking to me. "You're a nice young lady, Scout. If I was a young man, I would've enjoyed taking you out for supper at a fancy place."

"Aw, thanks, Swepty," I said to him. "I probably would've accepted your invitation."

"I should set you up with my son, Whit," he said, his big round face beaming at me.

I smiled shyly. "No, that's okay. I don't want a boyfriend."

"It's nice to talk to a sweet girl like you. Makes me feel young. You're not cynical about life yet. You're carefree and not jaded by life's harsh ways." Ha! If he only knew!

For the most part, I pay attention to the customers like I'm supposed to, like a waitress just trying to get a decent tip. I'm nice, but most importantly, I demand nothing from them, unlike the real women in their lives.

Another regular customer named Pete was complaining about his wife yesterday. "I work hard all day and Paula just stays home watching her stories on TV."

"Does she not have anything else to do?"

He laughed, his mouth full of BLT. "She drives the kids to school. She don't even clean the house anymore."

"She doesn't want to get a job?" I asked, pretending like I cared.

"She needs to. Or she should join a gym. If the kids are gone all day and she's not gonna do anything else, then she can at least go to a gym and lose thirty pounds."

It was then I realized that I wouldn't want to be married to a man like Pete, who'd tell some waitress such nasty things about a woman he's supposed to love. Pete, and a few others like him, usually don't start out saying such things about their wives, but eventually, after they know me better from coming in so much, these are the kinds of insights I get on married life and what some men are really thinking.

Since I don't know what it's like to be married, I simply listen and try to be nice and sympathetic. I don't listen because of any real interest in these men personally. I listen because I'm a waitress in a mom-n-pop restaurant that is slow at times. I listen because I'm genuinely interested in other peoples' lives, which I'm sure are much more interesting than mine. I listen because I'm a good listener and I like learning about how people see the world. I also listen because I'm just a nice person. Once in a while, I find myself really caring about whatever sad story I'm hearing.

I don't have any close friends but for Charlie. And my inner walls. Big, high, impenetrable walls. I don't see Charlie as much as I used to since I came to Raleigh and he stayed behind in Haddleboro to work for my daddy full time. Charlie is the only person I talk to about much of anything going on with me, but since long distance calls are expensive, and there's no extra money to drive home except for the college breaks, he's turned into someone I think about a lot — and miss always.

People who frequent this place like to tell me their problems as if I have the answers to life. I'm nineteen. If I have answers to anything, I wish they were the answers to my own problems instead. But it's nice to feel like someone finds me interesting and that I have something to say that's worth hearing. Plus, I might get a good tip and, as a college freshman from a working class family, I need the money.

It's mostly the older, married guys — wearing rings for God's sake! — showing me too much attention. It doesn't happen all the time, but it happens often enough to make me think that I don't want to be married. Unless I was to find someone like Charlie, who I'd never deserve anyway.

A couple of months ago, this man who looked older than my daddy came in and asked me if I'd want to meet him for lunch sometime.

"How old are you?" I asked him, a bit surprised.

"I'm forty," he said, smirking at me, wearing his middle age like a badge of honor.

"My daddy is forty-three," I responded, hoping he'd see the obvious, that he was too old for me.

"So what?" he asked, clearly not getting my point.

I turned him down, but wanted to ask him why a forty-year-old, gray-haired man would think a teenaged girl had any interest in going out with him. Well, that whole thought process was turned on its head the day that Rob came into Marty's Place.

It was getting late on a Saturday in November and I was working harder than usual. Football season was in full swing — and football at State is a big deal. We didn't have a great record, but Carter-Finley Stadium was still a Wolfpack howling haven on home game Saturdays, especially for this particular Saturday.

A lot of State alumni were in Raleigh for the homecoming activities for the weekend. The restaurant was busy. I typically work only three shifts a week and maybe a double on the weekend, but this specific weekend, I worked two doubles and was raking in the cash. Tired, after having been on my feet all day without any breaks, my pockets were heavy with change from so many tips. My hair was starting to come out of its ponytail. I felt my concealer, the only makeup I wore, sweating off of my face.

While balancing a tray with plastic cups full of tap water, my uniform got caught on something as I came around the edge of the counter where patrons were sitting. I lost the tray — right onto the lap of the most beautiful man in the world. No, not Mickey Rourke, the actor from that creepy movie, *Angel Heart*. But his twin, who I'd later learn is Rob Caralessi. Thirty-nine years old. Insurance Salesman. From Rocky Mount, North Carolina. North Carolina State University, class of 1970. And did I mention that he looked exactly like Mickey Rourke?

All six of my waters fell onto him as he sat at the counter slowly eating a barbecue sandwich. He wasn't one of my tables so we hadn't spoken. As he peered up at me with the front of his red State windbreaker soaked in water and his jeans looking like he peed himself, I burst out in nervous laughter. Embarrassed for both of us, I felt horrible. I had never done anything like this to a customer before.

My nerves, overwhelmed by his brown eyes as they bore through me, were just too much for me to maintain my composure. His eyelashes were so long, they had to be fake. No man has eyelashes like that. His face was chiseled and clean and perfect. He looked like the kind of man who would die in old age, still absolutely gorgeous.

As I stood there giggling, trying to make myself calm down so that I could apologize and offer him help, Felicia came over with a couple of towels.

"Sir, we are so sorry this happened," she said, handing him the towels and shooting me what-the-heck-is-wrong-with-you eyes. He put down his sandwich, accepted the towels from Felicia, and started wiping his windbreaker. I finally stopped with the laughter, not noticing anything else going on in the restaurant, including my own table of customers who were still waiting for their water.

"Sir, I'm so sorry," I stammered. "I'm sorry for spilling all that on you. My dress got caught. I swear I've never done that before."

He looked up at me, eyed my face a bit, and made me feel happy-nervous-excited, like how Brother Doug used to when he'd look at me across the campfire that last summer at Camp Judah.

My God where did this man come from?

Stricken speechless, I just stood there looking back at him, saying nothing, but with my heart racing a million beats a minute. I was so physically affected by everything about him — from his black high-and-tight haircut to his subtle cheek dimples and prominent chin dimple to his plump-for-a-guy kissable lips to the little dark hairs on his knuckles. I was possessed.

"Are you sorry you laughed at me?" he asked, his eyes softening on me, but his demeanor serious, like a professor.

I couldn't bring myself to answer. My entire body was suspended in this nervous excitement.

"Yes…"

Felicia went into the kitchen and the restaurant moved along busily as I started to come out of this bizarre fog. The man handed me the towels after he wiped himself up as best as he could.

"Y'all might want to wipe up this floor when I go," he said, pointing to a puddle of water beneath him.

"Yes, sir, of course."

"No 'sir' please. 'Sir' was my grandfather. I'm just Rob," he said, winking, bringing a calm to me. At last, he didn't seem so serious anymore. I was relieved.

I finally pulled myself enough out of my brain fog to clean up the cups and refill new ones to bring to my table. As I walked past him again, we looked at each other and some kind of powerful unspoken conversation occurred in the air between us. His mind said to me, "Don't spill that on me again." My mind replied, "I won't, I promise." His mind then said, "What time do you get off?" And my mind answered, "Whenever you want me to!"

At least, this was the cartoon showing inside my head, complete with word bubbles above.

We both smiled at each other, understanding all of the implied thoughts, replete with sexual tension. A big "thank you" to PSYCH 101 for also providing me with a word for that previously unknown feeling — "sexual tension." It was a brief, but intense exchange, almost knocking me off my feet, which would have caused me to spill all of my water again.

Shortly after I resumed working, Rob got up and went to the cash register to pay his bill. As he held out his money and check, I conjured up enough courage to approach him.

"Can I at least buy your supper for you?" I asked,

trying not to stammer.

He didn't look up at me and instead handed the dollar bills to the cashier. But with his wallet open, he pulled out a ten-dollar bill and extended his arm out, handing it to me while saying, "No, that's okay, Scout. Here's a tip for the towels though."

Scout. He knew my name. How did he know my name? Did he ask someone? Did he know my parents or something? *Dummy. Your nametag. He read your nametag.*

I was stunned. "Sir, I can't take this. First of all, I'm the one who got you all wet. And Felicia gave you the towels, not me."

He eyeballed me like before, saying nothing yet saying everything at the same time. Coyly, he still held out the ten dollars and said, "Remember, it's Rob, not 'sir' and I needed a bath anyway. You helped me out with that."

It was so cheesy and the worst comeback I've ever heard in my life. In that instant, I felt like he was my peer, a nervous college boy with no game whatsoever trying to flirt with me.

I thanked him for the tip and he walked out of the restaurant. But not out of my life.

ROB CARALESSI, AGE 39

Finding my way out of Raleigh and back home on a dark Saturday night after a great day, my mind was racing with whatever the hell that was back at that restaurant. "Run away, Rob. Run away" is what my head screamed at me. But the rest of me? The rest of me was running toward it.

With so many years of being the guy who always does the right thing, this one time I found that I was allowing myself — hell, even encouraging and applauding myself — to do the wrong thing. And boy did I pick a doozy.

In my case, the doozy is a girl named Scout. Scout? I knew a dog named Scout. She was so fuckin' adorable standing there looking at me star-struck, holding an empty tray, giggling this shy, raspy laugh because she had just spilled a bunch of water all over me.

Women have given me the star-struck look before and, being an insurance salesman, I do know how to use my charm to close the deal, but for insurance plans and insurance plans only. I have a good-natured way with people, a way that makes them feel like they're my friends. They are comfortable with me and I like that. So I use it to my advantage.

I've been told several times how much I look like that actor from that awful movie that Rita made me go see with her a while back. I suppose I lucked out in the looks department. *Three cheers to my parents for having sex.*

I'm certainly not stuck on myself, though. So while I try to use genetics and charm to my advantage in my career, I don't take advantage of anyone and certainly don't primp in a mirror or spend hours in a gym. I'm lucky to get in a long jog at the high school track once in a blue moon. Reality is that I'm just a regular guy who works a lot of hours in order to make good commissions so I can take care of my family of four. And for the first time in a long time, I got to have a full day with some old friends in Raleigh. We spent the afternoon at State for the homecoming football game and had a great time revisiting some of our old haunts in town, telling stories, remembering our glory days as young dreamers. In our day, girls were everywhere, all recently sexually liberated. It was a good time to be a guy, even a nice guy like me who had a conscience and was not the male equivalent of a whore.

We were ending the Sixties, a tough time in our country, and it didn't look like the early Seventies would be much better. I was lucky enough to have avoided the draft due to having some cartilage issue with both knees and a bum shoulder from my baseball days. *Three cheers for cartilage issues and bum shoulders.* I'd been recruited by State to play baseball — to pitch actually, but, unfortunately, I never got to step foot on the pitcher's mound at the new Doak Field.

If I had been drafted into the service, like some of the guys I grew up with, I would've done what I had to do. But lucky for me, I got to be a regular college student at State, going to class, partying from time to time, and having fun with the pretty coeds. Until I met my wife Rita, of course.

It was great being back with the fellas. I haven't been able to come to homecoming for several years, even though I only live like an hour away from Raleigh. Just been busy with life. And of course Rita always gave me shit about doing my own thing. I don't play golf, I can't be on a men's softball team, I can't get a gun and learn to hunt, and I would be divorced if I got myself a motorcycle. Anything to make her happy, I guess. "Happy wife, happy life" and all that. But she's right — the free time I have, I should be spending it with her and my kids.

This time, though, when my freshman-year roommate called, I took a deep breath and told Rita that I was going to the homecoming game.

"It's just for the day," I informed her, trying to handle it as delicately as I could.

She pulled out her infamous bitch glare in order to convey everything I needed to know about her feelings concerning the matter. "We have hardly even seen you for almost two weeks!"

This time, I looked away and said, "I'm going." She

was not happy.

I didn't care. I've worked my ass off to take care of her and the kids for many years now so she can just deal with me going to a goddamn State game for one goddamn time.

Afterward, the guys were going to some alumni function for dinner. I needed to get back home at a reasonable hour so Rita wouldn't give me more shit about it and then withhold sex from me for a couple of weeks as payback. So I decided to head back home after we had a few beers at a small bar near Cameron Village. Then because I was starting to dread going home, I drove around Raleigh to kill some time and then stopped at a restaurant that was a bit away from the campus for a quick bite to eat. It looked like an old diner, not a college pit-stop at all. So my plan was to have some Eastern North Carolina barbecue, and then go home to face the wrath of Rita.

Instead, I got my sandwich from the tall black chick who waited on me and then a lap full of water from the cutest girl I've ever seen. It wasn't like she was classically beautiful or some kind of pin up model — and maybe most guys wouldn't have looked twice at her. But there was something about her. Something interesting and mysterious and innocent about her.

I noticed her when I first sat down at the counter. She was waiting on a table behind me and I wondered if she'd be my waitress, too. When the black lady waited on me, I thought, "Oh well," but nothing more than that. The girl walked by me a couple of times, focused on her tasks at hand. And then I noticed her nametag said "Scout." That name only added to how cute she was.

Her hair was long and dark brown, pulled back into a ponytail. Her skin was flawless, pale with light freckles, not much makeup — hell, maybe no makeup at all. She had the cutest puffy cheeks, like they were something she should've outgrown by now. She was wearing a uniform so it was hard to make out her ass and tits, but from what I could tell, I'm sure whatever was underneath was just fine.

I didn't want to stare at her too much so I'd try to catch a glimpse when she'd walk by me. Typically, I don't look at girls or women like some horny twenty-one-year-old so I was surprised by how much I was actively taking in about her feminine details. Once in a great while, a woman will simply catch my eye, but this Scout had "a lil' somethin' somethin'", as my neighbor would say. I have a good sense about people, mostly due to all the years of honing my skills as a salesman, so I was pretty confident about my assessment of her. I could tell she was really young. Too young for me. Actually, I probably shouldn't have been looking at her like this at all. For Christ's sake, my son could've dated her in a few years when he comes to State.

After she had spilled the water on me, and we exchanged a couple of subtle glances, I tried to get out of there before engaging in the flirtation any longer. I knew she was interested in me. I could just tell. But an old married guy like me, who's been pursued a few times in his seventeen years of marriage, knows when he needs to move along and avoid trouble.

It's not like she was throwing herself at me or slipping me her number or indicating anything problematic toward me at all. But that giggle, the star-struck looks, the coy body language — a guy knows. Normally, I'll talk to a person quite a bit because I'm a people person, but I had to keep myself in check. So I didn't talk much at all. But I had a hundred questions to ask her. First one being: is she over eighteen? *God, I am going to Hell.*

I shouldn't have given her the ten-dollar tip. She wasn't my waitress, she spilled six cups of water on me, and then she laughed about it. I also shouldn't have told her my name. But I couldn't help myself. I was flirting with her. I knew I was, but I was doing it in a way to keep some kind of restraint. Even tried to make it like I knew she was a cash-strapped young waitress in the city and I was alleviating her of her guilt for spilling the water and making a rookie mistake. That's what I told myself anyway. Better than outright flirting. *Right.*

But I liked how she made me feel when she looked at me. It was warm and sweet and calming. Like she seemed to be.

I've had women flirt with me before and a couple of them have propositioned me — hell, I even had one grab my crotch once, totally surprising me. Didn't tell Rita about that one. She would've found a reason to blame me for it! Women have given me their phone numbers, one gave me her hotel key, and another time, an elderly customer, wrote me a love poem. *Yeah, a poem.*

I think there are a lot of lonely women in the world, and I probably could've had my way with more than my fair share if I wanted to only because I'm nice to them. But I don't. I don't want to. I'm faithful. I love my wife and my family. I'd do anything for them. I have integrity. I do the right thing. Always.

I left the restaurant that night and headed home feeling more alive than I had in years. Just a simple, but heavy, unspoken exchange, some kind of connection of sorts, with a fresh cute girl full of life and a little somethin' somethin'. She made me feel good. My right shoulder usually hurts with a nagging dull pain from my baseball days. Driving home, I felt no pain in it at all.

Raleigh isn't too far away from home, but I have no reason to go out that way unless it's a college-related function. Even my job doesn't take me there. So Scout the waitress was just a nice brief interlude for me, never to be experienced again. If I came back next year for homecoming, she'd probably be gone and I'd never see her again.

Or at least, that was what I told myself over and over again on my way home.

CHARLIE PORTER, AGE 19

I turned on the water in the deep sink in the side room, picked up a bottle of heavy duty hand cleaner, and poured it on my hands, rubbing it in really good. Scrubbing my hands after a long day here is the best feeling. It makes me realize that I spent my day well: hard work, helping people who need it, earning good money, even learning a few things once in a while. I've been working at Lee Webb Automotive for Scout's dad since I started high school and, after I graduated, Mr. Webb brought me on as a full time mechanic.

Mr. Webb's been like a father or an uncle my whole life. He's really the only man who took an interest in me, who wanted to see me make something of myself and not end up like a lot of the boys from here who just flounder around, getting into drinking and pot, knocking up girls, and dropping out of school.

That one summer a few years ago, when Scout was away at camp, Mr. Webb came over to my house on a Sunday afternoon. My mom was sitting on the front porch having a glass of freshly made sweet tea and she came into the house hollering for me. It was one of the only days while Scout had been gone that I had just hung around the house, played my guitar, and watched TV without my girlfriend Katie coming over.

I came downstairs and Mr. Webb was standing by the door. He was still wearing his church clothes.

"Charlie, you mind if I talk with you for a bit?" he asked me.

I was a little nervous because I don't really remember the last time Mr. Webb physically came over to my house in order to talk to me alone. Actually, I don't think he ever did. So I was pretty nervous what this was about and was wondering if something happened to Scout. "Sure thing, Mr. Webb," I said, following him outside.

Mr. Webb is quiet and confident with a cool, country demeanor. He's the sort of man who can be really funny out of nowhere with one comment. My mom called it "a dry humor", but he always looks and sounds like he means business. He isn't real tall. I tower over him by at least five inches. He isn't real muscular, but must've been a good athlete in his day. Just like Scout. His hair is dark brown with a little gray coming through and I suppose Miss Raelene thinks he's good looking.

He's never been cross with me or affectionate in any way, but he's always asked after my mom, like he just knew that life was harder on her than it should've been and it was his duty to check on us once in a while. I wondered if I wasn't best friends with his daughter if he would've even thought of us, but then again, he probably wouldn't have had any reason to really know us much at all. But the Webbs have always been good to us.

So we went outside and sat down on the two chairs on my front porch.

"Charlie, I've stopped by today to see if you'd be interested in comin' to work for me part time at the garage."

I was really surprised because we've never talked about cars and stuff like that before, but the thought of being able to get a real job was exciting. "Wow, I always figured I was just going to try and get a job at the Piggly Wiggly next year," I said to him.

"Do you want to work at the Pig instead?" he asked.

"Well, not really, but that's just what everyone else does. I never thought about an auto shop."

Thinking about it some more, I realized that I could stop being a paperboy and make a decent hourly wage. It would be better money and get me to the amount I needed for a car a lot quicker. Next June, I was going to turn sixteen, and I wanted to be able to hand someone a wad of cash for a good-working, used car.

"Charlie, have you been thinkin' at all about high school and what kinds of classes you might take?" he asked me.

I hadn't thought much about it because they are kind of assigned to you. "No sir," I answered. "I'm just taking the same classes as Scout, I think."

He continued, "Well, you know that you can take some classes at the high school that are more skills-related, like auto shop."

I knew that. "I think I can take auto shop next year."

"Do you have any idea about what you want to do with your life after high school?" he asked me, looking serious. "Do you want to go to college?"

I wasn't really the kind of boy who had any particular interest in college. I didn't know what I'd study there. We sure didn't have the money for it. I could go to the community college, but still, I had no idea what I'd study. I suppose I was more the vocational kid, the one who goes to work after high school and continues on with an adult life, skipping the whole four-year extension on being a kid. I was an okay student, but nothing special. I liked baseball and music and history and even science sometimes. I was good at math.

But what did I want to be when I grew up? The only thing that I ever thought about doing was going into the Army or being a cop.

"Mr. Webb, I don't know if I want to go to college. I've thought about going into the Army," I told him. "But nothing else really interests me."

"How about coming to work for me instead? Just while you're in high school."

"That sounds great, Mr. Webb. But I'd have an awful lot to learn."

He grinned at me. "Charlie, I know that you are a

hard worker and have all the smarts you'd ever need to do a good job as a mechanic. I'd teach you a lot and have no doubt you'd be great in no time. But I'd want to start you out slowly, just a couple of hours after school during the week and maybe some Saturday mornings. Four dollars an hour. I'd pay you under the table, just cash each week for the hours you put in."

I took it all in. I didn't know what he meant by "under the table", but I'm sure he'd explain it. It all sounded good to me.

"You can even keep your paper route if you want to, you know. That's in the early mornings. And, of course, you could cut back your hours when you needed to for baseball season." He paused. "It's still important for you to just be a boy. I believe that."

I nodded at him and thanked him for the job.

"How's Scout doing? Have y'all heard from her?" I asked him.

He looked thoughtful. "Well, son, we haven't gotten any letters from her. Not even one. It's not like Scout not to write a couple of letters each week when she's gone. So I don't really know how she's doin'. But you know Scout better than all of us. She's probably just soakin' it all in and having a great time."

That kind of surprised me. I had received only one letter from her and it was pretty short. Again, unlike Scout to write a short letter. Unlike Scout to write only one letter, too.

"Well, she'll be home soon," I said to him. "Then we'll hear all about it."

Mr. Webb stood up from the chair and my mom came out with a glass of sweet tea for him. He took a long drink from the glass, thanked my mom, and then shook my hand. "Charlie, tell your mom the good news."

My mom looked at me, curious.

"I just got a job at Mr. Webb's shop," I said, beaming.

She smiled at me with a burst of pride and thanked Mr. Webb for stopping by and for believing in her son.

"I have all the confidence in the world in Charlie, Ms. Porter," he said. "You've raised a good young man there. And I'm glad that my daughter Scout has him to look after her like he does. He is a real friend and those are awful hard to come by in life. Y'all have a good day."

Then he walked off down the street, headed back toward his house, which was a good distance away by foot.

Since that day, I've become a pretty good mechanic. I had enough money to buy my first car when I turned sixteen and I was the only sophomore at Haddleboro High with my own car when that school year started. It was also nice to be able to help my mom out with the bills, even though she would tell me to stop.

Since graduating, my life only consists of working and hanging out with some guys from high school. A lot of the kids I was friends with had gone away to college, either up in Chapel Hill or up in Raleigh or over at the community college, and some had gone into the military. I think my mom was a little bit disappointed that I didn't bother with any of that, but I told her that I just didn't know what I wanted to do. I wasn't going to go to college for college's sake. Scout knew what she wanted to do and her dad had saved up some money for her to go.

I spend a lot of time alone, more than I'm used to. I broke up with my girlfriend a few months ago when she went away to Chapel Hill. Well, actually, she broke up with me. She told me that she needed to be unattached when she went to college and didn't want a reason to come back to Haddleboro. I guess I understood that. No broken heart for me. She wasn't the only one with dreams of leaving this small town and seeing if she could have a different kind of life.

Scout went away to Raleigh back in August and I never get to see her and hardly get to talk to her anymore. I've been able to get up to Raleigh once to see her, but like me, she's always working. Plus, she's got classes and some other things she does so it's not so easy to get together. I did go see her on a Sunday and we walked around the campus and down along Hillsborough Street. She showed me everything she knew and introduced me to some interesting people she met while there.

"This is Brandon," she said, introducing me to a stocky boy built like a fullback. "He's from Australia. He's here on exchange."

"You mean like an exchange student, only for colleges?" I asked, shaking his hand.

"Yeah, I'm here studying for the semester," he responded, smiling and very friendly.

I knew Scout liked him because of the way he talked. She got all googly-eyed when he'd tell us about his life back in Sydney, which didn't seem that exciting at all, except for how he sounded when he talked about it. He said, "...and I was going to work" and it sounded a lot cooler than when I said the exact same words.

Beneath the accent, he seemed like a guy just like me, only he "went to uni and played rugby, which is a little like American football with no helmets. It uses an oblong ball, like your team called the Redskins."

I wasn't good at geography, but I knew where Australia was on the globe. And it was pretty far away from Raleigh, North Carolina.

When I got home that evening, it hit me that Brandon from Australia was the only person I've met in my entire life who was not an actual American. I realized how much bigger the world was and how I'd like to see a little more of it and maybe meet some other people like Brandon who aren't from Haddleboro, aren't from North Carolina, and aren't even from the United States. I'd like to see a city like Sydney or London or Venice or Tokyo and other places that I've read about.

A week after that visit with Scout, I drove over to Fayetteville to see the recruiter for the Army. I leave after the New Year for basic training in Georgia.

SCOUT

On November 12th, Rob-The-Mickey-Rourke Look-Alike came into Marty's Place in the late afternoon. It was a Thursday, and my classes were done before noon on Thursdays, so it was one of the days that I routinely worked in the afternoon until around 5:30 before the dinner crowd. It was a slow shift, but that was okay because I used it to study if I needed to.

I was behind the counter trying to fix one of the menus that got stuck underneath a table and had boot prints all over it. They were laminated so I figured it wouldn't be too hard to wipe it off and save it from the garbage can. It was a normal day, with cooling fall temperatures, but on the mild side, as we were nearing Thanksgiving.

As I scrubbed the menu, Rob walked in wearing a short-sleeved dress shirt and a tie. I always thought that men who wore short sleeves with a tie looked kind of shady, like used car salesmen. But his muscle-toned arms could handle the shady look just fine.

He was wearing navy blue dress pants and black dress shoes and I could tell that he must've been some kind of professional out and about on business, or maybe even a professor at State. This was only the second time that I'd seen him in Marty's Place so I had no idea why he was back. This really wasn't the guy-in-short-sleeved-dress-shirt kind of place and it was a little far from campus for even the professor types to stop in between classes.

He saw me immediately and walked over, sitting down at the stool in front of me. I looked up, feeling completely overcome with butterflies in my stomach and my heart in my throat — as well as a little stupid — so I tried not to speak for fear of something ridiculously sophomoric coming out of my mouth.

"Hi, Scout." He said it in a way that made me feel like we were old friends about to go on a boat trip together.

"Hey," I said shyly, trying not to look at him. I focused on scrubbing the menu with even more force than before. "Can I help you?"

"Yes, you can. I'd like some water," he said while studying me, clearly trying to get a reaction.

I couldn't look up at him. I was trying not to laugh or even smile. He was being witty and trying to make me laugh by asking me for water and I wasn't going to give in. All the embarrassment of last Saturday just came back at me and I felt like a foolish little girl, desperately trying to maintain my composure.

Then from somewhere deep within me, I conjured up a little confidence.

"Rob — it was Rob right?" I asked, pretending not to remember his perfect name. *Of course I remembered his name!*

He kept staring right into my face. I could feel his eyes on me like hot coals, daring me to look at him.

"I knew that you'd remember my name," Rob said in response. *Wow. The guy is pretty self-assured. I liked it.*

Quickly, I made him a cup of ice water and handed him a menu. Then I looked up at him. "Rob. What would you like?"

Smirking at me, he handed me a business card. It was simple with a white background and his name in black ink. Robert A. Caralessi, Agent. The phone number had a 252 area code and the address said "Rocky Mount." I turned it over and the card said, in male penmanship and blue ink, "You are beautiful, Scout."

Aside from the fact that no one other than my daddy ever tells me that I'm beautiful, and aside from the fact that I was caught by surprise and went into panic mode the moment I saw him, and aside from the fact that I hadn't eaten all day and was just generally an anxious person, falling over my feet and landing on my back, as I attempted to go back into the kitchen to scream into the walk-in fridge, seemed like a completely natural thing for me to do.

Rob got up from his stool and hopped behind the counter to help me up. No injuries, of course, thanks to the rubbery floor covering which helped prevent slips and falls. *Right.*

"Are you okay?" he asked me, his hands lifting me up by my arm. All that was going through my head were my usual rapid fire thoughts when confronted with a stressful situation: "Thank God this place is slow today" and "His hands feel like he's held a lot of balls" and "Why the heck would I think something like that and then have my mind go immediately into the gutter after I think it?" "I meant athletic balls, like baseballs or footballs." *Sheesh!*

"Yes, thanks," I said, mortified. Again. In front of Rob. Robert A. Caralessi, Agent.

His eyes bored through mine and I felt uneasy with him looking at me so thoroughly. I didn't know what to say to this man. I mean, he is so good-looking that I immediately go into that fog again. I've been around attractive men before and have not had this reaction so it can't just be his looks. It has to be something else about him. Is he a sorcerer or something? *No, he's an agent! But an agent of what?*

At this point, I didn't know what in the heck was going on. Was this the Rapture and Rob is really the Angel Gabriel and he is saving me from the impending Armageddon? *Don't think that was in Revelations, Scout.*

He came into my restaurant on a random Thursday, obviously from work and obviously from some place with a 252 area code. He came to see me. He came to give me his business card that informed me that it — or he — thought I was beautiful. Things like this do not happen to nobody girls from small towns like me. At least, not with an obviously older man, who looks like a movie star.

I was half expecting him to pull out a naval officer hat, stick it on my head, and carry me out in his arms like at the end of *An Officer and a Gentleman*.

So, because I wasn't in my right mind, I asked him if he sings.

"Do I sing?" he asked, curious as to why I would ask him such a question.

"Yeah. Do you know that song 'Up Where We Belong' from the movie *An Officer and a Gentleman*?"

He gazed at me, still holding my arm, and nodded with the obvious question of "Why?" in his eyes.

"Never mind," I said and broke free of his grasp.

Rob sat back down at his stool and Felicia came out of the kitchen. She looked at him, recognizing him as the man who I had spilled the water all over last weekend. Then she looked at me. Almost as if she was gifted with the proverbial sixth sense, or because she simply felt the "sexual tension" in the moment, she asked pointedly, "What's this about?"

I felt like a complete idiot. I usually feel like that anyway, but this bizarre situation overriding my mind and body was making me want to run out the door and down the street screaming for help.

Whenever a man flirts with me, and it certainly isn't all the time, but when it happens, I've taught myself to be calm and nice about it. Sometimes, I kind of like it. Unless it's a creepy person, then I just feel weird. But this obvious attempt at a pick-up was not the norm for me at all and my reaction was causing me the kind of distress I haven't felt since trying out for the high school softball team. I felt like I was going to throw up.

"I'm trying to ask Scout here if she'd like to have dinner with me some time," Rob said to Felicia.

Felicia, a beautiful black woman in her thirties who has worked here for about five years, has five children and a husband who drives a truck for Pepsi, responded sharply, "Do you know she is only nineteen?"

It kind of pissed me off that she said it like that. Like, so what? Age isn't everything. Just because I'm nineteen doesn't mean I can't have a good adult conversation and a nice supper with an older man who thinks I'm beautiful. And besides, *he* is beautiful. He is a professional. He has pouty lips that I want to touch with my finger and a deep chin dimple and his hands felt like he might like baseball, which was a requirement in any men I dated. Like I've ever dated anyone at all!

I hadn't allowed myself to go on a date all throughout high school. I was so pathetic that some of the girls whispered I might be a lesbian because I never had a boyfriend and I played sports. But I just didn't want one. I didn't want to go out with anyone. Going to prom with Charlie my junior year doesn't count and neither does going anywhere with Charlie for that matter.

"Yes, I'd like to go to supper with you," I blurted out

excitedly, as if I accepted an invitation to a Madonna concert — certifying that I am, indeed, only nineteen.

Rob smiled at me. "Can you today?"

I thought for a second. Yes, I got off in two hours.

"I get off at 5:30 today so yes. But I would need to go back to my dorm to change." I swore that Rob's face winced at the words "to my dorm" but it quickly recovered. "Can I meet you somewhere?" I asked him. "I have my own car."

"Are you a student at State?"

"Yes."

"What dorm are you in?"

"Lee Hall," I replied.

"I'll be there at 6:30. Is that enough time?" he asked, clearly knowing exactly what dorm I was in and how to get there. "I'll be out front waiting for you."

"Okay," I replied, not quite realizing what in the world just happened.

Then Rob winked at me, got up and headed out. Felicia stood there with her arms folded glaring at me, not at all pleased. I felt like she was my mom and was about to scold me or something.

"What are you doing, Scout? That man has got to be old enough to be your daddy and if not your daddy, then your uncle and if not your uncle, then your much, much older brother," she declared.

"I know, but I want to go to supper with him. I mean,

look!" I happily handed her the card. She turned it over and read it. Then she looked at me, me and all my naïve glory.

"Boo, you got to be careful. That there man is a lot older than you. He's paying you a bold compliment and that can mean only one thing."

I had no idea what "one thing" that could mean. Why couldn't it just mean that he liked me and wanted to take me out? That he too had felt the strong connection between us? That he thought I was beautiful? That he wanted to be my agent? Whatever that meant.

"It means he's probably married," Felicia said in a stern tone. "He's probably a man who's been married a long time and is bored, lookin' for some fun action with a young college girl."

I hadn't considered that, really. Unfortunately, I still failed to see the dark side of people as easily as I had hoped I would by now. I was still a girl who believed that people actually meant what they said because I meant what I said. Even if psychology class was teaching me otherwise.

"Well, I guess I will find that out then," I informed her.

Felicia put her hand on my chin. "You be careful, Scout. You're a nice girl — too nice for your own good. This world will eat you alive if you don't watch out for yourself. You can't trust people, especially a man in a short-sleeved dress shirt and a tie. You got to look at them with the belief that they are just trying to get something from you. Maybe they aren't, but you got to look at them like that so you don't get hurt. You protect that big sweet heart that the good Lord gave you. You hear?"

I nodded, taking her motherly advice.

She smiled. "He sure is fine, though. Mmmm mmm!"

We both laughed. He was fine indeed.

ROB

Sitting in my office in Rocky Mount, I regarded the piles of folders resting high on my desk. I propped my feet up and inched the folders over toward the edge with my left foot, wondering if I just nudged them into my trashcan, I'd be able to leave work for the day and go back to Raleigh.

I'm not a guy who pursues women. Never have been, even when I was single, which was a long time ago. I rarely allow myself the guilty pleasure of noticing other women's finer assets. I'm not saying that I'm blind, but unlike a lot of the guys I've hung with during my settled years, I had to program my brain to bypass that part in social situations, especially when Rita is around. She can't stand it if I say that some famous actress is beautiful. So it's easier for me to keep any thoughts I have about that kind of stuff to myself.

Whenever I have an evening where I'm watching a ball game or a race with a group of neighbors and friends and there are no women around, I don't generally participate in the discussions about Kathleen Turner's tits. I also don't have anything useful to contribute to the discussion about whether or not the hot babe in the latest movie would be good in a threesome. And I'm not all that concerned about Kim Basinger's lips and where they should go.

Married at twenty-two, right out of State, Rita and I met in an economics class our second year. I was immediately taken with her raven hair, red lips, and bright blue eyes. She, like me, was second generation American from Italian immigrants and very Catholic. She was also incredibly close to her huge Italian family. Unlike me, she wanted to move to New York and work on Wall Street.

Thinking back on those years, we were so optimistic and hopeful about everything. It looked like we would be able to graduate with no debt and go start our careers — her on Wall Street and me into some kind of sales with a lot of travel, maybe in medical equipment or pharmaceuticals. Then, after we saved some money, we'd get married and settle down. We just didn't know where. I certainly did not want to live in Manhattan or anywhere in New Jersey. But I knew that I wanted to share my life with Rita.

Growing up in Connecticut, my parents both passed away when I was young and my grandmother raised me until I went off to State. I had no siblings. Rita was a military brat with six younger brothers. Her father's last duty station was at Camp Lejeune, North Carolina. So when she graduated from high school, she decided to go to State because it had a good business program and cost her father very little. While Rita was a student, he retired from the Marine Corps and her parents and brothers moved to Florence, New Jersey to be closer to her huge extended family. I also think that moving to a town called "Florence" made them feel like they were back in The Old Country. Although, after the many times I have been to Florence, New Jersey, I can say with certainty that it looks nothing like Florence, Italy.

Rita eventually wanted to live near her family and work on Wall Street as the Princess of Colonel (Retired) and Mrs. Gianni Scotti. We started out like so many young couples of our generation and I can say that I had no doubts about Rita whatsoever. We shared the same values, faith, and outlook on life. She was beautiful, adventurous, and smart. Exactly the kind of woman that I wanted to marry. While she wasn't very domestic, like my Sicilian grandmother was, Rita had that subtle maternal quality that made her girlfriends always come to her with their problems. She was the one with all the right answers and a good pair of hands to rub their backs when they would cry. She could cook a few good dishes, though. I never told my grandmother that Rita's sauce was better than her sauce because it would break her heart.

But more than anything, I loved Rita. I was *in* love with her. Being around her made me feel alive. She would touch me and I'd have an immediate physical and even emotional reaction. Rita Scotti was the love of my life.

I appreciated that she was ambitious and not afraid to take on a totally male-dominated world like finance in 1970. She was tough, yet classy, and I thought, while her beauty would get her in the door, her smarts, tenacity, and relentless work ethic would keep her there.

Shortly before we graduated, Rita was offered an entry-level position with an investment firm. Then it happened — that unfortunate timing thing that happens sometimes to young people who are crazy in love: Rita found out she was pregnant.

In 1970, abortion was not legal and, even if it was, we were Catholic. There were no abortions to be had with us Catholics — at least not a Scotti Catholic. I'm not saying that the issue wasn't discussed, because we were both scared shitless. But it was never an option really.

So we did what you do in that situation, which is, we went ahead and got married. It's not like it was a real shotgun wedding though because we were planning to get married anyway. My son's entrance into this world just made a wedding happen a little sooner. And it was okay with me. I was happy and excited to marry Rita and become a father.

I got a job in sales for an insurance company in Rocky Mount, North Carolina so we settled there. All the Wall Street plans and traveling salesman plans went to the wayside. And to be honest, that was okay with me. I didn't need all that. I was a traditional guy with traditional values and traditional desires: wife, kids, dog, white picket fence. American Dream stuff. Plus, I liked North Carolina and its climate and the friendly, unassuming, easily-amused people.

But Rita? Well, becoming a housewife was not what

she wanted in life and, for the last seventeen years, every once in a while during an argument about the kids or my career or money or whatever, she makes it known to me that she had always been destined for something greater and gave it all up to become a wife to me and a mother to our kids. She did and I appreciated it. But she's always had a chip on her shoulder about it.

All along the way, I've loved my wife and my two kids and have done everything I can to be a good husband and father. I've worked long, hard hours and been present for everything my kids were doing whenever I could. I've attended mass every week and tithed and assisted with confirmation classes for our parish. I've coached baseball, football, basketball, and sat through more dance recitals than I care to count. I've sold Girl Scout cookies in front of the Kroger and dressed up like Santa Clause at the community center and did story time at the elementary school. I've had six little girls give me a facial, put twenty barrettes in my hair, and paint my fingernails pink at a birthday sleep over when my daughter Samantha was eight.

Rita is a wonderful mother and wife who takes care of us all; she's a dedicated volunteer in the schools, our parish, and in the community. My son Chase was now sixteen and Samantha was fourteen and I had everything a man could ever want in life.

So what in the world has possessed me to ask for Jim Richardson's accounts and even his fucking debit routes in

Raleigh? I don't go to Raleigh. I manage the accounts for the eastern region.

Jim announced his retirement last month and on Monday he asked me who I thought should take over the capital region accounts and management. His job is a lot harder than mine because he has a Raleigh commute several times a week. He kept requesting that our owner invest in a small satellite office, but that hasn't worked out yet. I told Jim to give his accounts to Godfrey West, who is the next best agent, in my opinion, and to hand off the debit route clients to a couple of the newer agents.

And then I thought about it further. If I took over the capital accounts, I would have a reason to go to Raleigh. Often.

So I went into his office and told him that I would take them over starting this week and would assist with reassigning my accounts and the entire eastern region management. Since I was highly respected and also being considered for partnership in the company, the owner would go along with whatever I suggested. And now here on my desk are about half of Jim's accounts.

Maybe I would have time to stop by that little restaurant to see if all that I felt on Saturday was real or just a byproduct of my middle-aged brain.

I was intent on this transfer, partly because I needed a change and partly because of this unexpected yearning to go to Raleigh, so I set up three courtesy appointments for

Thursday with a few of Jim's larger clients and the last one was near Marty's Place. After the last appointment, I stopped by the restaurant and peeked in the window to see if Scout was working. I saw her standing behind the counter wiping something ferociously.

Not quite sure what in the hell I was doing, I pulled out one of my business cards and scribbled something nice on it. I was planning to give her the card and tell her that I'd like to see her sometime if she was available — and if she was at least eighteen.

Since I hadn't thought through how I would approach this girl if I saw her again, I was winging it. Let's just say that it's been a long, long time since any woman has had this kind of effect on me. I took three deep breaths because my heart was in my chest, as if I were a fifteen-year-old boy about to ask a girl to prom. Then I put my wedding band in my pocket and walked in.

She was so fuckin' cute standing back behind that counter, trying not to look at me, pretending to not remember my name and being all coy and sweet. She tried not to smile when I said a little joke about the water. It was all I could do to not go back behind the counter and kiss her. I can't remember the last time I wanted to kiss a woman like I wanted to kiss her. Yes, the chemistry between us that I experienced on Saturday was real. My shoulder stopped hurting again.

That evening, I parked my car and walked over to Lee

Hall to wait for her outside. It was dark and she came out at exactly 6:30, wearing a pair of jeans and a sweater.

"I'm sorry I'm dressed so casual," she said, looking down shyly. "I don't get out much. Plus, any dressy clothes I have are back home."

"You are beautiful, remember?" I said in response and she immediately blushed.

I drove us to an old restaurant downtown that I used to frequent when I was a student here, a Raleigh staple, probably as old as the city itself. We went inside and sat down at a corner table and each ordered some Brunswick stew and hushpuppies.

"So, Scout, where are you from?" I asked her, starting us off in a normal conversation, as if I was trying to gauge her insurance needs at this point in her life.

"I'm from Haddleboro." Then she grinned, "I doubt you've ever heard of it."

Actually, I have. Being in insurance sales, you know where every little town and nook and cranny is in the entire state.

"Tell me about yourself. What are you studying?"

"Well, I'm just in my first year, but I want to go to the vet school and become a veterinarian," she answered. I realized that she was finally meeting my gaze.

"Doctor Scout," I said. "I find it adorable that a girl with a dog's name would want to be a dog doctor."

She rolled her eyes. "I am not named after a dog."

"Are you named after the girl in *To Kill a Mockingbird*?"

She smiled. "I am. It's an awful lot to live up to."

"I bet it is. Why do you want to be a veterinarian?"

She scooped some stew into her mouth, swallowed, and said, "Because I love animals. Especially dogs. I'd rather be around animals than people." She paused and added, "Animals are honest and you always know where you stand with them."

Not knowing quite how to respond to that little insight into her pretty head, I kept peppering her with questions about herself so she would feel at ease with me and reveal more to me about her life. Unlike in an initial client meeting, I was genuinely interested in everything about her.

"What's your family like?"

"My daddy owns a garage. My mom's a teacher. I have a little brother who's in high school," she said.

"Do you like music?" I asked her. She looked at me like I was an idiot.

"No. I hate music," she said, hiding her smirk behind a hushpuppy.

"Okay, that was a dumb question, I know," I said grinning at her. "Cute little smartass."

She laughed. "I like older music. Like The Eagles, Led Zeppelin, and Janis Joplin."

"Wow, really? That's music from my younger years," I reminisced. "That's impressive. You have good taste."

"You figured I'd just like Madonna or something?"

"I figured you more of a U2 girl. Passionate. Political. Social justice."

Scout laughed. "I do like U2. I like Madonna, too. I like all kinds of music. My tastes are eclectic."

Smiling, I replied, "That's too big of a word for an old guy like me." Suddenly feeling overly drawn to her, like any boundaries between us were now thrown away, I reached across the table and touched her small hands with my fingers. "I like U2 and Madonna, too, Scout."

When the discussion got to baseball, I felt like I had met my best trash-talking sparring partner yet.

"The Red Sox?" she asked, totally offended.

"Scout, I'm from Connecticut. That's a part of New England."

"Yeah, but the Red Sox are in Boston. It's not the New England Red Sox. You're not even from Massachusetts."

"You are a New York Yankees fan who is from North Carolina. The Bronx is in New York City," I said, with the emphasis on "New York" each time.

With a mouth full of hushpuppies, she responded with "Touché!"

"Why the Yankees?" I asked her, genuinely curious.

"Well, I know it's kind of silly, but my daddy grew up being a Yankees fan because it was the only games that my Pawpaw could get on the radio. So a lot of people down here like the Yankees. Or the Braves," Scout said, introducing me to this fairly interesting piece of cultural trivia.

I loved everything about her from her perfectly formed face to her almost whiskey-soaked voice with the subtle country drawl, to how anything we talked about did not seem to identify the glaring age difference between us. She seemed to know a lot about the same kinds of things that interested me and, despite the generation gap, she had no problem carrying on a conversation about current events and American history.

We talked for a good two and a half hours at that table and every time the waiter came over to ask us if we wanted anything else, we'd shoo him away.

The conversation ran the gamut and we had a back-and-forth as if we were Abbott and Costello in "Who's On First?" I'm a natural with people, but I have never felt as natural with anyone in conversation as I did with little miss Scout — and I had just met her. We talked like old friends who shared a common history with an underlying sexual chemistry that made me want to kiss her as I watched her lips move as she spoke.

After finally leaving the restaurant, we sat in my car to talk some more. It was getting late and I still had an hour-long drive to get home. Earlier today, I told Rita that I had no idea when I'd be home because of my appointments. Plus, I flat out lied and said I that might meet up with a friend of mine for dinner and a beer. She wasn't happy about it, but I needed a backup plan in case Scout said yes to dinner. Well, the backup plan was currently in force.

"Can I see you again?" I asked her, my heart seeming to beat much faster than humanly possible. I could practically feel a heart attack coming on because a part of me was afraid she'd say no.

Then she looked over at me with that adorable face — big brown eyes, soft freckles, those puffy cheeks — and smiled. "I would love to see you again," she said quietly. Her body language was so shy and reserved toward me, but her eyes were just the opposite, so hungry.

"Can I kiss you?" I asked her, but instead of waiting for an answer, I leaned over and did it. I was that sure she wanted me to, anyway.

As we kissed, I slid further over toward her on the front seat and took her face in my hands. It's been a very long time since I kissed my wife like this. But I wasn't thinking about my wife at all in that moment. I was thinking about this perfect girl in my car and how much I craved her since last Saturday. She kissed me back so sweetly, gently, and full of something deeper, some kind of longing within her that's been hidden for her whole young life. I don't remember the last time I felt this good.

She didn't care that I was twenty years older and that I wouldn't be able to see her that often. And I didn't care that I was married to a woman who I loved and was a father to two great kids who were old enough to be her friends. All I cared about was being wrapped up in this completely unpolished and undiscovered gem.

And, as we continued to kiss each other and then share the delicate intimacies of two new lovers caught up in the explorative passion swelling between them, I thought that this was the greatest I've ever felt in my life, or at least in many years.

My hands were gently touching the soft skin on her tight body and I slowly put my fingers underneath, along the edges of her sweater. My right hand then ventured up her bare back and I pulled her into me, wishing I could lay her down. I forgot how challenging it was to be with a girl in the front seat of a car. I felt the bottom of her bra strap and played with it, kissing her lips, her face, and then her neck. She easily surrendered and let me unsnap her bra and move my hands in front. I looked at her full young face, opening her dark eyes to gaze directly into mine. I continued to touch her, feeling her youth and all the freshness of her flesh. Had she ever even been touched by a man before? Was this virgin skin?

I awakened something within her and she rose to her knees. She leaned into me and kissed me with the fullness of a ripe apple in the fall and then began to put her hands under my shirt and onto my chest. They were furious, almost too rough for such a sweet girl, and as she slowed down and delicately rubbed my stomach with the palms of her hands, she looked at me and smiled timidly, almost embarrassed. I smiled back at her.

"Do you want to do this?" I asked quietly, my hands now at the nape of her neck, rubbing it slowly and giving her small kisses on her lips.

"Yes," she said without hesitation, putting her hands onto my face and kissing me.

As I lost track of the time and fell under the influence of the intensity between us, I pulled back from her and held her face. "Scout, I don't think we should do this here."

She looked up at me with what looked like faith. Trust. Belief. Dependence?

"I want to be with you, but not like this. Not in a car on the street. You deserve better than that. We deserve better than that."

She kissed my mouth and whispered, "Okay."

I absolutely had to keep seeing her. So I did.

CHARLIE

I was leaving for Fort Benning in a week and I still hadn't had a real conversation with Scout about what was going on with me, about the huge decision that I made in my life to go serve in the Army. I was sure her parents must've told her about it, but she never said anything to me, like it didn't interest her or anything.

Scout's been kind of distant and removed from me since she got home for her break right before Christmas and I didn't know if it was because she thought she was all hot shit now that she was in college and maybe thought she was better than me or because something else was going on with her. I figured the latter because Scout was never a snobby type of girl and I knew that she still cared about me. But she has been acting really weird and not herself at all the whole time she's been home. I didn't quite know what to make of it.

Christmas was over and the last time I went to her house, she said she needed to get to Raleigh so she could go back to work. She'd be able to stay at her aunt's house until her dorm opened back up for the second semester. It was almost as if she couldn't get back there fast enough.

We were sitting on her couch watching one of the stories she got hooked on at college, *General Hospital*. Whenever we watched TV together in the past, she used to sit kind of close to me and sometimes put her feet up on my legs or rest her head on a pillow on top of my lap. I loved watching TV with her like that because that's as physically intimate as she'd get with me. But this time, her body was all pushed up against the side of the couch, as far from me as she could be. So I decided to once and for all to talk to her about me going in the Army.

"Scout," I said, firmly enough to get her attention.

"Hmm?" she responded, eyes fixed on the TV.

"Do you realize that I'm leaving next week?"

She looked at me and said, "Yeah, I know. Daddy told me about it." She said it like I was just going off to the Pig for a soda. She was in some other world, her mind not here with me at all.

"You know it's the Army right? Like, I'm gonna be gone and probably not be back here for a really long time."

Scout suddenly came out of the absent state she's been living in. "What do you mean?" she asked, looking right at me with her pretty brown eyes.

"Well, I have basic training and then AIT, which is even more training, and then I'll get assigned someplace."

"You'll just get assigned to Fort Bragg. That's not too far away from here."

I smirked. "Scout. That might not happen."

"But Daddy told me that you'd get assigned there and I'd still be able to see you sometimes. At Fort Bragg, you'd be even closer to Raleigh!"

"No, that's not how it works. I don't know where I'll get assigned. I'm gonna be an infantry soldier, so I could get assigned to lots of places, maybe even Germany or Korea!"

Scout looked serious and then perplexed. I guess she hadn't said much to me about all of this because she just figured I'd still be close by.

"Charlie..." she started, her eyes starting to well up and a little quiver suddenly in her voice. "No..."

A part of me felt a little better when she said that because I realized then that she still cared about me. *Of course she still cared about me!*

We sat there looking at each other and I could see that she was holding back her tears. I didn't expect all that. I guess she didn't realize what me going into the Army actually meant or could mean for both of us. She just thought it would be like me simply changing jobs or something. But it's the Army so I don't know why she would've thought that it would be like nothing's changing.

She stared at me, like she was looking for something in my face, like she wanted to say what was in her heart, but couldn't find the words. Then she pulled herself away from the end of the couch and moved over next to me. She threw her arms around me like she was afraid she'd never see me again and buried her head in my neck. Then she started to cry.

Goddamn it, I cannot deal with her crying. I can't take it.

"Charlie, I didn't know. I didn't know you were going to be like really gone," she said, her tears melting onto my neck.

Scout's never been excessively affectionate with me, but she has been somewhat affectionate a few memorable times. Well, this was one of those times. She held me in her grasp and kept her forehead in my neck and I wasn't quite sure what to do. What I wanted to do was hold her, too, but I thought better about that. She'd been so different with me that I didn't want to do anything to ruin this moment where the Scout I knew and loved was back and holding me like I was her teddy bear.

Miss Raelene walked into the living room and saw Scout crying as she held me. "What's wrong?" she asked, walking over to us.

I looked up at her and said, "I was trying to tell Scout about how I might not be back here for a long time once I leave for the Army, that I wasn't sure where I'd end up."

She looked thoughtful. "Scout, he might end up right in Fayetteville, hon. It's gonna be okay."

But Scout wasn't convinced, I could tell. She pulled away from me and tears had been streaming down her face, a lot more than I thought.

"Charlie, I don't want you to go into the Army then," she said.

Miss Raelene interjected, "You two want something to eat?"

I didn't. Scout said that she didn't. So Miss Raelene gave Scout a quick hug and said, "Bless your heart, Scout. Don't you worry about this. Charlie will be right back here soon after his training."

But I wasn't so sure about that and, honestly, I didn't want to be assigned to Fort Bragg. If I was going to go serve my country, then I wanted to see a bit of the world. No need to put myself through all the hardships of Army life if I was going to end up being thirty minutes from Haddleboro. I know my mom would like that and I guess Scout would like that, too, but I was ready to go do something bigger with myself and my life. So many of my peers like Scout were trying to do special things with their lives. I wanted to do that, too.

Miss Raelene left the room, leaving me and Scout alone. She faced me and put her hands up on my cheeks, rubbing them with her fingers.

"Charlie, I've been an awful friend," she started. "I've been so consumed with myself and my own goals and college life and wants and..." she drifted off "...other things and people I've met." She sat back. "I haven't thought much about what's been going on with you at all and what you might want to do with your life."

Ouch. That hurt. Scout is always on my mind, even when I can hardly ever see her or talk to her.

"I go back to Raleigh in two days," she said. "I promise I'm going to do better with calling you and writing you. Especially during your training. I'm gonna write you all the time. Even if there's nothing to write about!"

I grinned at her and said quietly, "You are the kind of person who can make nothing sound like something great, Scout."

And then catching me by complete surprise, she leaned over and kissed me. She kissed me like a real kiss, like boyfriend and girlfriend kissing. My body tightened and I was flooded with adrenaline, both from the shock of it all and no doubt all the feelings I harbor for her deep inside. I love her. I am *in* love with her. I've always loved her and now she was kissing me in a way that told me how much she cared about me, too. Or at least I hoped she did. What was this?

I didn't know what to think because, all these years, Scout's kept a romantic distance from me. She didn't date any boys when we were in high school, so I never had to see any of that bullshit, thank God, but she also would never let herself be more than friends with me. Even prom junior year was completely platonic between us. All of our friends with were off together making out and doing God-knows-what-else and Scout and I looked like a brother and sister all dressed up for a fancy party.

As Scout continued to kiss me, I found myself kissing her, too, like I was finally filling my starving heart. It was so much better than the last time we kissed at eleven years old in my room. We kept going, caressing each other feverishly, like Jesus was coming back soon and there'd be no more kissing like this ever again. She moved her lips to my cheeks and my neck, my collarbone. She kissed my chin, my nose, my closed eyelids — all light, small kisses, fueled with an intimacy I don't think I've ever felt before with any other girl.

Suddenly feeling a little self-conscious because we were sitting in her living room and Miss Raelene had been in here and anyone could walk in on us, I stopped her.

"Scout, you got to stop, we can't do this here in your living room," I whispered, not really wanting her to stop at all.

Then she seemed to realize where she was and maybe even who she was kissing like this and got a horrified look on her face. Definitely not something I was prepared to see. Who did she think she was kissing? Someone else?

She sat back. "Charlie, I'm so sorry. I'm so embarrassed. I don't know what got into me."

I was sure my face was all red at this point and, while I've always wanted to kiss Scout like that, for real — dear God, had I wanted to — she seemed all ashamed and apologetic and now regretting that it happened at all. So that only made me feel stupid and foolish. I'm a fucking dumb ass.

During the last two days Scout was in Haddleboro, we spent a lot more time together: hanging out, watching TV, talking about life, going to see a movie, and simply being in each other's company — like the old days. And then, after a long and tear-filled goodbye, she got in her little old VW Rabbit that her dad fixed up for her last summer and headed back to Raleigh, to a life I wasn't much a part of at all.

But she didn't kiss me again like she did on the couch that day. And saying goodbye to her felt different this time.

SCOUT

What is wrong with me? What am I doing? Who am I? How am I even in this situation?

Laying in the dark, in my cousin's old bedroom at my aunt's house in Raleigh, I started thinking — obsessing, really — about what a mess I am and what a mess I'm in. And I don't know what to do about any of it.

I kissed Charlie on the couch the other day — really kissed him — and I don't know why I did that. I don't know if it was because I wanted to kiss Charlie Porter specifically or because I missed Rob so much. It was probably both. I've always wanted to kiss Charlie like that.

I was home for two weeks during the Christmas break and, because I have a job in Raleigh, I couldn't stay home for a whole month like so many of the other kids get to do while on their break. But really, I didn't want to be home at all. It just made me feel like I was still a little girl and not a grown woman with adult responsibilities and carrying on in an adult relationship. Even being around Charlie at times made me feel like a caged bird because he reminded me that I was still only nineteen, dependent on my parents, and always tethered to Haddleboro. And I didn't want to be any of that. I wanted to be in Rocky Mount with Rob, baking him cookies and making his bed and ironing his shirts like his wife gets to do.

My heart and my body just ached for Rob all the time. I missed him so much. His kisses on my face and his hands on the small of my back — which felt so familiar — and his chest on my chest and his shoulders — *my God, his shoulders!* — and our long, deep talks about life and our little inside jokes…and of course all of the incredible love making that I never wanted to end.

The man was irresistible. I had no idea that sex could be this amazing. Before Rob, I only had sex one time, the time with Brother Doug. And while the time with Brother Doug was amazing after I got past the painful beginning, sex with Rob was so much better, both physically and emotionally. We were a match, no matter our age difference, and I was older and more mature now so I could handle myself. I finally understood why a lot of kids had sex as often as they could and would go to great lengths to do it.

Rob was the most perfect lover. Whenever we were together, which was quite a bit more than I had anticipated over a month ago, it was just one memorable and beautiful experience after another. I could not get enough of him. And he told me that he wanted to make love to me every day of his life.

"Facciamo l'amore," he would say to me. It means,

"Let's make love" in Italian.

"Do you speak Italian?" I asked him.

He laughed. "Not really. But I know that one."

"I love you, little girl," he said to me a few days after our first time. When he said it, I put it out of my head that Brother Doug used those exact same words. Rob really loved me. He wouldn't say it unless he genuinely meant it. Would he?

We'd be together in my dorm room when my roommate Micaela went back home for the night. She was local but was able to keep a room because she was entitled to it through some kind of a scholarship. She slept at home at least a few times a week so Rob and I had the room to ourselves. He paid for us to use a hotel room a few times and I was surprised that I didn't feel like some trashy hooker, like I thought I would. When I told Rob that, he laughed.

"A hooker? Really?"

"Yeah, isn't that who goes into hotels during the day to have sex?" I asked.

"Scout, lots of regular people like you and me have sex in a hotel."

That made me feel better about it. But not really though. I didn't feel right about any of this even though I would tell myself that I did.

A couple of times, we were like two high school kids in his car, me straddling him in the back seat, hoping no headlights would come our way on the private side street of Raleigh. He didn't seem to be worried about the police walking up on us. I must've seen too many movies because I was always waiting for a cop to shine a flashlight on us and ask for our names.

I was so caught up in him. He was all I could think about, all the time. I didn't want to do anything else but be with Rob. Since I hadn't made many friends in school, Rob — either my dreams of being with him or the real live actual him — took up all my free time, but it wasn't noticed by anyone of substance. Because it's a big school, people probably didn't think much of the gorgeous man and the college girl going on the carousel at Pullen Park.

But by finals week, my grades were starting to suffer a bit and I was not doing as well as I thought. I tried not to get down about it, though, because I was happy, truly, overwhelmingly happy, and in love with a grown, caring man who was also in love with me and who rearranged his work life and life in general just to come spend time with me. He wouldn't do all that unless he really cared. Would he?

By the beginning of December, he had set up his work schedule so that he was able to come to Raleigh at least three times a week.

"I'll set it up so that I can see you on the days that you aren't working or you have an early shift," he explained. "Since your Monday-Wednesday-Friday classes are all done by 2:00, I can come on one of those days and get all of my work done before your classes are out. And then..." he stopped talking and kissed me. Then he was about to start talking again, but instead kissed me again. And again. Each time longer and more passionately.

"I just want to be with you. I don't care what we do. We can goof off. You can tell me what it was like for you when you were here," I said.

"I'd love to share that with you."

"And we have to find time to be alone together in order to make love as long as humanly possible," I said, leaning into his arms.

One day, right before I left for Christmas break, Rob picked me up from near the Bell Tower and drove us over to Reynolds Coliseum. He was dressed casually in jeans and his red State windbreaker, which was not the norm on his weekday visits. He said, "I want to show you something," and took me inside of Reynolds.

As a student, I hadn't gone into Reynolds before. I knew it was where the basketball team played and basketball here was a huge deal. The Wolfpack was good and always exciting and the rivalries between the other colleges around here were always fueled with so much energy.

In 1983, the team known as "The Cardiac Pack" won the NCAA championship, which was totally unexpected and one of the most exciting and memorable games in history. I remember my daddy looking at the TV, stunned, as we watched the legendary Coach, Jim Valvano, running around the basketball court looking like he needed someone to hug.

My daddy still talked about that game when March came around and all the tournaments began. He loved it. I had been so enveloped in my love affair with Rob that I hadn't even thought about this part of college life. I know my daddy would want me to go see a game at Reynolds.

Rob held my hand and walked me up to the entrance. He opened the door and we slipped in. I had no idea if we had any business being inside or if someone was going to say something, but we kept walking like we owned the place. Rob marched with purpose, as if he knew exactly where he was going. He turned down a corridor and into a section of seats and I could hear the squeak-squeak-squeak of shoes on the gym's wooden floors. He led me down a row and we sat down. It was pretty dark up where we were.

The lights shone down onto the floor where I could see tall young men, mostly black, doing some kind of sprinting drill. There was a rack of basketballs off to the side, a few men in track suits standing near the far basket, one player in a yellow shirt sitting on the floor with someone wrapping up his foot, and then a man with dark hair shouting something at the boys in the drill.

"That's Jim Valvano, Scout," Rob said to me as he pointed down at the dark-haired man.

I had figured as much.

"Listen, I forget that you are in fact just a college freshman sometimes," he said.

I winced. I hated to be reminded of this. I wanted to

be Rob's age. Maybe then all of this would be easier.

He continued, "College is a time to see and learn about different things, the kinds of things that you never really got to back in lil' podunk Haddleboro. This is the kind of stuff that college is all about: making friends from other places, joining clubs, trying new things, and enjoying the school pride at major sporting events. When I was here, I loved going to games whenever I could. Win or lose, there's nothing like being a fan of a college team when you're a part of the student body. And there is nothing better than college basketball in North Carolina."

I thought about what he was saying and knew that he was right. But since I got here, I had been so busy working and adjusting to being away from home. Plus, the big social scene really isn't my thing anyway. Ever since the summer of '83, I retreated into myself. Charlie was my social life. The church youth group, on occasion, was my social life. My dog was my social life.

I didn't get to go to a football game in the fall because of my job and, while I would love to go to a basketball game, I've just been so caught up with arranging my life to see Rob over the last month or so that these college kid things don't really cross my mind. I only wanted to be with Rob whenever I could. It was almost like I felt I was too old for the college life.

"I know, but I'd really rather be able to see you. You are better than any club I could join or friend I could make or game I could see," I told him.

Rob put his forehead against my forehead and kissed me. Then he wrapped his arms around my shoulders and pulled me close.

"I'll take you to a game sometime this season. It's early yet. But if you want to be a real State student, you've got to be a part of Wolfpack basketball for at least one game, okay?"

I kissed him and then put my mouth near his neck. "I would go anywhere and do anything with you." He had my complete trust. He had my heart. Did I have his, too?

"You have my heart, little girl," he said, as if he read my mind.

While I was home for my break, I couldn't call him because he wasn't at work and said that he would be in New Jersey. Work is the only place I can call to talk to him, but only briefly and only if really important. He calls me at either Marty's Place, because he knows my shift schedule, or he calls me on the phone in the dorm hallway.

The only real time we have together are times like in Reynolds or in his car or at Pullen Park or in my dorm room or in the little pockets of the State campus and beyond that we're able to find together. He said he didn't want to be seen by anyone he knows, so the campus area was the safest for him because people on campus were mostly students.

Right before Thanksgiving, after we had spent a couple of weeks being together, he told me that he was married and had been married for a long time. Felicia was spot on.

"I have two kids, both teenagers," he said, looking into my face to see what my reaction would be. "I know I should've told you all this up front, but I don't know...I didn't know how to." His confession made me feel a little weird, but I soon shut it out of my mind.

When he told me the truth about his real life, I wasn't all that surprised, but I was also waiting for him to say something like "but we are separated" or "but we aren't in love anymore and are staying together for the kids", but he never said anything like that. He never gave me some little sliver of moral justification related to our union in order for me to be able to accept that what I was doing was somehow okay. I knew that it wasn't okay, no matter the state of his marriage.

But whenever I'd think too much about it, I'd remember all the things he'd say to me and how he made me feel so, so happy and wanted and beautiful and mature and alive. He gave me purpose and I hadn't felt like I had any purpose to my life for a long time. So I locked out the gnawing sensation that I was, once again, some older married man's young little toy whore.

Whenever he would go back home to his wife after a wonderful afternoon or early evening together, completely wrapped up in each other in conversation, in kissing, and in love making, the self-hatred faucet turned on at full power and steamed throughout my body. It was stronger than any hot shower.

I detested myself. The angry, but true, words of Cammy DeHaan rang out in my head all over again. And then I'd think about his wife: the faceless, nameless woman who I was betraying, even though she didn't know me and I didn't know her. In the stillness of the late night hour, I would silently apologize to her for everything I was doing. But I couldn't break away. My bond to Rob was too strong now. I was in love with him and he made me feel like I was worth loving.

I knew that this was wrong in every way. At least when this happened to me the last time, I had a little bit of a defense because I was only fourteen years old. But who am I kidding? There was never any excuse for what I did with Brother Doug. I was a dirty, horrible, sinner and an abomination to God. There was no way for me to ever be clean again. Deep down, I knew how this whole thing with Rob would end: me with a broken heart, wishing I were dead. And this time, there would be no Charlie to hold me. He was going into the Army.

I would get what I deserved: a life with no one, a life all alone.

No Rob for two weeks left me in quite a funk all on its own. It was hard to enjoy Christmas with my family because all I could think about was how Rob was with his family, laughing, opening gifts and probably waking up naked next to his wife, telling her that he loved her, and saying to her the kinds of things he also said to me.

It was hard to be around Charlie. My daddy told me back at Thanksgiving that Charlie was going into the Army.

"He'll get assigned to Fort Bragg. Don't you worry."

But my gut knew better. I knew that Charlie was leaving home, leaving me, that he would probably find a girl to marry, and I'd lose him forever. So I kept a distance from him as much as I could. It just hurt inside and I was an anxious mess the whole time.

I was dealing with a one-two punch. One was the knowledge that Rob, a man who looked at me and kissed me and held me like I was the only girl in the world for him, was in fact with another woman who he actually did love and he would never, ever be with me. And the other was that I was losing Charlie to a whole new world.

Feeling sorry for myself and all alone, I knew that all of this emotional pain and misery was deserved. God just punishing me again, reminding me of what I am. A whore. A husband-stealing, home-wreckin' whore.

ROB

Driving to Raleigh on a cold, rainy, January day did not faze me. It wouldn't have mattered if it was snowing or sleeting. Growing up in New England did have its benefits. Drivers down here in the South are a joke, generally speaking, but in winter weather, they are a nightmare. Because so many of them are unable to do it, they stay off the roads entirely. A wet and rainy forecast had a bunch of people thinking that it might ice over. So the roads were clear but for the brave souls who felt like they had somewhere to be.

I had somewhere I needed to be. I couldn't wait to see Scout again. It had been way too long — really, a two-week eternity — and it was all I could do not to disappear from home last weekend and go see her at Marty's Place.

Rita started out the holidays with her bitch factor turned up a few notches and had been giving me a lot of shit about how much I've been going to Raleigh lately.

"I've explained this to you a thousand times. I've taken over the Raleigh regional accounts because of Jim's impending retirement. I have to travel there a lot. It's part of the job!"

"I can't understand why, after so many years of managing the eastern region, they decided to have their greatest asset switch locations. You're the one who has all the relevant relationships established. Can't the next in line just take over Raleigh?" Rita asked me, clearly frustrated.

At some point, after having to explain myself for what felt like the millionth time, I finally threw up my hands and said, voiced raised, "Hell Rita, it's just what they want to do — change it up! Who cares if it makes sense to you? It's not your job or your fuckin' company!" I don't ever talk to Rita like that so she looked at me, aghast.

It's exhausting being married to a woman who is smarter than I am and needs a thorough and detailed explanation of every decision that is made in my company. I'm more of a go-with-the-flow kind of person and rarely ask too many questions about anything.

"Why can't you just chill the hell out and let things be what they are? Why do you need to be able to see the reasoning behind everything? Who fucking cares why they are changing things? I guess an underused, bored, wannabe investment banker cares."

Rita was angry. Really angry. "That is a low blow, Rob. I don't know what your problem is that you would say something so nasty to me and use such a tone."

Raleigh was a rather long argument, the day after Christmas, at her parents' house in New Jersey. I think her mother was concerned that we were a little too feisty with each other. So much so that she later told Rita that she thinks maybe we should go away together for a romantic weekend.

Italians are a notoriously loud bunch and I'm actually not that loud at all, but when an Italian matriarch is telling you that you are too loud, then you are probably too loud.

Being away from Scout was torture. Not being able to call her and talk to her or hear her voice or see her face or touch her body was a living hell. It was the longest two weeks of my life and, as I pulled up to the campus to see her, I decided to park the car, go up to her floor, and surprise her at her room.

I followed a student into the residence hall and walked up the stairs to the second floor. My heart was pumping fast. I was so happy and excited to see my beautiful girl, my breath of fresh air, my baby-faced angel. I knocked on her door and Micaela, her roommate, answered.

She looked up at me and smiled. "Oh, hi. Scout's not here."

I was a little surprised. She should be in her dorm by now. I had her schedule down pat and she told me the other day, when I called her at Marty's, that she'd be in her room and would meet me outside at 1:00. Well, it was 1:00 and she wasn't here.

"Do you know where she is?" I asked.

"She said she was going to the library."

"That's odd. Classes haven't even started yet so why would she go there?"

Micaela shrugged, her light brown hair glided along her shoulders. "Sorry. I don't know."

I walked over to the library and roamed around the building until I found her, sitting alone in a study room. She was at a desk and had nothing with her, no books or notebooks or pens. Wearing a blue coat and jeans, with her Converse covered feet propped up on a chair, she looked so vacant and alone and like she had been crying. It was breaking my heart to see her like this.

As I opened the door, she peered up at me and immediately her face changed into that happy, bright face that I always want to hold in my hands and kiss. So I walked over to her, picked her up out of the chair and into my arms and, while holding her in the air, I started to kiss her like I haven't seen her in a year. Because, really, that's what it felt like to me.

"I've missed you so much, little girl," I said quietly.

Looking directly into my face, her eyes beaming with life, the distant stare now long gone from them, she said nothing and resumed kissing me. After a brief pause, I breathed, "Let's get out of here and go somewhere. I want to be with you so bad."

"Okay," she whispered, and we walked out of the building and into the chilly, wet afternoon.

RITA CARALESSI, AGE 39

What a strange Christmas we had this year. Well, it was actually pretty normal except for one person.

Rob was aloof this entire holiday season and, thinking about it even further, he has been acting this way for several weeks now. Being around him for twenty-four hours a day this past week has shown me how bizarre his behavior has become.

When we were trying to leave Rocky Mount in order to drive up to New Jersey to stay with my parents for Christmas, it took him an ungodly amount of time to get out of the house. Chase, Samantha, and I were all sitting in the car because we had expected to leave at the time that Rob said he wanted to leave. For me to be ready was not an issue. I am always ready on time and prepared. For my two teenaged kids, however, it was a small miracle. So even they were a bit perturbed with their father for seemingly rushing them out of the house and then not being ready himself. It was very unlike Rob.

After the eight-hour drive, which was excruciatingly quiet for a Caralessi family road trip, I determined that a pod had come out of a lab somewhere and taken over my husband's body. I didn't understand what was going on with him. Rob is and has always been a man who likes to talk with me as well as with his children. He is not a quiet person. I don't mean that he is loud because he's not. He just likes to talk about things, even things that do not need talking about.

On our many road trips to New Jersey over the years, he would sing along to the songs on the radio while he drives, start up annoying songs like "Ninety-nine Bottles of Beer on the Wall" with the kids, and play road trip games like punch buggy or count up how many vanity plates we can find. He would do voice impersonations. We'd usually laugh a lot and then, when we finally arrive at our destination, realize that the ride wasn't so bad at all — thanks to Rob.

He did not speak the whole way to New Jersey. He answered a question if I asked him one. He might've made a comment about our timing or what he thought might be a traffic hold-up near DC. But mostly, he simply drove. No singing, no talking, no anything. So eventually I took a nap and both kids either slept or read.

When we were at my parents' house, Rob watched a lot of TV. He used to help my mom a bit in the kitchen at dinnertime and he'd always do the dishes after a meal. He seemed to enjoy clearing the table and washing the dishes by hand because my mother didn't have a dishwasher. This time, he didn't do any potato peeling or onion chopping or marinade making. He didn't clear plates or do the dishes. He made Samantha do them instead. "It's time she does more chores and stops being so spoiled," he said to me, rather sharply, when I asked him why he was making her do the dishes.

My mother made sweet breads and some wonderful pastries, like her to-die-for cannoli, along with traditional Christmas cookies and other baked goods for the season. Rob would usually eat her out of house and home. "Mrs. Scotti, this is the best pastry (or bread or cannoli or cookie) I've ever had!" he'd say, over and over again during past visits. Then my mother, who like most women who meet Rob, becomes completely charmed and bakes him even more goodies, labels them with his name, and then packs them for the trip back to North Carolina.

Surprisingly, my parents were very understanding when Rob and I decided to stay in North Carolina and make our life there. All of my younger brothers and extended family live in the south and central New Jersey area, so I guess our little family of four not being with them didn't put much of a dent in their status as grandparents. They try to make up for it when we visit. They shower our kids with gifts and attention and Rob and I are always treated like gold. Not that we wouldn't be otherwise, but it's hard to be involved grandparents when you're a few states away.

It was difficult for us to accept that our Christmas traditions would need to be away from our own home in

Rocky Mount. Rob did not want that at all.

"I want my kids to wake up in their own house and go downstairs to their own tree to open their gifts," he said to me early on.

"Rob, I'm not going to live here in North Carolina unless I can spend Christmas with my family. Sorry, but that's a deal breaker for me," I said, putting my foot down on the entire matter. I was not *not* going to be with my family at Christmas.

So he finally understood that and accepted it. And we came up with other traditions leading up to Christmas, such as family baking and fudge making and the Christmas pageant. We also held a Christmas party at our home each year for our friends and some of Rob's clients. We would participate in something charitable each year, as well. Then, a few days before Christmas, we'd leave, with presents in tow, to spend the holiday with my parents and my six brothers and their families. We all grew to love it.

On Christmas Day, Rob always liked to be Santa Clause. When the kids were little, he ensured that they believed Santa knew that they were at their grandparents' in New Jersey rather than in North Carolina.

"But, Daddy, how will he know?" Samantha asked him, in tears, when she was only four years old. "And Grandpa don't have a chimney. How will he get inside with the presents?"

"Sammy, don't worry. Lots of kids don't live in houses

with chimneys. Your friend, Claire, lives in an apartment and Santa delivers to her just fine. Right?" he said, calming all of her fears.

He would make a big production of Santa's gifts versus our gifts, using different wrapping paper and handwriting on the tags. As they got older, and Santa was a thing of warm memories, Rob still made sure that he handed out all the gifts, one at a time, and we all ooo-ed and ahhh-ed as each present opened.

This year? Rob said, "They're teenagers now. They don't care about Santa Clause anymore. Who cares?" Samantha looked like she was about to cry when she heard him say that to me.

So the kids just ripped into their gifts like captive animals released for a spell and Rob, my parents, and I watched them. Then, the adults opened their gifts when the kids went to their room to go back to sleep.

My gifts from Rob were beautiful, as always, and very thoughtful. The priciest one was the diamond-encrusted bracelet that I mentioned I loved when I saw it at the jewelers in the mall not long ago. When I went to thank him for the gifts, I kissed his lips and he pecked me back like I was his sister. Later, he apologized to me. "Sorry, Reet, I'm not feeling well," he said, as he embraced me briefly and put his forehead to mine.

He didn't seem particularly excited about any of the gifts I gave him, or anything from the kids, or from my parents. He seemed out of it, detached and removed from the events of the morning. He barely touched his breakfast and, later that day, when everyone was over, he drank a lot of wine and listened to the commotion, but did not participate in any of the conversations. He didn't even want to play Pictionary! He loved Pictionary!

"What's up with Rob?" my sister-in-law, Celeste, asked me. "He's normally the life of the party."

"Yeah. I know. I guess, this year, he's the stick in the mud," I responded.

At some point the next day, I mentioned that all this going back and forth to Raleigh so much was too grueling. "Maybe you should go back to doing your previous accounts, which keeps you mainly around Rocky Mount with just the occasional trip to Greenville." The agents under him had done most of the travel in that region. Well, he got royally pissed off at me for suggesting it and, honestly, I was surprised by his angry reaction. Rob never raises his voice to the kids or me and he has certainly never talked to me like that. Dropping the "F" word on me, too! Twice! He never uses vulgar language around us and I was floored at how upset he was about it.

One of the nicest things about my husband's personality has always been that he doesn't have a hot head and he rarely, if ever, gets angry at anything. My mother used to say, "Rob is unflappable." He's always calm and cool, almost to a fault; and, while that can be a bit un-relatable for a Type A personality like me, it is truly one of those things about Rob that drew me to him for the long haul. He balances me out. I might not be a hot head, either, but, internally, I am stressed out all the time and I worry incessantly. Rob is a necessary part of my own internal peace and quiet.

He might be a good-looking man with ambition and confidence and intelligence and charm. But it's his kind demeanor, his sensitive manner, and the protective way that he cares for me that ultimately made me fall in love with him. Rob is a gentleman. He respects me, he respects his elders, and he respects women. While he has a lot of great qualities, the inherent respect and kindness within him is why I trusted him with my heart and vowed to him my very life as his wife. I gave up all of my own professional ambitions because I loved him that much.

Over the years, my female peers have been jealous of how good I have it.

"You're so lucky, Rita. You don't have to work and can be there for your kids' every scraped knee and sniffle," my friend Jackie once said to me early on.

"Yes, I'm lucky. I know."

"But even more than that, Rita. Everyone loves Rob. And everyone knows and can see how much Rob loves you. Most of us don't get to have anything like what you two have."

So yes, I do have it good. And I know it.

My suggestion about Raleigh being too much for

him was really more about how tired and irritable he seems lately. For the first time in the course of my marriage, I'm really worried about him. I hope he's not seriously sick or something.

SCOUT

Well into my second semester, I finally got to go see the Wolfpack play in a home game at Reynolds. I had been feeling a lot more alive and happy again ever since that day back in January when Rob came and found me in the library. It's crazy how all I needed to lift my spirits was one look at him. In an instant, my heart was revived and all of my shame and insecurities and fears and overall sadness, especially about Charlie, immediately went away.

Rob took me to a hotel that afternoon and we spent hours in there making up for all the time together we had missed. I don't think he left Raleigh until 7:00 at night.

As promised, he took me to a game. He decided that one of the best games for me to see would be the Duke game on a Wednesday night. State was good this season and a Coach K versus Coach V matchup would be especially memorable for my first game.

So off to Reynolds we went and, since he bought me a ticket, which I didn't need because I could get in as a student, I sat with him in the seat he paid for so we could be together. He was a little cautious because he didn't want anyone he might know seeing him there with me.

"Listen. During the game, we can't act like a couple. No kissing or handholding. For the next two hours, you're just a girl in the seat next to me. Okay?" he instructed me.

I nodded. I understood, of course.

Just as he said it would be, Reynolds Coliseum during a game was incredible. I had never been in an environment like that before. Baseball is outdoors, so it's a different kind of sports atmosphere. I've only been to a Durham Bulls game, anyway. Basketball in high school is in a small gym so it can get loud and exciting, but nothing like Reynolds.

State versus Duke was loud and rowdy and a lot fun. We won the game and, since it was nearing the end of the regular season and heading into the ACC tournament, the student body and the fans had an extra buzz to them all night. It was electric. I was so happy Rob made me do this and I couldn't wait to tell my daddy about it.

After the game, Rob still had an hour drive home so he'd get home late. He had no time to spare for me when it was over so it was a quick kiss in his car as he dropped me off. I didn't mind at all because I was on a winning high. It was different than a Rob high, but no less powerful. It reminded me why I loved sports so much and how much I missed playing them.

Charlie went off to Fort Benning and wouldn't graduate from all of his training until April sometime.

"My mom is going to drive all the way down here to

see me graduate," Charlie told me on the phone last week. "Your parents were going to come, too, but since your mom already had a commitment at the church and she couldn't bail on it, they decided to stay back. But they're sending a package of home-baked cookies for me."

"I wish I could be there, Charlie. I know your mom is so proud of you. We all are," I said, my heart torn in two. It was hard to talk to Charlie when I knew I was carrying on with Rob, living this big secret lie. "She wrote me a letter at school telling me about how much she had appreciated me and my parents all these years looking out for you and treating you like family."

"Yeah, she told me that she wrote you," he said, his voice a bit hoarse. "She says that she's getting along okay without me around."

"Well, I know she misses you. More than you'll ever know," I told him, knowing exactly what her letter said. It said that she missed him so much that some nights she found herself crying for no particular reason. I knew how she felt. I did the exact same thing. Not to mention the constant anxiety that I couldn't shake. I missed Charlie so much.

Why was I crying and feeling anxious again? Was it because Charlie was gone and I had only heard from him a few times? Once on the phone and the other times a couple of quick, scribbled letters telling me how much basic training sucked and how he wasn't sure he made the right decision. The more recent letters had been better than that, I guess.

Was I feeling like this because Charlie seemed so far away now and I didn't know when I'd ever see him again? Because I kissed him back at home and my feelings about him and Rob were so jumbled up? I knew I felt guilty because I was sure that I was in love with Rob and I was sure that I was in love with Charlie, too. But I'd never be good enough for either of them and I knew it.

Was I crying because Rob was married to a woman he loved and was telling me less and less lately that he loved me, too? That he seemed a little more interested in just having sex with me and not actually spending time with me, talking about stuff and having fun, and enjoying each other's company? That his kisses seemed less sincere than before and that he seemed to be going through the motions?

The Friday after the basketball game, Rob came to my dorm room in the late afternoon for us to be alone. Earlier in the week, he told me that he might not be able to come on Friday because of a commitment with his son, so I planned to watch *General Hospital* with the girls down the hall. Micaela was already gone for the weekend and I just got off work and felt grimy. Rob didn't seem to care that I wanted to take a shower. He immediately took off my clothes, then took off his clothes, and laid me down on my bed.

Because I had been feeling pretty insecure lately about the sense I was getting from him, I decided that I would try to talk to him after we were done. Well, he rolled off of me and, rather than lay there for a bit wrapped up together like we usually did, he got up, went over to the sink, and started to clean up. He was furiously washing himself, which he never did, so it scared me.

"Rob?" I said when he shut off the water. He was naked and beautiful. He needed a haircut because his hair had grown out quite a bit and was not looking as neat as usual. He wiped his hands on my small bath towel. "Hey," I said, trying to get his attention. He didn't seem to be with me in the room — not his head anyway.

So he looked over at me and I quickly slipped under the covers. I was very self-conscious about being naked in front of anyone, including this very man I'm in love with.

"What is it?" he asked me.

"Is everything okay?" I asked, cautiously.

He nodded his head yes.

"Are you okay with me? With this?" I asked him.

"Yeah, why?"

"I don't know. Just weird a feeling, I guess," I said.

Then he grinned a devilish smile and came over to the bed, got in under the covers, and started playfully biting my neck and making monster noises. He adopted a fake Dracula accent and started saying, "Scout, I vant to suck your blood..." and making little sucking noises on my cheeks. "I loooove your cheeks," he laughed.

I laughed uncontrollably because he was tickling me to death. Then he stopped and started kissing me passionately, like the many times he had before, and then kissed me all over the place. It put all of my gut feelings and fears to bed. At least for the rest of that day.

CHARLIE

Sitting on the floor of my barracks, I started cleaning my equipment. We'd just gotten back from a field training exercise, and my LBE, or Load Bearing Equipment, was caked with mud. I was finishing up my advanced training at Fort Benning and looking forward to the two weeks of leave I'd get to take right before I reported to my new duty station. I was assigned to the 24th Infantry Division at Fort Stewart, Georgia, the mechanized infantry, 11M or, as we called it, "Eleven Mike."

Boot camp sucked, but 11M school was great. I liked it a lot and looked forward to my first real assignment at my new permanent duty station. It wasn't getting me out of the country or even getting me out of the South, but at least it got me out of North Carolina.

When I first told my mom of my decision to go into the Army, she was surprised. I was making good money as a full time mechanic at Lee Webb Automotive, but I think she understood that, with Scout gone and no girlfriend anymore, there was no reason why I shouldn't get out of Haddleboro, too. I felt bad at first because I always thought it was my responsibility to be there for her and take care of her.

"No, Charlie. It ain't your responsibility or your place to do that. You're now a grown man and you need to go live your own life," she explained to me as she potted a plant in a huge ceramic bowl she made in a pottery class at the community college.

"But you'll be all alone, Mom. You've always had me."

"Charlie, I'm a big girl. And even though I'll miss you like the dickens, I will always be here for you. You always have a home here with me."

My mom wrote me letters while I was away and they helped me get through the long, hard days of no sleep and getting hollered at all the time. And, as she promised before she went back to State at Christmas, Scout wrote me, too. She wrote me a lot. She told me in her first letter that every Tuesday and Thursday would be her "write Charlie day" and she actually scheduled it into her homework and studying time. That made me feel good, knowing that she still cared so much about me. It had me thinking maybe that kiss meant to her what it meant to me: everything.

I was only able to write her a couple of times because of how busy I'd been. There wasn't any down time to write much in basic training, but during 11M school, I was able to do so more frequently. Scout seemed like she was doing okay, but her letters were not her usual, upbeat self. She seemed to be overwhelmed with her workload in school, her classes, and her job. And she also seemed to be lonely. I felt bad because there was nothing I could do about anything. If I could be at State with her, we would hang out together all the time and I bet that would've made her feel not so alone or overwhelmed anymore. It's a good feeling to share your burdens with someone who loves you.

She mentioned having a couple of girls that she knew down the hall, but, really, it seemed like she wasn't having a good time in college. She didn't have much of a social life that I could tell and the one club she joined earlier, she said she dropped out of it.

Before high school, Scout was real social. We were always out playing with other kids and being invited over people's houses, cuttin' up and all. She had lots of friends in school, too, but I was always her best friend. Then, when she went to high school, she kept to herself. While she did keep busy playing sports all four years, she wasn't friends with any of her teammates and it looked like I was her only friend in the whole world. Some of the girls were whispering that she was probably a lesbian or something. That pissed me off because it wasn't true.

But no one invited her to stuff anymore and, if she wasn't with me, she was all by herself. It wasn't like the other kids didn't like her or anything like that — people always thought Scout was a nice girl — it was more like nobody thought of her much like they did when we were younger.

But she always had me. I loved her. No matter how many girls I've met and how many girlfriends I've had for a spell, no one was Scout Webb or ever would be. When she first went off to State, I missed her like crazy, but I was also happy for her because she needed to meet some new people and make new friends. And she did.

"Charlie, it's so great. A bunch of the girls on the hall get together three times a week to do Jane Fonda aerobics tapes. They all have different color leg warmers," she wrote to me early on. I didn't understand the purpose of leg warmers. It seemed strange to me that women would exercise with little tube shaped sweaters on their legs. "We'll watch movies and soap operas in the afternoons during the week. And I joined a tutoring club that helps the children in the school near the campus. And I really like the ladies I work with at Marty's Place."

I took all of this in when I went to see her that one time in late September. Scout seemed like she was branching out more and I was happy for her. Then, when she came home for her break, she just seemed different, sad and lonely, like she was back in high school.

Once long ago, I tried to talk to her about what was up with her, why she wasn't as outgoing as she used to be.

"I'm just focusing on trying not to be such a sinner all the time. I need to stay in God's good graces," she said, tying her shoes before we headed out to school one morning.

"What's that mean?" I asked her.

"Nothing," she said, standing up. "Ready to go?"

I didn't know what that meant because I never knew

Scout to be anything other than the best girl in the world.

"Private Porter!" SSG Davis, my drill sergeant, ripped me from my thoughts.

"Yes, Drill Sergeant!" I replied forcefully, standing up at attention.

"Top wants to speak with you," he said, his voice back to a normal tone.

I got a little bit sick in my stomach at the thought of that. What the hell have I done?

"Go stand outside of his office, knock on his door and, when he tells you to enter, follow his orders," SSG Davis instructed me. "Dismissed."

I walked out of the barracks and over to the company's headquarters building. Soldiers were milling about and I intently looked for the room housing the Charlie Company leadership. I always thought it was awesome that I was assigned to Charlie Company.

I saw "1SG Zaharchuk" and "SFC Dillard" — my company first sergeant and senior drill sergeant — written on a piece of paper attached to the outside of one door. Standing outside, I knocked with authority, even though I was about to puke. 1SG Zaharchuk has never said anything to me in the thirteen weeks I've been here.

"Enter," I heard someone say.

So I walked in and, standing at attention, said, "Private Porter reporting as ordered, First Sergeant."

"At ease, Private Porter," 1SG Zaharchuk commanded.

I stood at ease and he started to speak. "I wanted to let you know that the cadre has selected you as our company's honor graduate for this class. You have exceeded all the standards in every aspect of your training and, overall, you are our top-ranked soldier in the entire company." He stopped speaking for a few beats as he watched me take that in.

Then he continued, "Private, this is a good thing. You will receive your first Army Commendation and that goes in your permanent file."

He came from around his desk and stood in front of me. "Congratulations. You've earned it. You will be recognized at the graduation ceremony on Saturday. Will anyone from your family be there? A girl maybe?"

"No girl, First Sergeant, but my mother will be there," I responded, my heart not quite sure if it was happy or sad or both because, while my mom would be there, Scout wouldn't be.

"Do you have any questions of me?"

"No, First Sergeant."

"Private Porter, I rarely come across a young man in my training company who I have such high hopes for. I hope you want to make the Army a career because you'd make an outstanding leader and we need outstanding leaders, especially in the infantry. It shouldn't be long until you're back here at the NCO Academy. You keep up all your hard work. Dismissed."

I snapped to attention, about-faced, and headed out of his office.

My mom would be here on Saturday for graduation and I couldn't wait to see her. I loved my mom so much and I know she'll be so proud of me for finishing my training and getting an honor like this. We both knew that the best thing for me was to break away from home and go do something meaningful with my life. This would only bolster those beliefs. This was good. This was right. She didn't want me to stay in Haddleboro just because of her. She was always a lot stronger than I'd given her credit for.

When I got back to the barracks, I immediately walked over to my footlocker, pulled out some paper and my pen, and wrote Scout to tell her all about what just happened.

ROB

As much as I cannot believe I'm thinking this, I've started feeling like the toll of the almost-daily trek to Raleigh is getting to me. No one tells you, when you decide to go ahead and live a double life, that trying to balance a busy family, a very challenging work schedule which has you on the road a lot, and then a beautiful, young, and nothing-but-sweet-and-good-to-me college girl on the side, starts to get exhausting.

Things between Rita and I have been strained since we had the big argument at Christmas. We don't argue much as a couple at all and I'm sure it's because I let her have her way all the time. It's easier that way. So the relatively few times we've fought over the years have tended to be pretty bad. The one at Christmas was right up there with the worst we've ever had.

Since then, she's been cold and distant toward me all while claiming that I've been cold and distant toward her. It's been nothing but a big, unbreakable circle with nobody budging or giving in and choosing *not* to be cold and distant. It's been several weeks since we've had sex and, other than when she was recovering from childbirth or using her little sexual manipulation over me in order to get her way, I don't think we've ever gone this long without it.

"You're moody and not yourself at all," she said abruptly to me the other morning in our bathroom, as she lathered up some lotion onto her long legs and I shaved my face in the mirror. "Maybe you should go get checked out by a doctor or something."

"I don't know what the fuck for," I retorted sharply.

"Dear God, Rob. Language. That's exactly what I'm talking about. Who are you?"

What is a doctor going to diagnose me with? Boredom? Adultery? A mid-life crisis? Caring too much about a nineteen-year-old girl? Being a completely stupid, selfish, shithead?

When I took over Jim's accounts, I hadn't thought it all through. It was just a spur-of-the-moment decision, knowing that it would get me to Raleigh. When I decided to take them on, I didn't know if Scout would have wanted to have dinner with me. That was how…just…taken by her I had been. Enamored. I was so stupid for making a major work decision on feelings. Am I even still a man then?

But my impulsive decision worked and, because of it, I got to see Scout a lot more than I thought I would. But Jim's accounts still included debit routes and getting the small cash payments each week from low-income people with small policies. It was so tedious and time consuming and ridiculous for an experienced manager and agent like me to be doing. There was a reason why the new blood did the debit routes. I think Jim's original idea had been to try to get a satellite office set up in Raleigh, but the company, a family-owned agency, wasn't ready to make that big of a leap yet. So Jim hustled all the time and lived with his commute. He also doesn't have a wife or family.

Rita's not stupid. She knew that taking on the debit routes was such an out-of-this-world concept at this point in my career. Her hammering me for spending each Monday wrapped up doing it instead of handing it off to a new guy was actually a valid complaint. But it was a complaint that I blew off because I knew that if I handed them off, it would be one less day with my State girl.

I've been trying to manage all of this chaos for too long now and I knew that something had to give. Scout was always so happy to see me and she treated me like I was the only thing that she had in the world. She rarely ever talked about her own family back home anymore and the only thing I heard about her friend named Charlie was that he had gone into the Army and she never heard from him. But she always wanted to know what was going on with me and my family, what my kids were doing, how my wife was doing. Almost like she felt like she was a part of it somehow.

I felt bad for Scout sometimes and other times I'd get so overwhelmed by my feelings about her that I wanted to eat her up and keep her with me all the time. She was so good to me: never giving me any shit about anything, never demanding anything from me, never complaining to me about failing her in some way.

"You know, you should join a softball team or do something fun with your friends," she said to me last week, as I held her soft and naked in her bed. Her hands were wrapped in with mine tightly and my right foot caressed her legs gently. "I bet you could still hit a ball pretty far."

I brushed her hair, which rested on my cheek, with my lips.

When I turned forty a couple of months ago, and I told Scout it was my birthday, she cupped my face into her hands and said, "You don't look close to being forty at all."

I kissed her lips and said, "Thanks for saying that, little girl."

"You don't! You look so much younger than my daddy."

That made me cringe. Then she realized how awkward that came off and started giving me little quick kisses all over my face. "You are *so* much better looking than Mickey Rourke. There's just *no* comparison."

She was never nasty to me if I had to break our plans because of some family or work reason. Everything about my relationship with Scout was easy. She made me feel carefree and at ease whenever I was with her. But her actual presence in my life also made it really, really difficult sometimes.

For a guy, I've always been in-tune with my own feelings. I certainly don't talk about them with anyone, but

I do know how I feel. And what I know is that I love Scout. I really do. My feelings for her are genuine and real and, to me, she is not some fling or an affair or a piece of ass. I know several guys who have their pieces of ass every now and then with their wives and kids at home. This is different. Scout's a girl who has my heart.

However, the truth is that I also love my wife. There are different kinds of love and I don't love Scout like I love Rita. I don't think I could, either, just because Rita and I have so many years invested in each other. We have such a long and blended history. The love we share is the kind that builds a life together and lasts and is strong.

If I met Scout when I was in college, then I bet I would've easily chosen to build a life and have this same kind of love with her instead. We fit. I knew it on the first night I took her for Brunswick stew and hushpuppies. I mean, I know that I should feel guilty about carrying on with her behind my wife's back, but I don't. Not at all. I've never felt like this was wrong. She's made me so happy. So how could it be wrong?

But the timing. What's the cliché? "Timing is everything." This whole thing just isn't reality. Reality is that I'm married — to Rita — and I love her. I'm not going to leave her to be with Scout. So what the fuck am I doing?

Scout has just about a month or so of classes left and then she is heading back to Haddleboro for the summer.

"I got my old job back at the Piggly Wiggly and I'm

gonna take off every Monday in order to come to Raleigh to see you!" she said excitedly awhile back when we talked about how difficult it would be to be separated for a few months.

"You're going to bust your ass six days a week making $3.35 an hour and then spend that money on gas and wear and tear on that Rabbit just to get up here to see me?" I outlined to her, trying to show her how crazy that sounded.

She nodded with those big brown eyes, which held all the trust in the world in me. "Of course I am. I can't go so long without not seeing you or talking to you. Christmas break about killed me!"

I pulled her into me. How can I not appreciate all the genuine heart and love for me that is within that sweet doll? And how can I actually consider letting that go?

But I know I have to. I can't continue to live like this.

Maybe she won't be able to do it and then maybe it will be easier for me to go ahead and wean myself off of her — and her body — and all the love she shows me — and her body — Jesus, that will not be easy at all! Who am I kidding?

Maybe it can end naturally and peacefully, nobody getting hurt, especially Rita and my kids. If Scout really loves me like she says she does, she will understand. We aren't in the same situations in life. We're in two different places. She is so young, with her whole life ahead of her. I'm forty years old, entrenched and entangled with so many things — and those things are all in Rocky Mount.

I won't talk to her about this stuff until it needs to be talked about. We will just enjoy each other for remaining time we have.

RITA

Rob and I have been in a stalemate for months. I don't ever recall things being so tense and difficult between us for this long. Maybe he doesn't notice the issues because he is a man and somehow this kind of thing just goes over his head and he has no idea what is going on or maybe he's just so wrapped up in this going back and forth to Raleigh and all the work related to it that he's forgotten that he has a family that needs his attention, too.

Every year for the past four years, Rob has been a coach for Chase's recreational baseball team and, before that, he coached his Little League and even tee ball teams. Because he was an intercollegiate-level recruit for pitching, and pitching was what got him to State, I would say that my husband knows something about the sport of baseball and about pitching, in particular.

Chase also plays varsity high school baseball in the spring and Rob has helped out with the pitchers there when he is able to. He goes to every game and practice he can and is very helpful to the boys by teaching these young players how to become better at their craft. Baseball has been a great father-son bonding activity for Chase's entire childhood. And Rob loved it because it allowed him to be involved with the one thing that he has truly loved his whole life. Baseball was also the one piece of his own father that he was able to carry with him since his father died of a heart attack, while umpiring a baseball game, when Rob was only thirteen years old. So, to say that baseball was just a hobby to my husband would be a complete misrepresentation of the truth.

Well, this is the first year that Rob is doing nothing with baseball.

"Why aren't you going to coach with the recreational team this year?" I asked him a few weeks ago, as we stood in the kitchen.

Rob opened the refrigerator, pulled out a beer and said, "He is seventeen years old now and he doesn't need me around for his rec-level team. He's only doing that for extra playing time anyway."

But then not even helping out with the varsity team? That blew my mind. It was so out of character for Rob to have absolutely nothing to do with Chase's baseball. He has come to most of the games so far, but he has also missed more games this season than in the last five years combined! He might think that Chase doesn't care, but that is not true at all. Chase notices and Chase cares.

Thankfully, Samantha's activities are more on the artistic side and she isn't interested in sports. It doesn't require much of a physical presence for a parent to look at her paintings once in a while or attend a play one Friday night. If Rob can't find the time to participate in Chase's one main activity, then I suppose Samantha would be lucky to even get a glance at this point. She has been going through her confirmation classes and is supposed to be confirmed in the Catholic Church in June.

"I wonder if you will be too busy to attend your own daughter's confirmation next month!" I said to him late last night, when he silently snuck into bed, thinking I was already asleep. "You had better step it up because my whole family is coming down for this and we have a huge cookout to plan for everyone."

He just grunted, "Okay."

Rob leaves early every morning and, most days, or at least it seems like most days, he comes home after dinnertime. He is always meeting someone he knows in Raleigh for dinner or trying to go to a basketball game or God knows what else that keeps him there so late. If I didn't trust him, and if I didn't know my husband, I would've thought that he had another woman on the side!

Today, I have to go to Raleigh and it wasn't at all planned. I hardly ever go to Raleigh and, when I do, it's not during the week. I'm meeting my old college roommate, Gail, for lunch in Cameron Village. It's been so long since I've seen her. She has been living in Chicago for the last fifteen years with her husband who is a patent attorney, but she recently came back to Raleigh to help her mother who was diagnosed with MS. She's only going to be here for a month so we decided to get together to catch up and share photos. She has three children, all under the age of ten, so I know she is going to have some stories to share with me.

I didn't think to tell Rob about my lunch date with Gail this morning when he rolled out of bed at the crack of dawn. I have rides arranged for both Samantha and Chase after school, even though I should be home in time to take care of getting them myself. They both have their own house key and I left them some cash to get a pizza delivered from Rocco's if, for some reason, I'm delayed at dinnertime.

Looking in the mirror in my beautiful bathroom with white and black accents, I began my morning ritual of face wash, face cream, and my Estée Lauder makeup application. Aging is no fun. I'm turning forty in November and the thought of that makes me feel ancient. Thankfully, I don't have any gray showing yet, but, because my hair is so dark, it will be the first big, loud sign of middle age when it does happen.

I've been fortunate to be blessed with good genes. I'm tall with long legs, which Rob loves wrapped around him in the bathtub. And I'm lucky that I don't have to exercise very much in order to keep my figure thin. A lot of my friends have put on weight that they claim they cannot get off. "Not even aerobics helps," they tell me. I've never had that problem.

I have my mother's blue eyes which Rob says is my

most beautiful feature. He's also told me, although certainly not lately, that when he dies, he hopes it is while drowning in the blue ocean of my eyes. I would normally think a comment like that to be terribly morbid, but the way Rob says it, and the way he looks at me when he says it, it is absolutely one of the most erotic things I've ever heard in my life.

Brushing my thick and wavy hair, I pin the sides into a lovely clip in the back. And after making my face as pretty as possible, I put on a simple black skirt, a white blouse, hose, and black pumps. If I had been brave and gone after my dreams back in 1970, undeterred by an unplanned pregnancy, this would probably look a lot like my work outfit for a high-powered job in the financial district in some big city. By now, I'd be wearing shoulder pads like the women I see on the news. But no, I chose love and family. I chose Rob.

I said a prayer before leaving. "God, please let things get better between us soon. I miss him."

SCOUT

Today, I got off of work at 3:00 because Felicia had to leave early. One of her kids got sick at school and I covered the rest of her shift until Judy got in. So I was late getting out of there and late meeting Rob. He called me at Marty's at about 2:30 when I still hadn't showed up to my dorm and I explained the situation. He understood, of course. He is so sweet and good to me. How did I get so lucky?

Rob told me, when I got off work, to come right over to La Dolce's in Cameron Village. He knew that I had finals coming up and wanted to feed me a late lunch or early supper, spend a little alone time after, and then head home early to be able to have supper with his family. So when I got off, I drove right over to La Dolce's.

I was pretty excited because I've never eaten there before, but I was in my stupid waitress outfit and felt like an idiot. La Dolce's was a nice restaurant. This time of day, though, it wouldn't be overrun with fancy diners — at least, I didn't think it would be.

School was ending soon and I would be heading back to Haddleboro for the summer. My parents were coming this weekend to help me move back. I already told Rob that I was going to drive to Raleigh every Monday to spend the afternoon with him. The thought of this separation and not getting to be with him very often was too much for me to bear, so I mostly put it out of my head and thought of his lips kissing mine instead.

The time we were apart over Christmas sent me into a deep depression. I couldn't go through that again. At least with this plan, I would always have Monday to look forward to each week. When I came back to school in August, we could continue seeing each other like we have been since November.

Last month, Charlie and his mom came up to see me in Raleigh. He was done with his training down in Georgia and was on two weeks of vacation before he had to report to his new Army post, also apparently in Georgia. It was a Saturday and Ms. Porter was like a whole new person. She had her hair done real nice and she looked like she was taking better care of herself. She didn't smoke one cigarette the whole time we were together. Charlie was still Charlie, but there was something different about him.

"You seem so much older," I said to him, while we waited for Ms. Porter to come out of the ladies' room.

"I do?" he asked, a little embarrassed, looking down at his perfectly spit-shined shoes.

"Yeah, you look more mature and very successful standing there in your fancy green uniform." I flicked his hair. "All your moppy, sandy hair is so short now." God, he was so cute.

Observing Charlie, all tall and lean and handsome in that uniform, I was so happy for him and full of pride. He had been selected as the best soldier in his whole unit and, while it was no surprise to me that he was, he seemed awfully surprised himself and very humbled by it. There was nothing boastful about Charlie. He was always so shy about people bragging on him. It was part of his sweet charm and more evidence of his kind and gentle soul. Yet another reason why everybody loved Charlie.

We had had a nice day together. Ms. Porter bought us lunch at the Chick-fil-A in the mall and she was so proud as she walked next to her Army son in uniform. It was almost as if Charlie's success had revived her. Ms. Porter was always such a sweet lady with a sad face and it was great to see her this cheerful for a change. I know she had a hard life and it looked like she was enjoying every single second of Charlie being home. Because soon enough, he was off back to the Army and no one knew when he'd be home again.

We never got to spend any time alone together and I know that he wanted to talk to me about what happened at Christmas between us. But I didn't want to deal with it because I had no idea what it meant myself. And if I talked about it and revealed my true feelings about him in any way whatsoever, I'd feel guilty about that, too. I knew I was in love with Rob. Plus, Charlie was just too good for me. I could never be the kind of girl he deserved to have.

Charlie knew nothing about Rob. No one did, other than Micaela and a couple of girls on my hall, and of course Felicia, who did not approve at all and made it her mission in life to convince me that he did not have my best interests at heart, was using me for his own sexual gratification, and would dump me in a heartbeat. He would never do that to me. He's even told me that he'd never do that to me.

Pulling into the Cameron Village parking lot, I saw Rob's car and pulled in next to him. I had butterflies in my stomach. He still made me tremble, even after all these months. The anticipation of seeing him made me so happy inside. Nothing else mattered.

Rob got out of the car and came over to my driver's side. He opened my door and when I tried to get out, he leaned in and kissed me, grabbing my hands. Then he pulled me out of the car and into himself, wrapped his hands around my waist and up my back and kissed me like I've just returned from a long trip. We were full on making out, all on display in Cameron Village, which is something I'm normally too shy to do in public. But since I was so caught up in him, I did it anyway.

Then he finally stopped and put his forehead against mine and said, smirking, "You smell so tasty, like barbecue." He was right. I did.

"You smell…like you," I said, sniffing his neck. God, I loved how he smelled.

Then he asked, "Are you hungry?"

Reading his mind, I replied, "Yes, for you."

"Let's just have some Ramen noodles back in your room."

He kissed me again and we both got back into our cars and drove over to campus as fast as we could.

Ramen noodles never sounded so good.

ROB

I knew my time with Scout was short and the thought of it was starting to eat me alive inside. I didn't want it end. I wanted to keep her, keep seeing her, keep talking to her, and keep making love to her whenever humanly possible. She made me feel so good whenever I'm with her and, for a while now, when I'm at home or work, I don't feel so good anymore.

I'm on my own a lot, so my office relationships aren't any fun. At home, no one has much to say and I don't know if it's because the kids are teenagers and that's how teenagers are — or if it's something else. And Rita is all frigid and snippy toward me all the time, making me feel like nothing I do is good enough. But she's right. It hasn't been. I haven't been there for her or the kids, physically or with what's going on in my head.

Chase has been wrapped up in his baseball season and I've been too busy with work — and Scout — to coach this year. That's another reason why I need to let Scout go. I have to get myself back on a normal work schedule so I can do the things I need to do with my son. If he wants to play college ball at State or anywhere else, I have to help him navigate that maze. I know his coaches would help him, but I'm his fucking father and I've been through the whole process myself. It's my job to help my own son.

Pretty soon, Rita's whole family will down here for Samantha's confirmation. That will be a week-long ordeal and, while Rita is the best hostess and party planner in the world, she needs my help. I enjoy helping her with things like this. We've always been a great team in any project we take on, especially party projects.

Rita needs me to be her husband again. My kids need me to be their father again.

I know all of this is true and right and exactly what I need to be doing, but it doesn't make my impending break up with Scout any easier. I love her. And I know she loves me, too. And I know I will be breaking not only my own heart, but hers, as well. And she doesn't deserve that.

And what will she do? Will she go crazy and tell Rita about us and then ruin my life?

Putting all of this depressing shit out of my head, I parked my car, and Scout and I walked to her dorm, hand-in-hand. I looked at her ponytail bouncing in the sunlight and said, "I can't wait to get you up there." I knew that this was going to be one of the last times, if not *the* last time that I would be able to be with her like this and I wanted to show her how much I cared about her.

Timing is everything.

RITA

And there, in the sunniest part of the Carolina daylight, on a Wednesday in early May, real life clocks me in the face and then punches me in the gut. Rob Caralessi, my husband, partner, and best friend for almost twenty years now, is passionately kissing a woman in a parking lot in front of an Italian restaurant in Cameron Village.

I just left a different restaurant after having a long, late lunch with my friend Gail. We got all caught up with each other and it was like no time had passed since we'd last been together. We simply picked up where we left off. I was feeling so good about our reunion and couldn't wait to see Rob tonight to tell him about it, even planning to suggest that we all go to Chicago this summer to visit her and her family for vacation. None of us had ever been to Chicago and we could have a wonderful and memorable Caralessi road trip like we did in the past. He knew Gail very well in college and always thought very highly of her.

The restaurant where we dined was directly across the street from where my Rob was standing kissing this... woman?...girl?...who had a long brown ponytail and was wearing an abhorrent, pale-colored dress. If we went to a different place, like we originally planned, I never would have seen this.

Is this some sick joke from God? Is this how he answers my obviously ill-conceived prayer from earlier today?

At first, I didn't think it was Rob because my Rob would never do this. My Rob was different than some of my friends' husbands who ran around on them while they did all the dirty work of staying home to raise their children and make a home or did both: work all day in a career and then come home to do everything at home as well.

My Rob was not that guy. My Rob respected me. He respected women. He respected himself. He respected family and the concept of fidelity and he believed in our union, which had been approved by God Himself. My Rob would not be kissing a strange woman in public and certainly not like he was about to rip her ugly dress off!

Feeling like I was watching a horror movie, I suddenly smelled popcorn. Then I felt like I ate too much popcorn slathered in that greasy butter from the movie theatre. I opened the door of my car, leaned over, and vomited my overpriced lunch onto the pavement. A man walking by was startled. "Are you okay, ma'am?" I slammed shut the door and looked again over at the gut-wrenching scene unfolding in front of me.

I watched them each get into their respective cars and drive off one behind the other. So I did what any scorned woman, currently in the throes of shock, would do and followed them on a stakeout.

They drove onto the State campus and each parked in what appeared to be some kind of student parking lot. Then they got out of their cars and walked — holding hands! — to a residence hall. Yes, if my memory served me correctly — and it's been years — that was one of the newer facilities when I was a student here. And then, as if the word "fuck" has been in my daily vocabulary all along, I said out loud to myself in the car, "He is fucking a college student," just to be sure that this was all real and I was not in a bad dream.

My Rob and his college whore disappeared from sight. And I was faced with my worst nightmare. In all of my life, I never would've believed that my husband would be unfaithful to me. Ever.

All I wanted to do was run out of the car and chase them down and scream at this little slut in the — let's face it, outright offensive — dress and then punch Rob until his face was bloody. How could he do this to me? To our family?

I sat in my car, and with tears streaming down my face, I went ahead and cried like a baby, something I haven't done since the death of my beloved grandfather in 1975.

*****

I didn't know what to do or how to handle this situation. It was 5:00 and I had been sitting here in this spot for an hour and a half. My mascara was dried to my cheeks and I had no more tears left in me. By now, Samantha would be home by herself, probably starting her homework. Chase would arrive by 6:30, after his baseball practice was over. I knew that my kids, at this moment, were okay and did not need me.

But I needed someone. Or something. A gun would've been convenient to have right now. I actually understood why some people lose their minds and kill their spouses' lovers. Or kill their spouses. It all made perfect sense to me.

How long has this been going on and I hadn't a clue? I knew Rob was different, stressed out, but this? And with, for all intents and purposes, a child? She couldn't have been much older than Chase, for God's sake! Rob had been running himself ragged with this Raleigh changeover since November. Was it so he could see this girl? Or did the girl happen after the changeover?

I had so many questions and so many things that were running through my mind. And then I saw Rob walking alone back toward the parking lot where his car sat.

Opening my door, I got out of the driver's seat. With hose over my bare feet, my pumps long ago having been thrown into the back, I walked right over to where we would intersect. As soon as he saw me, he stopped, mouth agape, eyes wide.

He was caught. And he knew it.

SCOUT

I always feel so blissful and content when I'm with Rob. He makes me feel beautiful, wanted, and loved. And then he leaves and I don't see him for a day or sometimes two days and I start to feel disgusting, dirty, and like a whore, which is exactly what I am. Picturing Cammy DeHaan's angry face and Brother Doug's blank dismissal of me, I shut my eyes to try to squeeze the eternally emblazoned images out of my memory.

When I'm with him, we are a couple: two people in love who belong together and who should be in their own bed and their own kitchen. When he is at home with his family, we are just another ugly lie in this world: a dirty little secret to be kept hidden with all its pain and misery awaiting its day of bloom from the soil.

It's a warm spring day here in Haddleboro. My mom's flower garden in front of our little old house is full and colorful. The grass is green and the trees are fat with leaves and blossoms again. I haven't been home since January, so seeing it all pretty like this fills me with nostalgia of my truly happy days, which seem so long ago. I actually feel like I've aged ten years since I've been gone.

I got home yesterday afternoon and my parents helped me move all of my stuff from my dorm back into my bedroom at home. It was an easy enough transition. I worked my last shift at Marty's Place two days ago and Felicia gave me her phone number.

"You call me sometime to chat. If you get to Raleigh, you come see me." Then she hugged me tight and kissed my cheeks when I was leaving. "I will miss you, sweet little Scout."

"I'll miss you too, Fee," I said hugging her tightly.

I liked having an older friend like her. She treated me like she really cared about me. I said goodbye to Micaela, who was a nice roommate to have because she was neat, clean, and hardly ever there. She also didn't judge me or say anything about Rob and then make me feel like a slut. We signed up to stay roommates in the dorm next year, too.

I thought for sure that Rob would come see me at least one last time before I left for home, but he didn't. It's really strange and I've developed a sick, anxious feeling in my gut that just won't go away. It has nothing to do with me missing him so much, which I do, but more to do with this unsettled feeling that something is wrong and he isn't telling me.

He has always assured me that everything was fine whenever I'd ask him. But this time is extra weird. This past Wednesday, we spent a truly wonderful afternoon together with all the passion and excitement of our first times together back in the fall. Then he left and I haven't even received a call from him. I tried calling him at work on Friday to remind him that I was leaving the next day, but he wasn't there. So something had to be wrong. Rob wouldn't *not* say goodbye to me. Would he?

It's been three days and I feel strangely deserted. I arranged to have off on Mondays to go up to see him. I haven't told my parents of this plan, but I have no way to confirm with him if I can't get in touch with him. So I'm going to just call him Monday morning at work and, if all was okay, I would go up there.

But something inside of me knew that things weren't at all fine. Something inside of me knew that things hadn't been fine for a while. My gut instincts would ring on and off over the last couple of months and, whenever I'd feel paranoid enough, I'd ask him about us. And he would say all was "fine" and then be especially attentive and sweet and loving to put my mind and heart at ease. And because I trusted him, and believed the things he would tell me, I would feel better, but only for a short time until the gut feelings started singing to me again.

I had a couple of days to myself before starting work at the Piggly Wiggly and one of my first natural responses to being home was to go over to Charlie's. My body was just accustomed to hopping on my bike or hopping in a car to zip over there. But then it hit me that this summer would be the first time since I can remember that I would not be with Charlie. At all. So between the awful doom-and-gloom feeling that was festering beneath the surface of my heart about Rob and the sudden slap in the face that there would be no TV watchin', front porch swing settin', Jasper Lake fishin', lunchtime visitin', bluegrass concert attendin', or late night star gazin' — all Charlie and Scout summertime livin' — I got pretty down and out.

Feeling totally alone, I decided to take a walk into downtown Haddleboro just to be outside and bring some kind of calm to my internal storm, now brewing at a feverish level.

"I'm gonna go for a walk into town. Do you need anything?" I asked my mom who was washing a few dishes in the kitchen.

She looked over at me and then opened the kitchen window in front of her.

"No, hon, that's alright. We're good. But if you see Miss Nelly outside her house on your walk, tell her I said 'hey.'"

I walked out, the screen door slamming behind me, and started rambling down our street. We lived in an old neighborhood where the houses were spaced out along a side gravel road, which eventually leads to a main road. All of our homes were a dusty white or pastel color, two floors, with big wrap around porches. We had an acre of land to ourselves and Daddy hated having to mow so much. He had Jonny take over that job a few years ago.

Once you get to the main road, you turn left and walk along the side, hoping no one will fly by too fast and knock you into the ditch. Just before you get into the downtown part of Haddleboro, there are some side streets leading into town. Charlie lives — lived — on the second street that had about ten old, red brick duplex-type houses on it, one after the other. Those houses had hardly any land around them, but they did have little front stoops and a small shed in the postage stamp back yard. Ms. Porter has rented her side of the duplex from her neighbor, Mr. Cullen, for Charlie's whole life.

Walking farther, you come across the town baseball field and then, after about a full mile and a half from my house, you get into the downtown part of Haddleboro, which has one stop light and all the basics: Piggly Wiggly, a breakfast restaurant called Casper's, a burger and barbecue place called Annie's Home Cooking, Dale's General Store, the First Baptist Church of Haddleboro, Markham's Hardware Store, and the Haddleboro Drug Store. We had one gas station, a small sandwich shop — which also served Hershey's ice cream and made the best milkshakes this side of the Mason Dixon Line — a Methodist Church, a Lutheran Church, a barber shop and a beauty shop, and Lee Webb Automotive. Ms. Porter worked at the hardware store.

As you go even farther down the main part of town, there was a small set of buildings that had the courthouse and sheriff's office in there, as well as some other government offices: the school offices, the post office, and the place you go to register for events and sports. And then there was the library, the elementary school, and some other small places: a used car dealership, a convenience store, a field where they had the farmer's market every Saturday and Sunday, the Senior Center, and the community college. And like most little southern towns, there was a black section, where most of the black folks lived. They had their own small grocery store and many attended the AME church with its happy and loud praise and worship songs. Unlike our church, the AME church's services seemed to go on all afternoon, long past Sunday dinner.

The high school wasn't near downtown. It was another three miles away. Charlie and I used to have to get up at 6:00 in the morning just to catch our bus.

The farther you got from the downtown area, the emptier the spaces were. There were a lot of small farms and good country folk who lived here, their families' blood running as deep as the red clay for generations. My mom's people were from here, but Daddy was from another town called Reidsville, up in the northern part of the state.

Growing up in a place like Haddleboro kept us young and innocent — until we weren't either young or innocent anymore. It's funny how you don't appreciate the place where you grew up until you leave it for a while. Being in a city is really exciting and all, but it's not personal there, even if the people are still friendly. It's different. In Haddleboro, everybody knows us Webbs and we know everybody. I actually liked it like that.

Taking in the smell of burgers on a grill somewhere, I walked upon a lemonade stand. Clay and Hannah Barwell were selling cups of it for a nickel each. They both attended my church and Hannah was pretty good with a fiddle. Handing her a dime, I said, "Keep the change."

"Thanks, Scout!" she said happily. It doesn't take a whole lot to please an eight year old.

Then I walked over to my church. I hadn't stepped foot in there for quite a while. The last time I attended a service was at Christmas. When Easter Sunday came around, I avoided going home and didn't even bother to go to one of the services at a church near campus. God seemed so far away from me anymore, like an old friend who moved away and never wrote or called after He promised that He would.

While I have nothing but good memories of my church days and the people who go there, I've been lost where God is concerned. I know part of the reason is because of how I've been acting and, if the Rapture came tonight, I wondered if I would be taken up with my family. Certainly, God wouldn't want anything to do with an unrepentant Jezebel like me. And it's not only the embarrassment and shame of knowing what kind of a girl I truly am and then having to face Him and explain myself on Judgment Day, but I'm also mad at God. I don't pray anymore and I haven't for a long time now. I can't quite put my finger on why exactly I'm so mad at Him. He didn't make me choose to have sex with Brother Doug and go running around with Rob. He didn't make me a whore who falls in love with other women's husbands. He didn't make me a sinner. I made myself a sinner. I'm just a lowly wretch, like in the song, "Amazing Grace." I don't deserve His mercy or forgiveness, just as I was taught in Sunday school.

Mr. Gaskins, an elderly man wearing a green tee shirt and denim overalls, who was always taking care of the church cemetery, was picking weeds near a headstone. He looked up at me, the sun directly in his old blue-green eyes.

"Well, I'll be. Scout Webb, how you?"

"I'm fine, Mr. Gaskins, hope you are," I said back politely.

"You home for the summer now?"

"Yes, sir. 'Til August."

He picked up a handful of tulips sitting in a vase next to a headstone. "Here. Beautiful flowers for a beautiful flower," he said, handing them to me.

"Mr. Gaskins, I think maybe those were left for Mrs. Annabelle Wallace," I said, nodding toward the headstone now devoid of its tulips.

"She ain't there, Scout. She's up in Heaven with the Lord. I bet she'd like a nice girl like you to have her flowers," he said, winking at me.

Figuring it was too much work to argue with him, I thanked him for the tulips and started back toward my house.

Monday, I was going to drive up to Raleigh. And if I still couldn't get in touch with Rob, then I was going to go to his office in Rocky Mount. And when I'd finally see him, I would tell him that I loved him with all of my heart but that I couldn't keep living like this. We needed to do something about our situation. And while I'd never ask him to leave his wife, and a part of me didn't want him to leave her either, I still hoped that he would want to be with me as much as I wanted to be with him.

ROB

After somehow surviving the worst five days of my entire life, I went into work to deal with the mess I've made there, in addition to the mess I've made at home. I needed to get my professional life back in order, hand off the Raleigh accounts to Godfrey, take over my old accounts, and get the fuck out of my house for a while. The dark cloud that has enveloped my family in there is starting to suffocate me.

When I saw Rita outside of Lee Hall last week, my life became a slow motion car crash. She was standing there in her typical classy Rita attire, but looking like she spent the afternoon in a washing machine full of black ink. I can't recall Rita ever crying before. She's not an emotional woman, more the stoic type. But if I ever doubted my ability to make her cry, well, I didn't doubt it anymore. I saw front and center how badly I could make her cry.

I followed her home that night, hoping that she wouldn't crash her car — or crash my car either. My heart was beating so fast realizing that my life as I knew it was over. There was no un-ringing this bell of betrayal. Here I was, about to do the right thing, and let Scout go for good.

I was choosing to be the kind of husband and father that I used to be until that homecoming Saturday last year. Instead of being able to bury my shame deep inside of my head and learn to live with all I've done, everything came out in full view. And Rita, the love of my life, got crushed. That was the last thing I wanted to happen in all of this.

Immediately, my brain went into survival mode and any thoughts about Scout were how I'd explain her to Rita — or how to avoid her for the rest of my life. I allowed myself to succumb to the sweetness of, and my foolish attraction to, a young, college coed. And now I had to figure out how to keep her away from me. I mean, she's not going to go away quietly, right? I have no idea what she'll do. But now that Rita knows, at a minimum, that I have been cheating on her, I guess it doesn't really matter what Scout does. It's all out there anyway and now I have to do whatever it takes to prevent Rita from leaving me and losing my family. Dear God, please don't let her tell our kids.

When we got home that night, Chase and Samantha were sitting in front of the TV watching a show and Rita told them both that they needed to go to their rooms. Chase looked at Rita like she must've been from outer space. She never looks frazzled or messy and, here in the kitchen, she looked like a homeless person who tried, unsuccessfully, to dress up.

"What happened?" Samantha asked, shocked to see her mother in this state.

"I need to talk to your father alone. Everything is fine," she said sternly. That's Rita — doing and thinking of everyone else first, trying to spare any pain for her children.

When the kids left, I started, "Rita..."

"Stop."

"I'm so sorry. I am so stupid — have been so stupid. I don't know what's wrong with me."

"I said stop, Rob. I don't want to hear anything you have to say to me."

She was so calm, it scared me. Aren't scorned women supposed to go insane? Throw things? Scream? The whole "hell hath no fury" did not seem to apply to Rita in this moment, which made it even worse for me.

She walked over to the kitchen sink, washed her hands and put water on her eyes. She patted her face with a kitchen towel and said, without looking at me, "I don't want to hear anything about your explanations or reasoning or your apologies. I don't want to hear your fucking voice. Stay away from me. Sleep somewhere else. I don't care if it's in the den or at your office or in a gutter on Main Street. Do not speak to me or come near me, ever again."

And with that, she walked off into our bedroom and shut the door.

The word "fucking" coming from Rita's mouth was all I needed to hear in order to gauge the level of her anger. She doesn't cuss. Ever. The crying and cussing both in one day meant that she's at a level of pain and anger that I have never seen in her before.

I stayed home. I took sick days from work, which I never do. In fact, the receptionist said, "Wow. You must really be pretty bad off."

"I am. Please have Godfrey call me at home when he gets into the office."

I spent the next several days hanging around the house: cleaning, fixing things, watching TV, and hoping Rita would say something — anything — to me. I had to repair this awful mistake and I was intent on doing so. Being at home and making myself present, but keeping the boundaries that Rita required of me, was the first step. So I slept in the den and kept my distance. I picked up Chase from baseball practice and went to both of his games. I helped Samantha with her algebra. Rita holed up in our bedroom, only coming out to get something to eat. But I could tell that she hardly ate anything at all. I told the kids that she was sick and to leave her alone.

The kids aren't stupid. "Dad, come on. It's obvious something bad is going on," Chase said to me on the way home from baseball. "I don't believe she's sick at all. You're not telling me what's going on. I've never seen Mom like this before."

I hoped that Rita wouldn't tell them what kind of man I am. I hoped she'd let me make this up to her somehow and forgive me and give me another chance to be the kind of man she deserves, the kind of man I used to be. I felt so bad, so sick that I did this to her, to my family. I wished I had some answer or some reason for doing what I've done. But I don't. There is no excuse. I'm just shit. All the good things I've tried to be my whole life all came down to this one big wrong thing I've done.

And then Scout. How do I tell Scout that it's over between us? She has done nothing but love me. She's not a whore, no matter what Rita thinks of her. She's a beautiful, thoughtful, and kind girl, who I care a lot about. I can't pretend that I don't. But I have to now. I have to put her out of my heart and my head for good. And how do I tell her all of this without destroying her? She trusts me.

I guess I don't. I guess I just ignore her altogether and hope she gets the hint and goes away and leaves me alone.

CHARLIE

Walking along the sidewalk in my combat boots and battle dress uniform and heading toward the chow hall, I looked over and saw a training bus pull into the parking lot. That indicated that the line to get in for lunch would be long today. Since I've gotten to Fort Stewart, life has been a lot better than when I was at Benning. I'm a regular soldier now, or at least I feel like one because I live in a normal, enlisted barracks for single men, which is like a dorm. My days are organized, but we have a lot of free time and it's been great getting to know new people from all over the country and going out and doing things.

Each morning, there is Reveille and we get up and head to Physical Training or PT formation. I'm a fire team leader within my squad and now at the rank of Private First Class. After we're all accounted for, we do unit PT and then begin our workday. Other than the mildly-regimented existence of garrison living on an Army post and going to work in a uniform, it's somewhat like I imagined college would be like. We live together in a building — at least, those of us who aren't married — work out together, eat in the chow hall, have our evenings to ourselves, and go out and do things young people do: parties, the enlisted club, the movies, the mall. Sometimes, we have special duties that take up a weekend, inspections, and of course we have periods of training out in the field, but for the most part, I feel like I've been at a different kind of college than the one Scout goes to, in a different kind of fraternity.

The guys I've met are from all over. My roommate is named Glenn Garrett from Texas, which sounds like the name of someone who should be singing country music. He, too, plays the guitar and we have nightly jam sessions. He oddly makes me think that I'm rooming with a younger version of my father. We were at Benning at the same time, mesh real well together and have a lot in common, other than the fact that he likes the Houston Astros and I like the Yankees. It's been nice getting close to someone who isn't Scout. There's an unspoken brotherhood here, something I've never experienced before. Much more profound than a baseball team or even a girlfriend.

I decided that I've got to find a way to break my heart's strings away from Scout. That kiss she gave me before she went back to school at Christmastime has done a number on my head. When I was done with my training and came home on leave, my mom and I went up to Raleigh to see her for a day. And while it was great, I found myself feeling strange around her, like Scout is hiding something from me. Who knows, maybe it was my mom being there, too.

Scout sends me too many mixed signals: telling me how handsome I was in my uniform and messing with my short hair and then becoming shy with me all of a sudden, like we haven't known each other our whole lives. Being away from her, with our only real contact through letters and some infrequent phone calls, I don't know what to make of it all. Part of me wishes I'd meet a girl at Fort Stewart or over in Hinesville who'd knock my socks off and take my mind off of Scout altogether. But I love her and I don't want any other girl. I want her and I want her to want me back in the same way.

This whole mess is my fault because I've never told her exactly how I feel. I want to spend the rest of my life with her. I could marry her today. I wish I had the courage to do it and don't know what I'm so afraid of. Rejection?

When we kissed at Christmas, it seemed that she felt the same way about me. I imagine hitting myself in the head every single day because I stopped her when we got hot and heavy on her couch. I should've never done that. We should've just kept kissing each other, even if Miss Raelene or, God forbid, Mr. Webb, walked in on us. Maybe they would've cheered, "It's about time y'all!" or something like that. But I didn't want to be disrespectful of them in their home. Why couldn't she have kissed me like that somewhere outside, during the millions of times we've been alone together? How many times she could've just rolled off the grass in the field and on top of me. I wouldn't have stopped her.

Missing Scout is a full time job, but I keep myself as busy as I can so it's more like a dull ache that I've learned to live with since the day she left for Raleigh. Then, when I get a letter from her, the ache goes away for a while. When I get to talk to her on the phone, the ache subsides and all is right in the world. But later, when I'm alone and thinking about her, it starts hurting all over again.

Ever since that day a long time ago when she came back from Camp Judah, I've felt like there is something deep down in Scout that I can't get to, no matter how hard I try. She never told me about what happened to her. But I knew it had to be bad.

Glenn, Damien, and Chester, my three closest buddies here, are sitting over in our usual section of the chow hall. After I went through the chow line, hoping to find some of that carrot cake from yesterday, but finding some banana pudding instead, I walked over to the bench to eat my lunch, hoping they will start talking about something so I could get my mind off of Scout.

RITA

I've spent the past week being "sick" in my bedroom. I know my kids weren't fooled because, one day, Samantha came in after school, laid down on my bed next to me as I remained curled in the fetal position under the covers watching a Fantasy Island rerun.

"What in the world is going on with you and Dad?" she demanded. In that moment, and all the moments before then, I sure wished someone would take me away to Fantasy Island on "da plane, da plane." But no one did.

"Your dad and I are going through a bit of a rough time," I told her.

She adjusted her head on her dad's pillow and held a piece of her hair in her mouth. "Are you getting a divorce?"

Well, we weren't at that point yet, but I had no idea what I was going to do about my marriage. I'm Catholic. We don't do divorce. But I could get one, I think, for adultery. I bet I could even get the whole thing annulled if I wanted to. I was so mad about everything, I wanted to pretend my marriage never happened and that my children were just products of immaculate conceptions.

"No, honey, we aren't getting a divorce," I said, rubbing her chin, knowing that I might be lying to her, but not wanting to traumatize her without knowing for sure what I was going to do when I didn't know yet.

I loved Rob so much. I never knew I could hurt this bad. When will this endless pit-in-my-stomach feeling go away? I can't eat, I sleep in thirty-minute increments, and I keep dreaming about braless college girls with perky boobs and Rob sitting in a strip club with a handful of dollar bills. Seriously? That is what I'm dreaming about now?

How could he do this to us? And with a girl not even that much older than our own son? He couldn't possibly love her. A man Rob's age and usual maturity level cannot actually love a girl that young. It had to be all about sex —

it simply had to! And while that didn't make it any easier to take, I know that sex is different for men than it is for women. Sometimes, sex means nothing emotionally to a man and is instead only a way for him to release whatever stress he's under. But Rob's not like that. Or maybe he is now? I have no idea who my husband is at all!

Sometimes, I withhold sex from him because I don't feel appreciated. And lately, I've felt so distant from him, like he hasn't wanted to be here with us. So we haven't had sex. And it's my fault. So maybe he was just getting his basic needs met by a girl who was willing to provide them? *What the hell is wrong with me? I am rationalizing his sordid and disgusting behavior and then blaming myself for it!*

While Rob was at work earlier in the week, I went out and consulted with an attorney.

"Mrs. Caralessi, you can separate from your husband and divorce him on the grounds of adultery. But you need to be separated for at least a year before filing for divorce. Also, you'd be entitled to ask the court for alimony and child support. And, really, because of the adultery and because you've been the primary provider of your children's care for their entire lives, I'm pretty confident you'd get primary custody," the attorney informed me.

As I drove home, I thought about this mystery girl who Rob was willing to risk his marriage and family in order to screw behind my back. Maybe she didn't know he was married or was just stupid and mesmerized by his good looks and personality. She certainly wouldn't have been the first woman to be charmed by Rob Caralessi. Maybe she was a hooker. Hell no, Rob would not pay for sex. Would he? Maybe she was a stripper. I was driving myself nuts.

The truth is, it didn't matter who this girl was. This was Rob's fault. Rob was the one who was married — to me — and he is the one who made vows — to me — in front of God and our families and he is the one who chose to kiss that girl like he was eating her face and then go into her bed, which was located in a fucking dorm room! He didn't have to choose any of those things. But he did.

I was surprised to learn that my anger was not really concerned with that girl because isn't that what we women do? Put all of our hate and ire at the "other woman" rather than our philandering husbands, who are the ones who actually betray us? No, it would be too easy for him — and even too easy for me — to just hate her. It's easy to hate someone or blame someone you don't care about or don't know.

My wrath was all pointed at Rob and what he did to me and our family. If he didn't allow that girl into his life, no matter who or what she is, no matter her age or place in life, then none of this horror show would be happening now. I doubt she stuck a gun to his head and demanded he cheat on me.

I knew some women who forgave their husbands of their transgressions or an indiscretion after they begged for forgiveness and promised them the moon and stopped seeing their paramours. Most of the ones I heard about were over a one-night stand. But I don't know if I was the kind of woman who could forgive this. How could I ever trust him again? And without trust, what is the point in being married at all?

Wallowing in my grief and pain over losing the promise of my life, I knew that I couldn't make any rash decisions about our family. But what I really wanted to do was run away to New Jersey and cry in my father's arms. I used to believe that there were two men who would never let me down. Now there was only one and he was more than seven hours away.

So rather than do anything at all, I kept to myself and let time do what time does: heal and reveal.

SCOUT

By early August in the summer of 1988, I left my house for the first time for a reason other than to go to work at the Piggly Wiggly. I was supposed to go back to State next week, but all I wanted to do was crawl into a hole and die.

Back in May, when I hadn't heard from Rob and he wasn't taking my calls at his job, it appeared like he had dropped off the face of the earth. On one of my days off, I told my parents that I was going to Raleigh to see Felicia for the day. They didn't quite understand why I'd use up my gas money to drive all the way up there for that, but it was my cover for going to Rocky Mount to see why Rob vanished from my life without a word. I was physically ill over Rob's disappearing act, could barely function on some days, and because I didn't know what to make of it all, I needed to see him and get a resolution about what was going on, what happened, what I've done wrong, and to find out if he still loved me.

When I found my way to Rocky Mount, after lifting my daddy's latest Rand McNally Road Atlas, I was able to locate the insurance company on Church Street. After finding his car parked on the side of the building, I sat outside to see if I could catch him going in or coming out.

At the time, more than a week had passed since I last saw him. Our final moments together were spent with so much love, our bodies knotted masses of contented tender happiness. When he left my room for the last time, he said to me, gazing right into my eyes, "I love you, little girl. I will see you soon." Then he kissed me like he meant it.

So something was definitely wrong. At first, I thought maybe he was hurt or even dead because what kind of person says, "I love you, little girl" and then disappears from that moment on?

I sat on the street for two hours and felt like a detective or a criminal or something. My stomach was in a pretzel and his car sat there alone and empty. It was brutally hot outside and my car had no air conditioning so I was sweaty and worried and nauseated the whole time. By lunchtime, a few people came out of the building and walked down the street, but still no Rob. Finally, at around 3:00, as I was about to pass out from heat exhaustion and starvation, I watched him come out of the building, get into his car, and drove off.

Keeping my distance, I followed him all the way into a nice neighborhood several miles away. He pulled into a driveway. By this time, my body was seized into a full-on panic attack and I could barely breathe. I probably shouldn't have been driving at all.

This must've been his house. It was so nice: big,

white with black shutters, huge trees in the front yard and a beautiful garden in front of the big wrap-around porch. It looked new, definitely not old like my house, almost like he was rich or something. There was a basketball hoop in the driveway and a flag over the mailbox that had a big red "C" on it. Caralessi.

A blue Volkswagen drove past me on the street and pulled into the same driveway. A tall, thin, and beautiful, dark-haired woman got out of the car. She was wearing a light pink shirt and khaki shorts. A girl with equally dark hair, who didn't look much younger than me, got out of the passenger side. That was Mrs. Caralessi and their daughter Samantha. What in God's name am I doing here? They both walked in the front door and it closed behind them.

No contact with me, my calls ignored and avoided, no attempt to reach out to me in any way. He is not sick or injured or dead and is okay and at work and at home with his family. My biggest fears came crashing down onto my head as I sat in my car under a tree on Rob Caralessi's neighborhood street.

He had abandoned me. He dumped me. He got what he wanted and was done with me. And without even the courtesy of a phone call or an explanation and a goodbye, I discovered that my own heart had betrayed me. I trusted him, trusted what he said to me, and trusted how I felt about him. All along, he had been using me. And once again, I realized that I meant absolutely nothing to someone who told me that he loved me.

That was a tough day, driving all the way back to Haddleboro, realizing that Rob never cared for me at all. After everything we shared with each other and all I gave to him. And in the end, I was an object, a piece of ass, just as Felicia feared and warned me about. I had been wholly involved with a married man, knowing full well that it was wrong, hating myself day-in and day-out for doing it, apologizing to his wife in my sleep and my prayers and my dreams, but doing it anyway because I loved him and believed him when he said he loved me. How could I have been so stupid? Felicia had also been right about her assessment of me. I was too naïve and too nice for my own good. I trusted that people meant what they said and let myself be taken advantage of.

The weeks and summer days following, I didn't hear from Rob at all. He never reached out to me to give me a sign indicating that what we shared meant something to him. Just like so many of the gossipy rumors that I've heard over the years about some folks in my home town, Rob was the same as them. He was just like Brother Doug, hiding behind his family. Another coward.

And so was I. If I had been brave, I would've gone to his house and told his wife everything and apologized to her for my part in all of it and then let him feel as he made me feel — alone.

One late July day, my mom came upstairs to my room

and sat down on my bed. I was sitting on the floor with a teddy bear that I've had since I was born and listening to Lionel Ritchie on the radio.

She sighed. "Scout, what in the world is going on with you? Are you depressed or something? Your daddy and I are real concerned and think maybe you should go talk to Pastor Rhodes."

"I'm fine," I replied.

"That is bull, young lady. You have been down and out all summer, keeping to yourself. You never go outside or go meet up with anyone. What ever happened to Maybelle?"

"Maybelle's fine. She finished hair school and moved to Sanford to live with her brother and works at a salon way up there now."

"You're mopey and you barely even speak! Is this because Charlie's gone?"

There was my way out of this conversation. Charlie. Saving me yet again.

"Yes, I miss Charlie," I said, which was not a lie at all. "It's not the same around here without him and so I'm lonely." All true.

She sat there eyeballing me, studying my face, obviously wanting me to say something more. My mom wanted me to open up to her, was welcoming it with open arms, but how in the world was I supposed to tell her what I really am? A home-wrecker and a whore who lets herself get used by older married men. She had no idea how filthy I was and I didn't want her to know the truth about me. They raised me in a good, Southern Baptist home and gave me a safe and honest upbringing. There was no reason why I should've ended up being such an abomination to God and the Webb family name. If she knew the truth, she'd find a way to blame herself for raising such a horrible daughter, trying to figure out where she went wrong, not knowing that this had nothing to do with her at all.

My dog Stretch had been my confidant. I could tell him anything. He would listen, not judge me, and then lick my face. But he was long gone now and we never got another dog. And now with Rob and Charlie gone, too, all I had left was this ratty teddy bear, a gift from my Mema when I was brought home from the hospital in 1968.

"You know, Scout," my mom started. "All of this reminds me of how you were after your last summer at camp. You never told me about what happened at Camp Judah, about what happened with Brother Doug. Your daddy told me something happened, but he wasn't real clear. I always hoped that you would say something to me about it because ever since then, you've never been quite the same person."

As if I could feel any worse than I had already felt about myself, the suffering of that particular moment in my life, which fertilized my self-hatred on a daily basis, swelled up within me. Coupled with the already grieving state I was dwelling within over the loss of Rob and the realization that he never loved me, I started to cry. And there was no Charlie to hold me this time.

"Mom, I don't want to talk about that," I said through tears.

"But why? I don't understand. What in the world happened?" She really wanted to know.

"Nothing, okay? I don't want to talk about that summer or Camp Judah or Brother Doug. Ever."

And I meant it. I didn't want to, even though I probably needed to. Those wounds were as fresh as the day they had been inflicted upon me like a much deserved bloody lashing and it had been five years ago.

"Alright, honey," my mom said, getting up and coming down on the floor next to me. She hugged me with both arms and pulled me to her. I let myself cry a little more into her shoulder. "If you ever decide that you want to talk about anything, I hope you know that you can talk to me. I know you don't think I understand stuff, but I was young once too. I understand more than you think."

That conversation, and my mother's genuine concern for me on that particular day, as well as her concern for me all summer long, and how I knew in the deepest parts of myself that I needed her now more than ever, all stuck with me as I drove myself to a Kerr Drug Store about thirty minutes away from Haddleboro.

I haven't had my period in over three months.

Part III

March - April 2003

"Watch out for false prophets. They come to you in sheep's clothing, but inwardly they are ferocious wolves."

Matthew 7:15, The Holy Bible, New International Version

SCOUT WEBB, age 34

"Jemmmmmaaaaa!"

I waited. No noise.

"Jem! Are you up?"

Still no noise from upstairs.

Sighing, I walked up the steps and put my ear to my daughter's door. "Jem? You up?"

Still hearing nothing, I opened the door and saw Jemma's thick black hair jutting out from underneath the covers still managing to hang onto her bed. Her big navy blue comforter was on the floor and she had Boo wrapped up under her left leg. Boo looked up at me, his eyes covered in fluffy white hair, and he proceeded to move and get off the bed. Jemma moved her head and then opened her eyes, looking at me.

"What time is it?" she asked, voice cracking.

"Time to get a move on! You're late and I have to go."

Jemma rolled slowly off the bed and Boo came out of her room with me.

After letting Boo outside, I yelled up, "Jem, I have to leave, so please don't miss your bus because I don't have time today to come back and take you to school."

"Okay," she mumbled. I could hear the shifting around, the stumbling out of her room and into the hall bathroom to get ready for school.

Boo followed me to the door, his little white paws in lock step with my paces.

"Be a good boy," I said to my white mutt, a sweet shelter dog who would've been put down due to overcrowding had I not rescued him. I patted him on the head. "Mama's gotta go. Long day."

Normally, I'd take Boo with me to work, along with whatever foster dog I had in my care, but I have to tend bar a bit early tonight at Flavia, a high-end Glenwood South restaurant with an extremely active bar, and don't have time to deal with getting him home in between jobs.

Last weekend, I had to say goodbye to three mixed breed eight-month-old puppies named Bubba, Copper, and Vedder. Jem and I had been fostering them for the past four weeks because their owner had to give them up due to an indefinite hospitalization. Needless to say, we found good homes for them through my day job and my night job, and now they were off making some other families happy. Saying goodbye to those three babies was pretty tough on both of us. But Boo, in his mature age, was more than happy to see them go.

I quickly looked in my duffle bag and saw that my black dress pants were folded neatly inside, as well as: a brush, my travel makeup bag, my little glass jar of perfume, and my black bartender shoes. "Long nights on your feet require confident, comfortable footwear," the dude at the shoe store had told me. I slung my duffle bag over my shoulder, grabbed my purse, and put the wire hanger carrying my white starched dress shirt, hanging up on the coat tree near the door, under my fingers. Kicking the door shut behind me, I walked to my white Dodge Neon sitting in its assigned spot here at the Chatham Pines Townhome development, just near the Raleigh city limits.

After loading up my car and reversing it from its spot, I spotted Boo's big, white face sticking out of the blinds upstairs in my bedroom. He was wondering why he wasn't coming with me today — because, as any dog owner knows, dogs talk to us and communicate their thoughts out loud. Sometimes, we will do the talking for them in a cartoonish voice and then answer ourselves in our own voice. Or are we the only ones who do this?

Jemma has softball practice after school and would be able to get a ride home with her teammate Haley, a senior who drove and also lived in our neighborhood. She's been a latchkey kid since she was eleven and, now at fourteen, she is a responsible little lady who takes care of herself, her dog, and her own mom sometimes.

I thought about how much growing up we did together. Having a baby at twenty sure changes the trajectory of your life. I was going to go to the Vet School at NC State and graduate a "Doctor of Pets." I was going to work with dogs and cats in my own vet practice and volunteer with horses and farm animals at the Fairgrounds in Raleigh whenever my schedule would allow. I was going to make my parents proud. After all, I had spent my whole youth working hard to make them proud.

I kept out of trouble, had good grades, was involved in school, served on Student Council, sang in the choir at church, had a part time job at the Piggly Wiggly, and stayed away from boys — except for Charlie, who wasn't just any boy. Then I went away to college. Far enough to get away from Haddleboro and spread my wings, but close enough to be able to get back home if I needed to.

I was doing well in college, studying hard and working good hours at Marty's Place. At the time, I was coming out of my self-imposed shell and hanging out with some girls I met in my dorm. I liked my roommate, Micaela. We did aerobics together when she was around, and the girls on my floor would get a Blockbuster movie every Friday night. We'd watch *General Hospital* together and, if I had to work, they would fill me in. I was actually enjoying my simple college life.

Then *bam*. Meet Rob Caralessi, fall madly in love, become possessed, forget who I was — my basic Christian morality, even — and why I was in college in the first place. In one moment, much like when I was fourteen years old, I resumed my amazing ability to go from being a put together young woman to being a big, flipping idiot in a matter of seconds. And I did this to the point where I started justifying my very intimate and completely inappropriate relationship with a married older man. Then after being discarded by him as if I had meant nothing, I discovered I was pregnant with his baby, at nineteen years old.

And it isn't just having the baby that changes the course of your life, which is enough. It's having the baby alone. No husband. No boyfriend. Just loving and perplexed parents who are beside themselves trying to rescue their fallen daughter, barely out of her teens, and help her figure out her messy hellhole of a life.

Driving down the two-lane back road to get to my day job as a satisfied veterinary technician, I looked at all the beautiful trees lining the way, finally starting to show some lively light green for the spring with a few white and pink blossoms poking through here and there.

Like the trees, spring makes me come alive again. I always feel better about myself this time of year, just for a little while. I hate myself a little less and feel remarkably ambitious. Maybe I'll apply to the Veterinary Doctor program this year! Heck, I even feel more attractive. I feel so much better about life in general that I try to do more with my hair and be more talkative with the patrons who frequent the bar at Flavia.

One little uptick in my life over the past several months has been a blossoming friendship with a very charming, funny, and profoundly interesting New York attorney who comes into Flavia each evening I'm working. He has been embroiled in some drawn-out, highly expensive litigation, which has him based out of a big firm in Raleigh and living out of an extended-stay hotel within walking distance from the bar. He and his wife live in Manhattan. He goes home most weekends, so either he's paid really well or his big time firm pays for it.

He's a lot older, but is attractive for a man in his fifties, at least lately I think so — and I can tell that he likes me. He doesn't come across at all like he wants to sleep with me or anything, but he has taken a real interest in me as a person. I find it refreshing and have never met anyone quite like him before. So I've allowed myself to get to know him and have allowed him to get to know me, which is completely against my nature.

So far, I've kept a good emotional distance, but it's been getting harder to do. Lately I've had to come to terms with the fact that I genuinely want to be his friend, even when he eventually goes back to New York. He's offered his family's hospitality and said that they would should show us everything in the city.

"Times Square, Ellis Island and the Statue of Liberty, Yankee Stadium, Central Park, the Empire State Building, the USS Intrepid, and the huge gaping hole that was the World Trade Center. It'll be so much better because you and Jemma would be tourists getting first-class treatment from

Manhattanites," he told me about a month ago over a late night cup of coffee in Flavia. "I'll have my wife pick out a Broadway show. There's no show like one on Broadway."

"That would be incredible," I said, truly impressed. I had never been to New York before and the thought of finally seeing Yankee Stadium gave me chills.

Early on in our friendship, he said to me, "Scout, you are one of the most interesting people I've ever met. And I've met a lot of people. You're a little mysterious, but I can tell that you're a really good person."

While I have no idea why he thought I was mysterious, no one else has ever come out and said things like that to me, so I was a bit taken aback. "Wow, um, thank you," was all I could muster as I looked down at the floor, embarrassed.

"I want to know everything about you and what makes you tick – what's in that head of yours."

I felt a little unnerved and strange at first with all of his attention and the kinds of things he'd say to me, but he seemed genuine and kind. Plus, he had this way about him that made people want to be around him and listen to his stories. Because I was always working whenever I saw him, I had no choice but to hear them all anyway. But I liked how he wanted to hear my stories, too.

Once, after a fairly long conversation — especially for me — I flat out asked him if he was married. He never wore a wedding ring, and I found myself liking him more than I probably should have. I wanted to be sure that I wasn't going to piss off yet another man's wife.

"Yes, I'm happily married, Scout. For a very long time." Noticing the thoughtful, maybe even confused look that must've come across my face, he added, "Listen. I promise. I'm only interested in being your friend. But I do feel close to you. What I'd imagine a real friend to be."

"What do you mean 'imagine?'" I asked him.

He smiled. "I don't think I've ever had a real friend my whole life, except maybe when I was a small boy. There's no one in my life that I'd consider a real friend or even a *best* friend."

I believed him; he was that convincing. And because he talked about his wife as if she were Helen of Troy, the most beautiful woman ever who sunk a hundred ships — or her face did...or something like that — how he is so in love with her after all of his years of marriage, and how blessed he is to have his grown children and a grandson, it was very easy to believe in his stated intentions toward me.

I gave him a friendly hug. "For my friend from New York," I said to him. *Who wasn't Charlie.* A friend who wasn't Charlie. What a concept.

The best...or worst...part — I haven't figured it out yet — is that his name is Tom Robinson. Only he doesn't spell it "Tom." He spells it "Thom." And I always want to call him "Thom" with the "Th" sounded out. Personally, I think it's pretentious when men spell "Tom" with an "h" in there. But since it was a Thom *Robinson*, I couldn't get past the irony of a Scout befriending a real live Thom Robinson. So I overlooked the harsh glare of his annoying name spelling.

When we met for the first time in Flavia, he ordered an expensive bourbon. After I passed him his glass, he put his hand on my hand as it paused across the bar.

"Young lady, what is your name?" he asked me, looking fiercely into my eyes.

Not accustomed to strangers touching me like that, I peered down at his hand on mine and then back up at him, replying, "Scout?"

"Scout?" he said, a little too loudly. I noticed that he didn't come back with the usual line of knowing a dog named Scout, like everyone else does. Instead, he laughed and then held up his Pappy Van Winkle and exclaimed, "I KNEW there was something special about you! It is fate that we met. You and me…will be bonded for life!"

Puzzled, I backed up a bit and smiled at him. "Really? Why is that?"

He threw his drink back, put the glass down on the counter and winked at me. "Because my name, little girl, is Thom. Thom Robinson. And it is very nice to meet you."

"Well, it's good that my father proved your innocence, despite all that you had going against you," I said still smiling. "Everyone in that court room knew you really didn't do it."

"All I had going against me was being a black man in a white world," he said, his eyes scrunching at me. "How is your old man these days?"

I marveled at this wild character sitting in my bar, who now had me wondering what ever happened to Atticus and Jem and Dill and the gang after the whole story was over.

Blushing from the attention he was giving me, I felt like I was the only person in the room. Everyone was looking at me. I kind of enjoyed it, but only briefly. It was nice to feel special, like the union of a Thom Robinson and a Scout meant something. He sure convinced me that it did.

It was nice to have someone who listened to me, wanted to know me, wanted to know how I was doing. Someone other than Charlie, that is. And it was nice to get to know a person from someplace else, a place I've only read about and have seen in countless movies and TV shows but have never been myself: New York, home of my beloved Yankees.

We had a great tit-for-tat, a parallel sense of humor, and a similar view of the world. We were a match in wits and, while I sensed that he thought I was cute (he commented once that he liked my hair styled a certain way and that his New York-based makeup artist son would be able to make me look like a movie star), I did not sense at all that he was interested in getting me naked. Which was a relief. It made me feel like I could be myself and have a friendship with a man who was not Charlie and that did not involve trying to get me into bed. It gave me some faith in men who frequented bars.

I looked forward to working my shifts at Flavia more and more every time. Thom knew my schedule and was always there the whole evening, keeping me company and talking it up with everyone. He made my job so much fun. We had even walked down the street for a hot dog at Snoopy's once, like friends do.

But other than this Thom Robinson character — and he *is* a character! — and of course my occasional lunch dates with Charlie, who's always working or spending time with his girlfriend, Stephanie, I enjoyed my work as a vet tech, volunteering with animal rescue, going to Jemma's softball games, and trying to make friends with some of the other parents. While I rarely committed to extra plans, everyone is always very nice and inclusive. I don't know if that's because we southerners are a friendly bunch by nature or if it's because Jemma is one of the best players on the team. As far as I can tell, I'm the only truly single mom. But no one treats me differently and, in fact, several have offered to give Jem a ride if she ever needs one.

Ever since I had my daughter, I have purposely kept a distance from establishing close relationships. Charlie has raised Jemma as his own and, other than my own father, he is the only father she's ever known. I've gone on a few dates and had two actual boyfriends, but I never let myself love them, so those relationships were ultimately doomed. My only focus has been on Jemma and trying to find a way to raise her with as little help from my parents as possible. After all, it isn't their fault that I was the winner of the "Dumbest Girl Who Ever Lived" award and who ruined everything I had worked for. All over a cruel and selfish man who looked like Mickey Rourke.

Jemma does not know her father at all — not even his name — and lately she has been asking me more about him: what he was like, if she looked like him (she does), who he is. So far, I've refused to tell her. Heck, my parents still don't know the identity of this mystery sperm donor. No one knows. Not even Charlie.

Lately Charlie has been trying his hardest to convince me to tell her about him. I guess I understand why he feels that way since he has his own daddy issues. But I am the one who knows what is best for everyone, especially my own daughter. And what is best for everyone, including Rob Caralessi himself, is that Jemma never knows who her father is — that *no one* knows who her father is — and that this secret dies with me.

I left his name off the birth certificate for a reason. She is my daughter, only mine, the only thing in this entire world that is mine. Rob Caralessi already has kids. He doesn't need my kid, too. The day he walked out of my life without even saying goodbye, treating me like the nine months we'd spent together never even happened, was the day I knew that he was just another coward in this world. My Jemma does not need a coward for a father. Having a dumb, home-wrecking whore for a mother is enough to be saddled with as a kid.

So, since I already caused enough problems in his life and he never cared about me anyway, it was best for us both when, three months later, I learned I was carrying our baby and never sought him out.

For so long, my shame and the never-ending agony over what happened with Brother Doug at Camp Judah and what happened with Rob five years after that have enveloped me in so many layers of walls. No one has been able to get through. Not even Charlie. And, dear God, he has tried.

Long ago, as I rested in a hospital bed, trying to feed a baby with the most perfect big head of black hair anyone has ever seen, Charlie said to me, "Scout, I need to tell you something." It was the softest and most serious voice I had ever heard come from his mouth.

I looked up at him, sensing the gravity of his tone. He stood next to me wearing a gray Army tee shirt and a pair of new jeans that had obviously never been washed before. His hair was freshly cut into a high and tight with the salty blond tips forming a patch of thin, smooth carpet. His boyish face, so honest and kind, looked down on me with an almost pained expression. If an outsider peered in at us, he would've thought that Charlie was taking pity on a girl holding a newborn. But I knew there was not an ounce of pity in his heart. Charlie was just scared to death.

"Jeez, Charlie, what is it? You're scaring me," I said, holding the little tiny bottle of formula to Jemma's mouth.

He eyed me with an intensity that I never knew was inside of him. He looked down at his feet and then looked at me again, his face softening. "Scout," he started, "I love you." And while I've heard Charlie tell me that he loved me before, this time it was different.

Chills came up over my body and I felt like I was naked in a room full of strangers without a blanket to be found.

"I have loved you my entire life and I wish I had told you this a long time ago. I want us to be together. Really together. I can take care of you and Jemma both."

He said those exact words. They are forever imprinted into my memory. And unlike Doug DeHaan or Rob Caralessi, Charlie Porter meant what he said to me. But I knew that I didn't deserve such a wonderful man to love me. A kind, tender-hearted, hard-working, honest, young soldier like Charlie deserved so much better than a college dropout loser with a bastard baby, like me.

Several months after Desert Storm, Charlie decided to get out of the Army in order to come back to Haddleboro to be closer to me and Jemma. By then, Jem was a toddler and he had spent all of his vacation time coming back to see us whenever he could. His devotion has never wavered over all these years. I knew Charlie had truly loved me back then, but I also knew that I could never be good enough for him. He didn't know what kind of person I really was and all the horrible things I had done.

Even all these years later, and despite his now serious relationship with this sweet woman Stephanie, I knew he still loved me. Even after I broke his heart and told him that I could only be his friend after he asked me to marry him after the church's summer picnic, I knew he still loved me.

He had been home for a brief leave to see me, Jemma and his mom. Our church always had a picnic in the summertime, and after Charlie and I had won the three-legged race, my mom told me that she would take Jemma home so I could spend some time with Charlie before he had to leave again.

We sat out under our dogwood tree, feeling sticky from the heat and humidity. He turned to me and, again, in that serious tone of voice, said, "Scout. You know that I love you and that I love Jemma. I think we've waited long enough." I knew what was coming next. He got up on both of his knees and faced me, took my hands in his, and asked, "Will you marry me?"

I knew that he would ask me someday because of what he told me when I was in the hospital. But other than Jemma getting a little older and my broken heart getting a little scarred over but never quite healed due to the passage of time, I was still as far away as I could be from being good enough for Charlie Porter.

My silence was awkward and Charlie and I were never awkward. So he said, "I figured it would be kinda silly for me to go get you some diamond ring since you probably wouldn't want to wear it."

I laughed quietly. He was right. He knew me.

"I'm sorry, Charlie," I said, not able to look at him at first. "You know how much I care for you. But I just don't feel like I can marry you."

Immediately, I could hear his breathing get a bit harder and I wondered if it was really just the sound of me breaking his heart with the anguish of my answer. I don't think Charlie would've asked me if he felt like I was going to turn him down. After a couple of minutes of silence and me trying to hold back all the tears rising into my eyes, Charlie stood up and handed me his dog tags.

"I'm pretty sure that I'll be deploying to Kuwait soon," he said in a normal Charlie cadence. With those words, my heart sank, and immediately, the tears that had been welling up streamed out onto my face. First of all, where the heck was Kuwait? All this time I never thought about the Army being really dangerous, about him going to an actual war. I always thought about how far away he was going to be from home and how much I'd miss him instead.

"I'm giving these to you because I love you and Jemma," he said, pressing them into my hands. "And even though you won't marry me now, I know you love me, too. This is a piece of me that I'm leaving with you so you and Jemma will always know that I'm with you, even on the other side of the world — and that I'm thinking of you all the time."

A part of me always wondered, after that night when I turned down his marriage proposal, if he would go ahead and leave Haddleboro once and for all and just leave me behind where I belonged, holding onto his dog tags. Maybe go find his father or a nice clean girl who did deserve him, a girl who deserved the precious gift of holding onto that piece of him.

I had to be honest and let him be free to go live a life that was worthy of him. I was still living at home with my parents, working as a receptionist, and trying to save some money to move out. I wanted to enroll part time in the community college to continue working toward my bachelor's degree. I was trying to get my life back on track and marriage to anyone was just another thing that I would no doubt destroy.

And now, all these years later, Charlie Porter was still too good for me. I was and would always be damaged goods. Even God wasn't interested. Charlie warranted a free and untainted woman who could give him all of herself. And I wasn't that girl. The Scout he loved was the Scout with whom he played baseball, the Scout he kissed with his first kiss, the Scout he held as she cried when her beloved Stretch died on a rainy winter afternoon when she was sixteen. The twenty-two-year-old Scout was a long-time tragedy with no hope of being fixed. And even at thirty-four years old, she was still a disaster, caught in the dead memories of her lost youth.

While Charlie has provided the only real friendship I have ever known and the closest thing to true love that I will ever get to experience, I refused to allow myself the simple pleasure or even the hope of another man's genuinely heartfelt affection, attention, even touch. I was basically ice. Not bitchy ice. Never mean. But emotional ice.

Thom Robinson was the first person I've met in years who began to thaw me.

***

After a tough day at Paw's Animal Hospital and Pet Resort, I jumped in the back office to take a quick shower. Mrs. Meyer's Great Dane named General Eisenhower did not react well to having his teeth cleaned. It took five of us to restrain him. Even "Paw" himself, our beloved elderly vet, was part of the cast of that production. Then, Mr. Gardner's precious Cardigan Corgi's last days were here, and I didn't do a good job of convincing him that he should have that loveable girl put down rather than extend her misery. He had Slinky for thirteen years, so I know it's a tough decision. A dog dying is harder on some of us than a person dying.

But now I had to put on my cute lil' bartender face and attitude so this extra income from Flavia would sufficiently pay for Jemma's travel softball fees and the softball camp up at Carolina this summer. The things a modern woman does for her daughter's dreams!

Slipping into my uniform and shoving my scrubs from Paw's into my duffle bag, I fixed my medium-length, sharply cut straightened brown hair into a high ponytail so I'd look younger than what I am. *Better tips.* I put some simple makeup on my face to cover the slight crow's feet starting up near the corners of my eyes and headed off for my evening of making cocktails, filling beer mugs, pouring bourbon and whiskey for relatively wealthy men who are going to just sit at my bar and not go home for one reason or another — and hanging out with my good pal for a laugh or two.

JEMMA WEBB, AGE 14

I was so relieved when my mom said that she had no time to deal with me this morning. I figured she wouldn't because I know her schedule as well as I know my own. Growing up in an organized, single-parent household, we abide by the schedule. From daycare drop-offs to after school programs to coming home alone with my own key in fifth grade and immediately having to call my mom at work and then my Mema at her house right after. If there was no phone call by 3:15 PM, everyone started to freak out.

Early on, I learned the importance of these things: the phone, a clock, and the appropriate amount of time to complete a task. Luckily, I managed to freak them out really bad only once, which was like a week after September 11th. Everyone was on edge and I forgot to call my mom. She wasn't able to leave work due to a vet emergency and no one else was there to deal with it. Charlie was out of town so she called my Mema, who then drove the ninety minutes to our house and got into an accident on the way because she was speeding. Then she called my Pop-Pop to leave the garage he owned, also ninety minutes away, just to see if he could find me. He had to close the garage because no one else was there that day. He finally got to my house only to find me up in my bed with Boo and my headphones in my ears, listening to some Shania Twain on my MP3 player.

After that, I felt awful about being lax on my phone calling responsibilities, especially because my poor Mema's car got totaled and she had to get another one. My mom gave me the riot act that day. But I know it's all because they love me and want me to be safe. I do wish they'd chill out, though, because I'm fine. I can take care of myself. I'm a lot more mature than other kids my age and have been that way my whole life. There aren't many fourteen-year-old girls with their own beeper! And I'm hoping that someone in authority in my family will see fit to give me my own cell phone soon enough.

I remember when I overheard my second grade teacher talking to another teacher about me.

"She is just so much more responsible than my other students. She's very neat, respectful, and mature way beyond her years," she said.

Standing behind a wall, I thought about how nice it felt to hear her say such good things about me. Not realizing I was eavesdropping on their conversation, the other teacher, who I didn't know said, "Well that's because she's had to grow up fast. Her mom had her right out of high school and no one knows who the father is. What kid wouldn't have to learn fast and early with only one parent who's barely an adult herself?"

That stuck with me. I knew my family situation was a little different than a lot of the other kids my age. Sure, some of them had parents who were divorced and living with one or the other or both. But it was common knowledge that I didn't even know my dad at all.

At the time, we lived in Haddleboro near my grandparents. It was a small town and my mom grew up there. My grandfather owned a garage there. My grandmother was a reading teacher there. Everybody knew everybody's business. And everybody, including me — especially me — wondered who my dad was. It was the great mystery of Haddleboro.

Well today, I am skipping school. Today, I am going to go meet him.

CHARLIE PORTER, AGE 34

"Coast is clear. Let's do this," Jemma said on the phone. Leaving my townhouse, which was not too far from Scout's, I passed by Mr. Gates who was walking his black lab named Scout — there's always a dog with that name! He looked up and waved. The people here appreciated having someone in law enforcement living in the neighborhood. It's like having a doctor next door. Someone is always coming to you for some kind of help. But I didn't mind. I liked helping people.

Today, I was helping one of my favorite people ever, Jemma. I am helping her with the most important thing I could ever help her with. At least, I think so. Far be it from me to encourage a kid to skip school or defy her own mother, but it's justified in this case.

For the last two years, Jemma has been asking — no, begging — her mom to tell her about her father. And still, Scout refused. I've played all my cards. I've staged an intervention on the issue that included her parents, Jemma, and the retired pastor who Scout's known almost her whole life. She would not budge. She knows my situation with my own father and how I've spent my whole life struggling with not knowing him, feelings of abandonment, having to be a man when I didn't even know what that meant. But, for whatever reason, on this matter, she is closed off. I haven't been able to get through to her. And if I can't, then no one will ever be able to.

There were no records, no names, no nothing. Jemma could have been conceived by a ghost for all we knew, that's how guarded the identity of this father was.

Then one day almost a month ago, Jemma found me at my house after softball practice. One of her teammates had dropped her off. While we live in the same sprawling neighborhood, my house is a good mile or so away from hers.

She handed me a piece of paper. It was a pretty old business card that said, "Robert A. Caralessi, Agent" in faded ink and included a phone number with a 252 area code. I turned the card over. In old, sloppy handwriting it said, "You are beautiful, Scout."

"Charlie, I think this is him," Jemma said, in between a look of excitement and horror at the same time.

"Why?" I asked her.

"I found it in an old storage box mom has hidden in her closet. There are some old photos in there of our family, but this business card was stuck behind a picture of her when she was young." She began speaking faster as she went on. "I went on the computer and found the website of an insurance company in Rocky Mount. There's a picture of this guy on the website. He looks just like me."

I looked at the name. "Jem, show me."

We went into my kitchen where my computer was housed and logged on to the Internet. She typed in the address from memory. It was a website for what appeared to be a large national insurance company chain. When she went to look at the insurance agents affiliated with the company, a photo of a good-looking man with jet-black hair, maybe in his forties, popped up. I looked closer at his face: pouty bottom lip, slight cheek dimples, prominent chin dimple. I wasn't fully convinced, but there was definitely a resemblance between this Robert A. Caralessi and my Jemma.

"Robert Caralessi Insurance Agency, Inc." Jemma read aloud. "Rob has over thirty years of experience in the insurance industry, establishing Robert Caralessi Insurance Agency, Inc. in 1995. As an agent, he specializes in home, life, long-term disability, and elder care insurance with National Coastal Insurance Company. He and his dedicated staff are here to help you with all of your insurance needs."

I stared at the website and kept trying to make a facial comparison.

"Charlie. It's him. Why would mom have a crumpled-up, old business card of this guy? And if it was just a business card because mom wanted insurance or something, there would be no 'You are beautiful, Scout' written on the back." She repeated the phrase in a funny voice, like she was imitating Yoda.

Jemma had a good point there. And I have certainly never heard of any guy named "Rob" in Scout's life before. Thinking about it, other than a "Dennis McCarthy" and a "Laz Lopez," there are no other men I've ever heard of in her life, past or present, which is a small list for such a pretty woman.

That day, Jemma called Robert Caralessi's office from my house. She didn't want him to see "Webb, Scout" come across the line in case he had caller ID. After she confirmed that it was his number, I set up an appointment to meet him to discuss my bullshit need for an insurance plan, an elder care one that I wanted to set up for my mother. If she knew that I had set up an insurance plan for her elder care, she would hit me over the head! So on my next day off, I drove over to Rocky Mount, met with Mr. Caralessi to go over what I felt my needs were, assessed him overall, and left with some of his hair that had been left on his sports jacket and an empty bottle of water that was in his trashcan. You can always rely on someone having to leave a room in order to take a piss at a certain time in the morning.

I took the hair and the bottle to the Crime Lab at the State Bureau of Investigation and had my geeky forensic analyst friend, Betsy, do me a favor so that we could have some kind of scientific proof that this Robert Caralessi was indeed Jem's biological father. Once that was established, and I told Jemma the results, we came up with our plan for her to confront him.

But first, I had to calm her the hell down.

She was jumping up and down, like Justin Timberlake was my new best friend and we were going to go meet him backstage. I thought she might have been a little freaked out by this news, but I think she knew the day she found him online that it was him and had already processed it. Now she was just excited about it. She really wanted to meet him and get to know him.

"Charlie, he is my father. Look at him. He looks like he's really nice," she said.

"Jem, he abandoned your mother. You know she was just a kid when she had you and had to drop out of college. If he's in his late forties now, then you know he was a lot older than her and probably just took advantage of her." I tried to reason with her, bring Jemma back to reality. "What if he doesn't want to know you? Are you prepared for that possibility?"

Jemma looked at me cockeyed. "How could he not want to know *me*? I'm amazing. I bet he doesn't even know I exist."

I thought about that. Maybe she was right. Maybe Scout had never told the guy she had his baby. That was a Scout thing to do — keep her secrets to herself. And she sure had been adamant for a long time about not revealing the identity of this man.

I smiled at Jemma. "You're right. He'd be crazy not to want to know you."

The plan: I was going to go in and meet with him again to finalize this elder care policy for my mother, while Jem sat waiting for me in the reception area. I was going to engage him in some small talk and, if I felt like it was a safe situation for Jem, I was going to call for her to come into his office. Then I would leave the room.

This was Jemma's moment and her confrontation alone. I wasn't going to take that from her. He is her biological father so she's already had too much taken from her by this asshole. Confronting him at his work place, where he wouldn't be able to scream at a young girl, was the best way for us to deal with it. If anyone was tough enough for this — or ready enough for this — it was my kick-ass kid Jemma.

So, we headed out to Rocky Mount as soon as I picked her up. I honestly felt like this was the day that Jemma's life would change forever, one way or another. It would be a defining moment for sure, something she has wanted and needed for a long time. I was a little jealous of her to have this opportunity to get to know her father and I hoped that he would embrace it, too, because Jemma Webb was the greatest kid in the world.

ROB CARALESSI, AGE 55

My alarm went off at 6:00 in the morning and I rolled out of bed to go for my daily run. Actually, at this point in my life, it was nothing more than a trot, but I was training for my first marathon and I have a history of bad knees, so a trot was just fine. Rita was sleeping next to me, her dark hair all heavy and smooth from going to the salon yesterday. I always loved how her hair felt when she got back from the salon.

My Blackberry was downstairs sitting in a charger and I had a missed call from one of my agents and a text message from Chase telling me that our trip down to Fort Myers to see the Red Sox play in spring training in two weeks was now booked and we were ready to roll. We will leave on a Friday, fly into Fort Myers, rent a car, stay in a hotel on the beach, and spend the weekend acting like two baseball groupies. We've been doing this trip for the past ten years now and I looked forward to it every year.

I left my house at about 6:15 and began my week six marathon training schedule. Today would be a four-mile run, then tomorrow I rest. Then Wednesday, a five-mile run.

So far, so good. My miles are slow, but all of this running I've been doing over the past five years has really helped me out.

When I turned fifty, I vowed to Rita that I'd start taking better care of myself. When I left the insurance company that I had been with my entire career in order to start my own company, the stress of that transition took over my life and she demanded — rightfully so — that I find a healthy hobby to get addicted to in order to manage my stress. That was her subtle reminder of what I did to her the last time I had too much stress in my life.

As I ran out of my neighborhood and down a long, empty side road, I did my thinking. Thinking about how grateful I am to be alive, especially after having to bury Rita's eldest brother, Sal, two weeks ago at the age of fifty-two. Thinking about my day and all I had going on at work. And thinking about how much I looked forward to Samantha coming home next week for a visit. She has been working up in Boston as a financial adviser in a national firm for the past three years and we haven't seen her since Christmas.

Today, I only had one appointment. Most of the time, I have my agents handle all the new business now, but this guy came in a few weeks ago and had specifically asked to meet with me. It was a little strange because he was from the Raleigh area, and he especially stood out to me because he's an SBI agent.

When he came in for his initial appointment, I asked him curiously, "Why are you trying to secure a long term care policy for your mother who lives in Haddleboro from a Rocky Mount-based company? You know you could've easily gotten a good one over in Raleigh."

"Yeah, I know, but an old client referred me to you."

"What was his name?" I asked him. I've had a lot of clients through the years.

"John Hardy," he said.

I put my hand over my mouth, thinking as far back as I could and could not for the life of me remember any John Hardy. But I sure did know the town of Haddleboro. And when he said it, my gut flared up with a sick feeling.

Coincidence or not, Haddleboro makes me think of Scout, the absolutely adorable and sweet State girl I so cruelly dumped without even a proper goodbye. I knew I had broken her heart all those years ago when I had pretty much lost my mind and became desperate to save my marriage.

I think about Scout now and again because I hate what I did to her. It was so unfair and wrong, but, at the time, I was so zoned in on keeping my family intact and trying to do whatever it took to convince Rita not to leave me that I wasn't thinking much about Scout's feelings at all. In short, I was a complete douchebag to someone who had been so nice to me. And while time has allowed me to learn to live with it all, I doubt I'd ever really be able to forgive myself. I didn't just hurt Rita in all of that. I hurt Scout, too. And she didn't deserve what I did to her.

At the time, the only thing I knew to do was just cut

her off and hope that she went away. She was a very young girl with no money and there was quite a bit of a physical distance between us so I thought that would be the easiest thing to do. I was scared for quite a while that she might show up and start throwing things or confront me in front of my family, but she never did. She just stopped calling my office and I never heard from her again. So my method worked.

Sometimes, I wondered what became of her. Did she ever become a veterinarian? Did she start going to more basketball games and hanging around people her own age? Did she go back to working at that little mom-n-pop place? Did she ever get married and have her own family? I wondered where she was living, what she looked like. Did she ever cut that long, brown hair? Did she grow out of those full cheeks? She was the nicest girl I'd ever met. Not a mean bone in her body. Over the years, I have admitted to myself many times that a big part of me missed her. What could've been if life had been different for us both, if the timing had been better, if she had been born in the 1940s or 1950s instead?

But I know I'm the luckiest man in the world with exactly what I have. After that whole mess I made, and a lot of hard work on my part and healing and forgiving on her part, Rita and I became stronger than ever. We went to counseling and I rededicated myself fully to her and the kids. It took a long time for me to be able to sleep in my own bed again, but, eventually, Rita did forgive me and we moved on. There is not a woman on this earth who is stronger or full of more love for her family than my wife.

After my run, a long shower, a good breakfast, and a nice kiss goodbye from Rita, I went into work a little early. When I got to my office, the SBI agent from Raleigh was already there sitting in reception for his appointment. There was a girl with him who looked up at me with a sharp intensity.

"Mr. Porter," I said shaking the man's hand. He was tall and lean with sandy blond hair and no trace of a receding hairline, which made him look younger than a guy in his mid-thirties. "Good to see you again. Give me a minute and I'll be right with you."

"Sure thing," he replied to me.

The girl still looked at me fiercely and I was starting to feel a little uncomfortable. To put us both at ease, I asked, "Is this your daughter with you today?"

"This is Jemma," Mr. Porter said.

"Nice to meet you, Jemma," I said to the girl, smiling and offering my hand. She just looked at me in my eyes and, with a gravelly sounding familiarity to her voice, she said, "Nice to meet you, too" and shook my hand.

When Mr. Porter came back into my office, I handed him the contract for the long-term care policy for his mother and waited for him to pull out a checkbook to write out the amount for the premium. Instead, he began to talk about the weather and then went to the door and motioned for the girl to come in. When she came into my office, Mr. Porter walked out and shut the door.

And it was in that moment, as that tightening feeling within my chest and gut started to spread out and take over my body, I realized that I wasn't having a heart attack or a stroke. I was looking directly into a mirror.

The girl handed me a manila envelope and said, "Hi again. My name is Jemma Webb. And you are my father."

SCOUT

"Hey, little girl," Thom said to me as he sat down at the end of the bar in what has become his permanent spot. "When you get a second."

I smiled at him and nodded, knowing that he wanted a Guinness.

The fact that Flavia was Brazilian didn't mean all that much. We celebrated St. Patrick's Day for the entire month of March. The bar was fairly busy for a Monday night, and I didn't know if that was because of a huge convention downtown or because of March Madness or because Thom had managed to acquire himself a following tonight. The man had everyone fully entertained with his grandiose stories and the crazy things that would come out of his mouth. I imagined him performing in court each day, a successful and accomplished trial lawyer who wins all the time because juries and judges and plaintiffs and defendants alike would have no choice but to love him.

Thom was the kind of person who would say things that everyone else is thinking but won't say out loud. Everyone listening to him is both horrified and amused at the same time. Get a few drinks in him and he got even funnier. I think the patrons appreciated how he was so free because he didn't care what anyone thought. I was envious of his ability to be like that.

But what I liked most about him was later, when the place cleared out and I was getting ready to leave, he would walk out with me and talk to me next to my car for a good thirty minutes. And he would open up to me. There was a lot more to Thom Robinson than being the main attraction in a courtroom or the centerpiece of the Flavia bar. While he might've been some high falutin' Manhattan attorney, there was something else about him that chipped at the thick walls around my heart.

He was not the kind of man who opened up to anyone, let alone some single mother from small-town North Carolina. He told me before that he was impossible to know.

"My own family doesn't really know me," he once confided. I understood how he felt, so it wasn't an odd statement to me. But for some unknown reason, he wanted me to know him and had told me so on this particular night.

"Little girl, you make me feel so welcome here in Raleigh. You are like my home away from home. Not Flavia. But you, you, you," he said, his kind face reflecting a bit in the street lamp's light. "I feel like I've known you my whole life, like we grew up together, down the street from one another in Brooklyn."

Thom never came across like he was trying to flatter

me. He always sounded so sincere, like he meant it, and there was not a hint of repressed sexual tension between us at all. That made me feel so much more comfortable with him because there was no way in the world that I was getting involved with a married man ever again. Thom respected me and neither of us had ulterior motives.

He was somewhat intoxicated so I asked, "Are you going to be okay? I mean, getting back to the Confederate?" The Confederate Suites was a family-owned, extended-stay hotel where he lived during the workweek. It was just one block away from Flavia, so I wasn't that worried about him, but as his bartender, I felt obligated to ask anyway. Plus, I cared.

Thom wore a white button up shirt and suit pants. He was fairly tall, easily a few inches over six feet, and looked like he had been a football player back in the day. His chest and shoulders were built up, indicating that he once spent his extra time in a weight room. His face was bloated, like how older men who drink a lot of alcohol seem to get bloated faces, and he reminded me a lot of Tom Selleck — *who spells "Tom" correctly* — with his yawning cavernous dimples but a much thinner mustache. His size made him look strong and in command, but his face made him look cute and approachable, like a big, friendly puppy.

He looked down at me and said, "I would ask you to walk me to the Confederate, Scout, but then there'd be nobody to walk you back to your car. So yes, I'm okay," he said, trying to be a gentleman despite his current blood alcohol level.

I usually worked at Flavia on Monday, Wednesday, and Thursday evenings and sometimes Fridays for the past two years. Once in a while, I worked a weekend, especially during the winter. This schedule has been mostly softball-schedule-friendly for me, so I don't miss many games, if any at all. Jemma had rides home from practices and I always did extra carpooling on the weekends or after the games. Everyone in the travel softball community and on the high school softball team was very helpful and accommodating. They had a "we are all in this together" philosophy, which is why I could pull all of this off as a single parent.

One of the reasons Jemma and I had moved from Haddleboro a few years ago, other than to finally separate myself from my parents — which I really needed to do — was that there was simply more money to be made closer to the city. The Raleigh-Durham-Chapel Hill area, also known as the Research Triangle, had exploded in population over the past several years, the county school system was nationally recognized for its innovation, and the travel softball opportunities for Jemma were so much better than where we had lived. A vet tech job paid a lot more in Raleigh, there was safe affordable housing, and this bartending job made ends meet, more than paying for our extras, which right now pertained mostly to Jem's softball. I was also closer to State, just in case I decided to get off of my butt and once and for all apply to the vet school to realize my own dream. Someday. Maybe when Jemma's in college...

Of course, the main reason I moved to the Raleigh area, which I would never admit out loud, was that Charlie had to move here for his job with the SBI. After his academy training was over, he was permanently assigned to the capital district, and my entire being needed to be near him no matter where he was living. Charlie was as much a part of me as I was.

So I bought a small two-bedroom townhome and Charlie bought a three-bedroom townhome, both in the same neighborhood. He wasn't really my neighbor because of how big the development was, but he was close enough to come over and close enough for Jemma if she needed him. *Or if I needed him.* It was my way of being married to Charlie, as screwed up as that sounds.

"Did you have a good weekend at home?" I asked Thom. We didn't get to talk a whole lot this evening, even though he was at the bar for all of my four-hour shift.

"I did. I got to take Zach to the Central Park Zoo for the first time," he said, beaming.

I smiled, knowing how much he loved his three-year-old grandson.

"What did you do?" he asked me.

"Jemma had a clinic up at Duke." He knew the whole softball mom ordeal from our many conversations about raising children and the things we do for them.

"We had a bunch of friends over Saturday night and I started thinking about how tired I am of that whole thing," he said, stretching his arms up over his head.

"What whole thing?"

"Entertaining people at my home. I like having a couple of friends over once in a while, but not... Honestly, every single Saturday night I'm home, she has a huge group of people over and expects me to be on, up, and in host mode," Thom said, looking around at the quiet night that blanketed us in its cool, dark air. "I'm fucking tired."

I looked at his weary face, desperately in need of a fluffy pillow. "When do you get to rest?" I asked him.

Thom laughed. "I get to rest when I die." Then he mumbled, "I don't even know why I go home." He seemed to be rambling a bit more than usual. Probably the alcohol. "Sorry, little girl. I don't mean to whine like a pathetic shithead. This case is wearing me out and then there's all the traveling and all the stupid bullshit I have to do when I get home. Part of me likes living as a geographical bachelor down here during the week, just so I don't have to answer to anybody for a few days."

"Aw, Thommy," I said in my best New York accent. "You know how much you miss your wifey and little tiny dawggie."

He smiled at me with that lips-closed-deep-dimpled smile only Thom can do. "What the hell was that?"

"Sorry, that was my best New Yawk accent."

"You sounded like a death row inmate from Chicago!"

We laughed. "Sorry, I guess I'm not so good at talkin' Yankee."

Thom shuffled his feet and looked down. I really wanted to get going, but he kept on talking and I felt sorry for him. He seemed so lonely, especially tonight.

"You know, I'd really like to leave Manhattan altogether and move down here, take a job with one of the firms, and try a slower-paced southern life. Maybe even play more golf and learn how to fish."

"You should! Lots of people from up north have moved down here. You'd probably find yourself a huge house for a lot less than your place in the city. Then one day, you'll be mowing your big, green lawn, and your neighbor will come over to talk to you. And you'll learn that you both grew up on the same street in Brooklyn." I stopped talking and looked behind me as I heard a car door close. Then I looked back at Thom, who was looking down at me, grinning. "You know what they say that Cary stands for?" I asked him, referring to a town right on the outside of Raleigh.

"What?"

"Containment Area for Relocated Yankees."

Thom smirked. "Well, I don't think my wife would go for it. She is Manhattan through and through. I doubt she'd know what to do without a Fifth Avenue." I liked how he said "Manhattan" in his Brooklyn accent.

I chuckled when he made that statement about his wife because I had no clue what kind of world he came from.

I knew Fifth Avenue was where all the expensive shops were, like Chanel and Gucci and Prada. But I didn't know what a Chanel or Gucci or a Prada even was, let alone own anything from them.

Thom continued, "Then I'd get to see you all the time. Maybe you'd invite me and my wife over for a barbecue," he said, putting his hand up on my shoulder. I thought about how nice that would be, inviting some people over for an afternoon of grilled chicken and beer, people who weren't Charlie and Stephanie.

"I'd like that," I said starting to look around, realizing that I needed to get going. It was late and I wanted to say goodnight to Jemma before she went to bed.

"Maybe one day soon we can do that," Thom added. "You live close to here, right?"

"We will, I promise. Thom, I have to go. Are you sure you're okay getting back to the Confederate?"

"I'm fine," he said, bear hugging me and then kissing my forehead.

A part of me felt bad for Thom. All that money he made, working so hard, and he had to spend all this time down here away from his beautiful, designer-clad, New York wife, his successful, grown, New York children and his adorable, New York grandson. He had basically been living out of a suitcase for more than five months now and I don't know how anyone drinks like he does and functions at any level, let alone a high level. I guess some people are just cut out for that. God knows I'm not. Two beers and I'm out like a light.

But during all of my years in the working world, and especially working with the public either in vet care or at a nice bar, I've learned that people are just people, simply trying to survive and get by, doing the best they can. And no matter how much money they make, they still have the same problems and want the same things. In particular, they want someone who cares about them, someone who listens to them, and someone to love. The same was true for Thom Robinson. He just drank more expensive bourbon and had better clothes than most of us.

When I got home, Jemma was in her room on her computer. I asked her how her day went. She was kind of abrupt with me.

"Practice was extra-long tonight and I had a lot of homework," she said with a bit of an attitude.

"Do you think you guys are ready?" I asked her, referring to her team's first game tomorrow.

"Yeah. Coach Lundy's got me starting at short," she replied, again with attitude.

I cleared my throat. "Am I bothering you?" I asked her.

Jemma turned around and looked at me. "No, I'm just busy," she said, obviously annoyed that I'd asked and even further annoyed that I hadn't yet left her room.

While in the shower, I thought about how I should

invite Thom over for a barbecue dinner soon. I trusted him enough to have in my home and to meet my family. I genuinely liked him and it's the least I could do since the poor guy has no life other than his case and the bar, living for his weekends at home. I do think Charlie and Jem both would like him a lot. Jemma would think he's cool because he's from New York and even cooler because he is a Yankees fan. When she finds out that he's offered to take us to Yankee Stadium for a game sometime and to meet Derek Jeter, a close friend of a client, she will think he is the coolest human being ever.

CHARLIE

Standing outside of Courtroom 8A, currently hosting the murder trial of Gregory Massa, a suburban dad from Cary on trial for murdering his wife Kimberly in December 2000, I held my cup of coffee and straightened my suit jacket. I was waiting for my name to be called by the county prosecutor so I could provide my testimony in the Massa case. I was one of the investigators at the crime scene two and a half years ago and I spent the last two weeks going over and over my notes so that I could make sure my memories were as accurate as possible. This is the thirty-fourth case that I've testified in, the twentieth murder, and I still get as nervous as if it were my first time.

Last Monday, I saw one of the best scenes I've ever had the privilege to witness. Being a part of uniting a father and his daughter for the first time, and having it go better than I ever imagined, was the stuff of fairytales. I know it all has something to do with my own missing pieces, but to see a grown man break down in tears as he held his child for the first time, a child that he never knew he had, made me reconcile the bullshit inside of me with my own lack of a father.

It was okay now. I was okay now. I gave Jemma her father instead and for me, emotionally, it was like letting my own father go for good. I was so happy to be a part of something so special.

Rob Caralessi was older than we thought. He had just turned fifty-five. And as Jemma had pegged him, he was a pretty nice guy. I met with him on Saturday so that I could listen to his story and try to figure out how we are going to deal with the Scout issue.

We met at a Waffle House, and he gave me the whole messy tale about how he met Scout while she was waitressing at Marty's Place.

"I started it all. I pursued the relationship with her. She didn't initiate anything with me and was just an adorable young girl doing her work and minding her own business. She had spilled a tray of water on me and something just changed inside of me, almost in an instant. I'd been watching her the whole time I was there for some reason and, I don't know, I've never been so smitten by someone before."

"She was barely nineteen," I said, looking at him like he was an idiot as I imagined Jemma in just five more years being pursued by a man my age and how disgusted that made me feel.

Rob leaned back in his seat. "I know. I didn't look at her like that though. I know it's cliché, but age can be just a number sometimes. That was how I felt about Scout. I came back a few days later looking for her to ask her out to dinner. She said yes and we both wanted to continue to see each other." He stopped, took a sip of his Coke, and continued, "I know it was wrong. Of course it was. But you have to understand that I really did care for Scout a lot, more than I should have. I never looked at what we shared as some kind of sordid affair, regardless of what that might sound like to you or to society at large."

All I could think about was the fact that I was working for her father during that time, about to go in the Army, missing her so much, loving her, and she was up in Raleigh messing around with this man who was almost as old as her own father.

Rob continued, "After several months, right before she went back home for the summer, I basically dumped her when my wife found out. I was planning to end it anyway, but then my wife saw us and I went into survival mode and was doing everything I could to save my marriage." He paused briefly and went on, his voice changing a bit. "I love my wife. I loved her through all of my time with Scout and I love her even more now."

"Loved his wife?" I thought to myself. "How is that possible? How can you love your wife when you're carrying on with another woman?" While I'm not the guy who knows the answers to such complex questions of life, I hoped that I was not the kind of man who would love one woman and then sleep with another behind her back. I didn't think I was. Not normally one to judge, because I've heard it all in my career, I concluded a while back that I simply didn't understand why people do what they do, for love or for anything else really. I mean, Scout was just as complicit in the whole thing, no matter how young she was. She knew better than to be involved with a married man.

"And this I want you to hear clearly: I did not know she was pregnant. She never told me. Plus, I was told by a doctor after my daughter was born that I couldn't have children anymore. Natural birth control." He sighed, took another sip of his Coke and said, "A part of me couldn't believe Jemma was mine and a part of me knew that she was absolutely mine the moment she came into my office." He paused. "Charlie, I have felt like shit every single day since for what I did to Scout. And what I did to my wife. It's something that I live with. The shame of it all never goes away."

I was impressed. Rob took total responsibility for everything he did. I doubt most guys in his situation would have done that. In my line of work, they always tend to blame someone else rather than themselves or at least try to make themselves look victimized in some way. Rob didn't do that.

"She was just a kid for God's sake," he said to me, shaking his head. "She was so innocent and sweet and, as far as I could tell, no one had ever even touched her before."

I nodded. "Yeah, I've known Scout my whole life and was with her all through high school. She never dated anyone."

Rob took the last bite of his burger and I finished my sandwich before saying, "I need to figure out how I'm going to tell Scout about what's going on. She's going to be really upset with me and, even though I know it was the right thing to do for Jemma, she's going to feel betrayed. I'm her only real friend."

Rob looked up at me. "I remember her talking about you. She said you had gone into the Army."

Goddamn that was a long time ago.

"Look, I know that you want to spend time with Jemma and get to know her. And you should. But I need to figure out this stuff first and make sure that things go as smooth as possible for everyone. Getting Jemma her own cell phone so she can at least talk to you at this point was a good idea, but I don't know if you should be coming to her softball games. I mean, what if Scout sees you?"

"I'll sit with the other team's side. She won't recognize me. It's been a really long time, Charlie. I'm an old man now. Jemma said she'd email me her schedule, so I'll keep my distance until we have all of this worked out. I do need and want to talk to Scout, though. So you've got to tell her. Don't sit on this. She's gonna find out one way or another and it's probably best if it comes from you."

Rob made sense. I was more nervous telling Scout about what I've done than I am testifying in this trial. I was even more nervous than in February 1991 when my Bradley Fighting Vehicle started moving through the Euphrates

River Valley. But I knew I needed to do it. And Rob needed to tell his wife.

"What about your wife?" I asked him.

"Well, that's something I'm trying to rev myself up for," Rob said, clearly not ready to do it. "It's going to bring up all of our old shit, her pain and suffering and, really, a whole new can of worms."

"What do you mean?"

"My kids don't know about what I did. They knew back then that we were having some marital problems, but they don't know that I cheated on her for several months. So dear old dad falling off his pedestal, coupled with 'Hey, here's your baby sister you didn't know you had...' is going to set off a few bombs in my life."

Rob stopped, picked at his fries, and continued. "But I trust in Rita. I know her, and she is strong. She can handle anything. I deserve to be humbled for what I did to her and I can never really forgive myself anyway. I know that she is going to be devastated at first, but I've been thinking about this nonstop for five days now and, no matter what, Jemma is worth it. She is my daughter and a gift from God. I know that my family is going to be upset with me, but when they all see that this is really about blood...about family..."

I laughed. "You think they will just embrace her?"

"Charlie, we are family people. Everything is about the family. My parents are dead. My grandmother is dead. No matter how good Rita's family is to me, I have no blood family other than my own children and grandchildren. Jemma is my blood. That matters more than anything to me. Plus, she is just a kid. She didn't ask to be born into this mess. I might not deserve her, but she does deserve to know me and her own family."

The waitress came by to refill our water and Rob asked me some questions about Scout.

"Wow. She never finished at State?" he asked, surprised. "She loved it there. She really wanted to be a vet."

"Well, she's a vet tech, so…it's close."

"But she never went back to school after Jemma was born?"

"She finished her degree eventually, but she didn't go on to vet school or anything. She has all but given up on that."

Rob looked down. His mouth curved a bit at the sides. He sighed, sounding like his brain was letting out some ancient compress of air. Jesus, he and Jemma looked exactly alike. Even their small frown and the accompanying deep sigh is the same.

"And all this time and she never got married? That's really sad. She's the marrying kind. Such a great girl. Would've made a great wife for some lucky guy," Rob said slowly, more deliberately than he had been before.

His mind was obviously recalling a different Scout than the one I knew. The one I knew was not the marrying kind. The one I knew would never let herself love any man, let alone a lucky one.

I think Rob began to realize that what he did to her ran a lot deeper than he ever imagined. He didn't just break her heart, which was bad enough. He also set her life on a completely altered course, one that was harsh and very difficult, one where she made different decisions and breathed different kinds of breaths because of what she had been put through — by him.

While he was off trying to be a better husband and father, redeeming himself at home, and continuing his success in insurance sales, a young woman barely twenty gave birth to his child and had to give up all of her own dreams, suffer through the humiliation of an unplanned pregnancy in a Southern Baptist household, live at home with her parents, work two jobs to give her daughter a better life, and worse yet, never let another person close to her again. I explained to him how she always had me, but she had kept things between us platonic.

He also didn't see how all that mess affected me. I didn't have to leave my promising career in the Army, but I felt like I needed to help Scout and be there for her and Jem. Plus, I wanted to be near Scout anyway. And if she wouldn't marry me, then the next best thing was to just be near her all the time.

JEMMA

Shagging balls in the outfield before a game sucks. It makes me feel lazy because it actually is lazy and all we do out here is gossip anyway. It's still a little chilly out this time of year, so I'm wearing a baggy and uncomfortable long sleeve shirt underneath my jersey. We're playing against a school that is supposed to be the best team in the conference this year so I don't know what to think about it. We have a good lineup and, because I'm only a freshman starting in a key position on a fairly decent varsity softball team full of travel players, I know that all the parents are going to be watching me closely and judging the job I'm doing.

But nothing — not even a loss, not even playing badly, not even a strike out or an error — is going to get me down today. Because on this day, for the first time in my life, my real father is going to come to see me play in a game. My Pop-Pop and Charlie have come to as many games as possible ever since I was a little girl and, as much as they've supported me and been there for me, they aren't my fathers. I've had one out there all along and now he's going to be a part of my life.

Meeting my him for the first time was the best thing that's ever happened to me. I knew when I saw him on the Internet after finding that card in mom's stuff that he was my father. And when we were standing together in his office last week, it was all I could do not to just dump the folder on his desk and run away and go throw up. But I didn't. I stood there with all the strength I could manage and said what I'd been practicing in the mirror for three weeks. But when I told him that he was my father, he didn't even bother to open the folder. He knew. Same as me.

Rob Caralessi stood there staring at me for a good long minute. He told me later when we were talking on the phone, while my mom was at work, and after he got me my own cell phone just so we could talk to each other, "I didn't want to speak. I was trying to take in the features of your face. You look just like me, like how Lisa Marie Presley looks like her father Elvis, but still looks like a girl."

I had to look up that whole reference because I had no idea who Lisa Marie Presley was or what she looked like. But when I pulled up her picture next to Elvis', I could see exactly what he meant.

As we both remained frozen while standing in his office, he finally spoke. "Is your mom's name Scout?" And I could see his eyes were welling up like he was going to cry or something.

And when I nodded yes, he kept repeating, "I didn't know. I never knew." Then he came around the side of his desk, looked down at me, and cupped my face with one hand. "How old are you?"

"Fourteen," I said. "Last month."

I could tell he was studying me, maybe doing some math in his head or trying to think about it more, and then, suddenly, he grabbed me, just as Charlie opened the door to come in to check on me. Rob held onto me in a full embrace, his hands pulling me tightly into himself, and before long he had tears coming out of his eyes. I've never seen a man cry before so it was a little weird. He was holding onto me like I was his long lost daughter — which I am — but that was exactly how it felt, too.

I looked at Charlie standing in the door and he was smiling, satisfied. This was the best outcome we could've hoped for. Soon, all three of us left the office together, and Charlie drove us around, per my father's — *Jeez! I like saying "my father's"* — directions.

First, he wanted to show me where he lived. It was a big, beautiful house in a nice neighborhood. "Are you rich?" I asked him.

"Not rich," he said, "but I do very well and own my own business. I've worked hard for a lot of years to build everything up to what we have today."

He told me that I had two siblings: a brother named Chase who was thirty-two years old and a sister named Samantha who was twenty-nine. "Chase has two sons named Dylan and Sean. So you have two nephews."

"I'm an auntie? How cool is that?"

As we drove around Rocky Mount, he told me about how he and my mom met when she was in college. "It was awful what I did to your mother. It's all hard for me to explain, but I know I hurt her. I've always felt bad about it because I really cared for her a lot." Then he paused, took a deep breath and continued, "And Jemma, please understand. This will be a very difficult thing for me to tell my wife and kids. I'm gonna need some time to figure it out."

"I understand. I'm just so happy that I finally got to meet you," I said. "Most people take it for granted."

"Take what for granted?" he asked.

"Knowing who their father is."

Rob turned around and winked at me. I knew that he wanted to know me, too.

At one point, he asked Charlie how I was able to get the SBI to help me. "The SBI investigates crimes. I might not be the best husband in the world, but I'm not a criminal."

Charlie laughed from the front seat. "I'm an SBI agent, but I have raised Jemma as if she was my own daughter for her whole life."

"So are you Scout's husband?" he asked.

With a twinge of disappointment in his voice, a sound I am very used to by now, Charlie said, "No, I'm just Charlie. Her best friend."

"From Haddleboro..." my father said.

"Yes, from Haddleboro."

After showing us around Rocky Mount some more, pointing out a few historical places, showing us the private school his kids had attended, taking us by some of the flooding damage that still remained from Hurricane Floyd, and talking about the next steps and how we could stay in touch, I suggested that Charlie get me a cell phone so I could talk to my father whenever I wanted.

Rob said, "That's a great idea," and we went over to a store where he proceeded to buy me one.

And just like that, I had a father and a cell phone.

I looked in the visitor's section and saw him sitting on the top bleacher with a Red Sox baseball cap on his head and wearing a pair of sunglasses. I guess that was his attempt at a disguise. I'm glad he wasn't wearing a fake mustache because that would be dumb and would make me laugh. So far, the only thing I didn't like about him was that he was a Red Sox fan. I mean, seriously. Why couldn't he have been a Yankees fan? He waved at me and I waved back. I was so happy. I've never been so happy in my entire life.

I was going to play my best game ever today, just for my dad, Rob Caralessi.

SCOUT

Retrieving the meat out of the fridge, I sliced open the clear wrapping and pulled out the chicken breasts and boneless thighs. I mixed together a marinade from a package and left the chicken to sit down inside the bowl for an hour.

The doorbell rang and Boo went to the door barking. Thom came in, immediately petting Boo, getting him to calm down.

"I've heard so much about you, boy," Thom said, rubbing Boo's ears. "You do live close to Flavia," he said to me, taking a quick scan of my living room.

"Yes, I do," I smiled. I was looking forward to this evening. Jemma and Charlie should be here any minute.

He followed me into the kitchen, and I handed him a beer. "I got exactly what I know you'd like, Mr. Robinson," I said.

He smiled and I found myself noticing how handsome he was.

"You look casual for a change," I remarked, my finger briefly touching a button on his chest. He was wearing a blue shirt and black jeans. He stayed silent and looked at me a bit earnestly for a second and, for the first time, I noticed that his eyes were a hazel color. "That's sad," I said.

"What's sad? That I'm not dressed like a lawyer today?"

"No," I grinned. "Almost six months I've known you and I never noticed the hazel color of your eyes until just now." Okay, Scout. You sound like you're flirting. Stop talking.

Ever since my Rob catastrophe, I've avoided older men like the plague. I've gone as far as imposing an age limit on myself whenever I'd consider going out with — or God forbid, outright dating — any man. Ten years. No more than ten years older. But I have no interest in dating Thom Robinson. I was self aware enough now at my age to realize that I had a thing for older men. But this relationship with Thom was different. I just liked him. Maybe more than I should allow myself to. But what the heck? If you can't let a good person into your heart once or twice in your life, then what is the point of living? This was my attempt to open up to people.

Thom set off no red flags in me and my gut told me that he was a good guy who had no malicious intent. We exchanged phone numbers a few months back and I think he liked having a friend in Raleigh. I didn't mind being that friend for him. It made us both feel a little less lonely, I gathered.

Ever since Charlie began dating Stephanie about a year ago, I don't see him as much. He was still involved in our lives, but this was the first serious girlfriend he has had in a long time, probably his first serious girlfriend ever. I knew Stephanie was a nice girl, and I did like her for Charlie, but a part of me knew that he was supposed to be with me. And I couldn't let that happen. Even after all these years and after all he has done to show me how much he loves me, I still didn't deserve him. He was too good for me. Charlie was the greatest man in the world and this was the first time I thought maybe he had found someone who is worthy of him.

I've talked to Thom about Charlie a couple of times and he had told me that I should tell Charlie how I really feel.

"Little girl, he won't know unless you tell him. You don't want someone like that to pass you by. It only happens once in life and that's if you're lucky," he had told me. "I don't know where I'd be without my wife. She is the greatest thing that's ever happened to me." It was excellent advice, but he didn't know the rest of my story.

I confided in him about Rob, although I didn't name him. "He was just this beautiful older man. And I was so stupid and naïve, believing all the crap that he fed me. He told me he loved me and treated me so well. And then to find out that I was just used for his fun and amusement...Well, that almost sent me into a depression I couldn't climb out of." I stopped talking and looked down at the floor briefly. "Jemma saved my life."

"And he doesn't know about Jemma?"

"No way. I never told him. No one but me knows who her father is. And I will take it to my grave."

Thom was so nice about it, just asking me questions and not judging me at all. He listened, offered a few thoughts of his own, and hugged me tight when I started getting emotional about it. He made me feel like he really cared and understood that I was doing what I thought was right, even if others in my family did not agree.

I told him more than I've ever told anyone about some of my deepest, darkest stuff, some of my internal struggles with self-worth and how I had lost my faith in God. I didn't go as far as to tell him about Brother Doug, but I certainly opened up to Thom Robinson more than I had to anyone else in my life. Charlie knew me better than anyone, but I never told him about Brother Doug. I was so afraid of losing him if I did.

I couldn't put my finger on what it was about Thom that made me feel so safe to talk about my pain. Maybe it was because one day he'd leave Raleigh and would go back to his life, forgetting that I even existed — right along with the stories I've told him. Maybe it was because I could tell that he cared and even empathized with me in some way. Maybe it was because I sensed that he lived with his own suffering, just as I did. We seemed bonded in that way. Maybe it was because I simply needed to talk to someone at this point in my life without the fear of losing him, and Thom had been presented to me on a leather-upholstered barstool.

We hung out on my backyard patio at my small bistro table and talked about everything under the sun. I started heating up the grill. Jemma hadn't come home yet, which was odd. She seemed to be staying later and later at practice lately with that coach of hers, which really bothered me. She had homework to do and I didn't like the coach. He was young and good-looking and I had an uneasy feeling about him.

Charlie still hadn't come over, either, and he should've been over at the same time Thom arrived. Then my phone rang.

"Scout, I can't come tonight. I'm sorry," Charlie said. "I got called in to work."

"Okay, another time then," I said. "Be careful, please," and we hung up.

Then the phone rang again and this time it was Jemma. "Mom, Coach Lundy is taking us to Cook Out. I'll be home later."

I went back outside and told Thom that it looked like it was just going to be me and him. "I'm sorry," I said. "Charlie got called in to work. Crime scenes are usually on their own time table. And apparently Jemma's not going to be home until later. She's with her team."

Thom winked. "It's okay, little girl. Now you'll just have to have me over for dinner again when everyone's free."

I got him another beer and began to cook the chicken. I pulled out a potato salad, nachos, and some steamed vegetables. He talked some more about his case and how he thinks he has another couple of months to go on it, how he met some great people through working on the case, and how his wife doesn't seem to miss him anymore.

"Sunday before I left to fly back, I told her that I didn't want a bunch of people over when I'm home. I'm just too tired and would rather it be quiet and relaxed, at least until I get back to Manhattan for good."

"She didn't agree?"

"She just got pissed, told me that it's ridiculous, and offered instead to go off for the weekends and not bother me so I could have my peace and quiet," he said.

I winced. "Where's she gonna go?"

"To the country with her friends," he said, his voice a little quiet. "She said she was even going to take the dog with her."

"What are you gonna do while you're all alone then?" I asked, feeling awful for him.

"I guess I'll just mess around the apartment, do husbandly types of things. She always has a 'honey do' list anyway. I'll see Bethany and Zach over on Long Island," he explained.

I felt bad for him. He works so much and spends his weeks down here, all alone without her, and then when he finally gets home, all he wants to do is relax and so she decides to go off "to the country?" What does that even mean?

"Well, I can tell you this. I will definitely miss you when you finally do leave Raleigh," I said emphatically. "My bar will never be the same! You actually make me look forward to going to work."

His face perked up when I said that, like it made him feel good that he would be missed.

"You never know. I really do like it down here. I'm going to talk to my wife about maybe making a move south. I wasn't kidding when I told you that the other night."

I laughed. "You remember saying that to me?"

"What do you mean?" he looked puzzled.

"You were quite inebriated," I said, smiling.

"Scout, I remember. I always remember everything when I'm drunk. Everything."

"Alright, only you would know that," I said, putting some plump and juicy chicken onto a plate. "Are you a breast man or a thigh man?" I asked him, realizing that I unintentionally threw him a double-entendre, which would easily be construed as flirting.

Thom looked up at me then looked down at my butt. He smirked and said, "Well, I'm really more of an ass man."

I put a breast and a thigh on his plate as I turned red.

"Now, now, behave," I commanded, trying to change the subject.

Eventually, Jemma came home and was very polite to Thom, shook his hand, engaged in some small talk about the Yankees, and then went upstairs to shower. Thom took another swig of his — *fifth?* — beer. "I need to head out now. I have an early morning. But thank you for the great meal and even better company," he said. "Will I see you tomorrow?"

"Yes, sir, I'll be there ready to serve you," I answered. "Are you okay to drive? I will gladly drive you back. It's not a big deal."

He laughed, "I'm fine, little girl. Beer doesn't do anything to me."

Then he walked closer, hugged me like he usually does and, rather than give me a sweet forehead kiss, kissed me fully on my lips, with a hint of sexual charge to it. I was so surprised by it — and it did feel nice — that I kissed him back. Then he left.

I spent the rest of the night wondering what the heck all that meant and then hitting myself in the head. No way, I am not letting this happen! I'm not getting sucked into some lonely man's fantasies again. "But it was just a peck, Scout. Chill out. It was nothing but a simple kiss between friends. That's how they do things in New York."

Yeah, that was it. It was just how they did things in New York. He didn't mean anything by it.

That was what I kept telling myself as I fell asleep that night.

RITA CARALESSI, AGE 54

Exactly one month ago today, my brother Sal passed away. He was fifty-two years old. He did exactly what all parents forbid their children to do: die first, die before them. I don't think any parent, no matter what age, is ready or equipped to deal with the death of a child. And it certainly doesn't matter that they have six other children.

Sal was larger than life. He was my father's oldest son, my closest sibling, and Chase's godfather. His wife and children were devastated by his untimely death and, even though I do feel all of my fifty-four years on some mornings, I cannot imagine being widowed even now — and definitely not at forty-eight years old with three children still at home. But this is why my big family is such a blessing. Celeste has all of us to help her and the kids through these tough times ahead. I just wish I lived closer to them.

Father Neville told me after mass last week, during a private chat, "God's reasons and God's timing of life's events do not always make sense to us. But everything is a part of some larger plan."

Of course, all of that sounds nice. And who doesn't

like the answers to life all wrapped up in a sparkly package from God? But it doesn't change the fact that some boxes, no matter how nicely wrapped, are still just empty inside.

"But I can't imagine why in the world God would take my brother in such a brutal and tragic way, leaving a wife husbandless and his children fatherless," I responded, holding back my tears and with a slight quiver in my voice.

Father Neville put his hands over my hands. "Rita, dear, it happens single every day to families everywhere. It was just his time. He had a wonderful and full life and you all were so lucky to have had Sal for fifty-two great years."

I knew that he was right.

So when Rob came home yesterday at lunchtime unexpectedly and said, "Rita, we need to talk about something very serious," my gut flared up in pain. What horrible thing was he going to tell me? What life changing information was going to some out of his mouth? Still raw and terribly vulnerable, I thought about Sal's death, my intense grief over his loss, how much I hated being away from my family who all lived up in New Jersey, how alone I suddenly felt inside now that my children were grown and gone, and how much of life is just made up of endless forms of loss. And then small gains. And then big losses again. Until the ultimate loss of our own lives.

"My mistake all those years ago," Rob started, like he was sitting in a confessional and I was his priest.

I didn't know where this was going, so I just asked,

"The very one that almost ended our marriage?" *As if there was any other mistake.*

Rob looked at me in my eyes and nodded. Then he peered down at his feet and told me that it had apparently produced another life entirely.

"I'm the father of a fourteen-year-old girl. I just met her for the first time a week and half ago."

If I had been holding shoes in my hands, they both would've dropped onto the floor.

"God never gives you more than you handle," Sister Mary Josephine once told me in St. Thomas Aquinas Catholic School near Camp Pendleton, California back in 1962. I would call upon those words every time I was handed a bag of shit from life. And far be it from me to refer to any child as a "bag of shit," but this unfathomable situation that Rob has presented to me is indeed a bag of shit.

He looked so pathetic sitting on our otherwise untouched white couch in the living room. His head hung low, his tie was undone, and he had sweat patches on his armpits like he went for a long run in his work clothes on his way home. I had come in from the backyard where I'd spent the morning cleaning up some of the winter mess in my garden to make way for the tulips desperately trying to get taller.

"Rita, I am so sorry. I know we went through so much back then over my…what I did…and we worked so hard to get past it. But…" He didn't know what else to say. And neither did I.

I was still fully in grief over Sal and now this completely unexpected explosion in yet another area of my life just made me become numb everywhere.

"How am I supposed to react to this?"

My husband has a secret fourteen-year-old daughter by a college girl he was screwing behind my back. My children have a younger sister that they never knew existed. Now they would not only be presented with this new flesh and blood human being as part of their family, but they would also learn what their father did to their mother and their family years ago. And they would hate him for it. Except for that one rather extensive time period, Rob has been the best father in the world. And here I am, yet again, trying to make things better for Rob no matter the mess he's made and the difficult position he's put us in.

"Rob, I don't know what you want me to say," I responded, after he clearly gave up talking altogether. My heart was stone now. It's really some kind of a gift that my heart can do that, I suppose. It would've made me a great investment banker in New York City, and it sure came in handy in dealing with the rather massive blows that have hit me during the course of my life.

That night, Rob stayed downstairs watching TV alone and I laid in my bed with the lights off, thinking. What I had gathered was that there was a young girl out there with Rob's face and black hair and her mother's voice. Her mother was not me. She had been raised by a single woman, who'd been barely an adult herself, and probably raised in some kind of poverty. Or maybe her parents helped her out. The girl was a softball player, something I have no doubt Rob was proud of in some way — even though he had nothing to do with it! — since he had always wanted Samantha to be a softball player. The girl and her mother lived in Raleigh. Her mother kept Rob's identity hidden all of these years. Some SBI agent had a DNA test done without his knowledge and Rob was definitely the father. And Rob was happy about this. He's happy that he is this girl's father. That, I could not wrap my head around.

How could he be happy that he is the father of some bastard child? And then I instantly scolded myself for even thinking that of any child. But we are talking about *my* philandering husband and *his* bastard child, not someone else's philandering husband and bastard child. It took me a long, long time not to remember, every day when I woke up, what Rob did to me. But, eventually, I didn't think about it much at all because I made peace with it and him. I'm old enough to realize that the inner struggles of our lives can manifest themselves in several different, sometimes destructive, ways. And now once again, here was my excruciating pain. Only this time, presented to me eternally, in the form of a real live human being.

Life is fragile. God knows I know that is true. Life itself is a gift. A child is a gift from God. Clichés exist for a reason; many of them are just polite expressions of truth. I knew that no matter what agony I was living in right now, either because of my brother's sudden death or because of the unexpected presence of my...*step-daughter's?*...life that the one value Rob and I shared beyond all others was that of family.

Little Jemma Webb was family.

JEMMA

After practice, my dad picked me up and we went to Cook Out, my favorite place, for a burger and a shake. He told me that he was going to get to every game he possibly can this season and that he would come and get me from practice at least once a week so we could have dinner together. I can't believe all these years I thought that my dad had abandoned us — and here my mom just wouldn't let me know him. I was so mad at her that I couldn't even stand being in the house at the same time. So I just stayed in my room all the time.

My dad tried to reason with me: "Jemma, it's just a complicated situation. You shouldn't be so hard on your mom. She was doing what she thought was best. Everything that happened was my fault."

"I know she thought she was protecting me, but I'm pissed off. I spent my whole life wondering who my father is and all along it was…you! You're not some deadbeat in jail or some drug addict or a rapist or something. You're a really nice man who would've loved me just like Charlie does. Maybe even more. And not only that, but you would've given my mom support to help with me. Then she wouldn't have had to work two jobs and live with my grandparents and everything."

He took a bite of his burger and with his mouth full said, "I told my wife about you."

My stomach clenched. "I guess that must've been hard."

He nodded, chewing. "Yeah. She's gonna need some time to deal with the whole idea of you before you two meet."

I understood that. Taking a long sip on my vanilla milkshake, I said, "It's okay. I mean, finding out that your husband unknowingly fathered a daughter out of wedlock probably sucks royally."

My dad smiled at me and said, "Hey. Look at me."

I looked up at him.

"I know my wife. She will come around and it will be okay eventually. Just might take a while."

I wasn't so sure. I wanted her to like me, but I could understand that accepting me into her life was just a constant reminder of what my dad had done to her all those years ago. It's like the worst kind of scar, one that you have to see all the time, remembering what gave it to you and how much pain it caused, and how ugly it is. It can't simply be covered up with some clothes or makeup. It's the kind of scar that mangles someone's face. And there's no plastic surgery in the whole world that covers up the scars of an unwanted child.

"What I did to my wife and also to your mom was wrong. But to me, you are the best thing that could've come from the whole mess. I mean that. You are not a mistake, Jemma. I don't ever want you to believe that. You are a gift from God," he stated with a voice full of conviction.

I appreciated him saying so, but I really wasn't the kind of girl who ever thought that way about herself. My mom made sure of it. Every night when she put me to bed, she'd rub my forehead and tell me, "You are my heart and my soul." I always knew that I was profoundly loved and wanted, no matter how I came into this world. And she had surrounded me with people who loved me: Charlie, my grandparents, the people in our church.

Since my mom has been working a lot of evenings at Flavia lately, and even missed one of my games, I've been able to talk a lot to my dad on the phone. We've really gotten to know each other, quickly. Even Charlie seems to like him and thinks that he will be good to me. I trust Charlie's judgment since he's pretty good at reading people and especially because he loves me like I'm his own.

Last night, I had dinner with him and his girlfriend Stephanie.

"So when are you gonna tell my mom about what's going on?" I asked Charlie.

He just sighed. "Girlie, I don't know. I don't know how to tell her. She's going to feel betrayed."

Stephanie said, "Charlie, you have got to suck it up and do it. Scout needs to know."

"I know, but it's not so easy. There are parts of Scout

that are a dark mystery and, while I know that the rational part of her will see that this was the best thing for Jemma, that other part of her… I don't know how it will affect her."

"Maybe I should tell her then," I said. "I'm not scared of her."

"Jem, I don't want her to hurt more than she already hurts. You don't know what it's like to be your mother and I don't want to approach her the wrong way and send her into some kind of a depression," Charlie tried to explain.

Stephanie seemed to handle, fairly well, the strangely complicated relationship that Charlie had with my mom. I liked to observe her because she was super confident and didn't come across like she felt threatened by my mom's presence in his life, like some of the girls Charlie had dated before. Also, Charlie bought Stephanie a ring and was going to ask her to marry him. I was the only person who knew about it. That was yet another thing he was scared to tell my mom. Two huge life changing things: one is that I know my dad and he is in my life now, and two is that Charlie loves Stephanie enough to marry her. I knew both would be big hits on her.

I'll never understand why she would never marry Charlie herself. I'm not stupid. I knew they loved each other.

We were all sitting in some kind of weird holding pattern about how to tell my mom about Rob. She was so busy working two jobs and trying to scrape together her time so she could be there for me, I doubt she noticed much of anything extra going on. Plus, she had that old man from New York over for supper the other night. I had no idea what the hell that was about. She had never brought any man home to meet me before. And while she told me he was her friend, that I'd really like him, and that he knew Derek Jeter, I got some other kind of signal from them, like they were both keen on each other. So that pissed me off.

There was something about him that I didn't like, something that bothered me about how he smiled at me and the kinds of words that he said. He didn't seem genuine to me, like he was a big fake. Maybe it's his accent. He sounded both tough and stupid to me, like he was really a big jerk pretending to be cool. Maybe it's not fair of me and I'm just partial to Charlie, but she could do so much better than that guy. My mom was really pretty and I knew that Haley's dad had a big crush on her. Her parents were divorced, and he was always standing next to her at my games, trying to talk to her. And even I thought he was pretty cute — for a dad.

So, because I wasn't sure how my life was going to change, or if it would change that much at all — other than having A REAL LIVE ACTUAL FATHER — I let myself enjoy all the time I spent talking to Rob, getting to know him, and seeing him from time to time.

But I couldn't wait for my mom to know already and for his wife to like me or something because I wanted to be able to go to his house and have a sleepover and meet my brother and sister and my nephews and learn a lot more about who I am. There's a whole side of me I have yet to explore.

I love my Webb side. It's great and I have the best family in the world. But I am half Italian, half Caralessi, and I bet that's pretty awesome, too.

But I will never like the Red Sox.

SCOUT

I called and called the house for Jem, but she was not answering. I beeped her beeper, telling her to get her little butt to a phone and call me. When she never called me back at work, I started to get the "oh no" feeling of terror and dread that all mothers get when they cannot get a hold of their child in this day and age. *I need to bite the bullet and get her a cell phone already!* I called Charlie's house, but he wasn't home. I called his cell phone and it went straight to voice mail. I texted him, "Pls call me. Cant get in touch w Jem."

The bar was insanely busy. John and Mel, two retirees who were always so friendly to me, came in tonight after a day of golf down at Tobacco Road. They come in at least once a week to watch college basketball. Mel likes the Tarheels and John doesn't give a rat's butt about any particular team. He likes to watch the games and criticize the officiating because he used to be a basketball ref once upon a time.

"Scout, you look stressed out," Mel said to me, taking a sip of his beer.

"I'm fine, thanks," I lied to his face.

Just then Thom came in looking the worse for wear.

He blew me a kiss, making me blush, and I fixed him a whiskey sour.

"Little girl, you just made my shitty-ass day," he said, taking a sip.

All the people in the bar were watching a March Madness game and getting a little loud. I swear, the owners should just dump the steakhouse part of this place and turn it into a sports bar. That's what it's become — this month anyway. I was running around with the two other bartenders like well-choreographed orangutans showing off our mad mixology skills when suddenly, my phone chirped. It was a text from Charlie. "Jems w me and Steph." Thank God for that. I think I needed a vacation.

When the current game ended and the TV turned to yet another game, some of the crowd dispersed. By 9:00, most of the people had left. I was relieved. There were just a handful of patrons and of course, my dearly drunk pal, Thom.

I served him too much tonight and wanted to stop making him drinks, but he'd insist. "Little girl, I'm just gonna walk on down the street," he said.

"Thom, please, just go to the Confederate now," I begged him. "I have to work extra late anyway. I promise, I will stop by to check on you."

"I swear, I'll just drink water until you get off," he said.

That made me feel better. It bothered me how much I

cared. I had to close the bar down, which I rarely ever have to do, and Thom insisted on staying the duration. Both of the other bartenders left and the place was basically empty. Thom sat on his stool, complaining about everything that happened with his case earlier today. "The judge is a fuckin' dick."

Since I wasn't quite sure of all the details concerning the litigation, but I knew it was in federal court and involved an insane amount of money, I just listened to him as he vented while I cleaned up. At one point, I had to go back into the kitchen to find more glasses to restock the bar. "Thom, I'll be right back," I said abruptly, ducking into the kitchen.

About to grab some cocktail glasses from the dishwashing area, and realizing it was so hot and steamy, I slipped out the back door onto the small stoop jutting over an alley and facing Peace Street. It was a crisp night, and the cooler air felt so good on my skin.

Suddenly, the back door opened and Thom came outside with me. He sniffed the air. "Wow. This is nice, Scout. A little spot to get some fresh air."

I sighed at him. He looked pretty rough, with bloodshot eyes and that putrid whiskey smell coming from his pores. I was sad for him. The guy works so much, is always under so much stress, is so far away from his family, and he has had to basically invent friends in a bar to get by from day to day. I grew to feel as if it were my responsibility to look after him while he was in Raleigh. I liked feeling that way, almost like

I was needed in some way.

"You going home?" I asked him, hoping he'd say yes. "I'll walk you home, Thom." The guy needed to go to bed. I'd walk with him to the Confederate and make sure he got into his room safely.

My heart started racing a little and suddenly, I began to feel very nervous. I didn't want to be outside in the dark on this stoop with him. The other night, he kissed me in my house and, while I tried to pretend that it didn't mean anything, I knew that it did. It had to have meant *something*. And I didn't want it to, but I also wanted it to at the same time. Dear God, no. Here I go again.

Thom made me feel so good about myself, a feeling I hadn't known in a long, long time. But he was married. As long as I kept my boundaries, we would be fine. He respected me and I was certain that he loved his wife by the way he talked about her. I had no interest whatsoever in being some lonesome man's fun time and I've never been the kind of girl who gets romantic with anyone just for the sake of having fun. My heart wasn't cut out for that kind of stuff. I was always one of those silly romantics who believed that sexual intimacy was an expression of love, no doubt more of my Southern Baptist upbringing. I'm so naïve...

I turned around to go back into the kitchen and Thom stepped in front of me. "Kiss me," he said. So I gave him a peck on the cheek. And I'm sure that this could've been forecasted by anyone with half a brain cell, but he kissed me back on my lips and did not stop. Like an idiot caught up in a bad romance novel, I followed his lead and kissed him too, taking him in the same way that he was taking me. And faster than I could shift my feet, his hands made their way under my shirt and then down my pants, and I let them continue on to wherever they wanted to go. What in the world was wrong with me?

It felt so good to have a man's hands on me like this, strong and sensual. He wanted me. And I knew that I wanted him, too. I let him touch me and kiss me and, before I knew it, he took my hands and put them onto him. It's been so long since I've touched a man that I almost forgot what one feels like. He was swollen and ravenous and I was lost in the moment just enough to go along with the flow of everything, not even thinking about the fact that I was doing exactly what I vowed I'd never do again! *How is this even happening?*

It was because he had been drinking. That's why this was happening. But I knew that it was really happening because I was allowing it. And it was also my fault because I'm the one who served him the drinks. I was a pathetic weakling with no will when it came to the charms of Thom Robinson. Because I felt so responsible for what was happening, I made excuses for him. He wouldn't have made a move on me if he had been sober. *Yes, he would! He did the other night!*

He was kissing me so fervently and with so much fury that at one point, as he pulled away and looked into my eyes,

I said to him, "Thom, what we doing?"

He whispered, breathless, "Having fun. I've wanted to kiss you like this since the night I met you."

We devoured each other and soon his mouth was on me in places that have not seen daylight since Abraham Lincoln freed the slaves. *My God, what am I doing? What are we doing? And why does this have to feel so amazing?*

I had no excuse for my behavior other than I wanted him, too, and no matter how strong I thought I had been, I was no match for this inconceivably mesmerizing man who had stealthily snuck his way into my heart over the past six months.

But I couldn't let it go further. I couldn't. I had to stop this. And when my conscience decided to make an appearance onto my face, Thom stopped to look at me and said, "Listen to me. You are the only one. Just you. I've never done this with anyone else before." Then he added, slowly, "I've fallen in love with you, little girl." He kissed me some more, but this time more tenderly, and his hands held onto my ribs and then slowly moved to my back, gently pushing my body against the outside wall. I took in all of his words, his wet thirst for me and believed him.

"I think I'm falling in love with you too," I whispered back to him. And I knew that in some way, not quite sure what way exactly, I meant it.

Then without warning, the Southern Baptist guilt showed up wearing a cape with a big "WWJD" on it and inserted itself like a force field around my body. I immediately stopped him, pushed away, and walked back into the kitchen, leaving him alone outside. As I went back into the bar while buttoning my shirt and trying to fix my pants, within a few minutes, Thom came through the door and into the restaurant, walked over to his bar stool, and grabbed his jacket. He stared at me and I kept my head down, wiping up the sink area, pretending not to feel his eyes on me. When I finally looked up, I watched him walk out of Flavia.

Mortified and feeling, once again, like the whore I've been before — because that's what I am and will always be! — I cleaned up as fast as I could, sped out, and headed home. I was full of shame and could hear Cammy DeHaan's screams of "slut, husband stealer, disgusting beast, cunt, horrid bitch, abomination to God" ringing in my ears as I drove to my house.

When I got home, Jemma was on her computer in her room. She was writing an email. When I opened her door without knocking, she minimized her screen and said, "Don't you know how to knock?"

Considering how awful I felt about myself, I snapped back at her little smart mouth. "Don't you dare speak to me like that. This is my house. If I want to open a door, I will open a door."

Jemma turned back around. "I have a right to my privacy!"

"Actually, no you don't. As long as you are my

responsibility, I have a right to YOUR privacy."

She scoffed. "This is my room!"

"That I work two jobs to pay for!"

"No one told you to work two jobs."

"Do you think some money fairy just shows up to provide a home and food and an education for you — not to mention your softball?" I challenged her. This kid had no idea how much it cost to provide for one child in 2003. I had no idea how people did it for more than one!

"Just go away and leave me alone!" Jemma shouted at me. Boo looked up from the bed, startled at how loud things were getting between us. We generally didn't yell at each other like this. Our mother-daughter spats were usually full of passive-aggressive statements and sarcastic commentary instead of heated words.

I was done. My daughter was hardly speaking to me lately, she was spending all of her time with either Charlie or her softball coach — and again, I did not like that at all! — I was working too much and feeling like I had been neglecting her, and now I've destroyed what I thought was a wonderful friendship, something that I was naïve enough to believe was real and would last. Plus, I was flat out exhausted. My work schedule was killing me.

So I shut Jemma's door, went into my room, took off my clothes, and went immediately under the covers. When I woke up the next morning, I had a text message on my phone from Thom that read, "C u later."

ROB

As much as I had been looking forward to this weekend away at spring training with Chase, I knew it was going to be difficult and that I was going to ruin it with my news. Telling Rita about Jemma was both the hardest thing and, in some strange way, one of the greatest things that I've ever done. Nothing is ever real to me until I share it with Rita. And while I knew it would hurt her, hurt me, hurt our children — the last thing I ever wanted to do to any of them — here was this girl who was mine and therefore *ours*, too. Blood. Family. And she was so amazing. It was surreal.

Jemma was a lot like her mother, only more self-assured and assertive. Spending time with her, either on the phone or the handful of times in person, she reminded me why I had fallen for Scout all those years ago. It wasn't just her unassuming beauty and innocence, all wrapped up in this little fireball sweetheart of a personality, but her mother had been the perfect blending of loud and quiet, embodied an intense thoughtfulness and a clandestine air, a girl who loved so hard and so soft at the exact same time. She was never just one thing, like so many people seem to be. Jemma was a lot like that, but also confident enough to be President of the United States.

Scout had brought out some of the best parts in me, much of which I kept under wraps, even with my own wife. I could always be myself around Scout, with no threats of criticism or interrogation or the subtle put-downs that go with being married to someone for a long time. She made me feel appreciated and accepted for exactly who I am and, a lot of the time, I hadn't felt like that with Rita, no matter how much we loved each other and how close we were to each other.

And now I had a piece of this back with Jemma in my life. She was my heart walking outside of my body, as much a part of me as Chase and Samantha. Her dark features, her face, and her build were mine. Even the whole Yankees thing was a cute addition. Rita's entire family were Yankees fans anyway. It amused me, and now I had a loveable rivalry between us, without her outright rebelling against me, like she would've had I raised her myself. Here was a girl who could talk baseball with me like an equal, just like her mother did during our short time together.

Jemma was so intrigued by the fact that she's half Italian and that her great grandparents came through Ellis Island right off of a boat. She wanted to know everything about my family and, my only regret about this part of her newly discovered history, is that they're all dead.

"Will you take me there?" she asked me last night on

the phone.

"To Palermo?"

"Yes. And all of Sicily."

I had never been to Sicily. "We will go someday, Jem."

Even the whole Catholic thing had her busy, asking lots of questions.

"I don't really understand the whole purpose of the Pope, but I love how you can go into a booth and tell the priest your sins and be absolved right then and there. You can hear his voice. That's better than being a Southern Baptist," she said. "You get it done and, rather than wonder if God heard your confession and prayer for forgiveness, a real live voice tells you what to do so you can go do it and then feel better, like you're free to forgive yourself, too. I always hate how I have to pretend that I hear God. I don't hear him! I want to, but I just don't."

I laughed. "You are a marvel, Jemma. You really think about things and don't just take everything at face value."

"I want to know how the world works: why the people in my family believe what they believe and where I fit into all of it."

Her maturity and insight into humanity blew my mind. I don't recall either of my other kids being so inquisitive or rational when they were her age. She wanted to be a spiritual person but she needed it to make sense, too.

How does a man make up for fourteen lost years, for having been nothing but a contributor to a scientific miracle? Scout had done it all herself, with help from her parents and Charlie, too, but Jemma is who she is mostly because of Scout and because of her love. And I knew that.

I wanted to know everything about her, just as she wanted to know everything about me. We talked about her grandparents, her life in Haddleboro when she was younger, but also about her mother and how hard she'd worked all the time: getting her Bachelor's degree in biology while working as a vet tech and raising Jemma, her moving them to the Raleigh area so Jemma would have better educational and softball opportunities, the fact she works two jobs to pay for it all.

She talked about her uncle and his new wife and she told me all about Charlie Porter, SBI Agent. She especially liked to talk about him.

"I doubt I could ever thank him enough for all he's done for you and your mom," I said.

"You don't have to thank Charlie. That's like thanking the Pope for being Catholic," she snickered. "People like Charlie just do what they do because it's who they are inside. They live what they believe rather than always sayin' it out loud."

Listening to her talk about him made me realize how much I failed them both. I knew I was a better man than what I'd done to Rita and Scout, but desperation and fear bring out the worst in people sometimes. It sure did in me.

Chase and I were sitting in some bleachers down in

Fort Myers, resting in between games. I hated to leave Rita at home alone after the bombshell I dropped on her and even more so because of the grief she's still dealing with over Sal. But she insisted, "Just go. I'm fine. It's actually better for me to be alone right now anyway."

I often wondered what it is about Rita that has made her so strong when she has been presented with some of the harshest realities that life has to offer, some of it directly from me. Her dad had been an officer in the Marines and they moved around a lot. According to Rita, he was not the easiest man to have for a father. Her brothers definitely had to be a part of her inherent toughness. Being the oldest of seven siblings — six of whom were boys — was sure to add a particular strength to a girl. I have no doubt that being a devout Catholic made her resilient, dancing around with all that guilt all of the time. Rita made sure she avoided doing anything that would ever make her feel guilty again, certainly after I knocked her up and we needed to get married. Nothing worse than being an unwed pregnant Catholic girl in 1970. Her mother was sweet and, while I wouldn't describe Rita as "sweet," I think that the sweetness come out in the tender ways in which she touches me, or during the few moments when I catch her looking at me — that's when she sees me as I am and loves me for it.

"Chase, I need to tell you something serious," I blurted out to my adult son.

Chase's head, with his Red Sox cap sitting firmly on

top, turned sharply, like those are the last words he'd ever want to hear from an aging parent.

"Jesus, what?" he asked, his eyes no doubt wondering if I was about to tell him I had cancer.

"Do you remember a long time ago when your mom and I were having some trouble in our marriage?"

He looked up at the sun, squinted his eyes, sneezed, and nodded. "The time you weren't around all that much? When we had that one Christmas that didn't feel much like a Christmas?"

"Yeah, the time I had disappeared a lot and there seemed to be a miserable cloud over our home for a while."

Chase looked across the field and shook his head. "Yeah, I remember all that I guess."

So I took a deep breath and told him about Scout, what I had done to his mother, how much I hated myself every day for what I did, how sorry I'd been, and how ever since then, I had done everything I possibly could to make it up to her.

"But your mom, she forgave me. She was able to move on and, honestly, we've been happier together than we had ever been before it all happened," I explained. "Your mother is a wonderful woman. She is strong and compassionate and you know how much she gave up to marry me and be your mother. I don't deserve her."

Chase didn't say anything for a while, but when he did, he asked, "Do you want a Coke from the snack bar?"

That night, we sat at a bar on the beach with the beautiful vista of the Gulf of Mexico during March in front of us.

Chase asked, "Why did you tell me all that shit about you and mom before? I could've gone the rest of my life without needing to know that, Dad."

I took a deep breath. "Because there's more," I added and took a sip of my beer.

"More?" he asked, looking directly at me.

"I just learned like a couple of weeks ago that my infidelity had resulted in an unplanned pregnancy."

Chase's head turned sideways, confused.

"You have a fourteen-year-old sister and, as big of a shock as this is to you right now, and to me when I found out, I promise that you will love her when you meet her one day, hopefully soon."

Chase sat there with his feet facing the beach, glaring at me with both shock and what I interpreted to be disgust. I was ready for whatever he would say to me, whatever rocks he wanted to throw at my face, and for a long silent treatment.

When a father hurts a boy's mother, the boy becomes the next defender of her honor. But I believed in the healing powers of the love within my family. I knew that they would come to see Jemma for what she really is — not some bastard product of their father's failures — but their sister, their blood, a gift from God himself. They would see her as I saw her. They would love her.

We would leave Fort Myers the next morning, and Chase didn't say much to me about anything. When he dropped me off at home after we got back from the airport, he simply stated in a monotone voice, dripping with disappointment, "I'll see you later, Dad."

SCOUT'S HONOR

433

SCOUT

I took a rare sick day from work at Paw's and, when Jemma went to school, I drove over to see Thom at the Confederate. I wanted to talk to him about what happened between us. Even though I had never been inside his room, I knew he was in suite six, so I walked down the hallway and knocked on his door. It should've been early enough that he'd still be there before going into his firm.

Thom opened the door and his friendly face lit up when he saw me, his deep dimples caving in just like Tom Selleck's do when he smiles — or does anything, really. He was wearing a white housecoat and smelled fresh and minty, like a Lifesaver. His short hair was damp and his face appeared freshly shaven. His mustache was neatly trimmed and this was definitely the most — intimate? — that I've ever seen him.

Still pretty embarrassed by what happened between us, and wondering if he remembered much of it at all, I walked inside. He immediately put his arms around me into a full embrace. Then he pressed me close to him, but it didn't seem sexual at all, just more like his usual bear hugs. Then he kissed my forehead.

Either I only imagined everything that happened last night or he doesn't remember any of it at all. I prayed for the former but feared the latter. He had been drunk. So maybe I could just forget about everything and we could carry on as friends.

"Do you want some coffee?" he asked.

"Uh, yes, that would be great, thanks," I responded nervously. My stomach was in knots.

He walked over to his kitchenette and brought me over a steaming mug of coffee. I thanked him and set it down on his little coffee table.

"Little girl, you are such a sight for sore eyes," he said, beaming. "I've barely slept. Been thinking so much about you, wishing you were here with me."

Jesus in Heaven above, why did he have to be so darn charming?

"Do you know why I've stopped by?" I asked, sitting down on the standard hotel-like couch in his tiny living room, which was next to a half walled-off bedroom. The TV sat on a wooden polished entertainment stand with the local news channel churning out the weather forecast.

He sat down next to me and put his arm around my shoulders, pulling me into him. Looking into my face he said, "To talk about last night?"

Oh well, I guess he did remember everything just like he says he does when he's drunk. Feeling like a fool, I nodded.

"Listen, Thom," I started, feeling both uneasy and then oddly seduced as he held my eyes to his. He was intense, a man with the "on" button always pressed down, and it was yet another thing I liked about him. Then he leaned into me and kissed my lips, all full and tasting of coffee. It was so nice.

He was so confident in himself, except for the few times when I found him to be emotionally exposed, only after he had a few drinks and always when talking to me out by my car in the dark. I liked him like that the best because it was when he seemed most honest. He was sweet, like he was trying so hard to be understood by someone. And he chose me.

But he was not vulnerable at all right now. He was fully in control of everything going on between us — and he knew it.

"Scout, we are adults. If you're not comfortable with this, being intimate with me like last night, I understand. I made myself abundantly clear on that patio outside. I want you. I want to have sex with you, make love to you, fuck you, whatever you want to call it. I want to make you feel good and happy and share all I that can with you while I'm here. You make me feel good and happy every day that I get to see you. But if me being married is an issue, or if my age is an issue, it's okay. I'm a big boy," he said, putting his finger on my bottom lip.

Why did this man have so much power over me? I felt like a child in his presence, wanting to please him and not disappoint him in any way.

Here I am, sitting on his couch, trying to do the right thing and have a grown up conversation about why I can't be anything more than his friend. And those reasons were completely legitimate! I'm not putting myself in this situation again. I've done enough damage to other people and already lived with enough shame and guilt as it is.

But I was attracted to him and I meant what I said to him last night. I do have feelings for him, but could live just fine without the romance. Since I live without romance all the time anyway, it's no big deal. I wanted to be his friend. So how can I convey that message from my heart without him thinking that it's acceptable for us to strip down and go into his bed? Obviously, we're on different moral planes and I was too stupid to figure out what he thought was right and wrong. He didn't seem to think that what he had done with me — as a married man — was in the wrong at all.

"Thom, I'm sorry," I said. "I do have strong feelings for you, but you're married. And you love her."

He sat back and turned off the TV.

"So if I didn't love her, would it be okay with you then?"

The guy never stopped surprising me.

"It wouldn't. You're married. That's the line I have to draw. You have to understand that."

Thom put his hand on my knee. "Scout, you aren't married. So you aren't doing anything wrong at all. You're betraying no one. You've made no vows, signed no contracts to anyone. I'm the only one doing something wrong, then. So it's all my choice here. I'm choosing to do something wrong and I can live with it. I'm choosing to be happy over being right. And you make me happy. You've wormed your way into my heart like no other woman I've met in a long time."

Jesus, he is good. I can see why he is such a successful trial lawyer. It's actually not a bad argument and I never thought of marriage and cheating that way before. But my choices have to align with my morality, not his. And my morality dictates that I cannot get romantically involved with married men ever again.

"You are good, counselor," I said to him, looking down at the carpet and putting my hand on his, gently rubbing it with my fingers.

He leaned into me and started softly kissing me. Helpless, I allowed him to and felt like I stepped onto an elevator to some kind of heaven. It was intoxicating to feel this good. Then, faster than I could protest, he had me on my back.

He unleashed the belt of his housecoat and slipped it onto the floor. He pulled up my shirt and unsnapped my bra and his hands made their way to everywhere they wanted to go. He pulled off my jeans and panties and, like a tidal wave consuming an empty beach, I let him flood my body with his lips and his mouth. His physical and emotional prowess overpowered me and any inhibitions I had were long ago on the wayside. He started to do things to me that hadn't been done in many years and I was at last reminded what it felt like to be ravaged by a hungry man who knows exactly what he wants, and then goes and gets it. I was happy to be his prey for just a little while.

Completely naked, he gently ran his strong fingers along my inner thigh. I could feel myself losing complete control. He whispered to me, "Go ahead, put me inside of you..." and as he kissed my lips, my conscience once again came out of its horrible hiding place and forced me to say, "No Thom, please don't. I want to so bad. I just...can't..."

Abruptly, he stopped kissing me. He pushed himself up off of me and then averted his eyes, like I had humiliated him. Then he got up off of the couch, pulled on his housecoat, and walked into his bathroom. Shutting the door behind him, he turned on the faucet.

Resting on his couch, I felt cold and horrible, embarrassed, and full of shame. Cammy DeHaan's face, all contorted, glared at me from near Thom's door. I quickly put on my clothes and waited for him to come out of the bathroom. Ten minutes went by and he was still in there.

I knocked. "Thom? You okay?" I asked through the door.

"Yeah, fine, thanks," he said back, sharply.

"I'm so sorry, I don't know what to say. I'm just not ready to..."

Thom interrupted. "Don't bother. It's fine. Just let yourself out. I need to get to work anyway."

He was so dismissive of me and I guess I understood why. I mean, I had let him get so far with me and then pulled out my "please don't" card at the worst possible moment, which was completely unfair. I'm sure I had humiliated him and now I hated myself for that, too. He's been so good to me, so kind and caring all this time. He opened up and told me how he felt about me, and like a selfish moron, I shut him down.

But I knew that I was doing us both a favor. I was doing the right thing. I cared about him too much to let him do that to his wife. I was fine with just being his friend because he was so great for me in every other way, and I believed he felt the same way. I didn't want to lose everything over — of all things — sex!

Awkwardly and painfully, I left. Later, I texted him to see if he could meet me for lunch. He never responded. Feeling paranoid, I called him. He didn't answer, so I left a voicemail. When I went into Flavia for my evening shift, he didn't come in. This was the first time he had not come into Flavia since the night I met him six months ago.

When my shift ended, I walked down to the Confederate, determined to speak to him. I knocked on suite six and a young, attractive, platinum-blond woman with her hair up in a bun, holding a glass of red wine in her hand, and wearing a black business suit answered the door.

"Hi, um, is Thom in?" I asked her, my heart in my stomach, about to heave onto the door. *Who in God's name is this?*

"Dad?" she yelled back. "Lady at the door." Her accent was thick New York.

She shut the door and I was about to pass out from shock. This gorgeous woman at the door was apparently his daughter and here I am showing up late at night to her father's place to talk to him about what's been going on between us! I had no idea she'd be visiting him. Thom never said anything. Standing there, not quite sure what to do, I thought maybe I should just leave.

Then she opened the door again and asked, "Are you Scout?"

I nodded. She came out in the hallway and shut the door behind her. She started to talk, then stopped and looked at me with what appeared to be pity in her face. Then she started again like it was some kind of rehearsed speech. "I'm sorry, but he said that if it was you at the door, to tell you that it was nice getting to know you, but he's not interested in the relationship anymore. He's tried to make it as clear as possible so could you please leave him alone."

I looked at her, stunned. What is she talking about? She read my face like she's seen this look before.

"Listen, it's better to go back home and leave him

alone. As you know, he's a lawyer, and I've known him to get restraining orders out on women before with no evidence that they're actually harassing him." She sighed. "For some reason, women flock to him and won't leave him alone when he denies their advances."

Denied my advances?

She continued, "I don't get it. I mean, he's kinda cute for an older guy, and he can be funny, and of course he's rich, but he's seriously just a total dick to people, and he can be so, so cruel sometimes. And once he's done with you, he's done with you. Forever."

Dumbfounded, I studied this striking young woman, a daughter who was making no excuses for her father's questionable ways. She could tell that I was having a hard time understanding exactly what was going on. How can this man tell me that he loves me last night, say all the things he said to me just this morning, and share all the personal confidences that he's shared with me over the past six months, gain my trust, and then never speak to me again? And why do I feel like I've been through this before? *It's déjà vu all over again.*

Reading my mind, she eyed me with that same pitying look on her face. "Look. That's just him. It's how he is. Don't beat yourself up about it and don't take it too personally. You aren't the only girl he's done this to."

Wait. I thought I had been the only one. He said I had been the only one. Oh my God, I am such a stupid little fool.

Realizing at last that I had been a toy for some man's sick games yet again and that I hadn't learned a darn thing in twenty years, it was all I could do to keep myself from breaking down his door and kicking him in his nuts. I don't think I've ever had a violent thought against another human being in my life before this very moment. Now, I was just mad at the coward on the other side of the door.

Slowly coming into my rational self, I looked down at the floor and then back up at her and said, "Listen, Bethany, right? It's Bethany?" I knew her name because of how much time I had invested in getting to know Thom.

She nodded.

"I want you to know that I did not sleep with your father."

I wanted to add, "I almost did. He almost got what he wanted from me. But he didn't get it." I thought better of it. She didn't need to hear from me what kind of man her father really was. It's evident that she already knew.

Taking a deep breath, I continued. "I don't know why I care what you think about me. I really did — do — um, care for him and wanted to be his friend. Just didn't realize...." I stopped talking, still shell-shocked about everything, and my voice got soft. "I'm so embarrassed and feel so foolish. I'm truly sorry for any pain that I've caused you."

Bethany half-smiled. "Don't sweat it. All the ladies care for him. They all want to be his friend or his girlfriend on the side. He just has a way with women, I guess, but other than sex and fucking with their heads for his ego's amusement, he's got no real use for them."

She looked down the hallway, eyeing a resident opening and closing his door. "Look, I'm sorry he's like this. I don't know what's wrong with him. Maybe he was dropped on his dick when he was a baby. He's been like this my whole life. He's fucked around on my mother for years with an infinite procession of stupid and even some well-meaning girls like you who get suckered in by that Thom Robinson charm. At some point, he just gets bored or whatever and drops them like a sack of potatoes. And that's how he handles pretty much everything else in his life, too."

Bethany unbuttoned her suit jacket and pulled out her blouse from her pants. "He knows my mom won't leave him. And since my mom knows that she's the only woman he truly loves, she turns a blind eye and lets him do whatever he wants. That's just how their marriage is. I guess it works for them because they've been married a long ass time."

Feeling a bit relieved in some strange way, I looked at Bethany and shrugged. I didn't know what else to say. It was no doubt one of the weirdest conversations I've ever been in.

She sighed. "Look. He's my dad and he's a good dad to me, a good grandfather to my son, and the only one I've got. I love him and I know that he loves me. His extracurricular activities ain't my business."

I thought to myself how odd it is to encounter a person who actually sees the truth. Most people don't want to know the truth, no matter how boldly it stares into their faces. Most embrace their illusions so they can continue to live in whatever fantasy they've created for themselves about the ones they love, and it doesn't matter what they have to live with in order to maintain it. Bethany Robinson was no such person. She saw her dad as he really was, no blaming me or accusing me of trying to seduce him or steal him away. She made no excuses for his behavior. She just loved him. Period.

I thought about everything she said to me about Thom and how both sad and even admirable it was that a woman could love her dad regardless of what kind of human being he is, that she was willing to accept whatever kind of father God handed her, even one who used his wife as some kind of window dressing to his soul and other women like objects to be conquered in order to feed his own revoltingly, empty self-image. And then toss them aside like cord wood when he's done. Thom was nothing but a parasite, a heart-and-soul-sucking vampire. I bet, the night he first grabbed my hand across the bar, he felt all of the brokenness inside of me and sensed that I'd be his next meal. And like a blinded idiot marching herself over a cliff, I was exactly that — another meal for him.

Silently, I hoped that Thom would never treat his own daughter like that. She was counting on him to be the one thing she held on to and hoped for: a good father and grandfather.

"Is Zach your son?" I asked her.

She lit up. "Yeah, he is."

"He's a beautiful boy. Your dad showed me pictures of him. Cherish him while he's young. It goes by fast."

She grinned at me, sharing the kind of understanding that only mothers can relate.

Then, as I turned away from her and was about to head down the hall, she said, "I'm sorry. You seem like a nice girl. I hope you find a good man for yourself someday."

I already had.

Looking back and nodding at her, I turned and sprinted down the remainder of the hallway and out onto the sidewalk in front, ran down the street to Flavia, got into my car and drove off thinking of Mrs. Robinson. What kind of woman is knowingly married to a monster like that? If his daughter knows what he is and accepts it, then certainly his wife does, too, and that was something I could never fathom and was glad that I couldn't. There were some benefits to naivety.

For the first time in my life that I knew for sure, I had met that elusive personality type I'd only learned about back in college psych class: a real live narcissist. And not only had I met one, but I'd been completely duped by one, a Manhattan trial lawyer named Thom Robinson. All that studying of the facts, and still, real life got me good.

Suddenly, I felt dirty and disgusting and couldn't wait to get into the shower when I got home.

CHARLIE

Yesterday afternoon, I got a call from Rob Caralessi informing me that he told his wife and his children about Jemma. "They aren't really speaking to me right now, especially my daughter Samantha, but I've told them everything, it's out there, and now it's your turn to tell Scout about me," he said with a level of demand in his voice that could've passed for that of a Company Commander. He was right. I had to get off my ass and tell Scout.

I sat in my cube with a mountain of files on my desk, files that needed some organizing and cases that needed reviewing. Feeling overwhelmed by my workload and all of the shit going on in my personal life, I unlocked the small strongbox underneath my desk and pulled out the little blue box that housed Stephanie's engagement ring. I kept it at work so she wouldn't find it in my house. I still hadn't worked up the courage to ask her to marry me, even though I knew she'd say yes, and now with all this Rob-Jemma-Scout shit going on, who knows when I'd proceed toward this next big step in our relationship.

But one thing was for sure. I wanted to. I was ready. I

loved Stephanie. She made me happy, and I knew she loved me, too. We were a great pair. She was very understanding about the unconventional parentage I had assumed with Jemma and my intricate relationship with Scout.

I had never met a girl like Stephanie before. She was so emotionally secure and laid back about life, and I knew that a life with her would be an adventure. Our personalities meshed like two peas in a pod. We shared the same values and wanted the same things, and we had so many things in common. She is the only girl other than Scout that I've ever loved.

The years have been tough on my heart since that summer evening when I had proposed marriage to Scout and she turned me down. I thought she'd say yes, or I never would've asked, so instead of giving her a ring that she didn't want from me, I just gave her my dog tags and headed off to Operation Desert Shield with my unit. Every day since then, I've felt the sting of her rejection. With every look she gives me, every intimate talk we have, every meal or simple moment with her, the rejection sits there between us.

When I met Stephanie and found that I started having real feelings for her, the constant sadness I seemed to endure, just sitting underneath my skin, didn't seem to hurt so much anymore. I saw that I could love someone else and that Scout wasn't the only girl in the world — maybe not even the only girl for me.

I never could understand why Scout didn't feel how I

felt about her. We spent our whole lives together. We knew each other like how people who've been married for seventy years know each other. I can finish her sentences and I know every line on her hands and her face, every look and what each one means, every inflection in her voice, every gesture and mannerism, and every story — because they're my stories too. And she knows mine. So why does she not feel it all for me like I do for her? Why didn't our hearts match?

Once I had talked to my mom about it all. "You and Scout are what they call soulmates. Scout loves you Charlie, exactly as you love her. I can just tell. I can see it all goin' on between you two whenever you're together. It's all over her face," she told me as she was raking leaves. "But there's something not right with Scout. There's somethin' that prevents her from being who she really is — somethin' dark and ugly. And I ain't got a clue as to what that could possibly be."

I had loved Scout so much for so long, with nothing really to show for it other than a life-long best friend who I could never have as a wife and lover — and a daughter who I loved like my own blood but wasn't really mine either. A best friend in Scout and a daughter like Jem is great and I'd never trade them for anything.

But what about that other depth to living that I deserve, too? The one that consists of a deep, abiding love between a man and woman, a love that is shared not just with an understanding but expressed with our bodies, our minds, our language, and our entire hearts? The one that goes both ways and is not one-sided, a little sad, and unrequited.

Stephanie and I had that kind of love and, no matter how hard it had been to accept, no matter how much I loved Scout and always would love her, I deserved to be with someone who loved me back like Stephanie did. And regardless of what my mom thought, Scout never gave me those signs about being "soulmates" and never let me into whatever darkness that consumed her so I could help her and understand her better.

I remember sitting in the desert in Kuwait, waiting for that short joke of a war to start, holding my photo of Scout and a tiny Jemma in my hands. It was the photo I'd keep in my Kevlar inside of an envelope to protect it. That certain letter every infantry soldier wrote to someone back home, just in case he died, was also in my equipment. It was addressed to Scout.

Scout was my girl and that was what I told the other guys when we'd talk about our girls "back home." But I knew that she really wasn't and it was all a big lie. All Scout was back then, and I was too love sick and stupid to see it, was a hope that I held onto, a hope that true love would come to me some day. And now finally it had.

That photo kept me living for a reason though, and so I'd always be grateful to Scout for that. But I'd also always be grateful to her for being honest with me back then and not marrying me if she didn't feel the same way. Because, if she'd done the safe thing, which would've been to marry me, a man who'd walk through fire for her and Jemma, then I would've never met Stephanie and have what I have with her today.

My cell phone rang from an unknown number. Since I'm not the kind of person who likes to answer unknown numbers, I let voicemail take it.

When the little envelope popped up telling me that I had a message, I listened to it.

"Uh, Charlie, this is Lee Webb. I'm at Harper Hospital in Fayetteville. Um, son, your mama collapsed at work, and they brought her in here by ambulance. You got to come as soon as possible." Mr. Webb's voice sounded odd and a little desperate.

SCOUT

It's always weird when I go back home to Haddleboro. Every time I go to my parents' house, I feel like I'm fourteen years old again, just a little girl with a daughter of her own. A child with a child. I sat on the bed in my old bedroom with my white dresser still in the corner. Jemma's duffle bag sat on the floor with a black dress lying over my old desk chair. The room was still the same pale pink color that it had been when Jemma and I moved out for good back in 1994 and into our first little above-the-garage apartment just a few miles away.

Jemma was outside with my brother Jonny who brought over his new dog, Leo. She hadn't seen her uncle since Christmas and, since he was moving to Atlanta next month, she was trying to make up for the time ahead that would no longer be.

Tomorrow was Ms. Porter's funeral. She would be buried at the First Baptist Church's cemetery, and Pastor Dan, the new young pastor who took over for Pastor Rhodes when he retired last year, would officiate. Charlie's been staying at his mom's house this week, trying to deal with some of her paperwork and the many details of an untimely death, when someone you love dies from an errant blood clot.

The day after I had been blindsided with the discovery of what exactly my "friendship" actually meant to Thom Robinson, I was at Paw's trying to get a fecal sample from Mr. Moody's German shepherd named Venus. My cell phone rang and, seeing that it was my daddy's number, I let it go to voicemail because I was holding a Popsicle stick smeared with dog poop at that particular moment.

Several minutes later, when I listened to Charlie's very deliberate voice tell me about what was going on with Ms. Porter, I finished Venus' exam as fast as I could and told Paw that I had a family emergency and needed to get to Harper Hospital down in Fayetteville as soon as possible.

When I got there almost an hour later, my parents were both with Charlie and I had never in my life seen him in such a state. His face was ghostly white, like life itself had disappeared from his body, and when he saw me, he grabbed onto me like he was a little boy again. Sandy-haired little Charlie with the big toy dump truck that we'd push around in the sun yellow kiddie pool.

Eventually, I got him to sit with me on one of the hard plastic chairs in the waiting room and my daddy told me that he and my mom were going to head up to Raleigh to let Boo out and go to Jemma's game. They would get her some supper and take her home afterward and would even stay the night if I needed them to, so I could tend to Charlie.

In my emotionally frazzled head, from both the bizarre drama the night before with Thom and his daughter and now this horrible tragedy with Charlie's mom, I hadn't even thought about the fact that Jem had a game today and that my parents were planning to come up for it.

"Will you call Stephanie?" my mom asked me. "We don't have her number and Charlie forgot his cell phone in Raleigh."

"Yes, of course," I said, my hands tight on Charlie's shoulders as he sat in the chair, frozen, paralyzed, by the horrible shock of his loss.

Charlie has dealt with a ceaseless amount of crime scenes and victims over the past several years — all kinds of deaths, murders, rapes, shootings, suicides, stabbings, and some of the ugliest things that human beings do to each other or do to themselves. His mother died of natural causes on an average sunny spring day while working at the hardware store and, instead of the thoughtful and stoic SBI agent, he just turned into that sad little boy again, the one with no father, the one who had come up to me at the church Easter egg hunt when we were five years old and asked me if he could have one of my eggs.

I remembered it like it was yesterday. I found ten plastic eggs during the hunt and each one was supposed to have jellybeans in it. A towheaded boy in desperate need of a haircut with a red and white striped shirt, blue shorts, and bare feet, walked up to me as I sat by myself under an azalea bush near the steps of the church's entrance. My mom had given me a plastic pastel-colored basket she bought for a nickel from a yard sale and I used it for this egg hunt, my very first one.

Eyeballing this scrawny boy who I had never seen before, and who had ketchup smeared on the sides of his mouth, I asked him who he was.

"Charlie Porter," he answered.

"Where's your mom and dad?" I asked him, with the authority of an adult.

He turned and pointed at a young blond woman in a peach colored sundress, sitting at one of the picnic tables by herself.

"That's my mom." Then he said, turning back at me, "I don't have a dad."

I considered that for a second, realizing that I had never heard of someone not having a dad before. So I handed this Charlie Porter boy one of my eggs. It was purple. He opened it and out dropped three jellybeans and a slip of paper.

"That's the special egg," I said to him, excited that I was the one who found it.

"What's a special egg?" he asked me.

"It's the egg with the paper in it. It means you get an extra prize," I said, recalling Pastor Rhodes' instructions before the egg hunt began. "Take it over to Pastor Rhodes and he will give you the prize."

Charlie held the jellybeans in one hand and the purple egg and piece of paper in the other. Then he handed the piece of paper back to me. "Here, you should have the prize. You found the special egg, not me."

He was right. I did find it. But there was something interesting about this strange little boy who was shorter than me and who made me feel like we had been friends before, once upon a time and in a land far, far away.

Not long ago, when I was in a drug store, I read something on a greeting card that said, "Souls recognize each other by vibes, not by appearances." That was the best description I ever came across about what transpired between me and Charlie Porter on that warm spring day so long ago.

Taking the piece of paper from him, I grabbed his hand and put it between our hands and held them together. I picked up my basket and walked with him hand-in-hand, leading him over to Pastor Rhodes who was standing next to the grill with the sizzling hotdogs.

"Pastor?" I said, getting his attention. Pastor Rhodes looked down at me.

"Yes, Miss Scout," he said smiling, holding a pair of tongs in his hand.

"Charlie and I have found the special egg," I said, unclasping our hands and giving him the piece of paper.

Three minutes later, we were sitting under a large

dogwood tree, sharing the biggest chocolate bunny I've ever seen. And now, twenty-nine years later, almost to the day that we shared that chocolate bunny and became the best of friends, I held him in Harper Hospital as he wept the kind of weeping that has no tears or noise, the kind of weeping that a grown man does when he loses his mom forever.

"Charlie, we should go. There's nothing we can do here. The folks here have everything under control. I'll take you to your mom's house and stay with you 'til Stephanie can get there," I said, facing him on my knees, holding his hands as he held his head down in sorrow. "If you're not okay to drive, I'll drive you. We can just leave your car here and get it another time."

Charlie looked at me, his eyes glassy and full of despair. Then he looked down again and said, "It's alright. I can drive."

"Okay," I said, standing up. "I'll follow you to Haddleboro."

****

When we got to his mom's house and went inside, I was struck by the fact that there was no cigarette smell anymore. Ms. Porter had stopped smoking several years ago and the smell that I grew up associating with Charlie's home was the stench of Camel cigarettes. She had left a coffee cup in the sink, not realizing that would be the last cup of coffee she'd ever have. Her house was neat and clean and simple, just as it had been for all the years I knew her, no signs of the subtle cruelties that life gave her.

After calling Stephanie to tell her what was going on, I thought about how telling it was that Charlie called me and not her to tell me his mother died. But considering our history and unconventionally shared life, I supposed it all made sense.

I had never been jealous of Stephanie, despite the fact that I loved Charlie more than life itself. She was good for him had helped him move on from me in some ways, gave him something special in life that was just his, and I loved how good she was with Jemma. And Jemma liked her, which spoke volumes. At last, I thought maybe Charlie found a woman who would be worthy of him.

But he was still my Charlie, no matter who he was dating, and I always knew that. He is approaching his thirty-fifth birthday and he'd never even been close to getting married to someone — and Charlie was indeed the marrying kind.

Had he been just waiting for me to come around, treading water, hoping I'd feel the same eventually and come in and rescue him? He never knew the truth: I did feel exactly the same for him. I shut him out of that part of me just to be sure that I could still hold on to him somehow. How unfair I've been to him all these years.

Charlie went upstairs and, when I didn't hear him moving around for a while, I went up to find him lying on his old double bed, his arms wrapped around his mother's royal blue housecoat. Seeing him like that reminded me of when I was stuck in my own unimaginable grief over Brother Doug and how Charlie came into my bed and held me. So I crawled over to him on the bed and held him.

****

A couple of hours went by and neither of us had moved. I wasn't sure if Charlie fell asleep, but he was as still as I had ever seen him. Stephanie told me that she wouldn't be able to get down to Haddleboro until tomorrow afternoon because of work and, after Charlie had gotten off the phone with her, I felt like I couldn't leave him alone until then.

The sun had set and the bedroom was dark. Thinking about everything, I could now see that I'd spent my days and nights since Camp Judah hiding within myself and coming out once in a while for some air. In the air, I'd find the brief relief I needed from my constant pain within the company of the two other Brother Dougs who came into my life: older married men who take an interest in me, either as a girl to talk to or as a girl to screw. And all along I had been foolish enough to think that one of them might really care about me, actually mean what they said. But that was never true. They never did. They got what they wanted from me and then threw me away.

But Charlie had never done that to me. Charlie was true-blue.

Lying there, holding the love of my life, my soulmate, my best friend and confidant, the only man I could ever trust and who would never fail me, I knew that he needed to know the truth. I loved him. I loved him like he loved me. I needed to tell him this, no matter what it would cost me. We both deserved it.

Eventually, Charlie got up and went into the bathroom. When he came out, he laid back down on the bed with his hands under his head on the pillow. He faced me and, in the moonlight coming in through his window, he looked in my eyes like we were a married couple, about to have an intimate conversation about our hopes and dreams.

"I love you, Charlie," I said to him, tears welling up in my eyes.

"I love you, too, Scout," he said back to me, his eyes unflinching.

Not able to contain my tears anymore, I went on. "No, I mean I love you. I love you like you've loved me. I love you like in the Bible, in First Corinthians 13. I love you so much — with all of my heart — and I always have." At this point, I began crying, almost sobbing, barely able to get all the words out.

"I should've married you when you first asked me. I should've said yes to you. I should've asked you to marry me instead and we could've raised Jemma like normal parents and been together like we were always supposed to be, like God had intended for us to be."

He moved his hands from underneath his head and held mine. I took a breath and continued, "You are the most wonderful man in the world, the best person who's ever lived. Even Jesus Himself doesn't hold a candle to you. You've loved me for so long and I've loved you, too — just the same, just as much. I just never felt like I was good enough for you. You deserved someone so much better than me."

All these words that have been secured and bound with chains inside of my heart for so many years, all because of my shame and fears, rushed out of me like a huge, roaring river breaking through an old, crumbling dam. Charlie released my hands, put his fingers up to my tears to wipe them away, and kissed me with a tenderness that I have never known before — and I knew that I would never know again. It was so different and more profound than any kiss by any other man I've had in my life. Right then, I was the only woman in the world. And he was the only man.

Kissing each other slowly at first, then eagerly, consumed with the lifetime of love that we had known for each other, all the kisses we never got to share, the big celestial heart that held us both within it — the one with the sign that says "For Soulmates Only" — became a seamless fusion of all that is right in the world.

We began to undress each other with our famished lips and eager hands, moving along the softness of our skin, everything between us so gentle and beautiful and unblemished — like two young virgins in love. He touched me like he loved me, truly loved me, like his hands belonged on my body and mine on his, and I felt all the years of our wonderful friendship, which was the perfect union of two souls meant to be — finally being consummated.

He lightly ran the pads of his fingers along my stomach, along my waist, barely touching my skin as he kissed me. I opened my eyes briefly to watch him. His eyes were shut and intent. Charlie and I were in another world, that one where there was just us and no one else. He kissed my neck and moved his lips along my shoulder blades and collar bones. My hands found the tightness of his chest and his back. He laid on his side, and I rolled next to him onto mine and began to kiss him with more love and longing than I had ever known. My mouth moved along his face, and soon I found myself on top of him, my lips kissing his, my heart melding to his, our bodies — at long last — becoming one.

As Charlie and I made love for the first time, I knew that I had wasted so much of my life hating myself instead of accepting the love he was always trying so desperately to give to me. It was always right there for the taking, in the palm of my hand.

I had never felt so at peace in my entire life as I did then in that perfect union with Charlie Porter — my sweet, flawless, devoted boy who I loved with every cell in my body — and with whom I was now ready to spend the rest of my life.

CHARLIE

I said a final goodbye to my mom on a Saturday morning as I put a red rose onto her casket, the very color she had always deserved from a man who loved her. I had been that man in her life. My mom was in Heaven now and no more sorrow or loneliness could ever occupy her days again.

She had actually done well for herself over the past five years. She managed the hardware store for the owners, bought her duplex from the previous owner who had rented it to her, and then rented out the other side of it to a single mother with a little boy. She was active in the First Baptist Church choir and in the women's ministry, helped out with the food pantry once a month, and had made some friends. She stopped dating assholes and had been seeing a nice guy — one she hadn't told me about yet — a good ol' boy named Rusty who lived over in Dunn. Apparently they had met on some dating website.

A lot of good folks came to her funeral and it made me happy to see how many people in this small town cared about her. When I was in the greeting line with Pastor Dan and his wife, almost everyone stopped to hug me and say what a sweet and wonderful lady my mom was. These are all things I already knew about my mom, but it was nice to hear it from other people.

The Webbs hosted a small gathering at their house for me and lots of people stopped by to pay their respects to my mom's memory and offer their condolences. Scout and Miss Raelene had taken care of all the details, ensuring there was enough food, paper supplies, and seats, and Scout had made an incredible photo display of my mom's life. She must've stayed up late the night before assembling it from all the pictures that my mom kept in shoe boxes in her closet.

Jemma had managed to charm everyone there with her ability to have conversations about absolutely anything with people of all ages. Stephanie helped me get organized, kept straight the names and addresses for thank you cards, wrote names on masking tape to put on the dishes of donated casseroles, and made sure that I had the right clothes with me for the funeral, viewing, and church service. Even Boo had a purpose, which was primarily comforting me. Dogs always know when someone is hurting.

When I was ready to leave, I kissed Stephanie goodbye so she could go back to Raleigh. She had to drive to Asheville for a work event the next day, and that's quite a haul. After I gave all the Webbs a hug, especially Scout, I went over to my mom's house so I could mow her lawn and lock up for now. I needed get back home and attempt to get my own life back in some kind of order.

Pushing the mower, I thought about what happened a few nights ago, the night I had dreamt about my entire life, the night when Scout told me her true feelings for me, the night we finally, at long last, were able to express everything we held inside of ourselves in every way. It was more than I had ever imagined it would be. It was not sex at all. It was the manifestation of our lifetime of friendship and the most honest and intimate kind of love between a man and a woman.

I had kept a tasteful and proper distance from Scout since that night, and she kept her distance from me. It was easy to do because we were all so busy dealing with my mom's arrangements, but it was best for me because of how conflicted I was about everything going on in my head.

The morning after Scout and I made love to each other, I woke up with her next to me. I was in a dream-like state. Her beautiful face with those full cheeks was up on my pillow with a calm and peace to it that had been missing for so many years. And then it hit me like a brick: I finally realized that I had, in fact, moved on from Scout Webb. It was too late for us. I loved her and would always love her. I know what Scout is to me, and no one can ever take that away or change it. But I loved Stephanie now and wanted to marry her and spend the rest of my life with her.

When Scout woke up, I was sitting on the edge of the bed, and with tears in my eyes, I told her how I really felt about everything.

"I'm so sorry, Scout. I just can't be with you at this point in my life. It's too late. I love you. I do. With all I have in me. And you'll always be the most special girl," I said. I couldn't look at her, but I could tell that she was looking at me. It was killing me to say this to her, knowing how much we really loved each other.

I continued, "I'm in love with Stephanie now. It took a really long time, but my heart found a way to make a place for someone new. I never thought it could happen either. I bought Stephanie a ring a few weeks ago and I plan on asking her to marry me."

Scout sat still and silent and I could feel a cold air come over me. "Jemma knows already." Then I looked up at her, her face soft and pale as she gazed over my head and out the window. "You know I love you and Jemma very much, and you'll always be a part of my life. But I have to be honest with you. I gotta follow not just my head but my heart too."

As I sat there, dealing with more difficult emotions consuming me at this one single time than I'd ever felt in my life, I watched Scout simply get out of the bed and then come over to me. She wrapped her arms around me, then let go, looked into my eyes, and kissed my lips.

"Thank you for being honest with me, Charlie."

With a tear slipping from her eyes, she held my chin in her hand. "I love you — forever — and I will always carry you with me no matter where our lives take us. I'm happy for you that you've found love and someone to share your life with. You deserve nothing but the greatest things. I want you to be happy. And if it's not with me, then I'm glad it's with her."

And isn't that, in the end, the real meaning of love? When your only hope is to see the one you love be happy, no matter how much it might hurt you? When your biggest desire is to see the one you love have what is ultimately best for him?

Scout did indeed love me. I knew it now more than I ever knew it before.

I didn't know what to say to her anymore because the truth is, my heart was torn between two women, two remarkable women who I could see myself waking up to every day, having children with, growing old with. Normally, I'd make a joke about becoming a fundamentalist Mormon. But in my grief and in my completely fucked up emotional state, I had no jokes in me today.

Can a man possibly love two women so much at the same time? I think the answer is yes, he can. Rob Caralessi tried to convey that message to me at one point. Right now, I understood what he meant. But I had to live my life as an honorable man. I had to choose only one. And I chose Stephanie.

Scout put on her work scrubs from the day before, which had been lying on the floor, and slipped on her black work shoes. She made the bed back to the way it was when I first laid down on it. I watched her move about my childhood bedroom, the place we shared our first kiss so many years ago. She folded up my mother's housecoat and set it on a chair, right in tune with her sweet rhythm, that precious melody that accompanies everything this striking woman does. And I knew then that it — whatever it was — was over between us.

About to leave for good, she kissed my forehead. "Charlie, thank you for everything you've done for me and Jemma. And thank you for having loved me."

Then she walked out of the room.

SCOUT

I helped clean up my parents' living room and kitchen and Jem took out the garbage with both Boo and Leo following her. We would spend the night here and then go back home after the Sunday morning church service. My mom begged me to stay and go to church with them since I hadn't visited in so long and everybody was so happy to see me and Jemma at Ms. Porter's funeral.

My mom had run out to the store, and my brother was watching TV, waiting for his wife Ginger to get back from somewhere with the car before they left for home in the next town over. I stood alone in the kitchen, drying dishes, sitting in my thoughts of all that had gone on in the last five days. The walls around my heart had served as ardent fortresses for times like this. If I didn't have them so fortified by now, I supposed I would have had a nervous breakdown over it all and have to be locked up in some mental ward.

Reaching into my pants pocket, I pulled out Charlie's dog tags, the same ones he gave me so many years ago before he went off to Kuwait, a reminder that in some ethereal way, we belonged to each other. I carried them with me all the time, my own wedding ring of sorts, a kind of grown woman's security blanket. On days like this, I felt like a little kid. And feeling the cold, long chain thread through my fingers made me realize that the depth to my pain could never be reached by anyone, not even me.

Just then, my daddy came in, picked up a towel and started drying dishes with me. We didn't speak, just wiped and sorted our dishes from the neighbors' dishes, all needing to get returned.

"Daddy," I said, breaking the silence between us.

"Yessum," he replied.

"What did the people at the camp say to you?"

He stopped rubbing a plate and looked at me. "What people?"

I looked back down at the sink and then out the little window above it, which displayed a colorful wind chime.

"The people at Camp Judah. When you came to pick up me and Jonny that last time — what did they say to you before we left?"

Daddy started drying plates again, putting them on top of each other neatly and then after a bit he said, "Scout that was a long time ago."

"I know, but what did they say to you? What did they tell you happened with me?"

He stopped messing with the plates and backed himself into a kitchen chair.

"Well, they said that you were chasing after the blond fella. What was his name?"

"Brother Doug..."

"Yeah, that's him, Brother Doug. He said that you had been pursuin' him for a long time because you had some kind of crush on him and it was really upsettin' his wife. He asked me to have you leave him alone for now on and stop writin' him letters." He paused, a rather long pause. Then he continued, "And then he told me that he'd talked to you a lot of times alone at the lake — about tobacco and drugs and alcohol because you'd been asking him lots of questions."

"Drugs and alcohol?" I asked a little too loudly, revealing that this was the first time I'd ever heard of such a thing.

"Yeah, he said somethin' about maybe havin' you talk to someone at church or maybe a shrink doctor when you got back home because you seemed to have some kind of trouble goin' on with you, an interest in drugs maybe."

He stayed quiet for a while, and I turned back toward him. "Did you believe it? What he said about me?" I really wanted to know. All these years had gone by and we never had this discussion.

"Well, honestly, at the time, I didn't really know what to think because you were just a nice girl who never gave me and your mom any trouble. But you were a teenager and I'm not real keen on knowin' much about teenaged girls, so I wasn't so sure about you being infatuated with the man or anything. But..." he stopped and poured himself a sweet tea. "But the drugs? The alcohol? That all seemed kinda off to me. The way he said it and the way he was phrasin' things about all that — and about you — was just givin' me a sour taste in my mouth. It didn't sound right, like he was makin' it up as he went along."

Drugs and alcohol. *Wow.* Strangely enough, that had never been any kind of an issue for me. I've never even tried pot and only enjoyed an occasional beer with a pizza. And ironically, I grew up to be a bartender in an upscale bar serving liquor to people who indeed have real issues with alcohol!

"I just kept an extra eye on you after all that and asked your mom to watch out for you, but we never saw any hint of promiscuity or you hangin' around the pot head kids. Hell, you never even smelled like you'd been smokin' cigarettes. And lots of kids your age were at least doin' that back then."

"Daddy, why didn't you ever ask *me* about what happened?"

He took a long sip of his tea and said, "I didn't know what to say to ya, Scout. You were so sad, all cryin' and whatnot. That blond fella was sayin' things to me that made no sense whatsoever. All I wanted to do was get you and your brother out of there as quick as possible and get back home. And y'all never went back there either. I told Jonny the next year that camp was over for you both, that we didn't have the money to send y'all anymore."

I started drying plates again and put some clean silverware in the drawer.

"The only thing I knew to do that would make you feel better when we got home that day was to give you an air conditioner for your room," he said standing up. "I'm sorry if it wasn't the right thing to do or if I could've done better, Scout. But I'm not real good about stuff like that, and I figured you knew that I loved you no matter what kinda trouble you'd been up to at camp."

Just then, I burst into tears — twenty long years' worth of tears — thinking that my daddy believed all the bad things Brother Doug said about me and knowing that the truth was even worse than any of the outright lies he told him.

I went over to my daddy and hugged him tight, crying into his shoulder. He held me back and let me sob for a while, and when I was done, he looked at me in my face and said, "I should've done this, just hugged ya. Instead of the air conditioner, huh?"

I chuckled at the pure, loving heart that had always lived within my daddy, no matter how much time had passed between us.

As I was about to walk out of the kitchen, he said to me, "Listen, Scout. I know you don't feel about the Lord like you once did when you were a girl. And I know life is hard, and it's been hard at times for you, for sure. I don't know a whole lot about whole lot, but one thing I figured out in life is that while we might not always understand why things happen as they do, or why it seems sometimes that God stays quiet, his love for us – and you – is like a father's love. We are his children. It's like how I love you. I don't care what you do. I love you. I know I don't say it often enough, but I've always been proud of you. My beautiful daughter, Scout Elizabeth."

"Thank you, Daddy," I said back to him, tears welling up once again. If he only knew how much I needed to hear that. "I love you."

JEMMA

Ms. Porter's funeral was the first one I've been to that I can remember. When I was two years old, my great-grandfather died, but I don't remember his funeral so I don't really count that. Death intrigues me — mostly because it's so final and no one really knows what happens afterward.

Do you go to Heaven to be with Jesus? Are there pearly gates? Do we all get mansions on a hill? Do you go to some place called purgatory instead? Do you become a ghost and kind of hang out some place and haunt the people who did you wrong? Do you become another person altogether, getting born all over again? Do you get reincarnated into some kind of animal? Do you become an angel and protect those you love? Or do you just simply cease to exist?

I don't know the answers to any of this stuff and I think that people who claim that they do know are full of crap. But I do understand why so many people all over the world need something to believe in, some kind of hope that there's a life after death and that we'll see the people we love again someday. I think it's hard being a person in this world sometimes, and finding comfort in some kind of supreme justice, like God or the Pope or some prophet, is no different than finding comfort in all the other things that we do or believe in to help us get through tough times.

When I was eight years old, I got baptized in the First Baptist Church of Haddleboro just before third grade started. It was a really nice day for me. I got to wear a white robe and Pastor Rhodes said all kinds of nice things about me as he stood in a little pool full of water called the baptismal. I went down the steps into the warm water with him and he dunked me "in the name of the Father, the Son, and the Holy Ghost." The people at the church all welcomed me as a new member and we had cake and punch down in the basement room where we'd always have church pot luck meals. My whole family was there, even my great-grandmother from all the way up in Reidsville.

Earlier that summer when school was out, I had accepted Jesus as my Savior and asked him to come into my heart when I did the Sinner's Prayer at Vacation Bible School. After that, I went to some classes on Sunday mornings to learn what it meant to be a Christian and what it meant to get baptized.

I was the youngest person in the class, which also had a boy in high school named Kieran who bagged groceries down at the Piggly Wiggly and a man named Andrew who had recently stopped drinking alcohol for good. It was a really interesting class, and a lot of it didn't make a whole lot of sense to me, but Pastor Rhodes told me that because I was so young, some of the teachings would make more sense to me when I got a little older. So I took his word for it.

Well, I'm a little older and some of the same stuff still didn't make any sense to me.

I didn't understand how if some kid who lived over in Africa — and who never heard of Jesus before and then died — couldn't go to Heaven just because he never accepted Jesus into his heart. That really didn't seem all that fair to me. So when I asked about that, Pastor Rhodes said, "It is our duty as Christians to go tell about Jesus in all four corners of the world." So I understood that to mean: that kid in Africa? — his blood would be on our hands.

Then I couldn't understand how some guy who has murdered a bunch of people and did all kinds of horrible stuff his whole life could be lying on his deathbed and accept Jesus into his heart and then go to Heaven. And then some young teenaged girl, who dies in a car accident, who never went to church because her parents never took her, but had been a good person who tutored little kids and volunteered at the food bank, doesn't get to go to Heaven because she never accepted Jesus into her heart. So Pastor Rhodes explained, "Jemma, it doesn't matter what we do on this earth that gets us saved. It's only by God's grace that we are saved and we have to accept that grace. Ephesians 2:8: 'For it is by grace you have been saved, through faith, and this is not from yourselves, it is the gift of God.'"

But the thing I had the toughest time with was how

God knew everything that was going to happen already. "God is omniscient," Pastor Rhodes would say. So, if God already knew how things were going to unfold in the world, then why bother praying for things to be different? I mean, they were going to end up how God already knew that they would, right? Praying for a different outcome wouldn't change any of that. And if it did, then how could God know ahead of time? And if He didn't know, then He couldn't be omniscient. And did I really have free will if God already knew what I was going to choose? Sometimes, I'd listen to the older folks in church talk about these things, and it would get me thinking – it would keep me up at night, actually.

Pastor Rhodes always seemed to have an answer for everything I'd ask him, but the answers were more mystifying than the original question I had. So after a while, I just stopped asking him because I was becoming more and more confused and frustrated.

When we moved to Raleigh a few years ago, I realized that my mom stopped taking me to church.

"How come we never go to church anymore?" I asked her one Sunday morning, as she made me an egg sandwich.

My mom looked thoughtful as she flipped over the eggs with a spatula. "I just don't see the point."

"What do you mean?" I asked, scratching Boo's ears.

"Jemma baby, I don't really know what I believe in anymore. Except one for thing. I believe in how much I love you. And I don't want you to grow up thinking that you're nothin' but a rotten, low-life sinner all the time."

I missed going to church in Haddleboro because the people there were so nice to me and had known me my whole life. No one had ever told me that I was a rotten sinner or made me feel bad about anything. I liked Vacation Bible School when I was little, and we were always doing fun stuff at church, like picnics and singing and games and helping each other out. The ladies in the church always gave me presents. Mrs. Dunston would always touch my hair and say, "Baby doll, you are fearfully and wonderfully made."

Whenever some of the girls on my softball team would talk about what their youth groups were doing in their churches, I felt like I was missing out on something cool.

***

Haley whacked the heck out of the ball and it flew passed the second baseman. Ground single. I was on deck. We have two outs, the game was tied, and Haley is the winning run. If I can get her in — or at least keep us alive for another batter — and then if Brittany behind me hits her in, the game is over. Nothing like a little pressure to keep me motivated.

"Next up for the Lady Chargers, number seven, Jemma Webb," the student announcer said into the microphone.

Coach Lundy was standing in the third base coach's box and signaling for me to do what I do best: drag bunt and run it out. Since I'm a lefty when at bat, and very fast, it's basically a guaranteed single. That would move Haley along to second and she might even try to take third because she's our best base stealer. I haven't done a drag bunt today so the other team wouldn't be prepared for it, unless they've been scouting us.

I looked over to the visitor's bleachers and could see my dad in his stupid Red Sox hat watching me. I gave him my "hi, Dad" signal, which was putting my right hand flat against the front of the visor of my batting helmet. Then he would respond by doing the same thing on his stupid Red Sox hat. I liked having a secret signal like that with my dad.

My mom was over in the home bleachers with Charlie and Stephanie. Charlie knew my dad was over there and he still hadn't told my mom about everything. My dad decided to give him a break on telling her because of his mom dying and all, which had been really hard on him. So we were still in a holding pattern on all of that.

The first two pitches were awful and I decided not to show my bunting intentions. This pitcher was tired and it was showing. When the third pitch came in, I went into a traditional bunt stance, pulling the infield in, to give Haley a better chance to steal second. It worked. Haley stole second easily.

Making them think that I wouldn't bunt now that Haley stole the base, I went ahead and drag bunted the next pitch down the first base line and ran out the single. Haley boldly took third base.

So now the winning run was screaming for a single.

"Now batting for the Lady Chargers, number eighteen, Brittany Espinoza."

As soon as the first pitch was released, I trotted over to second base. In softball, the catcher rarely bothers to try to stop a base stealer when a possible run is standing on third base, especially the winning run.

And then a gift was given to our team by the softball gods of Raleigh, North Carolina. A wild pitch got by the catcher, and Haley — always on her toes — took home for the win.

Our team was now tied for first place in the conference, so we would definitely be going into the playoffs in two weeks. Our school hadn't had this good of a softball team in several years, so Coach Lundy and the Athletic Director were really pushing us. Because of how well we were doing, more and more of the students were coming to the games, hoping to see us make it far into the state playoff run this year. It was an exciting time to be on this team, and the best part of all was knowing that my dad was watching it happen and sharing in the excitement.

When the game was over, I said to my mom, "We're all going to Cook Out."

"Okay, I'll come, too," she said.

"Mom, none of the other moms are going!" I protested.

She looked over at Charlie and said, "Alright. I'll just

go home and eat with Boo."

I hated lying to her, but it wasn't a complete and total lie. I was going to Cook Out, it was a "we", and no one else's mom would be with us. It's not my fault if she thought it was Coach Lundy and the team.

Charlie hugged and congratulated me and Stephanie gave me a double fist bump, which was our inside joke together. I had to be careful now when fist bumping with her because of the gorgeous diamond ring she was sporting on her left ring finger.

When I saw my mom head off to her car and drive away, I went over to my dad, who was waiting for me on the visitor's bleachers. He said, "Nice game, shorty" and then took off his stupid Red Sox hat and put it on my head. I would wear absolutely anything on my head as long as it belonged to him.

We headed off to Cook Out for some father-daughter bonding time.

SCOUT

After Jemma's game was over, I went home and took Boo for a nice, long walk and made myself a Lean Cuisine. Turning on the TV, I started to watch an old episode of "Friends," which ended up reminding me of what a stupid, stupid fool of a woman I am — even now, at my age — and all because of a scene that showed Monica and Chandler in Central Park. So I turned off the TV and decided to go upstairs to get Jemma's dirty clothes off the floor and into the laundry.

I went into her room with its unmade bed, messy desk, and clothes strewn all over and began to pile them into the hamper so I could carry them downstairs. As I was picking up her favorite light blue tee shirt from Limited Too, I heard a beeping noise coming from her desk drawer. So I went over to it and pulled out the drawer, which revealed a teal colored Nokia cell phone.

Jemma does not have a cell phone yet. I was planning to get her one this summer so we could get rid of the beeper. Why does Jemma have a cell phone in her desk?

Searching through the recent call history, there was only one number that she made as an outgoing call or received a call from — all from a 252 area code. *Why was that familiar?*

There were no names in her contacts assigned to this number and, in fact, there were no contacts at all. There were no text messages or voicemails either. I didn't know why the phone beeped other than the fact that it might need to be charged.

Sitting down on Jemma's bed, I held the phone and tried to think who this phone belongs to and what this number could possibly be. Some boy? But why would some boy she goes to school with have a 252 area code? Why would some boy give her a phone? Maybe it was a boy she met who just moved here? Maybe he had an extra phone?

And then I realized. Maybe it wasn't a boy at all.

Coach Lundy was from Greenville, which had a 252 area code. Coach Lundy went to East Carolina University and moved here two years ago to teach at the high school. Coach Lundy was a good-looking man in his mid-twenties coaching girls' softball. Coach Lundy has had my daughter in his car often over the past few weeks. Coach Lundy was always taking the girls to Cook Out. Maybe instead he had been only taking Jemma. Maybe Coach Lundy was... Oh my Lord, NO. She is repeating my life!

All of my fears about my inherent dislike and natural suspicion of her coach since day one were starting to rise within me to a fevered pitch of anxious rage. That son of a bitch was using his authority, influence, and good looks to attend to the slow seduction of an innocent fourteen-year-old girl. And not just any fourteen-year-old girl, but *my* fourteen-year-old girl. Why was he calling her so much? Why were they on the phone so much? Why had they been spending so much time together?

Because you selfish failure, you were at Flavia and neglecting your daughter, the one responsibility you have, the only person you're on this earth to protect, your reason for being on this earth at all. Instead, you were off working late in a bar and letting yourself get seduced and used and caught up into the mind games of some repulsive pig from New York! You've not only failed yourself time and time again, but now you've failed your daughter! Now your biggest fears are coming true: she is becoming you!

Grasping the secret cell phone with all of my strength and with angry, fearful, and guilt-ridden tears flowing down my cheeks, I sprinted out of the house and jumped into my car. Screaming out of the neighborhood, I sped over to the Cook Out near the high school to see if I could find her with that perverted, sick, piece-of-garbage coach. As I pulled into the parking lot, with the street lights shining, I watched my Jemma — wearing a Red Sox ball cap of all things — walk out of the restaurant with some relatively familiar looking older man with dark hair who was not Coach Lundy at all.

Who is that with Jemma?

I parked my car, opened the door, and got out, and as I slammed the door with more force than I knew I had in me and watched them head toward a car, Jemma saw me.

She stopped walking, looked at me, and then glanced over at the man next to her. Is that...Rob? Rob Caralessi?

Standing there under one of the lights in the parking lot of Cook Out, holding about twenty more pounds on his frame than when I knew him but still wearing the exceptional good looks of a Hollywood leading man, Rob Caralessi stood with our daughter, his twin with a ponytail.

Jemma said, her voice cracking, "Mom?" and Rob said, emphatically, "Scout."

I sat down on the pavement next to my car with the cell phone in my hands and began to cry out another lifetime worth of tears.

Epilogue

April 11th, 2015

"Above all else, guard your heart, for everything you do flows from it."

- Proverbs 4:23, The Holy Bible, New International Version

"Mom, do you think you can hold back this part of my dress behind me somehow so I can go over to the other room to get Kristin to fix my hair?"

Scout, caught in a daydream while looking out the window of the First Baptist Church of Haddleboro, turned back toward her daughter, standing barefoot in the choir room and looking breathtakingly beautiful in her white gown: long, form-fitting, and as fresh as white snow. Jemma stood awkwardly, needing some help to move around because she didn't have her shoes. Her maid of honor wasn't at the church yet and was in possession of Jemma's shoes.

Scout helped her daughter scoop up her dress so she could walk from the choir room to the pastor's office where Kristin, both Scout's and Jemma's childhood hairdresser, could fix the parts of the wedding up-do that needed fixing.

It was two hours before show time and Scout was feeling anxious, anxious like long ago when she would wait in the outfield for a batter to hit a hard fly ball to her.

Today, her smart, raven-haired, independent, and remarkably well-adjusted daughter would pledge her love to a wonderful young man named Eric Gage. Both twenty-six years old, gainfully employed, happy, and in love, Jemma and Eric met at Appalachian State during their junior year and have been together ever since.

They bought their own townhouse close to Charlotte, where Jemma's new job was starting next month. Eric was already working in Charlotte. They planned to leave the next day for a nine-night Caribbean cruise out of Florida. Jemma had never been to the Caribbean, so they were very excited about the warm, sunny weather and island adventures awaiting them on their honeymoon. This is exactly how the end of the story is supposed to go. Or the beginning of the story. Or simply the new path of one story that weaves in and out of many other stories, connecting us all.

Scout grabbed the folds of the dress and carefully held them back so that nothing would happen to them during the process of walking from here to there. Kristin stood in the pastor's office talking to Pastor Dan about the Easter Cantata she has planned with the choir. They both looked up at Jemma.

"You are a marvel to behold, Miss Webb," Pastor Dan said to her, smiling.

Jemma is not comfortable with compliments on her appearance and probably never will be. Shyly, she said, "Thank you, Pastor Dan."

Scout quietly followed with the rest of the gown and set it down gently near Kristin. Kristin started flicking at her earlier work on Jemma's hair. Feeling overwhelmed emotionally, Scout excused herself and went to the ladies' room down the hall.

Passing by the opening of the sanctuary, accented in

white daisies throughout, Scout caught a glimpse of Charlie and Rob standing outside the front of the church. Rob, now old enough to collect social security, had thick, mostly-gray hair and those still-pouty lips. He saw her and waved his hand. She waved back, knowing he would always have a place in her heart.

Scout went into the bathroom and looked at herself in the mirror. The day that she is truly saying goodbye to her partner-in-life for the past twenty-six years is here. Even after all this time, and all of the tears due to a life full of so much heartache, pain, and disappointment, not one gray hair erupted through her own head. Sure, there were a few wrinkles now over the faded freckles that once adorned her face and kept it pure. Her cheeks weren't quite as full anymore, the years finally wearing down those youthful identifiers.

After today, she would be alone. Jemma would be Eric's partner for life and, well, that is how it's supposed to be, of course. Circle of life and all that. Everything she did during the course of her adult life was for that girl.

Scout lost her entire childhood in one ill-fated summer moment because she was a silly, dreamy teenaged girl with a huge crush on a man she trusted, fully and naïvely trusted. She wasted even more of her youth in the quiet, desperate suffering of self-hatred through isolation and an unrelenting depression for what she was and what she wasn't anymore — and worst of all — what she believed herself to be.

She had been gifted with so much in life: a good family who loved her, faith, a best friend, intelligence, a touch of life's spoils — but never too much — and a God-given internal strength and fearlessness which had evaporated right along with her childhood. Right along with her honor, innocence, dignity, and self-respect. She lost these things to a young husband and father on the very day he stole them in order to gratify his own lack of honor, dignity and self-respect — and then offering her up as a virgin sacrifice in order to save himself.

After that, she lost any hope of regaining her youth because she fell in love with a much older man who saw her as a kind young woman, whose vulnerabilities and affections would allow him to escape from his own internal frustrations of a demanding adult life.

Both were men who should have known better. Both were men who then abandoned her when confronted with their own shame and faced with their own demons.

Ever since the events of the summer of 1983, Scout never felt the touch of God's love or the "peace that passeth all understanding", whether through her family, her friends, or anything else. She never felt worthy of any happiness or success or even the real love of a man. She didn't care much for God, either.

Those cemented feelings of shame and self-loathing went through life right along with her, like a cruel best friend who won't go away. It was a true battle of darkness within, not even healed by the miracle of her daughter's love. She knew the only thing that kept her from walking off into some kind of abyss all these years was the fact that she had Jemma and Charlie. Jemma had at least had been hers. Until today.

Charlie would always be there for her, she knew that. But Charlie, too, had his own life to live: a full career, a loving wife, and two boys who kept him busy. Charlie was not hers, either. Well, not technically, but they would always be bonded beyond the confines of time and space — that's how it is with soulmates. Life went on for Charlie. Life went on for Scout. It had to.

Rob was Rita's except for one brief period of time when the sun rose and set on their secret love affair, culminating in nothing but pain, misery, and heartache for everyone affected by it, which is what secret love affairs have a tendency to do, after they are exposed. The whole mess would be nothing but a faint heartbeat of melancholy memories if not for the fact that it produced this truly extraordinary young woman who was getting married today.

Scout's parents, Lee and Raelene, belonged to each other. Jonny belonged to his wife. Brother Doug was out there somewhere, probably belonging to someone. Who the hell knew who Thom belonged to? He belonged to himself, Scout supposed.

Scout knew that she had to move on and be her own best friend. And having herself as a best friend wasn't such a bad thing.

The family and guests began to gather in the sanctuary for the wedding of Jemma Webb and Eric Gage. Everything was so beautiful. Eric stood nervously at the front, rocking on his heels back and forth and joking with the organist. Scout walked down the aisle alone and sat in the front row on Jemma's side. Everyone started to head to their seats and the wedding party began to make its way down the aisle. Then the organist started "Here Comes the Bride."

Jemma, her veil hiding her angelic face, walked down the aisle with a dad on each arm —Charlie on the left, the dad who raised her as his own and who is the reason Jemma is so secure in male relationships. Charlie is as close to perfection in a man as one can get. He is why Jemma believes in her worth as a woman, why she is so self-assured and confident, and why she knew, from a young age, what she wanted in a husband someday.

Even though it was apparently God's will or Fate or the universe's big, cruel joke that they did not end up together, Scout knew that she ruined it. She had everything she could ever want in a man all wrapped up in Charlie Porter, but she came to that realization too late. The clichés were true: sometimes love's just not enough. Sometimes, it's simply too late. And while Charlie and Scout would always be, on some level, a disappointing ending to a Nicholas-Sparks-type of love story — the kind where the star-crossed soulmates indeed do not end up together — there was the satisfaction within them both that they knew exactly what they were to each other.

On Jemma's right arm was Rob, the dad who was deprived of the chance to raise her because of the early decisions of a scared and desperate college kid. Scout will always be grateful to Rob for his compassion toward her about everything that happened and will always appreciate him and his family for accepting and embracing Jemma as their own. He may not be able to get back the first fourteen years of her life, but he has the rest of them. He has done everything possible to be a good father to her: he was involved in her life from the day he met her, paid for her college tuition, came to see her play softball during her high school and college years, and always included her in family holidays and vacations. They had a real father-daughter relationship, probably better than so many others out there that started off the right way with a cedar box full of pink cigars and inside of a hospital nursery.

Rita sat a few rows behind with the rest of the ever-expanding Caralessi clan. After having to face the truth and accept the reality that her husband fathered a child none of them knew anything about, long after she had dealt with and forgiven her husband's affair, she also began to attend Jemma's softball games, participating in her life, and treated her as a part of their family. Rita was the consummate family woman: the mother to everyone, she who held everything together, the glue. Time has a way of healing even the ugliest of stories, but Rita Caralessi was one woman that Scout admired quietly and from afar. Jemma was lucky to have a strong woman like that in her life, one who could see past her own humiliation and pain and do what was right for a girl who was flesh and blood, who was family, and do so with open arms.

Being a part of Rob's life was Jemma's birthright and Scout knew that she had been selfish in keeping it from her. She couldn't have asked for a better outcome to the whole situation.

It was in that moment, watching the three of them arm-in-arm, that Scout realized for the first time that she was not alone. She was not losing Jemma. She still had her. She had her parents, her dogs Ranger and Joe, her brother, his wife, her niece and nephew, and Charlie and his family. She was in a great family, a part of something beautiful and much larger than herself, no matter what happened to her in her life or what she has done or not done with it.

She was worthy of love, she knew that. All of the sacrifices and tough choices and challenges she faced, she did so all out of love for everyone around her, everyone who had come into her life and touched her soul — whether they deserved her love or not. Her pure and genuine heart was the very definition of love. And isn't that the essence of God? Isn't that what Jesus was all about?

She looked down at the Bible resting in the pew and

turned it to First Corinthians 13, the very passage that Pastor Dan would read during this service.

"If I speak in the tongues of men or of angels, but do not have love, I am only a resounding gong or a clanging cymbal.

If I have the gift of prophecy and can fathom all mysteries and all knowledge, and if I have a faith that can move mountains, but do not have love, I am nothing.

If I give all I possess to the poor and give over my body to hardship that I may boast, but do not have love, I gain nothing.

Love is patient, love is kind. It does not envy, it does not boast, it is not proud.

It does not dishonor others, it is not self-seeking, it is not easily angered, it keeps no record of wrongs.

Love does not delight in evil but rejoices with the truth.

It always protects, always trusts, always hopes, always perseveres.

Love never fails. But where there are prophecies, they will cease; where there are tongues, they will be stilled; where there is knowledge, it will pass away.

For we know in part and we prophesy in part, but when completeness comes, what is in part disappears.

When I was a child, I talked like a child, I thought like a child, I reasoned like a child. When I became a man, I put the ways of childhood behind me.

For now we see only a reflection as in a mirror; then we shall see face to face. Now I know in part; then I shall know fully, even as I am fully known.

And now these three remain: faith, hope and love. But the greatest of these is love."

Scout said quietly to herself, "The greatest of these is love." She had always loved others in place of, and instead of, loving herself. She knew that it was time to do both.

If God Incarnate had been standing next to her in the pew, He would have announced loudly, "Scout, this is your ah-ha moment!" and then given her a framed certificate and maybe the keys to a new car.

Scout smiled the kind of smile that she hadn't worn in many years as she watched Pastor Dan and the bride and groom go through the rituals of a wedding. He was talking, but she wasn't listening. In some ways, she was missing her own daughter's wedding due to the sudden and unexpected emancipation from one destructive mindset — and then bonding herself to a new and better one. Something that had eluded her for years began to envelope her like a warm blanket on a crisp Carolina morning and, once again, Scout felt the presence of God. It isn't defined by a book of books or a prophet or a pastor in a church or even a prayer. It is defined by the peace residing within an individual heart.

All these years of trying to find a way to just...feel better...by hiding in her work and hiding in her daughter and hiding in her animals and even hiding in her attachment to Charlie, desperately trying to heal from old wounds and getting nowhere. The whole time she was waiting for her honor to show up in a box, wrapped with a pretty bow, left on her doorstep by an unnamed suitor or the UPS guy or God Himself — or, hell, even Brother Doug. But that's not how honor works.

Her honor has always been inside of her. No one can give her that and no one can take it away, either. It was hers to claim and to own this whole time.

At long last, she felt it. Honor. Her own honor. Scout's Honor.

****

Scout stood near the head table, all covered in white linen, inside the church's basement, which now served as the wedding reception for the newly announced Mr. and Mrs. Gage. The guests were all waiting for the bride and groom to come downstairs so that the reception could begin.

During the whole ceremony, and now as she waited for her married daughter, Scout's thoughts were nestled in all the love she had in her heart for the people who have been there for her entire life, who loved her no matter what happened to her at fourteen or nineteen or what poor decisions she made as a grown woman, or how long it took her to come to terms with it all and, at long last, love and accept herself. She was overwhelmed. As her Mema would've said, had she been alive, "My cup runneth over."

As she stood there alone, watching the guests wandering about as they waited, she was silent and removed from everything that was going on around her. She was making plans in her head: today she would go home and start the file so that she could apply to the vet school at NC State at the next available application period. She was ready. She would start planning a trip to the Grand Canyon, somewhere she had always wanted to go. She would sign up for ballroom dancing lessons at the community center, something she had always wanted to try. She would start her garden. She would learn piano. She would start running again and train for the next big Raleigh half marathon. She would...

Suddenly, she felt a hand touch her shoulder. Scout was startled out of her racing thoughts and turned her head to face a tall, very dignified-looking man in a black suit, burgundy striped tie, and with salt and pepper hair who looked to be in his late forties. He had a chiseled chin and warm brown eyes. She had never seen him before.

He said to her, in a baritone voice, thick with a southern drawl, which sounded a touch more Texan than North Carolinian, "Are you Scout? Mother of the bride?"

Scout nodded, smiled, and felt a bit out-of-sorts. He stood fairly close to her, somewhat in her personal space, and Scout noticed how good he smelled.

"We're sitting next to each other," he said, pointing

at his name placard on the table, which sat next to Scout's placard. "I'm Jonathan Cordova." Then he paused, looking for some sort of recognition in the expression on Scout's face. There was none.

He continued, "I'm Jemma's boss?" He paused again. Jonathan seemed a bit surprised that Scout looked as if she had never heard of him before. "Well, I'm sorry, I thought Jemma would've mentioned to you that she invited me to her wedding. I sure am gonna miss her when she heads to Charlotte. Anyway, people call me Buddy," he winked, showing a confident smile.

Scout's heart jumped. Jemma's boss is here and he is *really* handsome. And she has never said anything about this. These past couple of years she has worked for him in Fayetteville and not one word! And she invited him to her wedding? And she sat him next to her on purpose? And she knew that she has never, in her entire life, met a man who goes by "Buddy" who wasn't just…an absolutely great guy.

She turned toward Buddy, who was looking around at the all the people he didn't know, hoping that Scout would engage him in some kind of a friendly conversation.

But Scout's mind was jumping in all kinds of directions: surprise at her witty little smart-ass Jemma's bold move here, pure happiness at how good she felt for the first time in years about everything in her entire life, pride in having such an amazing daughter, a little dumbfounded because of how good this ridiculously attractive stranger standing next to her smelled, and wanting to laugh at the irony that she is being set up with a man who also goes by a dog's name. She looked at his left hand. No ring. Of course, nowadays, that doesn't mean anything.

"So what do you think?" Scout asked Buddy.

"What do I think about what?" he responded.

Scout looked at him and grinned. He had a friendly look to his face and a calm demeanor.

"What do you think about the obvious set-up that Jemma has done on both of us here at her own wedding?" she boldly asked him, picking up their name placards and holding them up next to each other. She determined on this day that life was too short and she was too old to not just say what she was thinking.

Buddy chuckled. He took his placard from Scout, pulled out a pen and crossed out the name "Jonathan." Then he hand-wrote "Buddy" in black ink, while saying, "Ms. Webb, I have just met you, but I'm a good judge of people off of first impressions." Smirking, he put the placard back in her hand and said, "I think you and me are like a couple of two playful, slobbering, big yellow Labs rather than some formal couple at a big round table full of formal couples."

Scout laughed out loud.

"How 'bout today we be 'Buddy and Scout' rather than 'Jonathan and Scout?' Don't you think that sounds more fun?" he asked, also coming to the realization that his young ambitious employee has just set him up with her mother. Yes, that definitely sounded more fun. "That kid — she is just trying to help fate along," Buddy said and winked at her.

The End. The Beginning.

Acknowledgements

Thank you to my family:

To Eric, Abigail, and Allison for your love and support over the past year and a half as I went through this (at times) overwhelming process of writing and publishing my first novel. I never would have accomplished this personal achievement without the life we've all shared together over the last twenty-plus years. To my mother and brother for always believing in me, whether on a court or in a field or with a ball or with a rifle or with a pen and a notebook, and for living kindness each day. To my father for teaching me how to make doughnuts with my dirt bike, soap up car windows on the streets without getting caught, talk myself out of speeding tickets, and for ensuring that I would always be able to take care of myself in any situation. To all of my in-laws who have accepted me into your family. To Stretch & Slinky for always being so happy to see me, even after I've locked you in a crate for hours, and for being my loyal and unfailing confidants. I've learned rather late in life that sometimes the only true friend a girl will ever have for sure in this life is her dog…or in my case, dogs.

Thank you to my editor, Rachel, for all of your hard work, for helping me think deeper, and bigger and figure out why I really wrote this story, for believing in my book and for giving this first time author a chance. Thank you to Dionne and the French Press Bookworks staff for your diligence and support in helping *Scout's Honor* come to life. I will forever be grateful to you all for giving me this incredible opportunity.

Thank you to my teachers and university professors who always encouraged me. I know it is tough to be a teacher these days, but I hope my teachers know that their impact on me was profound. Thank you to all who have supported my writing, all the people I once knew and all the people I've met along the way.

Thank you to Jenny O'Brien for helping a Jersey girl write a Carolina story, Phil Crisp of the Phil Crisp Insurance Agency, Inc. in Chapel Hill for all of your expertise, Mel and Jo Wright for your insights and southern contributions as well as your friendship, Lorrie Marro for your excellent observations and suggestions and also for my muddy hiking boots, and novelists Mark Ethridge and Heather Carnassale for your sound advice in getting started in the fiction writing world. I've met some other great writers through this process as well.

I know this is long, but it's my first book, so please bear with me. If you've read this far, thank you so much for supporting my work – there is so much more to come. I've started two more and can't wait to see what they have to say. I hope when they are put out into the world, my characters and their stories will touch your heart. That one dream – to touch your heart, and maybe making a friend along the way, is really all I seek on this writing road.

-Dori

About the Author

Dori was born and raised in New Jersey. She graduated *magna cum laude* with a Bachelor of Science in History and is a veteran of the United States Army. Dori currently works in the legal field in North Carolina, where she resides with her family. She is a member of the North Carolina Writer's Network.

Scout's Honor is her first novel.

www.DoriAnnDupre.com

Go Social with Dori:

Twitter: @DoriAnnDupre

Facebook: /DoriAnnDupre and /ScoutsHonorBook

Instagram: @dori_dejong

Pinterest: @DoriAnnDupre

Youtube: Dori Ann Dupre, Novelist

Blogspot: finding-dori.blogspot.com

Did you like this book?

The best way to let an author know you've enjoyed their hard work is through a review. You can log onto sites such as Amazon, Barnes & Noble, iTunes, Kobo, and GoodReads to leave Dori Ann Dupré a few thoughts about what you've just read.

A review is an invaluable tool. It gives the author feedback as well as telling other readers what you thought about the book. If you have a book blog, booktube, or bookstagram account, you can tweet us your review - @ fpbookworks – and we will add it to our social media roll call.

If you want to know more about French Press Bookworks, log on to http://www.frenchpressbookworks. com.

CPSIA information can be obtained at www.ICGtesting.com
Printed in the USA
BVOW02s1407130416

444084BV00003B/57/P